IMPROPER

DARCY BURKE

ZEALOUS QUILL PRESS

ADVANCED READER COPY

IMPROPER

Society's most exclusive invitation...

Welcome to the Phoenix Club, where London's most audacious, disreputable, and intriguing ladies and gentlemen find scandal, redemption, and second chances.

Dissolute rogue Tobias Powell, Earl of Overton, has just inherited a sheltered, proper young ward for whom he must find a husband. And that is only the start of his problems. His father's will demands Tobias marry within the next six weeks, or he'll lose his mother's house, a treasure so dear that Tobias can't consider defeat. Surely he can rehabilitate his scandalous reputation, secure a match for his ward, and find the sophisticated woman of his dreams before it's too late. Except his ward is a hellion who cannot behave. She can, however, make him laugh.

Provincial Miss Fiona Wingate is eager to swap her boring small town for an exciting London Season. Until she realizes her new guardian, a dashing earl, plans for her to wed with the utmost haste. Fiona has no interest in marriage—she's only just been liberated from her lifelong isolation! But when she causes a near scandal and Tobias comes to the rescue, an unexpected attraction sparks between them. Except romance between a guardian and his ward would be most improper…

Don't miss the rest of *The Phoenix Club*!

Love romance? Have a free book (or two or three) on me!

Sign up at http://www.darcyburke.com/join for members-only exclusives, including advance notice of pre-orders and insider scoop, as well as contests, giveaways, freebies, and 99 cent deals!

Want to share your love of my books with like-minded readers? Want to hang with me and get inside scoop? Then don't miss my exclusive Facebook groups!

Darcy's Duchesses for historical readers
Burke's Book Lovers for contemporary readers

CHAPTER 1

London, February 1815

Tobias Powell, fifth Earl of Overton, smiled faintly at the brush of his mistress's fingertips along his shoulder. He didn't open his eyes. Instead, he pressed himself into the bedclothes as if he could hug the cozy softness of the bed. He was particularly tired today, but then it had been a viciously late night.

"What time is your ward arriving?" Barbara, his soon-to-be-former mistress, asked from behind him.

Bloody hell, his ward. His eyes shot open as he pushed himself to a sitting position, the bedclothes falling away from his nude body. "What time is it?"

"Three."

"In the afternoon?" Of course, in the afternoon. They hadn't even come back to Barbara's lodgings until the sun was rising over London.

Tobias scrambled from the bed and ran about plucking

up his carelessly tossed clothing. Foregoing smallclothes since he couldn't seem to find them, he pulled his breeches on. Then he threw his shirt over his head and haphazardly tucked the ends into his waistband.

From the bed, Barbara held up the missing smallclothes, her wide red lips parting in a teasing smile. "Don't you need these?"

"You kept those from me on purpose."

She shrugged, her elegant shoulders arching, which made her rather large breasts also move.

Tobias groaned. "I have to go. My ward could already have arrived." This was not how he'd intended things to happen. He was supposed to be on his best, non-scandalous behavior, both to support his ward's debut and to find his own wife. "You are far too tempting, Barbara." He narrowed his eyes at her as he tugged his waistcoat on.

"Your buttons are not aligned." She laughed softly as she leaned back against the head of the bed, making no attempt to cover her exposed upper half.

Tobias looked down and saw that she was right. Cursing softly, he started over. "This is your fault. You're a terrible distraction."

She stretched one arm up over her head, which again accentuated her breasts. "You like me that way."

"I like you every way, but you know this is our final meeting. It has to be."

Lowering her arm, she at last pulled up the bedclothes to cover her chest. Pouting, she said, "Because you must marry. *Immediately.*"

Flinging himself into a chair, Tobias began to don his stockings and boots. "Within the next five or so weeks, yes." Because his father had decreed it in a surprising change to his will before he'd died in December.

Tobias had to wed within three months of the former

earl's death, or he'd lose the one property that was not entailed—Tobias's mother's house, the only true home he'd ever known. He would do anything to keep it in his possession. Which meant he had to find a wife with nearly impossible haste.

And it was only *nearly* impossible because of his own behavior the past two years. While there were many who would gleefully accept an earl's suit, he didn't want just anyone. He wanted a wife of sophistication and wit, one who was kind and caring.

Someone he could love, even if he didn't at the outset. Because he had no bloody time to fall in love. He needed to find a suitable woman, settle the betrothal, have the banns read, and complete the marriage ceremony within five weeks. All while any woman worth having would likely turn her back to him.

Reformation was the plan, and so far, he was failing. He'd tried to break things off with Barbara the other day, but he'd encountered her last night, and she'd been incredibly persuasive.

Finishing with his boots, he stood and drew on his coat. His cravat was also lost, apparently. No matter. It would have been a horribly wrinkled mess. He grabbed his hat and gloves from the top of her dresser and went to the bed.

"This really was the last time, Barb. You know it has to be."

She exhaled, her dark eyes meeting his with a shadow of sadness. "I'll find someone else, but they won't be you. They'll be serious and boring, and they won't know me at all."

Tobias brushed a dark blonde lock from her cheek and bent to press a kiss to her temple. "They'll come to know you, and you'll cure them of their dullness." He straightened and set his hat atop his head.

"Perhaps I'll take your generous settlement and just wait for you to change your mind." She smiled up at him, and Tobias suffered a moment's regret. He didn't love Barbara, but she made him feel good and that was a lovely thing.

He turned and left her rooms, then practically sprinted down to the street where he hailed a hack. Three in the afternoon! He really hoped his ward had not yet arrived. It was a long journey from Shropshire, and the winter weather could have delayed her. Yes, he'd hope that was the case. Hadn't that been one of the arguments Barbara had used the night before to persuade him to go home with her? She'd cooed that his ward was likely stuck somewhere due to a washed-out road.

Not that it had taken much to sway him. He'd fallen eagerly and completely into debauchery without a shred of regret. That his behavior would have frustrated his father—and did while he was alive—only made it more attractive. After Tobias had failed to wed two years ago, his father had harassed him incessantly about taking a wife. Hence, his dying decree that Tobias marry or suffer—by losing the one possession that meant something incredibly dear to him.

And so his father would win as if this had been a game the past two years. It hadn't been, not to Tobias. He thought he'd fallen in love, only to have the lady in question turn on him and make him doubt everything he'd felt. Was it any wonder he was not inclined to court anyone else?

It was, however, time he did.

The hack stopped halfway down Brook Street, and Tobias leapt from the vehicle. He dashed through the gate and up the steps to his house, rushing inside as Carrin opened the door.

He stopped abruptly, facing the butler. "Is she here?"

"Miss Wingate?" Carrin shook his head. "Not yet, my lord."

The stress rushed out of Tobias's frame, making him feel as if he might slide down to the marble floor. "Thank God. I'm going to take a quick bath." He removed his hat and strode through the archway into the staircase hall.

"I believe she's just arrived, my lord," Carrin called just as Tobias put his foot on the stair.

Closing his eyes, he gripped the railing. "Bollocks."

~

"Oh my goodness, that's Hyde Park!" Fiona Wingate pressed her nose to the window of the coach, her pulse racing.

"How do you know?" Mrs. Tucket said without opening her eyes from beside Fiona.

"Because I do." Fiona had studied maps of London for as long as she could remember. Indeed, she'd studied every map she could get her hands on. "It's so big and wonderful." She splayed her gloved palm against the glass as if she could somehow reach through and touch the trees, their spindly limbs still bare.

Mrs. Tucket leaned against her, and a quick look showed she'd opened one eye long enough to peer past Fiona at the park. "Harumph. You can't see anything of import."

No, she couldn't see Rotten Row or the Serpentine or any of the ton's ladies and gentlemen who would be out and about during the fashionable hour. She doubted they'd be out today anyway. It was quite early in the Season, with Parliament just starting their session a few days earlier. And it was too cold to promenade.

At that moment, rain drops splattered the window. Certainly too rainy.

Fiona didn't care. She'd take London in the rain, the snow, even in a hurricane, if such a thing were possible. The point was, she didn't care about the weather or that the park was not yet in full bloom. She was in *London*. Most importantly, she was no longer in Bitterley, where she'd spent the entirety of her almost twenty-two years.

Mrs. Tucket exhaled loudly as she worked to push herself into an upright sitting position. She'd slumped rather far down in her seat since their last stop some miles back. "I suppose I must rouse myself from the travel stupor."

Fiona kept her face to the window until they reached the corner of the park. Even then, she craned her neck to look back at it, marveling at the archway leading inside. She would get to promenade there or mayhap even ride. Perhaps her guardian would drive her in his phaeton. If he had one. Surely all earls had phaetons.

The coach continued along a bustling street—Oxford Street, if she recalled the map correctly. And she was certain she did. Shortly they would turn right down Davies Street into Mayfair, the heart of London's most fashionable neighborhood.

They passed stone and brick-faced houses, some with elaborate doorways and others with wide windows. Some were narrow while others were twice as wide. When they turned left onto Brook Street, the houses became quite elegant, with fancy wrought iron fencing and pillared entrances.

At last, the coach drew to a halt in front of the most glorious house yet. An iron gate with a large O worked into the design at the top guarded the walkway leading to the front door where a pair of pillars stood on either side. The door of the coach opened, and a footman dressed in dark green livery rushed through the gate to help her descend.

Fiona tipped her head back and counted four stories stretching into the gray sky. A raindrop landed on her nose, and she grinned. Then she glanced down at the part of the house below the street. Five stories in all.

"I think my legs have completely gone to sleep," Mrs. Tucket said, grasping Fiona's arm to steady herself.

The footman held the gate open and indicated Fiona and Mrs. Tucket should precede him. Holding her head high, Fiona made sure Mrs. Tucket had a good hold on her before moving through the gate onto the short path that took them to five steps. Fiona went slowly so Mrs. Tucket, who had an aching hip, could keep up. This was more than fine since Fiona's heart was beating even faster than it had been in the coach as she contemplated how her life was about to change.

She was the ward of an earl in London on the brink of her first Season. It was, in a word, unbelievable.

The door stood open and another man in dark green livery was positioned just inside. "Good afternoon, Miss Wingate, Mrs. Tucket. Welcome to Overton House."

"You've arrived!" The booming masculine voice sounded through the marble-floored, wood-paneled foyer before Fiona could see the man himself. But then he, presumably the Earl of Overton, was there, striding through a wide archway directly across from them.

Fiona stared at him, surprised at his youth. No, not his youth, for he was likely almost thirty. No, she was surprised to see that he was...handsome. She'd expected someone like his father, whom she'd met a dozen or so times over the course of her lifetime. But where the former earl had been dour-faced and without any exceptional physical traits, the current earl possessed a lively gaze and eyes the color of pewter. His dark hair was damp; artful waves contrasting against his light forehead. He tugged at his coat and fidgeted with his simply knotted cravat as he came to stand in the center of the foyer.

Recalling her practice with Mrs. Tucket, Fiona sank into a

deep curtsey while her arm was still in her maid's grasp. "My lord."

"Well done," he said, grinning. "You are nearly ready for your presentation to the queen."

Fiona had started to rise but she nearly toppled to the floor. "My what?"

"You're to be presented to the queen?" Mrs. Tucket began to breathe heavily, so much so that Fiona feared she would faint.

"Can she sit?" Fiona asked, searching wildly for a chair.

Lord Overton's brow creased as he hurried forward to take Mrs. Tucket's other arm. "In here." He ushered them to a sitting room to the right of the foyer. Decorated in warm yellow and burnished bronze, the room welcomed them like a sunny afternoon.

Together, Fiona and the earl brought Mrs. Tucket to a chair near the hearth where coals burned in the fireplace. "Better?" Fiona asked.

"A drop of sherry would not come amiss," Mrs. Tucket said, untying her bonnet beneath her chin.

The earl stalked back to the doorway and asked someone to fetch sherry and tea. "Carrin will be along presently. That's the butler. He was standing just in the foyer when you arrived. I'll introduce you to the household a bit later, if that's all right."

"Yes, thank you," Fiona said, trying not to gape at the splendor of the room with its multiple paintings, rich window hangings, and lavish furniture. She'd known the earl would have a large house and fine décor, but she hadn't realized how large or how fine. And now it was her *home*. Her heart started to pound again.

Mrs. Tucket coughed. "Were you jesting about my Fiona being presented to the queen? Surely you must have been."

"Not at all," Overton said with a smile. "It is expected that young ladies entering upon their first Season are presented to Her Royal Highness."

Now it felt as if Fiona's heart might actually leap from her chest. The queen!

Mrs. Tucket's dark eyes widened, and she stared at Fiona in something akin to horror, which was just a wee bit annoying. "She doesn't know a thing about how to do that!"

The earl continued to smile placidly. "Do not fret, for Miss Wingate shall have ample opportunity to prepare. Her presentation is not until next week."

"Next week?" Mrs. Tucket squeaked as she drooped in the chair. She pressed the back of her hand to her cheek and muttered something unintelligible.

Moving to stand near Fiona, the earl murmured, "Er, is she all right?"

"Yes, she's just being dramatic," Fiona whispered. "She does that."

"Oh. Then I daresay it's wise that I've procured a chaperone and a sponsor for you. You'll meet the former shortly and the latter tomorrow."

"Did I hear you say you've hired a chaperone for my Fiona?" Mrs. Tucket sounded aghast. She pursed her lips most strenuously. "*I* am her chaperone."

The earl smiled affably. "Certainly, but I thought she might benefit from an additional chaperone. Someone acquainted with London and Society." He darted an uncertain look at Fiona as if he were looking for support.

"An excellent idea, my lord," Fiona said as she went to sit in another chair near the hearth. She reached over and patted Mrs. Tucket's hand. "How can I not prosper with two chaperones?"

"Harumph." Mrs. Tucket narrowed her eyes at the fire.

Fiona looked up at the earl. He was frowning, one hand on his hip and the other stroking his chin.

The butler arrived with a tray bearing tea and a glass of sherry. The earl scooped up the latter item and brought it directly to Mrs. Tucket. "Your sherry, ma'am."

She took the glass and downed half the contents without a word. Holding the sherry against her chest, she settled back against the chair and closed her eyes.

Fiona slowly rose and tiptoed back to the center of the room where the earl stood staring at her maid. "She'll likely fall asleep in a moment. The key will be to catch the glass before it falls."

The earl's dark brows climbed just before he nodded. Turning, he gestured for the butler to move the tray to a table in front of the windows that looked out to Brook Street.

A snore rattled the air, and Fiona dashed to catch the glass of sherry as Mrs. Tucket's grip slackened. Just one small drop of the contents splashed over the side onto her skirt. Fiona considered that a victory.

When she joined the earl at the table near the window, he inclined his head with appreciation. "Well done."

"It is not my first rescue."

The earl held her chair as she sat. "I see, and here I thought you had someone taking care of you."

"She does take care of me, but it's true that I also take care of her. More in the last year or so. She's quite tired, I think. She all but ran our household the past six years after my father died and then later when my mother became ill."

The earl, seated across the round table, handed her a cup of tea the butler had prepared before leaving. The entire activity—the delivery of the tea, organizing it and a selection of food on the table, and his departure had occurred with such ease and precision that Fiona wondered how the butler had done it all without her really noticing.

"How long since she's been gone?" Overton asked before sipping his tea.

"Not quite two years. She'd hoped to come to London with me for my Season, but, ah, your father didn't extend the invitation until just before she died. And then, well…" She didn't need to tell him about how things had happened. "I didn't mean to imply anything by that."

"Of course not," he said benignly, reaching for a biscuit. "You need never fear voicing an opinion about my father. You'll find I have many, and few of them are good."

"Oh." Fiona didn't know what to say to that, so she decided to find another topic. It wasn't hard, for she had a thousand questions. And that was before she'd learned she was to be presented to the queen or that she would have a new chaperone and a…sponsor? "What does a sponsor do?"

He finished chewing and waved his hand, still holding the biscuit. "An excellent question. You are quite fortunate to be sponsored by one of Society's most influential ladies, Lady Pickering." He waggled his brows. "She will come tomorrow, and you'll discuss all things of import, including your presentation to court, your wardrobe, and, of course, invitations."

Fiona had just picked up a biscuit and promptly dropped it into her teacup. "I already have invitations?"

"Not yet. No one knows who you are, and the Season has barely begun. Lady Pickering will see that you receive invitations. Once you're presented, there will likely be a flood."

Fiona picked up her teacup and frowned into the contents where the edge of the biscuit was visible just above the liquid.

"Let's just pour you a new cup." He reached for the third cup that was likely for Mrs. Tucket, who wouldn't be needing it. After pouring the tea, he added a bit of milk and sugar, then swapped it with her cup with an efficiency and care she would not have expected from an earl.

She couldn't help but smile at him. "You're quite jovial." She didn't recall his father being so likeable. He'd been rather serious.

"I try to be." He finished the rest of his biscuit while Fiona sampled her new cup of tea.

"Better?" he asked.

"Much, thank you." She set her cup down just as he picked his up.

"THE BLOODY QUEEN?"

The outburst from Mrs. Tucket caused the earl to spill his tea right down the front of his cravat and waistcoat. His eyes widened with shock as he darted his gaze toward where Mrs. Tucket still slumped in her chair. "Is she all right?"

"Oh, yes. She does that." Fiona picked up her napkin and went to the earl, dabbing at the tea on his front without thinking.

"Er." His gaze met hers—they were rather close—and Fiona realized this was highly improper.

"Sorry!" She dropped the now-soiled napkin in his lap and dashed back to her chair, heat rushing up her neck and cheeks.

He plucked the napkin up and continued where she left off. "It's fine. I appreciate your quick reaction. Mrs. Tucket often shouts in her sleep?" He looked toward her again, one brow arching. "She *is* still asleep?"

"Most certainly. At this time of day, she typically naps an hour or two. And, yes, she is known to call out. Usually with a profanity."

His hand stopped wiping at his waistcoat as his gaze fixed on her. "Truly?" At her answering nod, he let out a wonderfully warm laugh. Fiona couldn't help but join in.

When their laughter subsided, he set the napkin on the

edge of the table. "Well, it's good that I've enlisted additional help. You will require a chaperone who does not fall asleep and make exclamations using inappropriate language."

Fiona leaned forward slightly. "You can't dismiss her. I won't allow it."

The earl studied her in silence a moment. "I'm afraid it's not up to you to allow things," he said with a subtle edge of steel. "However, it was never my plan to dismiss her. I understand she's been with your family quite some time. She will simply take on a new role."

His plan. It wasn't up to her. Perhaps Overton wasn't as likeable as she thought. "Thank you, my lord," she said as sweetly as possible. "What role is that?"

"Whatever you deem it to be. Just know she will not accompany you to Society events. That will be Miss Lancaster's responsibility."

"Miss Lancaster?"

He stood. "Come, I'll introduce you now." Looking toward Mrs. Tucket, he pressed his lips together. "Should we wake her? I can have Mrs. Smythe, the housekeeper, see her upstairs."

Fiona went to assess Mrs. Tucket's situation. She didn't look particularly comfortable, but Fiona knew that didn't matter. What did matter was not interrupting this most important afternoon nap, particularly after their long, arduous journey over the past week. "She'll sleep another hour at least. Would it be possible to have a maid check on her periodically so that she doesn't startle when she awakens? She may not recall where she is."

The earl looked alarmed. "She's forgetful?"

"Occasionally, but so is anyone nearing seventy. This is a new place and we've only just arrived. I fear *I* might not recall where I was."

"Fair enough." He gestured to the door. "Shall we?"

The tea had stained the folds of his cravat, and parts of his maroon waistcoat were darker than the rest because the fabric was wet. She would feel bad if his clothing were ruined, but then he could surely afford to replace both items without a second thought.

He led her from the sitting room back into the foyer. A liveried footman stood near the door like a statue. They turned to the right, and there was an actual statue in the corner, a life-sized rendering of a muscular young man in a brimmed hat, winged sandals, and a cloth draped in an artful fashion covering his most intimate parts.

"Is that Hermes?" she asked.

"You know your Greek gods." He sounded impressed. "My father liked Greek mythology in his youth. Or so my mother said."

He led her into a large hall in which a wide staircase climbed up the right side. Portraits lined the wall ascending to the first floor.

"I seem to recall that about him when he visited my father. They discussed Greek philosophers too." She looked at the paintings as they went up. "Are these your relatives?"

"Yes." He pointed to the one at the top. "That's my grandmother. She lives at the dowager house at Deane Hall. She rarely comes to London anymore."

The likeness was of a woman past the blush of youth but not yet in middle age. Her gray-blue eyes were very similar to that of her grandson, including a certain sense of exuberance, as if she were ready to meet whatever came her way. "She looks lively."

"She has many opinions and will share them whether you want to hear them or not." At the top of the stairs, he continued onto the next flight. "Your room is up one more."

The staircase up to the second floor was not quite as

grand, and the paintings were of landscapes. There was also one of a bowl of fruit.

"Just to the left here." He led her to a doorway and stepped into a small, well-appointed sitting room decorated in pale pink and green. Once inside, he gestured to the right. "Your chamber is through there. And here is Miss Lancaster."

The woman who was to be Fiona's companion walked into the sitting room from a door on the wall opposite the one to Fiona's chamber. Miss Lancaster was taller than average with dark blonde hair and a narrow face. Her pale, gray-green eyes were wide, however, and fringed with long, dark lashes. There was a steel to her, perhaps in the way she stood or the manner in which she held her head with an air of resolve.

Fiona moved toward her with a warm smile, wanting to start their relationship off well, even if she did feel a bit like the woman was edging Mrs. Tucket out. "Good afternoon, I'm pleased to make your acquaintance."

Miss Lancaster dropped into an easy curtsey. "I have been eager to meet you, Miss Wingate. And to be of service."

"I will let the two of you become acquainted," the earl said. "Dinner is at eight."

"So late?" Fiona asked. "Mrs. Tucket will be quite famished by then, I should think."

"We don't keep country hours here in town," Overton said. "But we'll do our best to accommodate Mrs. Tucket. I'll see she has whatever refreshments she desires. As soon as she wakes," he added.

"Where is her room?" Fiona glanced toward the door from which Miss Lancaster had emerged.

"Across the gallery overlooking Brook Street. I'm sure she'll find it more than acceptable. See you at dinner." He turned and left before Fiona could ask any more questions.

Instead, she addressed Miss Lancaster. "Is that your room

there then?" Fiona inclined her head toward the door that didn't lead to Fiona's chamber.

"Yes. His lordship thought we should share this sitting room so as to form our, er, bond." Miss Lancaster shifted her weight, and Fiona saw the crack in the woman's façade. She was nervous.

Fiona relaxed, for she was nervous too, and it helped to know she wasn't alone. It also helped that her new companion appeared to be just a few years older than her, rather than someone with several additional decades. Fiona loved Mrs. Tucket, but it would be nice to have someone young to talk to. "How old are you, Miss Lancaster?"

"Twenty-five."

"Is that the age of most companions in London?"

"Er, yes?" Miss Lancaster sounded uncertain.

"You don't know? I thought Lord Overton said you were an experienced chaperone."

"Oh, of course. Just not here in London." Miss Lancaster abruptly turned. "Come, I'll show you your room. I'm sure you're anxious to see it."

"Thank you. I should like that very much, Miss Lancaster."

The taller woman looked back over her shoulder. "Please call me Prudence."

"All right, but you must call me Fiona then. Especially if we're to be friends." How she hoped they would be friends. Fiona hadn't had one in a very long time. Not since Abigail Harding had moved to Ludlow after getting married four years ago.

Prudence's gaze softened and some of the tension seemed to leave her frame. "I would like that."

"Wonderful." Fiona grinned and then gasped as she stepped into her bedchamber. It was more than twice as large as the one in their cottage in Bitterley on her cousin's estate, perhaps three times, actually, and decorated in beautiful rose and gold. There was a large bed, a writing desk, a dressing table, and a grand armoire along with smaller dressers for her things. What she owned wouldn't fill even a quarter of everything, but then she supposed her new wardrobe would.

Turning to face Prudence, she clasped her hands together. "I have so many questions but let me start by asking when we can go to Bond Street." There were so many things Fiona was eager to do and experience. Why not start with something close?

"I'm not sure, but soon. His lordship said you would require a wardrobe for the Marriage Mart."

Halfway to the dressing table, Fiona stopped. If the earl thought she was a biddable young lady eager for the marital yoke, he was going to be quite shocked.

Fiona would try not to be amused.

CHAPTER 2

Tobias climbed the stairs of the Phoenix Club with more speed than usual. Was he eager to join his friends in the members' den or running from his obligations at home?

Both.

As soon as he entered the spacious room that occupied more than half of the first floor, he was greeted by Ruark Hannigan, the Earl of Wexford. Tall with a wiry frame, Wexford was an excellent pugilist with a slightly crooked nose from having it broken more than once. With his black hair, blue eyes, and devilish smile, he was extremely popular with the ladies. As far as his Irishness allowed, that was. He was acceptable enough to flirt with, but an English earl was preferable to an Irish one.

"Overton, I wondered if you might not join us this evening because the arrival of your ward wore you out."

"I know you are in jest, but it was a distinct possibility. She is full of enthusiasm." She'd bombarded him with questions at dinner, mostly about things to see and do in London.

The poor chit had been horribly isolated in the country. He'd agreed to escort her to the British Museum on Monday.

Tobias followed Wexford to the back corner of the room. A window nearby overlooked the spectacular garden below where lanterns flickered and a rectangular pool with a statue of Aphrodite in the center reflected the light. One of the six chairs at the round table was already occupied by Dougal McNair, another of their friends.

Dark-haired MacNair was a pugilist like Wexford, but his shoulders were broader and his nose still straight. He greeted Tobias and signaled to a footman to bring drinks for the new arrivals.

"Evening, MacNair." Tobias dropped into one of the leather-cushioned chairs next to the Scotsman.

Wexford took the other chair beside Tobias. "Tell us about the ward. Am I going to want to change my marriage plans?" He grinned, for he'd been clear about not taking a wife until he reached the age of thirty. Which meant he had a good three years left.

Tobias narrowed one eye at him. "Could I tell you anything that would do that?"

"No." Wexford laughed. "But tell us about her anyway."

The footman arrived with a decanter of brandy and two glasses, which he promptly filled before departing. MacNair already had one that was half full.

Lifting his glass, Tobias took an eager sip. The activity in his house had been a tad overwhelming, particularly since he'd only just raced home right before his ward's arrival. An uncomfortable quiet had settled over the household following his father's death, but Miss Wingate's presence had completely changed the atmosphere.

"No Lucien?" Tobias asked, glancing around. Lord Lucien Westbrook was the owner of the club and his closest friend.

"He hasn't come down from his office yet," Wexford said in his Irish lilt. "I take that back. He just came in."

Tobias's back was to the door, so he swung around and saw the tall figure of his friend enter the members' den, where he was immediately waylaid by a pair of gentlemen. People often sought his company, and not just because he was the owner of London's most exclusive club. He was also well-known for granting favors to people in need, as he'd recently done for Tobias.

"It's a damn good thing he found a chaperone for Miss Wingate," Tobias said, shaking his head. "The one she brought with her from Shropshire is worse than I expected."

"Worse how?" Wexford asked.

"Well, she dozes off rather easily and, while sleeping, cries out, usually profanely."

Both of his tablemates laughed.

"What is so amusing?" Lucien asked as he took the chair next to MacNair. The footman delivered a fourth glass with alacrity.

"Overton was just telling us about his ward's unfortunate chaperone."

Lucien's dark eyes widened. "How can that be? Miss Lancaster is excellent."

"Not that chaperone," Tobias clarified. "The one from Shropshire. It's a very good thing you introduced me to Miss Lancaster. Mrs. Tucket would not have been acceptable here in London."

Lucien's brows climbed. "I see. I look forward to hearing what Lady Pickering thinks of Mrs. Tucket."

Lady Pickering was the sponsor who would shepherd Miss Wingate through her Season. A close friend of Lucien's family, she was a well-respected lady in Society with excellent connections. The only person Tobias could have asked— and did—was his grandmother and, as expected, she'd refused to come to London. Lucien had rushed to the rescue, as he did so often.

"Mrs. Tucket wasn't very enthused to learn of Miss Lancaster," Tobias said. "She feels as if she's being pushed aside."

"Which she is," Wexford pointed out helpfully.

"I can't imagine how she'll react to Lady Pickering tomorrow." Tobias couldn't decide if he was dreading or anticipating it.

"Lady Pickering has the patience of a particular bird of prey," Lucien said with a smile.

"And the brutality of one if you cross her." MacNair's shoulders twitched as he picked up his brandy, and Lucien laughed. "Not that I've ever been on her bad side, mind you. I think I'd run from London and never return." MacNair leaned toward Lucien and lowered his voice to barely above a whisper. "Why hasn't she ever responded to our invitation to join the club?"

All four of them were members of the Phoenix Club's secret invitation committee. They, along with Mrs. Renshaw, who managed the lady's side of the club, and two anonymous members, decided who within Society and without were invited to join.

Lucien shrugged. "There are those who look down at the club." He also kept his voice low.

Wexford snorted. "Because they're jealous. That can't apply to Lady Pickering, however. Why would she be jealous of anyone or anything?"

"While you're probably right, I suspect she doesn't want to align herself with the club because it may alienate some people with whom she would prefer to remain connected. And she won't decline because I suspect she doesn't want to hurt my feelings." Because she'd been a close friend of his mother's. That made sense to Tobias.

A brief smile passed over Lucien's lips. "Furthermore, I believe she very much supports the fact that the club includes women, even if we keep the sexes mostly separate. Indeed, that fact is what keeps us respectable."

"I would think she'd join eventually," MacNair said quietly. "The ladies' club has four exceptionally admirable patronesses. Lady Pickering would fit right in."

Lucien snorted softly. "Don't think I haven't presented that argument. Mrs. Holland-Ward is a good friend of hers." She was one of the patronesses along with Lady Dungannon, Lady Hargrove, and Mrs. Renshaw.

"You still haven't told us about Miss Wingate," Wexford said, raising his voice back to a normal volume. "Are she and Lucien's sister going to be rivals to be named the Season's diamond?"

Lucien snorted. "Cassandra will gleefully cede the attention. She's not terribly enthused about having her Season, but our father will not allow her to push it off any longer."

"Especially since you've completely rejected his efforts to see you wed," MacNair said. "He has to manage someone."

"I suppose it's possible Miss Wingate could be the Season's diamond." Tobias had been surprised and perhaps a bit unnerved by her beauty. With a heart-shaped face graced with a slender nose and pink lips that formed a perfect bow and a gently curved figure, she possessed the form and features of an ideal English miss. But her dark red hair contrasted against the fair cream of her countenance made her stand out and demanded one ponder whether her temperament matched the serenity of her countenance. Or perhaps it was the spark in her brown eyes. With unmatched curiosity, her gaze assessed everything she encountered as if she were committing each item to memory.

"She's pretty?" Wexford asked.

"Some would think so," Tobias said carefully. While he

was eager to marry her off, he didn't want any of his friends seeking her hand. Not that he ought to worry since none of them had declared an interest in the Marriage Mart this Season. "It's the red hair. Some will find it off-putting, I imagine."

"Then they aren't worth her time," MacNair said. He was well-used to people judging him based on the almond color of his skin, or at least regarding him as if he were out of place in Society.

Wexford raised his glass. "Hear, hear."

They all shared in the toast.

"Enough about my ward," Tobias said. "I've far more pressing matters than dealing with her. Thankfully, Lady Pickering will have things well in hand so that I may focus on my own predicament."

"Ah, yes, the need for a wife," Wexford said. He leaned back in his chair and, smirking, looked toward Lucien. "What about Lucien's sister?"

Lucien glowered at him in response.

Tobias shook his head at Lucien. "You do realize she's going to wed, and you won't get a say."

"I know that." He scowled. "But none of you can marry her, do you understand?"

"I don't even want to get married," MacNair said defensively.

"Nor do I," Wexford put in. "At least not yet. Your sister is safe from us, and I won't joke about her anymore." He rolled his eyes to punctuate the statement—which told Tobias he just wouldn't joke about her marriage prospects in front of Lucien.

"You didn't say anything." Lucien speared Tobias with an expectant stare.

"I've no plans to marry my friend's sister. Besides, she's far too young for my taste." She brought to mind the woman Tobias had planned to marry two years ago. Until she'd accepted someone else's proposal first. The entire affair had been humiliating. He'd believed they were perfectly suited only to discover her father preferred another suitor, the heir to a dukedom. And when Tobias had suggested that they elope to Gretna Green, she'd revealed herself to be a woman lacking maturity and demonstrating a hunger for notoriety. "I would prefer to court a lady who is not in her first Season. I might even prefer a widow."

"I suppose that removes your ward from consideration," Wexford noted.

"You can't jest about that either," Tobias said. "She's my *ward*. That would surely be...improper." He picked up his brandy glass and looked around the table. "Now, give me some names. I don't have much time."

"Six weeks?" MacNair asked over the rim of his glass.

"Five." Tobias winced. He couldn't lose his mother's house, the location of every single one of his happy memories. He'd been sixteen, away at school, when she'd fallen from her horse. Her death had been utterly shocking, and the loss had left a hole in his heart that had never fully healed. Losing the childhood home that he'd shared with her would be a devastation he didn't want to contemplate. That his father had put him in this predicament—using the place Tobias loved most to bend him to his will—had turned Tobias's mild dislike of the man into seething contempt.

Wexford grunted. "Not much bloody time."

"Precisely." Tobias looked to MacNair beside him. "I need names."

"You're looking at me? A man with no interest in the parson's trap?" MacNair laughed, then sobered when Tobias only narrowed his eyes. "Fine. What about Mrs. Drummond? She's a widow."

"She's also at least fifteen years older than me. I need an heir."

"Older women are quite lovely though." Lucien grinned, and the other two chuckled.

"You lot are no help." Tobias moved on to Wexford. "A name. And don't be flippant."

Wexford touched his chest. "Me? As it happens, I've an excellent suggestion—Miss Jessamine Goodfellow."

Tobias tried to recall her and couldn't. "What's wrong with her?"

"Nothing that I know of. She's just a wallflower. She has two younger sisters who are already married."

"How do you know her?" Tobias found it odd that he wasn't aware of her while Wexford, who was every bit a rake, was.

"I go to Society events," Wexford said with a measure of exasperation. "I am certain I danced with her once or twice last Season. If I remember correctly, she is rather intelligent. Didn't mutter a thing about any of the Fs."

Fashion, food, and flowers. Most young women stuck to those three topics. And occasionally the weather.

"How refreshing," Tobias murmured. "Thank you for the worthwhile suggestion, Wexford." He turned his gaze to Lucien. "Who do you recommend?"

Lucien rubbed his fingers along his jaw. "Lady Alford has just joined the club. She's a widow."

"Doesn't she have several children?" Tobias asked.

"Yes, but you didn't specify that your potential bride *not* have children."

"No, I did not, and I suppose it isn't an obstacle."

"It also shows she *can* have children." Wexford inclined his head. "Since providing an heir is likely important to you."

Tobias rested his elbow on the table and pressed his forehead into his palm. "I hate this. My father has ensured I approach this like a shopping excursion in which I search for the best product with an excess of haste." The loathing he felt for his father heated anew.

"*You* want to fall in love," Lucien said softly. "Again."

Dropping his hand to the table, Tobias raised his head and glared at him. "I wasn't in love."

Lucien shrugged. "You said you were."

"I was wrong. So nice of you to remind me of that."

"My apologies," Lucien said, bowing his head briefly. "I thought you had moved past Lady Bentley."

Of course, he'd moved past Priscilla. After he changed his mind about eloping, she'd gone and told everyone that he'd tried to kidnap her. No one quite believed the kidnapping part, but when she'd insisted he'd tried to convince her to elope, they'd eaten that up like marzipan at Christmas. Overnight, he'd become a rogue, a scoundrel, an utter reprobate. And since they seemed to delight in casting him in such a role, he'd decided not to disabuse them of their assumptions. He'd immersed himself in dissolution and depravity.

"Lady Bentley is an unfortunate memory. My attention is on the present and future, specifically the next few weeks. Indeed, I will need to formalize a betrothal in less than a bloody fortnight if I'm to schedule a wedding within the necessary timeframe." Tobias tipped his head back and groaned. "This is impossible."

"Bloody reading of the banns takes forever," MacNair muttered.

"You could try for a special license," Lucien suggested.

Tobias lowered his head. "I don't want to rely on that, but it's good to know the possibility exists. This is so damned frustrating." He finished the rest of his brandy and refilled his glass.

MacNair leaned forward and grinned. "You could also

dash off to Gretna Green. I've got cousins near there who'd celebrate with you."

"I shall hope the special license will work rather than risk a long journey while it's still winter. But I do thank you for the kind offer of your family's hospitality." Tobias gave him a silent toast before sipping his whisky. Setting his glass down with a muffled clack atop the tablecloth, he said, "All right, I'll start with Miss Goodfellow. Please let me know if you think of or meet someone else. I can't afford to pin all my hopes on one woman." Not to mention, he may find Miss Goodfellow completely intolerable. Or perhaps she'd find *him* intolerable. In any case, he really needed to find someone with whom he would suit.

And yes, he supposed he did want to fall in love. Or at least develop some sort of affection for the woman who would be his wife. He didn't want a cordial but dispassionate union like that of his parents. They'd both been happier when the other was someplace else. That was why he'd spent so much time with his mother—just the two of them—at the house she'd inherited from her grandmother.

Lucien cupped his hands around his glass on the table and leaned forward, his dark gaze on Tobias. "This is a wonderful plan but, forgive me for asking, are you certain you'll receive the invitations you need to accomplish this feat?"

Since he'd reinvented himself as a rogue, his invitations were not always of the best caliber. He hadn't cared. In fact, he'd reveled in his ignominy, particularly because it had irritated his father, who'd tried to press him into an unwanted marriage after he'd been jilted by Priscilla.

But now his reputation mattered. He could practically hear his father chortling from beyond. Indeed, he'd probably anticipated this problem when he'd changed his will. Which meant he expected Tobias to fail and thus to lose his beloved mother's house. And this was after he'd swindled the property from his father-in-law, demanding it as Tobias's mother's dowry. Tobias believed his mother's bitterness toward her husband stemmed from losing the estate to him in the marriage contract. She'd often lamented that she wasn't able to leave it to Tobias.

Yes, his father was almost certainly laughing.

Tobias curled his lip. "I've been on my best behavior since my father died. No gaming hells, no phaeton racing, and I gave up my mistress."

"Have you?" Lucien asked. "I heard you were seen running from her lodgings just this afternoon."

Glaring at Lucien, Tobias demanded, "Do you know *everything*?"

Wexford snickered. "Yes, he does."

Lucien sat back in his chair. "Lady Pickering should be able to assist you, but you'll have to do your part. The slightest misstep, such as continuing to see your mistress, and you'll ruin your chances."

"As well as that of your ward," MacNair said rather unnecessarily.

It was too much. His father hadn't even told him about Miss Wingate until he lay dying. He'd been the young woman's guardian for two years and hadn't said a word. Tobias wondered if he'd ever known the man at all.

"While you're considering potential wives for me, I will also take suggestions on how to mend my reputation."

"Align yourself with Lucien's brother." Wexford's brows darted up as he exchanged a look with MacNair, who chuckled.

"Brilliant idea," the Scotsman said.

Lucien groaned. "God, I wish that was a terrible suggestion. You do realize he's mostly insufferable."

Tobias couldn't help smiling. The relationship between

the two brothers seemed complex, but then Tobias had no siblings, so what did he know? "He's always pleasant to me."

Lucien grumbled something unintelligible before finishing off his brandy.

Wexford clasped his hands on the table. "A fortnight to secure a betrothal with the wedding to follow three weeks later. We'll make sure you find a wife, Overton."

"Thank you."

But would she be the woman he'd always dreamed of?

CHAPTER 3

*D*idn't he have any maps at all?

Since breakfast, Fiona had searched all of the lower shelves in the library. Time to employ the ladder and see what she could find up high.

Pushing the ladder to the end of one long shelf, she began her methodical investigation. Perhaps there was a book of maps. Or a book with at least one map.

She pulled a large tome from the shelf and balanced it on her hand as she opened the cover and read the title, *The British Isles*. That looked promising. Carefully turning pages, exultation bloomed within her as she finally came upon a map.

"What are you doing up there?"

Startled, Fiona lost her grip on the heavy book and watched in horror as it tumbled to the floor. She scrambled down the ladder and, in her haste, slipped.

It was an absolute miracle that the earl managed to reach her in time, catching her in his arms before she landed on the floor. And it was an absolute shock to find herself in his embrace. The rich scent of sandalwood washed over her along with a surprising heat.

Embarrassment. It had to be embarrassment, of course.

Overton set her on her feet. "All right?"

She nodded. "Yes, thank you. You surprised me is all."

He bent to retrieve the book and studied it for a moment.

"Did I damage it?" She'd feel just awful if she had.

"Not that I can tell." He flipped open the cover. "*The British Isles.*" He looked over at her. "You're interested in learning more about your homeland?"

"I was looking for maps, actually."

"Maps?"

"I like them. Very much."

He smiled as he set the book on a table. "Well, then let me delight you."

Something about the way he said those words sent a shiver along her spine. She didn't want to be delighted by him or any other gentleman.

He's your guardian. Think of him like a father or an older brother. It's perfectly natural to be delighted by a family member and not at all dangerous.

Dangerous? Is that how she thought of gentlemen? No. But maybe *this* gentleman was different.

The earl went to a bookcase with drawers beneath the shelves. He opened the lowest one and pulled out several oversized pieces of parchment. "It's not a large collection, but it's better than none." He set the maps on the table next to the book and opened one, laying it flat.

Fiona rushed to join him, any hesitation she might have possessed forgotten. "This is the Empire of Russia." She paused in reaching for the map, her fingers hovering above the paper.

"Unfortunately, it's from before Catherine the Great, so it's no longer accurate."

"That's all right. I like maps of all kinds, even if they are out of date."

"You can touch it," he said softly, eyeing her hand.

"I'll be careful. Not like I was with the book." She winced. "I'm terribly sorry about that."

"Don't be. I startled you with my arrival. I'm glad I was able to catch you before you sustained an injury. How would you dance if you'd twisted your ankle?"

He made a good point. "I am grateful for your quick action. I would like to be able to dance."

"Of course you would." He said it as if every young woman wanted nothing more than to dance. While it was true about her, she hoped he hadn't made other assumptions. "Have you always been fond of maps?"

"Yes, but we didn't have very many. When I see how you live here, I confess that I wonder how our fathers were friends."

He pivoted, resting his hip against the table as he crossed his arms. "Why is that?"

She found his gray eyes rather distracting. They seemed to possess the ability to see straight inside her, which was ridiculous. He would observe only what she wanted him to. "My father was not wealthy. He was an academic, and we lived on the support of his older brother. After my father died, my uncle took his library in exchange for a settlement for my mother. He permitted me to choose a handful of things to keep—they were all maps."

The earl frowned. "That sounds rather unfair."

She lifted a shoulder. "My uncle wasn't a very caring man. I believe he saw my mother and me as a nuisance. He thought he was being kind enough by allowing us to continue to inhabit our house, which was on his estate."

"He died recently?"

"Just before my mother passed. Thankfully, when my

mother died, his son allowed me—and Mrs. Tucket, of course—to continue living there." He'd also suggested she marry, but she wouldn't mention that for fear it would invite discussion on a topic that didn't remotely interest her. "I was quite relieved when your father's kind invitation for the Season arrived." He'd apparently sent it just before he'd died, giving his son no choice but to shepherd her through a debut.

Well, she supposed the current earl could have refused and left her to rot in Bitterley. She was glad he hadn't.

Overton uncrossed his arms. "My father didn't tell me a thing about you until he was dying. I have no idea why our fathers were friends. He only told me they'd met at Oxford, and that, as your godfather, he'd agreed to look after you and your mother when your father died. They must have formed their friendship at Oxford. I can't even imagine it because I can't see my father in that way."

"What way is that?"

It took the earl a moment to respond. When he did, he seemed uncertain. "Friendly, I suppose?"

It seemed the relationship between father and son was not close, but before she could ask about it, the butler announced the arrival of Lady Pickering.

Overton pushed away from the table. "Excellent. Please show her to the drawing room and make sure Miss Lancaster joins us."

"And Mrs. Tucket," Fiona said. She would not leave the beloved woman out, even if she was to have a limited role.

"Of course, yes, Mrs. Tucket." The earl sent her a look of apology, which she appreciated.

The butler departed, and the earl offered Fiona his arm. "Shall we go upstairs?"

Fiona cast a longing look at the map.

The earl chuckled. "You may have access to the library—

and the maps—whenever you choose. I'll also have all the atlases and books with maps moved to a more accessible location. That way, you'll be safe." He winked at her, and once again, the warmth of embarrassment flushed through her.

She clutched his sleeve more tightly. "You have atlases? As in, several of them?"

"Yes, I believe so. I'll dig them out later."

She'd never felt so delighted to be anywhere in her entire life. "Thank you. Sincerely."

He blinked, then gave her a lopsided smile. "It's my pleasure."

A few moments later, they entered the elegant drawing room on the first floor. Overlooking Brook Street, the rectangular room had tall windows cloaked with pale gold draperies. Several seating areas occupied the space with comfortable chaises, tables for games or refreshments, and chairs and settees for conversation. She'd first seen the room yesterday when the housekeeper had given her a tour of the house. Then and now, Fiona easily envisioned a proper London family enjoying their evenings in this room just as she saw more formal entertainments. At least, she assumed those would be commonplace. What did she really know about any of this?

"Lady Pickering, how wonderful of you to come," Overton said as Fiona withdrew her fingertips from his arm. He strode forward to take the woman's hand and bowed. Then he pivoted to look toward Fiona. "Allow me to present Miss Fiona Wingate."

Lady Pickering, between fifty and sixty years with a regal bearing, stood in front of a settee. She was of average height, but the sophisticated style of her still-brown hair and the quality of her clothes made her seem imposing. Or perhaps that impression was due to the manner in which she assessed

Fiona with her green-blue eyes, as if she'd seen a great many things and possessed both the experience and character to pass judgment on anyone.

"Miss Wingate, it's a pleasure to make your acquaintance and to sponsor you for the Season."

Fiona dropped into a deep curtsey. "I am honored by your attention and support, Lady Pickering."

"You've started without me?" Mrs. Tucket ambled into the room, and Fiona wondered if she really wouldn't benefit from a walking stick. She'd broach the subject later and hope the suggestion would not be greeted with disdain.

"Not at all," Overton said brightly. "We were just making our introductions. And here is Miss Lancaster too." He looked to Lady Pickering. "This is Mrs. Tucket, Miss Wingate's, er, chaperone from Bitterley, and this is Miss Prudence Lancaster, her new chaperone for London."

"How lovely to meet you both," Lady Pickering said. "Shall we become acquainted?" She lowered herself to the settee, and the skirt of her blue and gray grown draped perfectly about her lower legs and feet without any effort whatsoever. Patting the place beside her, she looked up at Fiona. "Come and sit with me, Miss Wingate."

Fiona attempted to sit as elegantly as Lady Pickering had but still had to adjust her skirts.

"Keep your legs pressed tight, dear, from waist to foot. Angle your knees a bit." She surveyed Fiona's movements and smiled softly. "There you are."

"She knows how to sit," Mrs. Tucket said with a touch of defensiveness.

Lady Pickering's expression remained benign. "Yes, of course. Do you like to play cards, Mrs. Tucket? There is a wonderful game every Sunday afternoon. I'll ensure you're invited."

Mrs. Tucket's lids fluttered in surprise as she sat in a chair near Fiona's end of the settee. "Thank you. I do like cards. I played every Saturday at the vicarage." While Fiona scoured the vicar's library. By the time she'd left Shropshire, she'd read everything in it—well, everything that interested her—at least twice. Sadly, the library had possessed only one map encompassing western England and Wales.

"Wonderful." Lady Pickering turned her attention to Fiona. "Lord Overton told you about your presentation to Her Majesty, the Queen? The drawing room is next Thursday."

That was in just a week. Fiona's stomach took flight. "Yes. He said I am to have a court dress made." She glanced toward him, seated near Lady Pickering's end of the settee.

"Indeed. We will visit the modiste shortly."

"Today?" As keen as she was to visit Bond Street or any shopping area, she was surprised at the speed with which everything was happening.

"A court dress is quite extravagant, Miss Wingate. Yards and yards of fabric, and there will be much embroidery. We will also need to select jewelry, but most of it I will loan to you for the occasion since you won't need to wear anywhere near that much again." She paused to smile. "And there will be feathers, of course."

"Feathers? Where do those go on the gown?" Fiona tried to imagine and came up with a rather ghastly costume.

"In your hair," Lady Pickering clarified with a smile. "The taller, the better. I know the perfect place to commission your headpiece."

Goodness, this sounded terribly expensive. Again, Fiona looked toward the earl. Prudence sat in another chair between him and Mrs. Tucket. Like Lady Pickering, she sat very prettily, her hands clasped demurely in her lap. Fiona copied her.

As she checked her hand position, Fiona noticed a loose

thread at the hem of her sleeve. She tugged it gently in the hope that it was simply loose. More thread came out of the sleeve, but it seemed to still be attached to the dress. Glancing up, she saw that Prudence was watching her. Blushing, Fiona squashed the thread between her fingers and stuffed it inside her sleeve.

"What of the rest of her wardrobe?" Mrs. Tucket asked, pursing her lips. "Or is she to wear this court gown to balls too?"

Lady Pickering smiled patiently. "Goodness, no. Wearing a court gown anywhere other than the queen's drawing room would be highly inappropriate. Miss Wingate will need many gowns. For calling, for promenading, and, of course, for evening events such as balls and the theatre." She blinked at Fiona. "Do you ride?"

Fiona's mind was still riveted on Lady Pickering's response, as well as the fact that Mrs. Tucket could not have acted as a chaperone, or anything else, for the Season. Reining in her thoughts, she responded to Lady Pickering's question. "Well enough, yes."

"Then you shall need riding habits."

Habits plural? Again, Fiona looked toward her guardian. He must be very wealthy indeed. She didn't even own *one* riding habit. She only rode occasionally when her uncle had permitted her to use a horse from his stable.

"As well as accessories, shoes, and undergarments," Lady Pickering went on.

Fiona suddenly realized her guardian would be funding her undergarments, and she wasn't sure how she felt about that. Perhaps she could persuade Lady Pickering that she didn't require new chemises or corsets. Except new outerwear would demand undergarments that complemented the fit of the clothing. Fiona knew at least that much. Her mind swam.

"What will our first event be?" Overton asked pleasantly.

Lady Pickering's brow gently creased in a pensive expression. "It is still early in the Season, so it is likely too cold to promenade in the park for another fortnight. And of course, no Vauxhall or other outdoor entertainments. The larger balls will not be scheduled for several weeks."

Overton looked disappointed. "That long?"

Cocking her head, Lady Pickering regarded him with curiosity. "Has so much time elapsed since you participated in the Season? I had thought it was just last year that you were...occupied."

Having sufficiently cleared her thoughts, at least for the moment, Fiona looked toward the earl. Occupied how?

"I'm afraid I'm the worst sort of gentleman who doesn't pay close attention to such things."

"Precisely why you should seek a wife, my lord." Lady Pickering gave him a knowing smile.

Was he looking to marry this Season? Given his age, it seemed he should. In fact, she wondered why he wasn't wed already.

"As to upcoming events," Lady Pickering continued, "I have procured an invitation for Miss Wingate and even for you, Overton." *Even* for him? What did that mean? Why hadn't he already been invited? Weren't earls invited to everything? Fiona had so many questions. Or perhaps she had too many assumptions.

"Excellent," the earl said without revealing any reaction to what Lady Pickering had said. "When is this event?"

"A smaller ball on Saturday evening hosted by Lord and Lady Edgemont." Lady Pickering looked to Fiona. "That will be an excellent foray into Society."

"So soon?" she asked, her insides twisting anxiously.

"Don't fret, Fiona, you will be a grand success," Mrs. Tucket said with a bright confidence that made Fiona feel better. Of all the people here, her opinion mattered the most because she knew Fiona. Her words would not be empty platitudes. "You won't be alone either. You'll have Lady Pickering and Miss Lancaster at your side."

But not Mrs. Tucket, and it seemed her former maid knew that. Fiona felt a bit sad, but if Mrs. Tucket was all right with it, she would be too.

"That's right," Lady Pickering said. "And don't worry about it being early in the Season, the Marriage Mart is still open." She winked at Fiona, whose insides turned to ice.

Did they expect her to wed immediately? She'd only just arrived in London. She understood—vaguely—that young ladies had Seasons in order to find a husband. But weren't there other reasons? Couldn't a young woman have a Season to meet people and make friends? To experience new things and learn? To dance and promenade without any pressure to wed?

She wanted to ask but didn't dare. Because she feared she already knew the answer.

～

*L*ater that night, Fiona walked into the sitting room she shared with Prudence after paying a visit to Mrs. Tucket in her room. Prudence, seated in a high-backed chair near the fireplace, looked up from the book she was reading. "How is Mrs. Tucket?"

"Quite well, actually." Fiona sat in the other chair near the hearth. "She confessed her relief to not have to accompany me to Society events. She was also pleased to learn that the card game every Sunday is not with women such as Lady Pickering." This had been a chief concern, for Mrs. Tucket was, at heart, a country maid of all work and wasn't interested in moving in Society circles. On the way to the modiste, Lady Pickering had clarified that the game consisted of retired housekeepers and ladies' maids, women like Mrs. Tucket.

It seemed Mrs. Tucket was now retired, and the only question that remained was whether she would remain in London or return to Bitterley. For now, she wanted to stay here with Fiona. If she wouldn't be her chaperone, she at least wanted to provide support—and love—as the only person who truly knew her.

"How nice," Prudence murmured, demonstrating again that she was a woman of few words and low volume. Indeed, she'd uttered barely a handful of sentences the entire time they'd been shopping that afternoon.

Fiona regarded her for a moment. "I can't decide if you're shy or reserved."

Prudence appeared confused. "Aren't they the same thing?"

"I think shy is something you can't help, and reserved is something you do. Perhaps because you're shy." Fiona laughed, and Prudence smiled in response.

"Then I am reserved."

"Splendid. I am not."

Prudence elevated her brows in a thoroughly wry fashion. "No, I wouldn't say you are. However, you are also not completely forthcoming."

Fiona rested her elbow on the arm of the chair. "No?"

"When are you going to tell his lordship that you don't wish to wed?"

Sucking in a sharp breath, Fiona made a face as she looked toward the fireplace. "Why do you think that?"

Prudence surprised her by laughing softly. "Are you really going to deny it? After that reaction? No, you aren't shy or reserved, nor are you adept at hiding your thoughts and emotions. At least, not completely."

Exhaling, Fiona leaned back in the chair. "Very well. No, I don't want to get married. Not immediately anyway. I only just left Bitterley, where I had no choices about my life."

"We're women. Choice is not something we are typically afforded. Especially when you are lucky enough to have a Season." Her tone was matter-of-fact but without any bitterness or envy. She was merely stating the truth—Fiona *was* lucky.

Fiona drummed her fingers on the arm of the chair. "So I am learning. I had no idea there would be expectations." She'd been foolish to think otherwise, but how was she to know? She no longer had a mother, and Mrs. Tucket had demonstrated her complete lack of knowledge about such matters. Indeed, the only advice Fiona's mother had ever imparted was to be wary of who she wed, that it was the most important decision she would ever make and, once committed to, could never be undone. The counsel wasn't necessarily earth-shaking, but the earnest manner in which her mother had delivered it had always stuck with Fiona.

"There are always expectations," Prudence said with a touch of darkness. "You should tell his lordship soon."

"Perhaps he'll change his mind and send me back to Bitterley." The thought of that made her want to weep.

"Or not." Prudence lifted a shoulder. "I shan't tell him."

Fiona looked at her in surprise. "But you work for him. Surely you feel a sense of loyalty to your employer."

"Yes, but my duty is to you. My loyalty is to *you*."

The sense of solidarity sank into Fiona, filling her with a gladness she hadn't felt in some time. "Thank you. I have just decided you are the very best thing about coming to London."

Prudence smiled. "I think I'll go to bed." She started to rise, but Fiona lifted her hand.

"Wait, one moment, if you please. Would you be up for an early morning jaunt tomorrow?"

"What do you have in mind?"

"I am desperate to go to Hyde Park. It's not that far. We can walk, can't we?"

"Yes, but ladies don't go to the park in the early morning. Are you hoping to see a duel?"

Fiona shot forward to the edge of her seat. "A duel?"

"They are typically fought in the park at dawn."

"How horrible. I don't think I'd *want* to see that."

Prudence wrinkled her nose. "Neither would I. Particularly when we can observe men being idiots just about anywhere."

Fiona laughed. "Oh, I do like you. I only wanted to see the park. But if you think we should not—"

"I didn't say that. We'll just go for a brisk walk that happens to take us into the park," she said airily as she stood.

Staring up at her chaperone, Fiona felt a renewed surge of excitement for the Season. "You have quite shocked me this evening, Prudence. You are not at all what you seem."

Prudence's eyes glimmered with something indescribable. "See you in the morning."

Fiona could hardly wait.

CHAPTER 4

*T*obias walked into Lord and Lady Edgemont's house near Berkeley Square, trailing his ward and her chaperone and sponsor. Miss Wingate looked lovely this evening, dressed in an ivory ballgown trimmed in pale green and gold. Her dark red hair was expertly styled, proving her new lady's maid, recommended by Lady Pickering, was a welcome addition to the household. Tobias didn't want to think about how much money his ward was costing him. It didn't bear consideration because his father had set aside a rather large sum for precisely this purpose.

Why his father was so willing to invest in this young woman was baffling. Tobias supposed it was simply because of the affection he bore Miss Wingate's father, but since Tobias had never witnessed any sort of warm feeling from him—toward *anyone*—it was hard to believe. Or perhaps it was only difficult to accept that he'd apparently liked his friend from Oxford better than his own family.

Lord and Lady Edgemont greeted them in their grand staircase hall.

"So many lovely young ladies having their first Season,"

Lady Edgemont exclaimed after meeting Miss Wingate. "You shall have a hard time choosing a wife, Lord Overton!"

He smiled blandly before offering his arm to Lady Pickering so they could climb the stairs to the ballroom. Or what was likely, in a house this size, a drawing room and another chamber opened up together to create something approaching the breadth of an actual ballroom.

"How did Lady Edgemont know I am in search of a wife?" he whispered to Lady Pickering.

"Because you are." She sent him a scolding look. "Why else would you be back in Society after your...respite?"

The word respite made his activities seem positively benign. "So it's obvious I am looking for a countess?" He'd hoped to conduct his search without the pressure of Society watching his every move. But Lady Pickering was right—his return to Society after nearly two years of skirting the edges would be noted. And questioned. And endlessly remarked and speculated upon. He groaned inwardly.

"It is the logical conclusion. Particularly since you have recently inherited the earldom." Lady Pickering pressed her lips together. "On second thought, perhaps people won't make that assumption. Logic isn't found in the greatest abundance in the ton."

Tobias grinned as they reached the drawing room. There were already a few dozen people in attendance, and the musicians were warming up.

Lady Pickering looked back at Miss Wingate and Miss Lancaster and inclined her head toward the wall where a tall window looked over Charles Street below. A line of carriages moved slowly beside the pavement.

"Now, Miss Wingate, do remember everything we discussed. You must accept every invitation to dance until your card is full."

Miss Wingate nodded.

"Are you feeling nervous?" Lady Pickering asked.

"Only about some of the dances."

Apparently, her mother had taught her to dance, but with no occasion to practice or become proficient, the lessons had faded from Miss Wingate's memory. Resultingly, she'd spent yesterday afternoon and a good portion of today with a dancing master.

Lady Pickering gently patted her arm. "You'll do fine. Now, let us make the rounds and do your best to remember everyone's name."

Tobias again escorted Lady Pickering as they circulated the room, introducing Miss Wingate—and Miss Lancaster as her companion—to everyone they encountered. The higher the rank, the longer they stayed to converse. By the time they'd nearly reached the door again, Miss Wingate had received four invitations to dance. Then the music started, and Mr. Mansfield came to lead her onto the floor.

Tobias pivoted to excuse himself. He needed to extend his own invitations to dance.

"Just a moment," Lady Pickering said. She edged closer to him, lowering her voice to a bare whisper. "Are you aware that your ward was seen walking in Hyde Park yesterday morning?"

Evidently that was bad, given Lady Pickering's disdainful expression. Her dark brows were pitched low over her eyes, which flashed with mild irritation.

He looked toward Miss Lancaster, who stood far enough away that she couldn't hear what they said. In addition, she'd fixed her attention on the dancefloor. "Er, no. I didn't even realize she'd gone for a walk at all."

"This must not happen. Ladies do not walk in Hyde Park before the afternoon. Do you know what sort of nastiness happens in Hyde Park in the morning?"

Tobias looked at her blankly. "I often ride on Rotten Row in the morning."

"Precisely. *You* are a man. And an obtuse one at that. You must instruct Miss Wingate, and more importantly, her companion, that they are not to do that."

"I'm certain it was an oversight." Except Miss Lancaster should have known better, shouldn't she? But then Tobias didn't know her that well. He'd relied entirely on Lucien's recommendation.

"Good. You'll need to keep a much closer eye on your household, particularly if you want to achieve your own goals. Regarding that matter, who are you considering?"

"Ah, Miss Goodfellow perhaps?" He still didn't know who she was.

"Then why aren't you dancing with her?"

Tobias glanced about, which was absurd since he didn't even know who he was looking for. "She's here?"

Lady Pickering sighed. "Have you even met her?"

"Probably."

"Can you pick her out?"

"No."

She exhaled with exasperation. "Come with me."

He held up his hand. "Wait just a moment and then you may introduce us. Or *reintroduce* us." He shook his head. "If you have other recommendations, I'd be interested to hear them. Just no young ladies in their first Season."

"Why?"

"I prefer someone with a bit more experience."

Lady Pickering's brows climbed.

"Not *that* kind of experience, though a widow would be acceptable."

"I see. You want a woman who already knows who she is and what she wants."

"That would be wonderful, actually."

"I will keep that in mind. And I do have suggestions. I'll introduce you to one or two of them tonight if they are here." She gave him a sharp stare that made him want to fidget, and he never fidgeted. "Why *are* you in a rush to marry suddenly?"

He shrugged, not intending to tell her, or anyone else, the true reason. "I just am."

"There is more to it than that, but I won't demand an answer." She narrowed her eyes. "Yet."

Pausing to tell Miss Lancaster they were going to mingle, Lady Pickering led him to the refreshment area and introduced him to Miss Goodfellow. If Tobias had met her before, he didn't remember. He also didn't remember her mother, who stood alongside her. Both were attractive women, taller than average, with bright cobalt eyes.

Tobias asked Miss Goodfellow to dance the next set, and she agreed. In the meantime, he noted the arrival of Lucien's brother, Constantine, the Earl of Aldington, and their younger sister, Lady Cassandra.

"If you'll excuse me for a moment, Lady Pickering, Mrs. Goodfellow, Miss Goodfellow. I'd like to speak with a friend briefly."

Miss Goodfellow curtsied, and Tobias bowed in response. He quickly made his way toward Aldington.

"Good evening, Overton," Lucien's brother said with a warmth that was not reflected in his hazel eyes. There'd always been something off about Aldington, as if he were eternally uncomfortable.

"Good evening, Aldington, Lady Cassandra." He bowed to the young lady and felt sorry for Lucien because he seemed bothered by the prospect of his sister marrying. And she would marry—she was far too beautiful and charming to last long. Plus, she was the daughter of a duke and in possession of a large dowry. That alone made her a sought-after bride.

Lady Cassandra rose from her curtsey, her sherry-colored eyes sparkling. "How lovely to see you, Overton. I'd almost forgotten you aren't Deane anymore."

"I will still answer to that." In fact, he rather preferred it to Overton, which in his mind was his father, not him. "You must meet my ward, Miss Wingate, when she is finished with the set. It is her first Season too and she is new to London. Indeed, it's the first time she's left Shropshire. She's in the ivory gown with the ribbons."

"Green and gold ones or pink?" Lady Cassandra asked.

Tobias squinted. "Oh, I suppose there is another ivory gown with ribbons. The green and gold ones. I should have just said dark red hair." She was the only woman in the room with such vibrantly colored locks.

"I look forward to meeting her."

Turning his attention to Aldington, Tobias clapped him on the shoulder. "We must catch up. Perhaps later we can have a drink—" He abruptly cut himself off before saying at the Phoenix Club because Aldington was not a member. It wasn't that Lucien wouldn't have invited him, but Aldington had made it clear that he would never accept. As a result, they hadn't bothered.

Aldington seemed to know what he meant, for his eyes narrowed very slightly.

"At White's," Tobias said. He was still a member there, even if he hadn't entered the building in nigh on two years.

"You'd come to White's?" Aldington asked dubiously.

"Certainly! I'll see you there later." He bowed to Lady Cassandra before returning to Miss Goodfellow.

After greeting her and her mother once more, he asked if Miss Goodfellow would like to take a turn about the room. The current set was nearing its finish, and there would be a short break before the next.

"That would be amenable," she said with a slight nod. She

had an intense gaze, but her demeanor was...measured. Yes, that was the best word to describe her.

Her mother smiled approvingly as Tobias offered Miss Goodfellow his arm.

Tobias looked at her askance as they began their circuit of the room. "You are quite tall."

"So I'm told." There was no inflection to the statement, but Tobias understood her meaning.

"My apologies. That was not only unoriginal; it was a ridiculous thing to say."

The edge of her mouth curved up. "You're fairly tall, though not the tallest man I've met."

He laughed. "Touché. Tell me, what do you like to read?"

Her gait slowed momentarily, and she looked at him as if he'd sprouted another ear. "Newspapers. Pamphlets about matters of the day."

"Indeed?" Tobias's eye caught his ward on the dance floor just as the set came to an end. Her partner bowed to her, then took her hand. His gaze lingered on Miss Wingate's chest before he led her from the floor. Tobias felt the urge to go and knock him down. How dare the scoundrel look at his ward like that?

"Is something amiss?" Miss Goodfellow asked.

Tobias blinked and refocused on the woman at his side. "What? No. I have a ward, and I'm afraid I'm new to this guardian business. My father didn't give me much notice on that front."

"Your father recently passed away, is that right?"

He nodded. "In December."

"Yet here you are, mingling in Society so soon after. I'd be shunned if I did that." Her jaw tightened, and he felt the ripple of tension that passed through her.

"It's not fair, is it?" he asked, thinking she'd probably fit right in at the Phoenix Club. It's too bad she wasn't eligible.

They did not invite young unmarried ladies. They did, however, invite spinsters. Not many, but a few. When exactly did a woman pass from marriageable to spinster? More importantly, *why*?

He surveyed Miss Goodfellow and judged her to be approaching her middle twenties, if not already there. She was likely seen, at least by some, as on the shelf, meaning she was past the point where most men would take an interest in her. Tobias understood her quiet outrage and, frankly, shared it. There shouldn't be an expiration on a woman's marriage-ability. There certainly wasn't one on his.

"Fair is subjective, isn't it?" She cast him an enigmatic glance.

"I suppose it is. However, I think I can state, without argument, that when it comes to expectations of men and women in Society, they are not held to an equal standard."

"On that we agree, my lord."

They'd reached the opposite corner of the room. He turned and started back the way they'd come. In doing so, he had a clear view of his ward speaking with Lady Cassandra. Lady Pickering and Miss Lancaster stood nearby. Likely Lady Pickering had taken care of the introduction then.

"Lord Overton?"

Tobias pulled his attention from Miss Wingate. "Yes?"

"Have you reentered Society so soon after your father's death because you've decided to take a wife?"

Bollocks. She'd cut right to the heart of his intent. Logic may not be rampant amongst the ton, but he'd selected a lady with a keen intelligence. He looked forward to discussing the "matters of the day" with her when they danced.

"I am an earl and must marry at some point," he said diplomatically. "And who knows, perhaps my countess is in this very ballroom." He gave her a broad smile before darting another look toward Miss Wingate. Her arm was linked with

Lady Cassandra's. They looked thick as thieves already. He wasn't sure if that was good or bad. Lady Cassandra was, after all, Lucien's sister. She was also Aldington's, so her behavior could go either way. She could be the best possible influence on Miss Wingate, or she could be a problem.

Now they were leaving the ballroom together. Suddenly, Tobias wondered at the wisdom of them meeting.

Alas, the music began. He'd have to play guardian after.

~

*F*iona had only collided with one dancer but had stepped on Mr. Mansfield's feet at least twice. As he escorted her from the dance floor, she noted her guardian was strolling the perimeter of the room with a tall, rather pretty woman with dark hair. Was he looking for a countess? She hoped so. Perhaps he'd focus on that instead of trying to marry her off.

Mr. Mansfield delivered her to Lady Pickering and Prudence. He took Fiona's hand and bowed over it. "Thank you so much for the dance. I shall look forward to next time." He smiled at her, keeping his mouth closed. She'd caught sight of his somewhat crooked teeth during the dance.

"Thank you." She dipped into a brief curtsey before he turned and departed.

"Well done," Lady Pickering said. "I want to introduce you to someone who will be a good ally for you this Season." She led Fiona and Prudence to a beautiful young woman and a rather stoic gentleman. "Lord Aldington, Lady Cassandra, may I present Miss Fiona Wingate? She is Lord Overton's ward. And this is her companion, Miss Lancaster." She looked to Fiona. "Lord Aldington is the heir to the Duke of Evesham, and Lady Cassandra is his sister."

Lord Aldington was dressed very conservatively in all

black with a dark blue waistcoat. His tawny hair was styled neatly, if not terribly fashionably, and his hazel eyes regarded her with interest, if not warmth. Conversely, Lady Cassandra wore a stunning coral ballgown with embroidery on the sleeves and seed pearls sewn into the bodice. Her dark hair was artfully arranged with more pearls, and she wore a beautiful coral necklace. She was like a bright flower waving in the sun. Fiona had thought her own gown was lovely and that her curled and styled hair looked nice, but Lady Cassandra commanded attention. She also possessed an air that said she didn't particularly care about getting it.

Fiona instantly liked her.

Lady Cassandra held out her hand. Uncertain, Fiona glanced toward Lady Pickering, who inclined her head. Fiona took the young lady's hand, and Lady Cassandra gave her a warm squeeze. "I'm delighted to meet you. Navigating the Season together will be such fun." Her eyes danced with enthusiasm, and Fiona couldn't help but smile.

Letting go of Fiona, Lady Cassandra gestured for her to come stand next to her. She looked toward her brother. "Con, aren't you going to say something?"

He arched a tawny brow at her. "May I?"

"No, no, you don't get to say that." Lady Cassandra rolled her eyes. "I am not monopolizing the conversation. However, I intend to, so say something now."

Aldington gave Fiona a slight bow. "I'm pleased to make your acquaintance, Miss Wingate. You are quite fortunate to have Lady Pickering sponsoring you." He sent an approving look toward Lady Pickering.

"I think so," Fiona said. "Who is your sponsor, Lady Cassandra?" It occurred to Fiona that it was probably her mother. She oughtn't assume other young ladies were like her and no longer had mothers.

"My aunt. She's here somewhere." Lady Cassandra

glanced briefly about the room, but without any apparent intent of finding her. "She rarely stands still."

"Like you," her brother murmured.

Fiona couldn't tell if Aldington was being kind or not. Without any siblings of her own, such relationships were foreign to her. But Lady Cassandra's answering laugh said she wasn't offended by what he'd said. "Just so, Brother. Now, if you'll excuse us, I must visit the retiring room, and Miss Wingate is going to accompany me."

"Fiona, when is your next dance?" Lady Pickering asked.

"Not this set but the next." She had plenty of time to visit the retiring room, and she wanted to ask Lady Cassandra a thousand questions.

"Go along with them, Miss Lancaster," Lady Pickering said with a gentle smile.

Lady Cassandra looped her arm through Fiona's and led her from the ballroom. "How was your dance with Mansfield?"

"Fine, I think. I did step on his feet a few times. I have not had much experience dancing."

"You're new to London then?" She directed Fiona up the stairs.

Fiona glanced back to make sure Prudence was following. Of course, she was. "I just arrived from Shropshire the other day."

"And you're already out? My goodness, Overton didn't give you much time to prepare."

"It's quite all right. I've spent my entire life in a small town without much family. I am *eager* to be out."

Lady Cassandra flashed her a smile as they reached the landing of the next floor. "Then this will be an exciting Season! It's my first one too. I presume the goal is for you to wed before it ends." She waved her hand. "It must be. There is no other reason to have a Season. If you don't want to marry, you may as well be Miss Lancaster." She turned toward Prudence. "My apologies, I meant no offense. Indeed, I envy you in many ways."

"I have no complaints about my current station," Prudence said pleasantly.

Lady Cassandra led them into a room arranged with chaises and chairs, as well as several mirrors. There was lemonade, pitchers of water, and a maid to presumably provide assistance.

"Would you mind fetching a plate of biscuits or similar?" Lady Cassandra asked. "I'm feeling a bit peckish."

The maid curtsied and took herself off.

Fiona would never have realized you could ask for something like that. "There was food in the ballroom."

"Oh, I'm not really hungry. I just wanted her to leave us alone. Servants often gossip." Lady Cassandra winked at Fiona. "How can we get to know each other if we're thinking about whether our words will be repeated?" She looked at Prudence. "You don't gossip, do you?"

Fiona answered for her. "Prudence is my friend. She would never." She didn't really know that, but she couldn't see Prudence sharing information. Particularly given her assistance yesterday morning when they'd walked to Hyde Park. To see one of London's primary attractions firsthand had been exhilarating. Fiona couldn't wait for her first promenade during the fashionable hour.

"Wonderful!" Lady Cassandra sat on a chaise and leaned back, bringing her feet onto the cushion. "Is Mansfield on your list of potential husbands?"

Fiona perched on another chaise but didn't lie back. "I don't have a list." She wanted to tell her she had no plans to wed but also didn't want to sound provincial or silly. "Do you have one?"

Lady Cassandra laughed briefly. "No. My father does, but

I choose to ignore him. It's a miracle I persuaded him to let me wait this long to come out. I'm twenty-one, for heaven's sake. Almost on the shelf."

It definitely seemed as though Lady Cassandra's mother was no longer living, but Fiona wouldn't ask about it tonight. Hopefully this would be the beginning of a friendship in which they commiserated about a great many things. "Is that true? I'll be twenty-two in just a few weeks."

"I'll be twenty-two in May, and yes, we are not as young as we ought to be." She snorted. "But can you imagine being chained to a husband at seventeen or eighteen?" She shuddered.

"No, but then I can't imagine being chained to a husband now." She clamped her lips together as if she could somehow stop the words, but it was too late, of course. "Nor can I imagine anything about being in London, but here I am." She forced a laugh to cover her mistake.

Lady Cassandra swung her feet back to the floor and sat up. She did not angle her legs as Lady Pickering had instructed. And she leaned slightly forward, her eyes animated. "Miss Wingate, do you even wish to marry?"

Fiona wanted to expose her true feelings to this new friend, but Lady Cassandra was the daughter of a duke. On the other hand, she'd also asked for biscuits to keep a maid from eavesdropping on their conversation. Squaring her shoulders, Fiona said definitively, "No."

Clapping her hands together, Lady Cassandra rocked back with a delighted chortle. "Oh, this is excellent! You are being forced into this absurdity just like me." She straightened and looked directly into Fiona's eyes. "Now we don't have to do it alone." Her gaze shot to Prudence, who stood to Fiona's right. "But I suppose you weren't anyway. You have a supportive young companion—a friend." She sounded...envious.

"And now I have another friend. You must call me Fiona."

"Then you must call me Cassandra. We will make the best of the time we have left. Hopefully we can delay having to accept a proposal until the very end of the Season."

"That would be lovely. I, er, haven't told Lord Overton that I don't wish to wed. I don't think he'd understand." Then again, Fiona hadn't been sure Cassandra would either.

"Probably not. Men like him have a duty to marry, and women like us are expected to fulfill that duty." Cassandra lip curled ever so slightly. "And why don't you want to marry?"

"It's so…final. And limiting? I've been stuck in a very small town with very few options for so very long."

"That's a great many verys."

"It's so *very* lovely to be somewhere else. With other people."

"You want to experience some freedom," Cassandra said with an understanding smile. "As much freedom as we're allowed anyway." She looked toward Prudence. "What are you doing to help Fiona?"

"We walked to Hyde Park yesterday morning since she hadn't been there."

"An excellent start." Cassandra turned her gaze back to Fiona. "Monday we must go to Gunter's."

"Lord Overton is taking me to the British Museum on Monday. I can hardly wait."

"Tuesday then. We must also visit Hatchards, Fortnum and Mason, and it would be ever so wonderful to take you shopping in Cheapside." She frowned. "I'm not allowed to do that, but my aunt has secretly taken me twice."

Fiona grinned, so glad she'd met Cassandra. "That all sounds splendid. I want to see everything."

"And the Phoenix Club!" Cassandra exclaimed. "That's the best part of finally having a Season. Now I can see for myself what takes up so much of my brother's time."

"What is the Phoenix Club?" Fiona asked.

"For us, it's like Almack's but *so* much better." Cassandra paused, riveting her gaze to Fiona. "Are you familiar with Almack's?"

"Only that there are weekly balls later in the Season, and one of the patronesses must invite you or something."

"That's about right. It's very exclusive and is the premier location of the Marriage Mart. It's also dreadfully boring, and the food and drink are atrocious." Cassandra made a face. "Not that I've been yet, of course, but that's what my brother says."

Fiona tried to follow everything Cassandra said. There were so many places and people to remember. "Aldington goes to Almack's but spends most of his time at the Phoenix Club?"

"My apologies, I have two brothers," Cassandra said with a smile. "Aldington thinks Almack's is pleasant—that's what he says about most things, which renders his opinion almost moot—and he's never been to the Phoenix Club because he isn't a member. My other brother, Lucien, owns the Phoenix Club, and he finds Almack's dreadful. I suppose that's one of the reasons he founded his club."

Her mind swimming, Fiona wanted to know more about this club that Cassandra was so keen to visit. "What's so exceptional about the Phoenix Club? And why wouldn't Aldington be a member if your other brother is the owner?"

"The club is very exclusive, perhaps even more so than Almack's, though not at all in the same way. Members of the Phoenix Club are more likely to be found on the periphery, or even on the outside, of a ballroom. People like my eldest brother—staid, respectable heirs with every possible privilege—are not generally invited to join."

"How fascinating. Do people like Aldington want to be members?"

"Some do. Others pretend they're above it, that its membership is lacking." She lowered her voice to a conspiratorial volume. "I suspect those people are envious and would enthusiastically accept an invitation if it were offered."

"I wonder what prompted your brother to establish such a place." Fiona rather liked the sound of it.

"He and Con are complete opposites. Where Con is solemn and restrained, Lu is gregarious and…indecorous." Cassandra grinned. "On occasion. Lucien found the typical gentlemen's clubs a bit too stiff. The Phoenix Club is his answer. The best part is that the club has a ladies' side. A women's version of White's, if you will."

"Indeed? How marvelous. You said you were glad to finally be able to see it now that you're having a Season. Does that mean I can go too?" Fiona hoped so.

Cassandra's mouth compressed into a brief pout. "No. And neither can I, unless it's to attend one of their assemblies, which they host every Friday starting in March."

"Then we'll do that," Fiona said eagerly, despite hearing the edge of pessimism in Cassandra's voice. "Unless there's some reason we can't?"

"Our sponsors must be members of the club for us to attend an assembly. Unfortunately, my aunt is not a member, and I don't think Lady Pickering is either."

"My goodness, the Phoenix Club does sound exclusive," Fiona said. "And wonderfully progressive. I'm astounded that women have their own side of the club."

"And they are allowed to enter the men's side on Tuesdays."

"We can't be members?" Fiona was certain the answer was no but wanted to be sure she'd understood everything correctly.

Cassandra shook her head. "We must be married or widowed." She pursed her lips a moment. "Or perhaps we can be spinsters. I can't recall. In any case, an assembly is the only time we can see the interior, and we'll be kept to the ladies' half of the building and the ballroom, which is shared with the men's side. We are not allowed to visit any other part of the men's portion. What I wouldn't give to see all of it, but especially the men's side, where my brother reigns supreme. Or so I imagine."

"Perhaps there's a way for us to steal inside," Fiona suggested with a grin.

Cassandra laughed, a devilish glint in her eye. "I do like how you think." She sobered and cast a glance toward Prudence. "I really hope you don't gossip."

"I do not," Prudence said. "That would be a most unwelcome trait in a companion."

"I assure you, she's completely trustworthy." Fiona smiled at Prudence just as the door opened.

The maid had returned with a plate of biscuits. She was also followed by two guests.

"Here you are, my lady." The maid offered the plate to Cassandra, who plucked a biscuit from the top.

"Thank you so very much. These are my favorite." Giving the maid a bright smile, Cassandra nibbled the biscuit before rising.

Fiona also stood. Taking a biscuit for herself, she silently asked Prudence if she wanted one by inclining her head. Prudence gave a slight negative shake. Then the three of them quit the retiring room.

By the time they'd returned to the ballroom, Fiona was feeling even more excited about the Season ahead. It wasn't just because of all the places Cassandra had mentioned, it was finding Cassandra. A friend.

After several more dances, multiple glasses of warm lemonade, and making the acquaintance of more people than she could ever recall, Fiona made her way to the coach on aching toes. Lady Pickering said good night and went to her own carriage, while Fiona, Prudence, and the earl climbed into his.

Fiona and Prudence situated themselves, and Overton sat on the rear-facing seat. He reached up and loosened his cravat the barest amount. Fiona suspected he would like to remove it entirely, but to do so would probably be improper.

"What did you think of your first ball?" the earl asked.

"I'm glad it was smaller. There is so much to remember. Particularly the dancing."

He chuckled. "You'll get better."

"I should have practiced more."

"Perhaps I should have practiced with you. My apologies." He leaned back against the seat. "Did you have a favorite dance partner?"

"Mr. Rowntree, I think. He was the most adept at avoiding my missteps."

"That bad, eh?" the earl asked, wincing. "I really am sorry I didn't help you prepare. We'll do that before the next ball."

"Speaking of the next ball, I heard about the Friday assemblies at the Phoenix Club. Will we attend one?"

His gaze arrested on hers. "No."

Disappointment doused Fiona's enthusiasm. Cassandra had quite provoked her anticipation to attend. "Are you not a member?"

"I am. A founding one, in fact. Lady Pickering, however, is not, and as your sponsor, she would need to accompany you."

"Why isn't she a member? Cassandra made the club sound quite popular. I would imagine she would belong."

He hesitated in answering. "I'm not sure. You'd have to ask her."

"Can someone else sponsor me for that assembly?"

Again, he took his time answering. "Let me think on that. The first one isn't until the first Friday in March." He folded his arms over his chest and studied her for a moment, the light from the lantern hanging in the coach casting a warm glow over the planes of his face. "Finding someone to sponsor you—indeed, retaining Lady Pickering as your sponsor—will depend upon your behavior."

Fiona's pulse quickened. "Did I do something wrong tonight?"

"Not that I saw, and I do recognize this is a huge change for you. But it has come to my attention you were seen walking in Hyde Park early yesterday morning. That is not something young ladies do." He transferred his disapproving gaze to Prudence. "I would have expected you to know better."

"She did," Fiona said, coming forward from the squab. "She said I couldn't go, but I insisted. I said I'd go without her." She glanced over at Prudence and hoped she wouldn't contradict her. "It was my fault, not hers." Fiona stared squarely into the earl's eyes. The pewter looked almost silver in the dim light.

"I see." He cast a dubious frown toward Prudence. "I expect you will be more persuasive in the future?"

Prudence stiffened. "I will try, my lord."

Fiona felt terrible. She would not risk Prudence's position ever again.

Turning her head as her heartbeat finally began to slow, Fiona stared out the window. This *was* a big change from the life she'd known. Was it so bad that she wanted to experience every moment, to see as much as she could?

"I am sorry, Lord Overton," she said quietly.

"Just be careful, Miss Wingate. You wouldn't want to ruin your chances."

For marriage. He hadn't said that, but that's what he'd meant. For a brief moment, Fiona wondered if ruination might be better.

CHAPTER 5

Tobias could still feel the excitement radiating from his ward as they left the map room at the British Museum. They'd spent all of their time in just this one place, and she still hadn't seen everything she wanted to.

"I'm sorry we didn't view anything else," she said a bit sheepishly as they made their way along a gallery, her hand curled about his forearm. "And I'm glad Prudence didn't come, for then I would have bored two people instead of one."

Lady Pickering had assured Tobias that he could escort his ward to the museum without a companion or chaperone since he was her guardian, and it was a very public place.

"I wasn't bored at all." He'd enjoyed perusing the maps with her. In all honesty, he probably would have enjoyed just watching her delight. "Besides, I've been here many times, and we shall return."

She beamed at him, her deep brown eyes gleaming with joy. "This is the best day I've ever had."

Tobias felt rather humbled by her statement. It was, after all, just a trip to a museum. Except he supposed it was much more than that for her. She'd spent a few hours poring over maps, which was apparently her favorite thing to do. "I'm glad you enjoyed yourself. Since you like maps so much, I wonder what you think of cartography."

"Well, obviously I support the endeavor," she said wryly. "If you're asking if I'd like to create maps, I've never considered it."

"Would you like to read about it? Perhaps you could start with Ptolemy's *Geographia*."

She slowed, and he had to drastically reduce his stride lest he drag her along. "I'm afraid I did not have an extensive education. I did read all that I could, but I am not familiar with that book."

Humility returned as did a bit of regret. He didn't want her to feel embarrassed about not knowing things. "Are you familiar with Ptolemy?"

"He was an astronomer, I believe?"

Tobias nodded. "Also a geographer, mathematician, and astrologer, among other things. He wrote scientific treatises on a great many subjects."

"It's too bad he couldn't settle on one thing."

Tobias smiled in response. "You would find his *Geographia* interesting, I think. He explains how he used data to create a map of the known world."

"That sounds fascinating. How can I read it?"

"I'll procure a copy."

She stopped altogether then and pivoted toward him. "I can't believe how lucky I am. Thank you. For everything you've done. For bringing me here—to London, I mean. I know your father made a promise to my father and that the guardianship was made in writing, but you don't have to do all that you are. You certainly didn't have to escort me here today."

"It is my pleasure to do so."

"How will I ever be able to repay your kindness?" She blushed slightly. "Well, I can't ever actually repay you—that court gown alone is beyond my comprehension of expense—but I should like you to know how grateful I will always be."

"When you are married well and happily settled, that will be all the repayment I require." He patted her hand and started walking again.

"Lord Overton, Miss Wingate," a gentleman Tobias recognized as Mr. Rowntree called as he strode toward them.

Tobias tipped his head slightly toward Miss Wingate and whispered, "Didn't you dance with him the other night?"

"Yes," she murmured as they came to a stop.

Young and spry with a sharp chin and a warm smile, Mr. Rowntree bowed to Miss Wingate and inclined his head toward Tobias. "Good afternoon. Lovely day to visit the museum. Are you enjoying the exhibits?"

"Yes, thank you," Miss Wingate replied. "Do you have a favorite?"

"I do love the Greek antiquities. I'm just headed there."

"Miss Wingate likes maps," Tobias said. "We've just come from the library." He felt her stiffen and wondered if he'd said something wrong.

"Oh, indeed? How marvelous. Are you interested in travel, Miss Wingate?"

"I think so, yes. For now, I'm enjoying exploring London. There is so much to see and do."

"You would like my home near Durham. It has a large library with many maps." He winked at her. "And Durham is a lovely city. The cathedral is perhaps the finest in England."

"Durham is quite beautiful," Tobias said. "And your library sounds magnificent."

Miss Wingate turned her head toward him and gave him a puzzled stare. She returned her attention to Mr. Rowntree and gave him a pretty smile. "I'm keen to see Westminster Abbey and St. Paul's."

"Both are splendid. Perhaps I may escort you to one of them. Or both?" He looked at her with unabashed hope.

Tobias felt a surge of glee—this was a definite suitor! Or potential one, anyway. He glanced over at his ward. She could do far worse. Rowntree wasn't titled, of course, but she couldn't really expect that. Tobias imagined her father would have been quite pleased with this match, as would Tobias's father. The latter was almost annoying. Tobias hated doing anything that would please his father.

Yet wasn't that precisely what he was doing by looking for a wife? No, Tobias was holding on to the best parts of his life—his mother and his memories of her.

Tobias belatedly realized that Miss Wingate was staring at him. He couldn't imagine why. Pursing her lips, she returned her gaze to Rowntree. "It seems as though my guardian must consider whether I may be escorted to Westminster Abbey or St. Paul's."

Damn, had he missed a question while he'd been congratulating himself on finding a potential husband for Miss Wingate? He thought back...Rowntree had suggested escorting her...

"I'm sure we can arrange something," Tobias said.

"Well, if it isn't Lord Overton!" Two ladies came toward them, the older of whom had spoken.

Tobias bowed to the new arrivals, recognizing Lady Fairweather and her daughter, Miss Fairweather, whom he'd danced with the other night. "What a pleasure to see you here, Lady Fairweather, Miss Fairweather. Allow me to present my ward, Miss Wingate."

After a brief curtsey, Miss Wingate gestured to Mr. Rowntree. "This is Mr. Rowntree."

Rowntree bowed. "I believe we met at the ball the other night."

"We also danced," Miss Fairweather said, her dark lashes fluttering.

"Ah yes, we did." Rowntree smiled. "I was just on my way to the Greek antiquities. If you'll excuse me." He bowed again, extending himself deeper toward Miss Wingate. "I look forward to our next encounter, Miss Wingate." He looked toward Tobias with a slight nod. "Overton."

As Rowntree departed, Tobias couldn't help but notice that Miss Wingate relaxed beside him. Did she not like the gentleman?

Lady Fairweather directed her animated gaze toward Tobias. Her blue eyes were so intense that he nearly took a small step backward. "What have you toured at the museum today?" she asked.

Tobias needed to direct his attention at the petite and pretty Miss Fairweather, not her somewhat intimidating mother. "Just the library."

Before he could say anything about maps and Miss Wingate, she said, "And we are on our way out. I'm quite fatigued. I hope you'll pardon us."

Well, damn. He couldn't suggest they take a walk through the Egypt gallery now. While Miss Fairweather was a bit young for his taste, he acknowledged that he ought to at least attempt to see if they would suit.

Lady Fairweather's mouth turned down in a distinct pout. Suddenly Tobias was quite happy to avoid a promenade with the lady and her daughter. The only thing worse than an immature bride was an overbearing mother.

"I am sure we'll see each other again soon," Tobias said smoothly. "Perhaps the weather will improve, and we'll be able to take a turn around the park."

"I do long for warm days in the park," Miss Fairweather said. "I love when the trees blossom in spring."

"I'll look forward to seeing you there, Miss Fairweather." Tobias bowed again. "Lady Fairweather."

He started walking with Miss Wingate once more, increasing their pace to leave the museum. "Are you really tired?"

She kept her gaze trained forward. "Somewhat."

"Is there something wrong with what I said about you liking the maps? I noticed you tensed when I mentioned it to Rowntree. In fact, I noticed you were tense around him in general."

"I think I was a trifle nervous."

Tobias chose his words carefully, lest he increase her discomfort. "He seems interested in perhaps courting you."

She stumbled, as if her toe caught something. Tobias reached around her with his free hand to steady her, his fingers clasping her waist.

"All right?" he asked.

"Yes, just a bump in the floor or something."

Something being this discussion perhaps? "Is there anything you'd like to say?"

She glanced over at him, her eyes slightly narrowed. "*You* seem interested in Mr. Rowntree courting me. His library sounded 'magnificent'? 'Large' and 'many' are relative terms. They are hardly 'magnificent.'"

"I was simply making conversation." He frowned. "Do you not like Mr. Rowntree? I thought you enjoyed dancing with him."

"It was the least disastrous dance of the night. I would not describe that as 'enjoying' dancing with him." Her brows pitched into a V. "Or with anyone," she muttered.

"I am expecting too much of you too soon."

"Yes," she answered a bit testily. "Just because you have a duty to wed doesn't mean I do too."

Tobias clenched his jaw. He *did* have a duty, and his life would be easier if she was also settled. Hell, his life would be easier if she wasn't here at all. Glancing at her profile, he felt a pang of guilt. None of this was her fault. But then, none of it was his either. It was all his father's doing, a master of manipulation from beyond.

Still, she was a young woman in need of a husband. "Rowntree's family is excellent, and he has five thousand a year. You will be well taken care of."

"Have you already married me off then?" The question carried an edge of disappointment but also of irritation that made Tobias frown.

"It is my duty, as your guardian, to see you wed. I take that responsibility very seriously and will see it done. You'd do best to reconcile yourself to that fact." He tempered his tone lest she think him an autocrat. She simply needed to understand the way things were.

They'd reached the coach, and he helped her inside before climbing in after her. Rather than sit beside her on the forward-facing seat, he sat on the opposite side.

"All I am asking for is a little time to acclimate myself to this life. Two months ago, I could never have foreseen any of this. My goodness, I am meeting the queen in a few days."

Hell. Now he felt that tinge of guilt again. Exhaling, he stared out the window until they were driving along Oxford Street. When he directed his attention toward Miss Wingate, he speared her with an expectant stare. "I will allow you time to become used to this life; only remember that my father made a promise to your father. I will not force you to uphold it. If you are not ready to marry or don't wish to, I will be happy to send you back to Bitterley. Just say the word."

"Because there is no reason to have a Season unless I

intend to wed," she said softly, her dark eyes glittering in the filtered light of the coach.

"Correct."

She shifted her gaze to the window and folded her hands in her lap. "Then I appreciate your *kindness* in allowing me to adjust. I'm sure I'll find my way, and when I do, my...enthusiasm for marriage will rise to the surface."

Satisfied with her response, even if it had been sprinkled with sarcasm, Tobias settled back against the squab. He needed to speak with Lady Pickering. Miss Wingate required more guidance than he'd imagined.

And in the end, perhaps he'd end up shipping her back to Bitterley.

~

*S*he was *not* going back to Bitterley.

Neither did she wish to marry. At least not yet.

Fiona had thought of little beyond those things since her frustrating visit to the museum the day before with her guardian. Not all of it had been awful. The hours in the map room had been absolutely sublime. That part truly had been her favorite day ever.

Until Overton had ruined it by being a dictatorial wretch.

Perhaps he hadn't been that bad, but he didn't understand her desire to simply enjoy her newfound freedom. It was as if she were a butterfly finally free of her chrysalis, and he meant to clip her wings.

Fiona frowned at his back as they walked into Lord and Lady Billingsworth's house on Park Street for tonight's musicale. Prudence gently touched her arm, and Fiona brought her features into a more serene expression. Or at least one that didn't demonstrate her displeasure with her guardian.

Poor Prudence had listened to her lament. She understood Fiona's need to find her place before she committed to marriage, even while she explained Fiona's duty to wed.

Once they were inside and had given over their outer-wear, they were guided up the stairs to the drawing room. At the top of the stairs was a long gallery filled with people. Fiona immediately picked out Cassandra.

"My lord, if you don't mind, I'm going to speak with Lady Cassandra," she said, provoking Overton to turn.

His gaze surveyed the gallery until he found Cassandra. "I'll accompany you as I've a mind to speak with Aldington."

Fiona suppressed her disappointment. She'd hoped they could go their separate ways once they got there.

"Oh, Fiona!" Cassandra greeted her with a wide smile, and they clasped hands. "I'm so pleased to see you. What a fetching gown." Her gaze swept over Fiona's pale yellow dress.

"Thank you." She looked a bit enviously at Cassandra's vivid blue gown. None of her dresses were that dark in color. Lady Pickering had said she must wear light colors. She had one purple gown that was her very favorite. It wasn't dark, but the color was lush and vibrant. She was saving it for a special occasion, not that she knew what that was yet—perhaps her first ball at the Phoenix Club, for she was intent on going to one. Which meant she had to find an alternate sponsor for it.

Cassandra linked her arm through Fiona's. "Come, let us meander before the music begins." She smiled toward Prudence. "Good evening, Miss Lancaster. I'm so pleased to see you again too."

Prudence dipped a brief curtsey. "The feeling is mutual, Lady Cassandra."

"Don't be late for the performance," Overton said from beside Aldington.

"We won't," Cassandra said jauntily, preventing Fiona from responding in irritation.

As they walked away, Fiona leaned close and whispered, "Thank you. I fear I would have said something obnoxious."

"I saw the glint of annoyance in your eyes," Cassandra said. "What has Overton done to earn your ire?"

"Only try to force me into courtship." Fiona was perhaps exaggerating with her verb choice, but she didn't correct herself.

"It's to be expected, unfortunately. I shall hope for your sake that he will continue to refrain from presenting you a list like my father has to me."

Fiona made a noise low in her throat that would have horrified Lady Pickering. It was probably good that she was unable to attend this evening. "I fear that won't be far off. I believe I've persuaded him to give me at least a modicum of respite. This is all such a change for me after coming from the country without any expectations."

"I can only imagine. I've been raised to do just this." Cassandra raised her voice slightly in mock enthusiasm. "Have a sparkling Season where I dazzle a myriad of suitors before settling into marriage and motherhood." She rolled her eyes.

"I suppose it's worth it if you fall in love," Fiona said. She couldn't imagine marrying without doing so, but it seemed it wasn't necessary. In watching Overton, she didn't have the sense he was looking to find a love match. He was simply in a hurry to find *any* match. Or so it seemed. She really couldn't claim to know him that well. Why would he tell her his plans or confide his intentions?

In fact, with whom would he discuss any of it? His friends, she supposed. Just as she had Cassandra.

"Love is a fairy tale," Cassandra said.

"You don't think it's real?"

"I do, but I think it's special and extraordinary. And I don't think everyone is fortunate enough to experience it. My parents shared a mutual affection, but I would not describe it as love, and my brother didn't marry for the emotion, nor has he found it since." She glanced back toward where they'd left Overton and her brother.

This was only the second time Fiona had met Aldington, but she noted that his wife hadn't been present on either occasion. "Is Lady Aldington here?" Perhaps she was somewhere else in the house.

Cassandra shook her head. "She's still at Hampton Lodge where they spent the holidays. I expect she'll arrive in the next few weeks. Or perhaps she won't come at all. Con hasn't said."

"Why do you call him Con instead of Aldington? Do families address their siblings differently?"

"The story goes that when I was learning to speak, I couldn't pronounce Aldington or Constantine, his Christian name, so I called him Con. He has been Con to me and to Lucien ever since. My father has only recently stopped flinching when I use that in the presence of others." Cassandra grinned.

"Your father sounds rather terrifying." Fiona almost hoped she never had occasion to meet him. She'd yet to meet a duke. But then she was going to meet the queen the day after next, so a duke shouldn't be intimidating. A tide of anxiety tried to wash up her throat.

Cassandra gave her a reassuring nod. "He can be quite surly, particularly with me and my brothers, but he'll be pleasant to you."

Fiona thought of her own father, who'd died five years ago. He'd been involved in his studies, never having much time for her, but he'd always been kind.

They'd reached the end of the gallery where it was far less

crowded. A door stood partially open, neither inviting nor dissuading them to enter.

Cassandra moved toward it and peered inside. Turning her head toward Fiona, who couldn't see past her into the room, her eyes danced with anticipation. "It's a ladies' card room. Shall we?"

"What's a ladies' card room?" Fiona had heard about card rooms at balls and other entertainments, places where gentlemen gathered to play and wager.

"The same as a regular card room, except it appears this one is inhabited entirely by ladies." She lowered her voice. "I wondered if there might be one here tonight. Lady Billingsworth is known for her gaming—her mother used to have a faro bank years ago."

Fiona had no idea what that meant and didn't want to ask at the moment. She wondered when she would stop feeling like such a provincial. Or if she ever would.

Cassandra reached for the door, and Fiona felt a hand on her arm. She turned her head to see Prudence watching her with consternation.

Taking her arm from Cassandra's, Fiona murmured, "Just a moment." She took a few steps away from Cassandra, and Prudence followed.

"Is something wrong?" Fiona asked.

"I'm not certain you should go in there." Prudence glanced past her toward the gaming room.

"Are you truly uncertain, or are you trying to politely tell me to run in the other direction?"

Prudence smiled. "I am uncertain, which is probably bad since I should know these things. I just can't imagine gaming is encouraged for a young, unwed lady?"

Cassandra joined them. "I'm afraid I have frightfully good hearing. Playing cards with other ladies at a party like this is perfectly acceptable. The important thing is not to play high stakes, which we won't. If we play at all." She looked at Fiona. "Do you even know how?"

Fiona shook her head.

"Then probably not. We can, however, watch." Grinning, she linked her arm through Fiona's once more before turning to address Prudence. "Does that meet your approval? I don't want you to be uncomfortable. After all, Fiona is your charge."

"She isn't really. I am her companion, not her sponsor. Though I may act as her chaperone, it really isn't my place to dictate her behavior. I shall leave that to Lady Pickering and Lord Overton."

"Is it all right if we go inside?" Fiona asked. "I will only observe."

"If Lady Cassandra says it's acceptable, I bow to her judgment." Prudence gestured for them to precede her.

"Don't be nervous," Cassandra said as they entered the card room. Six tables were set up, of which four were occupied.

"What are they playing?" Fiona asked.

"Loo. It will be easier to explain after you watch it for a time." Lady Cassandra led her to a table to the right of the door. Keeping her voice low, she said, "Lady Hadleigh is a highly regarded player. She's the one with the two ivory feathers in her hair."

Fiona nodded as they took a position near the table. They fell silent as they watched for a few minutes. After a while, Fiona began to understand what was happening. It looked like great fun.

"They're only wagering pennies," Fiona whispered.

"For now. I suspect on the next round the stakes will rise. But that's because of Lady Hadleigh's presence."

"Does anyone want to join our table? We need at least two more," a voice called out.

Fiona looked toward the woman, who was perhaps ten years her senior, but didn't recognize her.

"Should we?" Cassandra asked, her voice rising with excitement.

Fiona glanced toward the doorway. "What about the musicale?"

"I'm sure we still have time." Cassandra looked to Prudence. "Would you mind going to check?"

"Oh yes, that's a brilliant idea." Fiona smiled gratefully at Prudence. "Thank you."

Prudence nodded before taking herself off with alacrity, while Fiona and Cassandra made their way to the table that was seeking players.

"Don't tell them you've never played before," Cassandra said softly. "If you get stuck, just nudge me under the table, and I'll try to help you."

Fiona clutched Cassandra's arm more firmly. "I don't have any money."

"Don't worry, I do." She waggled her eyebrows at Fiona.

They'd arrived at the table where three other ladies had already sat down.

Cassandra made the introductions—at least to the two women she knew—while she and Fiona took their seats. The third was then presented, and everyone exchanged pleasantries.

The dealer tossed three chips onto the center of the table before dealing the cards.

The oldest player, Mrs. Montgomery, on the other side of the table from Fiona, inhaled sharply, her gaze on the doorway. She muttered something that Fiona couldn't hear, but the woman to her left nodded.

Cassandra picked up her cards and silently told Fiona to do the same, her eyes darting down toward the cards on the table in front of Fiona. Plucking up her hand, Fiona promptly dropped the cards again as soon as she heard the voice behind her.

"Pardon me, but I've come to fetch my ward for the musicale."

Fiona's blood turned to ice. She slowly turned her head, and her gaze connected with a rather inappropriate area of her guardian. Lifting her chin so she wasn't starting at his crotch, she looked into his face.

And immediately wished she hadn't.

His eyes were a positively glacial shade of gray, even though his mouth was curved into a slight smile. There was no humor in it, just a façade meant to convey something opposite to what he was feeling.

For that, she was grateful.

"My goodness, I didn't realize it was already time." She turned back to the table. "Forgive me, I must go." She sent an apologetic glance to Cassandra before standing.

Overton held her chair, then offered her his arm. She would have rather walked out without touching him, but to do so would invite curiosity—and probably his ire. More ire than he already possessed.

Holding her head high and staring straight forward so she didn't see anyone's reaction to her being fetched from what appeared to be a ladies-only chamber by her male guardian, Fiona departed the card room on his arm. Prudence stood just outside, her lips pressed into a firm line and her gaze inscrutable.

Fiona wasn't sure what had happened, but she didn't blame Prudence. "I lost track of the time, my lord."

The earl looked to Prudence. "We'll join you in the drawing room."

With a slight nod, Prudence turned and left.

The gallery was empty. Presumably everyone had gone into the drawing room.

Overton pulled her along, then diverted into a small sitting room. He withdrew his arm from her grasp and closed the door.

Fiona turned, her mouth open to apologize, but the earl's features had grown even stonier since they'd departed the card room.

"Don't bother saying whatever you meant to say. Just what on earth did you think you were doing?" He shook his head. "Never mind. It doesn't matter."

"Are you angry because I lost track of the time when you told me not to be late to the performance?"

"Yes. I'm also angry because you apparently think it's acceptable to gamble at loo during said performance."

"It was my understanding that playing cards, and even gambling, was acceptable, provided the stakes weren't high."

"How were you even gambling at all? You have no money."

"Cassandra has money."

He wiped his gloved hand over his face. "I am beginning to think Lady Cassandra is a bad influence. I will speak to her brother at once."

Fiona stepped toward him. "Please don't do that. I'm sorry I lost track of time," she repeated, growing frustrated. "It looked like fun, and I've never played cards before."

Some heat returned to his gaze. "They would have devoured you whole. It's good that I interrupted you. Sometimes the ladies can be more vicious than the men." He closed the distance between them, moving to stand directly in front of her. "Miss Wingate, Fiona, you must stop these…antics."

"I fail to see how—"

He held up his hand. "Yes, you fail to see anything of import. Your behavior must be absolutely above reproach. A duke's daughter will be excused for things that you will not.

Following Lady Cassandra about will only get you into trouble. Then what will you do?"

She blinked at him. "What do you mean?"

"What will you do if your reputation is ruined? You won't be able to marry. Do you want that?"

"I don't want to get married." There, she'd said it as plainly as possible, and it felt glorious. A weight lifted off her chest, and she nearly smiled.

His eyes widened and then narrowed. "You're being foolish and immature. You *must* marry."

"Why, because you say so?"

"Would you prefer to return to Bitterley? I'm sure your cousin can still find you a nice country vicar to wed."

Her blood chilled. "Still?"

"That was his plan before I wrote to him requesting you come to London for the Season."

Fiona gasped. Her cousin hadn't told her that. Her shoulders sagged as the victory she'd felt a moment ago evaporated like steam. "Is it terrible that I just want to have some fun for once?"

Exhaling, he rubbed his hand along his jaw. "No. However, you must choose your fun wisely. Visiting the map room at the museum is acceptable. Gambling at loo during a musicale is completely unacceptable.

"I still don't understand how that will get me into trouble."

He leaned toward her, and his masculine scent of sandalwood filled the air around her. "Perhaps it won't, but you aren't where you're supposed to be, and that's when bad things happen."

She tipped her head back to look up at him and swallowed. "What sort of bad things?"

"Things like you leaving the card room by yourself and being dragged into a room by a gentleman who wishes to take liberties." His gaze briefly dipped before snapping back to hers.

"Like this?"

"I am not taking liberties," he said softly. "Nor would I. You are my ward. That would be highly improper. But you can see how easy it would be for someone to bring you here and kiss you."

Fiona swallowed again, suddenly feeling warm. He was embarrassing her again. He was quite good at that.

"Then you'd be compromised. And if the gentleman refused to wed, you'd be ruined."

"I shall be more careful."

Nostrils flaring, the earl took a step back. "You're damned right you will. And you'll marry as soon as possible"

She shook her head. "I won't."

"You will. You can either find someone here in London or return to Shropshire and become a vicar's wife. I'll leave the decision to you." He took a deep breath and smoothed his hand over his hair. "Let us attend the performance." He offered her his arm once more.

She glared at him instead of taking it, then she turned and stalked from the room. She wasn't going to marry anyone, nor was she going to return to Shropshire. There had to be another option.

Fiona just had to discover it.

CHAPTER 6

The last thing Tobias wanted to do after the discomfort of sitting through the musicale next to an angry Miss Wingate was visit White's to have a drink with Aldington. However, doing so was crucial to the rehabilitation of his reputation, and so here he was scanning the room for the earl.

Tobias ignored the cluster of gentlemen surrounding the table in front of the bow window where Brummel held court. Aldington wouldn't be anywhere near there. When Tobias had visited a few nights ago, Aldington had made a point to disdain the spectacle that often clustered around Brummel. It had briefly occurred to Tobias that Aldington might actually prefer the more casual atmosphere of the Phoenix Club where no one behaved sycophantically.

"Here again, Overton?"

Turning his head at the sound of his name, Tobias inwardly cringed at seeing Philip Trowley. Outwardly, he summoned a bland smile. "Evening, Trowley."

The older man stroked his hand over his rotund belly as he moved closer to Tobias. "I was just mocking a wager someone had entered about you marrying by Easter. Who would take that bet?" He chortled loudly, drawing the attention of others around them.

"I haven't looked at the betting book," Tobias said with a patience he only barely possessed.

"Coming here twice in one week after so long an absence following your fall from grace... I daresay you are trying to improve your reputation so as to make the best possible match." He sidled closer, lowering his voice as his madeira-soaked breath wafted over Tobias. "Tell me, is that true?"

"Perhaps I'm here to forge political connections," Tobias replied mildly as he took care not to breathe through his nose. "I'm new to the Lords, and I'm taking my new position rather seriously."

Trowley stared at Tobias a moment, seemingly at a loss for words. Then he erupted in laughter once more and smacked Tobias on the back hard enough that he had to grind his heels into the floor to keep from pitching forward. "You almost had me! I'm for the betting book." He took himself off, tottering a bit uncertainly.

Exhaling, Tobias turned and continued his search for Aldington. At last, he caught sight of the man at a table near the corner. As with the last time Tobias had visited—just four days before—the earl was alone.

"Evening, Aldington," Tobias greeted him pleasantly. "Mind if I join you?"

The earl's hazel eyes narrowed slightly as he looked up at Tobias. "You're here again?"

"Yes. I am a member." Tobias sat down, and a footman immediately offered him a glass of port, which Tobias accepted.

"Who hasn't visited White's in years until a few nights ago." He sipped his port, peering dubiously at Tobias over the rim of his glass. "And you sought me out then too."

"Because I intended to. Did I not tell you at the Edgemont ball that I would meet you for a drink here?"

Aldington set his glass down. "You did. What's your reason tonight?" Though he didn't bear a strong resemblance to his younger brother, they shared the same hooded eye shape and thick brows, which could work in concert to make them appear both devilishly handsome and uncomfortably intimidating. Aldington was currently the latter.

The truth was not only boring; it wasn't something Tobias wanted to admit, particularly since others were wagering on his behavior. Instead, he broached a topic that was also important. "I wanted to speak with you about Lady Cassandra. She took my ward into the ladies' gaming room this evening."

"Yes, I did learn my sister was in there. While I don't personally find that to be an acceptable activity for an unwed lady, it is not my place to instruct her. Our aunt is managing such things."

"Yes, well, she even funded my ward's participation. Miss Wingate is not the daughter of a duke whose debut has been anticipated for several years. She's a..." Tobias stumbled over his words. He'd been about to say she was a provincial miss from the middle of nowhere, but that was grossly inadequate, as well as unfair. She didn't deserve to be described in a way that would demand certain expectations of her. "Miss Wingate is new to London and is trying to make her very best impression."

"I understand. However, entering a gaming room is probably not the best impression."

Tobias nearly scowled but schooled his features into a serene expression. "No, which is why I'd like your sister—my ward's newest and apparently dearest friend—to guide her more appropriately."

"You can't expect Cassandra to act in the manner of

companion or chaperone, let alone sponsor. Isn't Lady Pickering managing your ward? I should think she'd be more than up to the challenge of bringing a country miss to heel."

Gritting his teeth, Tobias curled his hand around the stem of his glass. "She's not a dog, Aldington."

"Of course not. My apologies." Aldington exhaled and took another drink of port. "The musicale gave me a headache, I'm afraid. I would not have bothered to go if Cassandra wasn't having her Season. Deuced annoying to shepherd these young women, but it's our duty, alas." He fixed his gaze on Tobias. "I imagine it must be even more frustrating for you since your ward isn't even a relation. How did she come to be your ward anyway?"

Tobias had been frustrated upon learning he had a ward, but he wasn't anymore. He liked Miss Wingate, even if she had...frustrated him this evening. "She was my father's ward. Her father was a dear friend of his."

"I will speak with Cassandra and encourage her to be mindful of her new friend and their differences as to how Society might view them and their behavior."

"I do appreciate that, thank you." Tobias lifted his glass in a toast before taking a drink.

Aldington laid his palm flat atop the table, his fingertips on the base of his glass. "I'd thought you were coming here to demonstrate you'd settled down and were ready to take on the responsibilities of your title."

"That is certainly an added benefit," Tobias said with a smile.

"And are you?" One of Aldington's thick brows rose. "Settling down?"

"Since I have inherited, I fear it's time."

Aldington glanced down at his glass as he traced his finger around the base. "Have you given up your mistress?"

Tobias was momentarily confounded. That wasn't a question he would have expected from the man. "Er, yes."

"I was only curious. Many do not."

"Have you kept yours?" Tobias doubted the man had even had one but couldn't help asking. If Aldington was going to be curious about such matters, he would have to expect the same in return.

"I have never kept a mistress." His tone was cool, but his eyes didn't meet Tobias's.

Tobias didn't know what to make of that. He didn't know much about Aldington or his marital situation beyond the fact that he and his wife seemed to spend little time together. That fact and Aldington's query about Barbara was why Tobias had considered that perhaps Lucien's brother was not as staid as they believed him to be.

Aldington finished his port. "You must excuse me. I'm afraid this pain in my head insists I retire." He stood. "Will I see you here in another few days?"

"Perhaps sooner," Tobias said, wondering if he could bring himself to suffer another visit so quickly. It wasn't that White's was terrible, but the Phoenix Club was so much more than a club where men gathered to drink, gamble, and converse. And not just because Lucien had included women in the entire plan, though that was a large part of it. The purpose of the Phoenix Club was to include those who were often excluded, to offer a haven to those who had nowhere else to find comfort and camaraderie.

When Tobias had been at the butt of a scandal two years ago, many people he knew, including some he'd thought were friends, had turned their backs on him because it was the fashionable thing to do. Lucien, on the other hand, had founded the Phoenix Club and made sure that Tobias was one of the first members, along with Wexford and MacNair, who were also treated as outcasts from time to time. Since then, inviting people who were often on the outside looking in had been one of the primary objectives of the club. Tobias was proud to serve on its membership committee.

"Is there any information you'd like to impart that might help me win a wager?" Aldington smiled—a rarity in Tobias's experience. "I jest, of course. I do not make wagers."

"Of course. And no, there is nothing to share." Tobias picked up his glass as Aldington inclined his head and bade him good evening.

Alone at the table, Tobias swallowed the rest of his port, eager to follow Aldington out. He'd done his duty for the evening. Now he needed a proper drink with proper company.

~

A short while later, Tobias entered the library on the first floor of the Phoenix Club and poured himself a glass of smuggled Scotch whisky. As he'd walked from White's, his mind had turned to Miss Wingate. His earlier annoyance with her had faded, but he was still troubled by the events of the musicale.

He hadn't asked to be her guardian, nor had he promised *anyone* that he'd see her wed. Perhaps he'd really been annoyed with his father. No, not annoyed, *livid*. He'd completely tossed Tobias's life into shambles.

"Dipping into the whisky, eh Deane?" Lucien strode into the library. "Damn, I mean Overton. I was doing so well too."

"I'd insist you call me Deane, but I know you won't. Do you want a drink?"

"Yes, thank you. And I would call you Deane if you really want me to."

Tobias finished pouring and handed Lucien the tumbler.

"Tempting. My loathing for my father is particularly sharp this evening."

"Has he visited some new horror upon you?"

"No, just the same manipulation from his grave. I should have postponed bringing Miss Wingate to London until after I was wed. Then she could be my wife's problem."

"Your poor wife," Lucien said, smirking.

"Why? Managing young ladies is far more suited to a wife than to someone like me."

"You just referred to Miss Wingate as a problem. That sounds like a...problem."

Snorting, Tobias went to the collection of chairs near the hearth and dropped into a wingback chair. "She's out of her element completely."

Lucien sat opposite him. "Isn't Lady Pickering schooling her?"

"Yes, but in hindsight, I should have delayed Miss Wingate's introduction to Society and given her more time to learn what's expected of her."

Lucien shrugged. "You still can. Have her focus on her studies for a fortnight or however long. Then, when she's more comfortable, she can reenter."

Stretching his legs out and clutching his whisky on the arm of the chair, Tobias pondered his friend's suggestion. "Perhaps I should. I was so hellbent on seeing her wed so that I could focus on finding a countess that I failed to see she wasn't ready."

"Did something happen this evening?" Lucien asked.

"We went to the Billingsworth musicale." Tobias glowered at his friend. "She went off with *your* sister, and I found them wagering at loo. Since Miss Wingate had no money, Lady Cassandra supplied her with the necessary funds."

Lucien exhaled. "My apologies. But really, there's no harm in what they were doing. Unless Cass was throwing in with the high stakes ladies? Lady Billingsworth is known for her deep play."

"No, they were playing for pennies, but I still don't like it. Miss Wingate's father is not a duke. She doesn't even have a father. She's a nobody from the country." Tobias realized he hadn't paused to censor himself as he had with Lucien's brother.

"Whose guardian is an earl and whose sponsor is the inestimable Lady Pickering. She is also, apparently, a close friend of that daughter of a duke. I think you underestimate Miss Wingate's standing."

"Perhaps." Tobias took a long, satisfying drink of whisky.

Wexford tossed himself into a nearby chair. "What's worrying Deane?" he asked no one in particular.

Lucien chuckled. "I called him Deane too."

"Oh hell," Wexford said, laughing. "Was bound to happen."

"He'd rather we call him that."

"Done." Wexford eyed Tobias's glass. "You're almost out, and I forgot to pour myself something." The Irishman stood. "What about you, Lucien? Need a refill?"

"Not yet."

As Wexford stood, Tobias threw the rest of his drink down his throat and held out his empty glass. "It's the Scotch whisky."

Wexford made a face and a gagging sound. "Disgusting bilge water. Doesn't come close to Irish."

"Then why is there still so much of yours in the cellar?" Lucien teased.

Wexford snatched the glass from Tobias's fingertips. "Because I hide it so you lot don't drink it all." Chuckling, he went to the cabinet where the Phoenix Club's butler restocked the supply every day.

"Deane is frustrated by his ward," Lucien said. "And my sister, who has befriended his ward."

"Is Lady Cassandra causing trouble?" Wexford called from the sideboard.

Lucien's brows pitched into a deep V. "Why would you say that?"

Wexford returned with two glasses and handed one to Tobias, then the other to Lucien. "Because she's *your* sister."

Tobias snickered. "He has a point. And she did take my ward into Lady Billingsworth's card room."

Turning when he'd reached the liquor cabinet again, Wexford swept up his glass of presumably Irish whisky and started back toward them. "Lady Billingsworth? I hope you didn't give your ward much pin money, Deane."

"I didn't give her any. She was only able to play because Lady Cassandra supported her."

Casting himself into a chair and sipping his drink, Wexford looked to Lucien. "Sounds as though your sister *is* causing trouble." His vivid blue gaze darkened. "I know all about troublesome sisters." Because he had four of them.

"She's not, but I'll talk to her nevertheless."

"No need. Aldington said he would do it."

"You spoke to him about this?" Lucien asked. "Ah, he was at the musicale. I'm so glad I'm not the heir," he murmured before taking a drink with a thoroughly smug expression on his face.

"He was, but we discussed the matter at White's. I stopped in there before coming here."

Wexford goggled at him. "*Why?*"

"To improve his reputation," Lucien said with a snort. "As if a few visits to White's to drink with my brother will erase the past two years of his debauchery."

Tobias tossed a glare to each of them. "I'm beginning to think your brother was better company." This earned him laughter from both men. Tobias glanced toward the door. "Where's MacNair? He's less annoying than you two."

"He had business outside London," Lucien said. "How was my brother?"

Sipping his whisky, Tobias settled into his chair. "He had a headache. And he asked if I kept my mistress."

In the process of lifting his glass to his lips, Lucien's movements arrested as he pinned Tobias with a puzzled stare. "He did?"

"I found it odd too. I asked if he kept his, and he assured me, quite sternly, that he's never had one."

"That is certainly true. At least to my knowledge." Lucien took the drink Tobias had interrupted. "Perhaps I should accompany him and my father with Cassandra to the queen's drawing room tomorrow so I can pester him about why he asked you such a thing."

"You can't do that." Tobias looked at him in exasperation. "I don't want him to think we're talking about him."

"But we *are*," Wexford pointed out. He looked to Lucien. "You'd actually go to the drawing room just to investigate that?"

"Not really. I would be utterly redundant. So glad I'm not the heir," he muttered again.

"I thought Her Majesty rather liked you," Tobias said.

"She does, but that doesn't mean I need to attend her drawing room and watch a score of young ladies preen." Lucien's shoulder twitched. He'd never been interested in participating in Society or the Marriage Mart. His father, the duke, wanted him to wed, but as the spare, Lucien felt no pressure to do so.

Wexford lifted his glass in a toast. "Hear, hear." Lucien joined him in drinking.

Tobias frowned at his whisky. He missed the days when he was not consumed with thoughts of marriage, whether his own or that of Miss Wingate. He'd feel much better when she was settled and no longer his concern.

"Can either of you think of a well-regarded gentleman who is looking for a wife? He doesn't need to be titled, but he must have a good reputation." Tobias wouldn't marry her off to a scoundrel.

He realized many in Society regarded him that way, or as a rogue, at least. Dammit. He *was* trying. He hadn't seen Barbara in a week, and he'd focused the bulk of his energy on establishing his presence in the Lords.

"For Miss Wingate, I presume?" Lucien asked. "I'm trying to think of gentlemen who've joined the club this Season."

"What about Witney's spare? I met him at Brooks's the other night." Wexford waved his hand. "Yes, I still go there on occasion. Call me out if you must."

Lucien laughed and cast a look of mock disdain at Tobias. "At least it isn't White's."

"Anyway, his name's Lord Gregory Blakemore," Wexford continued. "He's an unassuming sort. He's been teaching at Oxford but may become a rector. I gather he is considering taking a wife."

"It's easier to obtain a living if you have one," Lucien noted.

"He's a scholar then?" Tobias thought of Miss Wingate's interest in maps and wondered if they might, in fact, suit.

"Definitely," Wexford said after swallowing some whisky.

"Sounds promising." And as the second son, he likely wouldn't care that Miss Wingate wasn't in possession of an impeccable pedigree. Plus, she had a sizable dowry thanks to Tobias's father. One that would grow even larger if Tobias didn't wed.

Bloody hell, it kept coming back to that, didn't it? He drank the rest of his whisky in one long gulp, then stood.

"Are we driving you away?" Lucien asked.

Setting his glass on a table, Tobias straightened his waist-coat. "No, just time to turn in."

Wexford glanced toward the clock standing between a pair of windows that looked down on Ryder Street below. "It's early yet."

"I'm a respectable gentleman now," Tobias said, brushing his sleeve. "I must keep respectable hours."

Snorting, Wexford lifted his glass once more. "Better you than me."

"Hear, hear," Lucien said, echoing Wexford's earlier words before taking a drink himself.

As Tobias made his way downstairs, the port and whisky caught up with him. The sounds of the gaming room called to him like a siren, but he held fast and went to the entry hall where a footman fetched his hat and gloves.

Donning the accessories, Tobias thanked the footman before stepping into the cold night. Thankfully, it sobered him slightly. But only slightly. Brooks's was a short walk away, as were any number of other entertainments, including the lodgings of his—former—mistress on Jermyn Street.

He could walk there or to St. James's to grab a hack. Both held temptations. He'd walk up to Piccadilly instead.

"'Evening, Toby," came a familiar feminine coo.

Closing his eyes briefly, Tobias exhaled, his breath curling from him in a wisp of steam in the chilly air. "Barbara, why are you out in the cold?" She wore a thick cloak, but there was truly no reason for her to be out here.

She sauntered close to him. "Just out for a stroll."

He shook his head as her familiar scent battered at his defenses, already weakened by the liquor he'd imbibed. "I'm not walking you home."

Curling her hand around his waist, she smiled up at him. "How about I walk you home? To my lodgings, that is." Her fingers brushed against his backside.

Typically, his body would jolt with awareness at her touching him like that, his cock hardening. And part of him *did* want her—the part that was warm and addled with whisky. The rest of him didn't want her, and he wasn't entirely certain why. Perhaps he was finally ready to actually be the man his father wanted him to be.

No, not that. Never that. Giving in to a flash of rebellion, Tobias lifted his hand to stroke his gloved fingertips along Barbara's soft, round cheek.

Fuck his father and his machinations.

Except if he truly wanted to win, he needed to wed, and this was not how he would accomplish that.

Tobias stepped from her embrace. "Good night, Barbara."

He turned and quickly made his way to Piccadilly and the boring safety of a hired hack.

CHAPTER 7

*G*oing down the stairs had been challenging. Climbing into the coach had been only slightly better than getting out. As Fiona maneuvered the massively wide skirts of her court gown into the antechamber outside the throne room of the Queen's House, she prayed she wouldn't lose her balance. How she wished Prudence were here, and not just for her help, but for her calming and supportive presence.

After they'd returned home from the musicale the night before, Prudence had apologized profusely for revealing her presence in the card room to Overton. In Fiona's opinion, she'd had no choice—he'd encountered her when he'd gone in search of Fiona, and Prudence had, smartly, told him that Fiona was with Cassandra. Fiona had thanked her for not jeopardizing her position and then admitted that her reasoning was self-serving, for she didn't want to contemplate navigating London without her. Which was precisely what Fiona was doing today, unfortunately.

The gown was a monstrosity and not just because of its size. It combined the high waist of modern fashion with the wide, hooped skirts of thirty years before, and the effect was that Fiona looked ten times her size. Or that her upper portion was a tiny bird sitting atop a massive rock. It was, in a word, unappealing.

White with a pale peach overskirt that exposed the center of the skirts of the gown, the garment was as heavy as it was unwieldy. Fiona was grateful for the support of Lord Overton's arm.

"Careful there, Miss Wingate," he murmured, his features creasing in a slight wince.

Fiona loosened her grip on his sleeve. "My apologies. This is a treacherous costume."

Lady Pickering looked from the four pale yellow feathers in Fiona's hair style to survey the room where perhaps a dozen other young ladies were already queued to see the queen. "Yes, four feathers was just right. And the cameo was a brilliant touch, if I do say so." Her gaze dipped to the several necklaces draped about Fiona's neck, which also contributed to her sensation of feeling as though she were a human anchor. Indeed, she'd wondered how she was going to leverage herself off the seat of the coach when they'd arrived. Thankfully, the earl had provided a great deal of assistance.

"Pardon me for a moment," Lady Pickering said. "I must speak with Lady Hargrove."

Fiona glanced about, wondering if any of the other young ladies felt as ridiculous—or frightened—as she did. And where was Cassandra? She was also being presented today.

A lady in her early forties and, presumably, her daughter approached them. "Good afternoon, Lord Overton. May I present my daughter, Miss Judith Nethergate?"

The earl bowed most elegantly, extending his leg in a way Fiona had never seen him do before. "Lady Corby, Miss Nethergate, I am pleased to make your acquaintance." He gestured to Fiona. "Allow me to introduce my ward, Miss Fiona Wingate."

Fiona dipped into a rather shallow curtsey. She didn't dare come close to the depth that would be required in the throne room.

Miss Nethergate was a very pretty and wholly proper English rose with pale blonde hair and sparkling blue eyes. Her blossom-pink lips perfectly matched the ribbons and ruffles on her ivory gown. It was every bit as ostentatiously absurd as Fiona's. In fact, Fiona suspected it might have been slightly larger. Miss Nethergate also had *five* feathers in her hair—four ivory and one pink.

Lady Corby's gaze slid to Fiona. "I didn't realize you had a ward. How charming."

"Yes, I assumed responsibility for her after my father passed. Miss Wingate is enjoying her first Season so far." He looked to Miss Nethergate. "And how is your Season?"

Miss Nethergate fluttered her lashes prettily. "This is my first outing, my lord. I am looking forward to the Basildon ball tomorrow evening. Will you be there?"

"Indeed we will."

Fiona wondered if she could get her eyelashes to do what Miss Nethergate's had done. She'd ask Cassandra to teach her. Surely she'd be able to do it.

"Your gown is lovely," Miss Nethergate said, eyeing Fiona's dress.

"Thank you. They're quite large though, aren't they?"

"That is the way of court dress," Lady Corby said with a patient smile. "If you walk correctly and curtsy with grace, the gown will flow and sway beautifully. Like birds showing their plumage."

Well, the feathers certainly brought birds to mind. Though they'd have to be particularly fat ones.

"Oh, it's time," Lady Corby said, her smile evaporating

and her brow creasing as she pivoted toward the doors of the throne room, which had just opened.

"Good luck," Miss Nethergate said before turning with an effortless poise that made Fiona want to weep.

"Don't worry," Overton whispered. "You've practiced plenty. You'll comport yourself beautifully."

She cast him a dubious stare. "Like a bird?"

He laughed softly. "Please don't."

Fiona smiled in spite of her nerves.

Lady Pickering rejoined them. "Ready? We'll wait to be called."

Scanning the room again, Fiona saw that Cassandra had finally arrived. And it was a good thing because her name was called next. Fiona met her gaze as she walked past, and Cassandra winked at her.

"Good luck!" Fiona mouthed.

How did Cassandra look spectacular in her overlarge gown? White with minimal gold and red accents, her dress was simply magnificent. It was the lack of fussiness, Fiona realized, that made it look less…garish.

No, she didn't look garish at all, especially given the way she glided across the floor as if she regularly walked around in such a dreadfully uncomfortable state. For even though Cassandra's gown might be the loveliest one here, it was still a death trap as far as Fiona was concerned.

Suddenly, Fiona heard her name. Every part of her turned to ice, and she feared she was too frozen solid to move. But then the earl nudged her, pulling her along into the throne room.

Rectangular, with people lining the sides as if they were spectators at a sport, the room seemed to grow longer with each step. At the opposite end was a dais upon which Queen Charlotte sat surrounded by her ladies in waiting.

Fiona's breath caught. As ridiculous as she felt, this was a moment she had never imagined and would never forget. She was a nobody from nowhere and here she was about to meet *the queen*. Everything after this would be somehow less.

The weight of everyone's stares pressed down on Fiona, joining the frightful burden of her gown and jewels and feathered headdress. At last, the dais seemed to be close. She caught sight of Cassandra to her left but didn't dare turn her head. Keeping her gaze pinned to the floor of the dais, Fiona put one foot in front of the other until Lord Overton came to a stop.

"Lord Overton and Lady Pickering," someone intoned.

The earl presented an even more elegant bow than he had in the antechamber. "May I present my ward, Miss Fiona Wingate."

Lady Pickering sank into a curtsey. "I am pleased to be Miss Wingate's sponsor, Your Majesty."

Now it was Fiona's turn. She'd practiced all this dozens of times—until her thighs and calves had ached. And while she'd done it wearing the hoops beneath her gown and a headdress with two feathers, she hadn't been wearing the actual gown or this headdress or any of these jewels.

Fiona carefully moved her right leg behind her left and slowly lowered herself toward the floor. When she'd finally reached the appropriate depth, she felt a surge of giddiness. Almost there!

But her left leg went numb suddenly. She feared for her balance. Panic rushed through her as she wobbled. She took a deep breath and silently told herself that she could manage this—she had only to rise. Only her legs were immovable, as if they were locked in place. She didn't dare look toward the earl or Lady Pickering. She was to keep her head pointed forward, her gaze directed at the queen's skirts.

Fiona heard a murmur to her right. She'd been down too long. She had to stand up!

Clenching her jaw, she squeezed her hands into fists and straightened her leg. The movement was too fast however, and the balance she'd fought so hard to maintain completely gave way.

Since she was closer to the floor than not, her body simply collapsed into a heap of ivory and yellow disaster. In that moment, she truly hoped the gown was large—and monstrous—enough to swallow her whole.

Alas, it was not. Nor did it prevent the sounds of people gasping from reaching Fiona's ears. Almost instantly, Overton's hands were on her, helping her, or more accurately, pulling her to her feet. He said nothing, but a quick glance toward his face said he was concerned.

Lady Pickering touched her arm. "We beg your pardon, Your Majesty. Miss Wingate was feeling a trifle overheated before she was summoned. Please accept our deepest apologies."

A heavy silence fell over the throne room as the queen surveyed Fiona. She kept her gaze averted just enough so that she wasn't looking directly *at* the queen. But the queen was definitely staring straight at her.

"Are you well, Miss Wingate?" the queen asked in faintly German-accented English.

Fiona clutched at Overton's arm, grateful for his presence. Lady Pickering's explanation, that Fiona was overheated, was certainly true at the moment. Still, she answered with a pleasant, "I am. Thank you, Your Majesty."

"Come forward," the queen said softly. Since she was only looking at Fiona, who was now returning her gaze, Fiona felt she should approach on her own.

She glanced toward the earl and gave him a determined look before taking her hand from his arm. Moving slowly, she approached the queen. "Your Majesty," she said, bowing her head and wondering if she should have attempted another curtsey. They hadn't practiced for this!

"Where are you from, Miss Wingate?"

"Shropshire, Your Majesty." Fiona was in awe of the queen's regal beauty. She wore a tall white wig, and her gown was made from a gorgeous blue brocade. Court dress looked absolutely lovely on *her*.

"And how long have you been an orphan?"

"Two years."

"Am I correct in estimating that you were not raised to expect a London Season?"

Was she that transparent? "Yes, Your Majesty."

"You are very brave to come here today. You've acquitted yourself well. I'm sure your parents would be proud. Do not be disappointed if you return to Shropshire unwed, for this will be the adventure of a lifetime." Her dark eyes gleamed with warmth and perhaps a tinge of excitement.

Fiona didn't know what to say. What had started as a nervous occasion and deteriorated into calamity was now culminating in something she could only describe as joyous relief. "Thank you, Your Majesty. I am thrilled to be in London and plan to make the most of my time here."

"Brilliant. You do just that." She turned her head and spoke to one of her ladies in a low tone so that Fiona couldn't hear what was said.

Clear that she'd been dismissed, Fiona did her best to turn as elegantly as she'd seen Miss Nethergate do in the antechamber. She was pleased when her skirt only wobbled slightly. Perhaps she would master this just in time for it all to be over.

The queen's words echoed in her mind as they made their way to stand on the side of the room so they could become spectators instead of the show.

The adventure of a lifetime.

Yes, this London Season was precisely that, and Fiona wasn't going to waste a moment worrying about being marriageable. She didn't mean to run headlong into ruin, but she wasn't going to be cowed into not enjoying things that other young ladies did, such as making small wagers in a perfectly acceptable gaming room. Of course, to do that, she needed funds. Why *didn't* she have an allowance?

She looked askance at the earl, who stood to her right. He looked different in his court costume of dark grey velvet, with a silver-embroidered green waistcoat, and an intricately tied cravat with lace. *Lace.* He should have looked effeminate, but the entirety somehow made his masculinity stand out even more. Rather, more than she'd noticed. Not that she hadn't noticed he was a man. But today was different. Today, he looked like the men who'd expressed interest in her. Which was preposterous because he hadn't demonstrated *that* at all.

No, but he'd shown care and concern here as he'd helped her up from the floor. As if he could read her thoughts, he looked in her direction, his eyes silently querying if she was all right.

"Thank you," she whispered. "For saving me."

"It was my pleasure. I will gladly do it again. I am your ally, Miss Wingate."

She hoped so, for she far preferred him in that role than as a foe. If she'd learned anything since coming to town, it was that having more people in her life was a good thing.

It was also just a little bit complicated.

❧

Tobias reached for one last sheaf of papers to read before going to the Phoenix Club. Glancing at the clock, he wondered if he should go now. Or not go at all. It was getting late, and it had already been a long day with the queen's drawing room.

He'd thought of Miss Wingate's topple countless times. She'd seemed mortified, but by the time they'd reached the coach afterward, she was already laughing about it. He admired her sense of humor and ability to not take things— or herself—too seriously. It was a good reminder, for life with Tobias's father had been nothing but serious.

Probably because the former earl had spent the bulk of his time immersed in his duties in the Lords. Tobias was finding it interesting so far, but he didn't see himself becoming consumed by any of it. For better or worse, he enjoyed taking time for amusement and relaxation, which was why he'd go to the club tonight.

A gentle knock on the half-open door to his study caused him to look up.

Miss Wingate peeked her head past the edge of the door. "Am I troubling you?"

"Not at all, come in." He stood from the desk and went to the hearth where a cheerful fire burned. "Shall we sit?"

"Oh, certainly, thank you." She seemed mildly surprised.

"You look far more comfortable than earlier." He hadn't seen her since they'd returned from the drawing room. He'd taken dinner at Brooks's with a few other gentlemen from one of his committees.

She glanced down, her hand smoothing over the spring-green skirt of her gown. "A thousand times more comfort-able, yes." She laughed softly before sitting in one of the armed chairs situated near the hearth. "It's a shame to spend all that money on the court dress only to never wear it again."

Tobias sat in the other chair opposite hers. "Unless you go to court again."

Letting out a stark laugh, she shook her head. "I can't imagine it."

"Someday you may need to present your daughter."

"I doubt that, but if that comes to pass, I shall hope the costume will have evolved into something far less dangerous."

"You can at least wear the headdress again this Season," Tobias noted. Or so Lady Pickering had indicated.

"Yes, I'm to remove one feather so it's slightly different. I'm glad for that economy at least." She straightened and again smoothed her hand over the skirt of her gown, skimming her lap.

Tobias hadn't ever noted how long and slender her fingers were. "Did you ever play the pianoforte?"

"No, we didn't have one."

"Would you like to learn?"

She blinked at him. "I never considered it."

"There isn't one here, but I could have one brought from Deane Hall if that would please you."

"Perhaps I ought to try playing one before you go to the trouble."

"That's probably a good idea. I'll ask Lady Pickering if she has one."

Miss Wingate nodded. "I wanted to thank you for the book on Ptolemy. I've only just started it, but I'm already fascinated."

Tobias grinned, glad she was finding it interesting. "Wonderful. I look forward to discussing it with you." He thought of Lord Gregory and how they would likely suit. Then she'd discuss Ptolemy with him. For some reason, Tobias found that mildly disappointing.

"I would like that." She fidgeted with her gown, her fingers pinching the fabric on the side of her knee. "I wondered if I might, ah, ask you about an allowance."

Surprised by her question, Tobias didn't immediately respond. He supposed he should have thought of that. "Is this so you can make your own wagers?"

Miss Wingate's eyes widened briefly, and dots of pink appeared in her cheeks. "No. I mean, perhaps. Don't young ladies receive allowances?"

He'd meant it in jest, but since they'd argued about it, he realized he perhaps should not have. "Pin money, yes. I will determine a fair amount and see that you receive it tomorrow."

She smiled as her shoulders dipped with relief. "I deeply appreciate your generosity. Truly."

"It was my father's intent that you enjoy the best Season possible. And that you marry well, of course."

"I will always wonder as to the source of your father's largesse. My impression from you is that he was not a kind man."

"I am baffled by it too, and I admit a part of me could have very easily ignored his wishes just to spite him. However, I shouldn't want you to suffer because of the enmity between my father and me."

"Why were you at odds?"

Tobias exhaled and pressed his back against the chair. "I was always closer to my mother. She spent most of her time at Horethorne, her grandmother's house in south Somerset. Before I went to school, that is where I spent most of my time as well." He closed his eyes for a moment and saw the swing that hung from the oak in the park, smelled the grass and summer flowers, felt the rush of warm air as he flew through the air, and heard his mother's laughter as she pushed him higher.

"You're remembering something," she noted softly.

He opened his eyes to find her watching him intently. "Yes. I miss my mother very much. Perhaps the closeness of our relationship was a stark contrast to what I shared—or didn't share—with my father. He was unflinchingly stern and demanding."

"How long ago did you lose your mother?"

"When I was sixteen." So long ago. "Nearly twelve years has passed."

"I'm so sorry for your loss. I'm sure she was brilliant, since you loved her so much."

"She was indeed. And how was your mother? You've already indicated your father wasn't terribly fatherly, for lack of a better word. Seems our fathers had that in common."

Tobias had a sudden thought. They were close friends and had remained that way since their Oxford days. That they'd been friends at all was surprising, given their backgrounds. He wondered what else they'd had in common. Perhaps their friendship had been very deep indeed. That might explain his father's puzzling dedication to Miss Wingate, the only child of his close friend.

"Yes, it seems so. No wonder they were dear friends," she said with a shake of her head. "My mother was caring, but she was also distracted. She was never quite...content. I'm not sure how to describe it. She always made sure our home was warm and comfortable and that I was happy. When I think back, it seems she didn't have much of a life of her own and that makes me a bit sad."

Tobias's heart went out to her. He'd hate to think of his mother not having her own life. She'd had Horethorne and him, and that had truly seemed to bring her an excess of satisfaction and joy. "I should think so."

"I suppose that's why I'm so very grateful for this opportunity you've given me—the ability to see things I never would have. To experience an adventure." Her mouth quirked into a brief, wide smile. "That's what the queen said to me today."

Tobias leaned forward. "I'd meant to ask you what she said when she asked you to approach. I wasn't sure if you'd want to share."

She lifted a shoulder. "I don't mind. She said this was the adventure of a lifetime and that I should enjoy it. I felt such relief when she said that. I'd begun to despair that a London Season is really no more than a business transaction. A young lady receives clothing and experiences, and in return, she must marry to the best of her ability."

The uncomfortable truth of her assessment pierced straight into Tobias, making him shift in his seat. "I suppose it really is just that," he said a bit hesitantly, as if not agreeing with her would make it less true.

Her gaze met his, and she didn't blink. "As I told you, I don't wish to marry, at least not right now. However, I also don't want to return to Bitterley. I fear my life might turn out like my mother's."

Another direct hit. Tobias pressed back against the chair and scrubbed his forehead. It occurred to him that he was forcing something upon her that she didn't want, not now anyway. He was no better than his father. Damn if that didn't sting worse than anything she'd said to him.

Before he could come up with a thing to say, she continued. "I will wed, however. *Because* I don't want to return to Bitterley. All I'm asking for is some time to enjoy the Season and my, er, freedom. It is my hope that in time I will meet someone with whom I will suit."

How could he argue with such a sensible plan? "You must forgive me, Miss Wingate. I fear I've been rather wrapped up in my own problems, and I failed to recognize what a drastic change this is for you. Yes, please take time to adjust. I was actually thinking that you might benefit from a respite from the demands of the Season. We have the ball tomorrow night, but after that, we'll decline your invitations for the next week or two so you may become more comfortable."

Her brow furrowed, and she rested her elbow on the arm of her chair. "I was rather enjoying the events of the Season. Even today's drawing room."

He smiled. "I'm glad. I'm not asking you to become a hermit. We just won't attend any more invitations until March. You're welcome to visit with Lady Cassandra and take outings together. Weren't you planning to go to Gunter's soon?"

Her brow was still creased, and he suspected she didn't like what he was suggesting. "Yes, we are still planning that as well as a few other things." Fiona drew a breath. "Lord Overton, is this some sort of punishment for—"

He sat forward in his chair. "Not at all. I thought you *wanted* time to adjust. This seemed like a good solution." Except she seemed to be enjoying her Season just fine, even if he thought she needed more tutelage. "It's only for a short period." Besides, with her safe at home, he could focus on finding his bride.

Her features finally relaxed, the lines in her forehead smoothing until they disappeared. "You mentioned you had problems. Is there any way I can help?"

He glanced toward the fire. "I, ah, need to marry this Season."

"'Need' to? Is there a reason for your urgency?"

He didn't want to reveal his father's dying edict. It was one thing for people to conclude that he was countess-hunting given his reentry into Society and his improved behavior. However, to share his father's machinations and the fact that he was manipulating Tobias from the grave was far more than he wanted to acknowledge.

"Now that I've inherited the title, it's time," he said. "I

thought I could see you wed and then focus on my own marriage hunt."

"I see." She pressed her lips together and turned her head toward the fire.

Was she angry with him? Why wouldn't she be? He'd treated her as an afterthought and had all but admitted it just then. "I apologize, Miss Wingate, for thinking of you as a task and not a person. It is important to me that you enjoy your Season. And your freedom."

She looked back at him with a slight smile. "I realize this is also new for you and not something you expected. I am grateful you heeded your father's wishes and gave me this astonishing opportunity. And for my expanding exposure to maps." She clasped her hands in her lap. "I shall keep an open mind regarding marriage, particularly if I meet a gentleman who isn't put off by my background or interests. It may be that no one in London will want me." She laughed softly.

"That won't happen," Tobias said with firm certainty. "You're beautiful, intelligent, witty. Why, any gentleman would want you. If you actively sought a husband, I predict you'd be betrothed within a fortnight."

Her eyes rounded, and her face lost most of its color.

He rushed to alleviate her distress. "Only if you wanted to. We are agreed that you will take your time. I will focus my energies on myself." He was the one who needed to be betrothed within a fortnight! Less than that now. "It's good that you will keep an open mind, just in case you meet the man of your dreams."

Laughing, she tucked an errant curl behind her ear. "I don't have a man of my dreams."

"Then you should think of one."

"Do you have one?" she asked. "A woman of your dreams, that is."

"I do, actually." He cast his head back and looked at the

ceiling. "She's smart and funny. She's mature so that she knows what she wants and is not easily swayed. I suppose she's also strong and confident." He lowered his gaze and met hers once more to find she was staring at him.

"You've thought about this."

Because he'd made a mistake two years ago, and he wouldn't repeat it. "I have to. I'm an earl. It has always been my duty to wed and have an heir. That I didn't do so sooner was a thorn in my father's side. What if I *died* without issue?" He slapped his palms to his cheeks and gaped at her.

She giggled. "We shouldn't be joking about death."

"Why not? It happens to all of us. If we can't laugh at life —and death—what point is there?"

She grew serious, returning her elbow to the arm of the chair and resting her chin on her hand. "You make a compelling argument. I'd rather laugh. Take today's debacle, for instance. I was so wound up with anxiety and fear that I almost forgot to have a good time. I met the queen, for heaven's sake! And yes, I fell on my arse, but—" She clapped her hand over her mouth. "Sorry."

Laughter erupted from him, and once he started, he couldn't stop. It was the combination of the horror on her face from saying "arse" and the memory of the horror on her face when she'd collapsed in front of the bloody Queen of England.

Thankfully, she joined in with him, her face lighting up with humor and joy. And of course she did. He'd meant it when he'd told her she was witty. His eye caught the clock on the mantel. If he was going to the club, he should probably leave…

He didn't want to.

When his laughter began to fade, he sat forward to the edge of his chair. "We're still going to a ball tomorrow night. How is your dancing coming along?"

"Well, I think. I practiced with the dancing master every day except today."

He stood and offered her his hand. "Show me."

She slipped her fingers into his palm, and he felt a surprising jolt. Her gaze ratcheted up to his, and he tugged her from the chair.

Leading her to the center of the study, he stepped back from her. "What dance do you prefer?"

"None of them."

He arched a brow. "You don't like dancing at all?"

"I like dancing. I'm just awful at it."

"You can't be that bad. Have you waltzed?"

"No. Lady Pickering said I would learn that last, and, in the meantime, I'm to say I don't have permission. Doesn't that make me sound dreadfully provincial?" She shuddered.

"No." He laughed again. "All right, maybe. I'll teach you."

"Really?"

"Why not?" He moved closer to her. "There are a few ways to conduct a waltz, but I'll show you the version I prefer." He took her left hand, clasping it within his, then placed his palm against the flat of her back. "You put your other hand on my shoulder."

She complied, looking up at him in slight surprise. "We're so close."

There were still several inches between them, but he supposed this was closer than she'd ever been to a gentleman. "Now you know why permission is required." He gave her a flirtatious smirk, such that she might expect from a gentleman on the dance floor.

She smacked him on the shoulder. "Don't do that!"

"Do what?" he asked with faux innocence.

"Behave like one of the young bucks who might wish to court me."

"I was once a young buck." Who flirted with every lady he met, regardless of her age or marital status.

"You're my guardian."

Yes, he was. And for a fleeting moment, he'd found that disappointing.

"Right. Then allow me to behave like a guardian and teach you to waltz." Lifting his chin and stiffening his frame, he focused on her hairline. "The most important thing to remember about the waltz is keeping time to the music. You can count one-two-three in your head. But don't get too caught up in doing that or you won't be able to exchange witticisms with your partner."

"You assume my partner will be capable of being amusing."

"One can hope. Dancing with a dullard is truly awful."

She nodded, her expression effusive. "Yes, you're stuck together for so much *time*. Abysmal."

"I'm going to guide you around the room," he said. "We'll move in a clockwise direction."

"And pretend there is music playing."

Tobias pressed his hand against her back and clutched her hand more firmly, then started to move. A melody came to his mind, and he began to hum.

She stumbled, and he had to clasp her even more tightly to keep her upright. "What are you doing?" she asked.

"Dancing."

"No, the sound you're making."

"I'm humming." He started up again as he steered her in a small circle, which was all the room would allow. They risked becoming dizzy.

She stopped so abruptly that he nearly fell. Digging her fingers into his shoulder, she started laughing.

"We're barely dancing! How can you be laughing?"

"Because you sound like a cat in mourning."

He stared at her, shocked, but he was already starting to laugh.

She sobered. "My apologies," she said solemnly. "To cats. I think that was perhaps insulting to them."

"Fiona!" The laughter spilled out of him then, and it was far more debilitating than the last time. Moisture pricked his eyes as he fought to gain his breath.

She grinned as she watched him. Then, gradually, she began to laugh too. A long moment later, they stood together fighting to catch their breath, their hands still clasped.

"You did not call me Miss Wingate," she managed to say.

He took a deep breath and wiped the back of his hand over his eyes. "And I apparently sound like a dying animal."

"That is not what I said!"

"Is it wrong?"

She shook her head, another giggle escaping her.

At the precise same moment, they both looked down at their still-joined hands. Their amusement came to an abrupt and rather obvious halt.

They released each other and took a step back.

"Well, that was nearly as disastrous as my presentation to the queen," she said.

"That bad? I was rather enjoying it, or at least the few seconds I was allowed to." He rubbed his hands together for he could still feel the heat of her palm against his. He could also smell her lavender scent.

He darted a glance toward the clock and decided it wasn't too late after all. "I must be on my way to the club. Thank you for the, ah, memorable *dance*."

She curtsied, dipping as deep as she had that afternoon. However, this time, she rose with grace and precision. "Haha! I did it. See, it *is* those infernal gowns."

"I never doubted it," he said. "Or you. See you tomorrow, Miss Wingate." He turned.

"Good night," she called after him.

A few minutes later, wrapped in his great coat and a hat stuffed on his head, Tobias pulled on gloves as he strode toward Bond Street, where he would still be able to catch a hack. He hadn't wanted to wait for his coach to be brought round from the mews.

Now that he was going to ease up on matchmaking Miss Wingate, he needed to plan for what could happen. No, what *should* happen. He would marry in the coming weeks, and Miss Wingate would come under the new countess's oversight.

And just who would that countess be? Bloody hell, he needed to set his sights on someone and move rapidly to a betrothal. It seemed he was destined for a special license wedding at this point.

Tomorrow at the ball, he must be singularly minded. Hopefully Miss Goodfellow would be there. And who was the other woman Lucien had mentioned? Tobias thought of the young lady he'd met at the drawing room that afternoon —Miss Nethergate. He shuddered. No, she was far too young. He wasn't going to repeat the errors of the past.

Resolved toward his goal, Tobias inhaled a deep breath of cool night air. Oddly, he could have sworn he smelled lavender.

CHAPTER 8

"Cassandra!" Fiona greeted her friend as soon as she entered the Basildons' ballroom with Prudence at her side. It felt good to have Prudence back, as if nothing horrendous would befall Fiona as it had at the queen's drawing room the day before.

Cassandra stood near the wall. Her aunt, whom Fiona had met briefly at the Edgemont ball, was deep in conversation with another lady nearby.

"Fiona, I'm so glad to see you. I worried you may not come tonight after what happened yesterday. But then I decided that was silly because you would never let such a thing affect you that much." Cassandra's brow puckered. "Are you all right?"

Fiona laughed gaily. "More than. Think of the story I have to tell for the rest of my life."

"What did the queen say to you? Everyone was dying to know."

"If I tell you, do you promise not to share? I'd rather people continue to guess." She winked at Cassandra, who grinned.

"I do like how you think. It is no wonder we are friends."

"As it happens, she told me I was having the adventure of a lifetime, and she's right. A country girl like me having a London Season. Who could have imagined that? I took it quite to heart and informed Lord Overton last night that I would not be rushed into marriage."

Cassandra's dark brows climbed her forehead. "Did you? What did he say?"

"He agreed." Fiona glanced toward Prudence. "However, he also said that after tonight, I shall be taking a break from accepting invitations for the next week or two." Fiona pushed her lips into a brief pout.

Cassandra looked crestfallen. "That is utterly unfortunate. Events like this won't be the same without you."

"He said we can still take all the outings we planned. I do believe he is relieved to not concern himself with me, since he's focused on finding his own wife. At least that's what Prudence and I deduced."

Prudence nodded in agreement.

Cassandra's eyes lit with mischief. "Do you know what I should do? I should flirt with Overton and make a courtship seem imminent. My brothers would have fits." She laughed, then tapped her finger against her lip. "So tempting." Blinking, she focused beyond Fiona. "Speaking of brothers, here comes Lucien. You haven't met him yet, have you, Fi?"

Pivoting, Fiona saw Lord Lucien coming toward them. "I have not." He looked more like Cassandra than like their brother, Aldington. Dark-haired and dark-eyed, Lord Lucien moved with the predatory grace of a cat stalking a bird.

At that moment, Cassandra's aunt turned from the woman she'd been speaking with. "Lucien, since you're here, I may take myself off." She waved to Cassandra. "See you later, dear." Her gaze landed on Fiona and then Prudence with a bit of surprise. Apparently, she hadn't noticed their arrival. "And your friend is here with her companion. Yes, you will be quite taken care of. Splendid." Smiling, she left in the company of her friend without waiting for anyone to respond.

"I see Aunt Christina is as helpful as ever," Lord Lucien noted with a wry shake of his head.

"Always," Cassandra drawled. "Lucien, allow me to present my dear friend, Miss Fiona Wingate."

Lord Lucien took her hand and bowed elegantly. He did not press a kiss to her glove, which Fiona would not have minded. In fact, she would have found it thrilling. There was something rather magnetizing about him. But he was also her newest, dearest friend's brother, and she would cease to think of him as attractive immediately.

"I have heard a great deal about you, Miss Wingate," he said, his deep voice rippling over her.

"Have you?"

"Overton is a close friend." He looked toward Prudence. "Good evening, Miss Lancaster. You are looking well."

"Thank you, my lord. It's nice to see you."

Prudence knew Lord Lucien? Fiona was dying to know how, but she'd have to wait to ask her about that.

"Lucien, it's good that you're here," Cassandra said. "I've been wanting to speak with you about the Phoenix Club assemblies." She glanced toward Fiona. "I would like to go but, as you know, Aunt Christina is not a member. Neither is Miss Wingate's sponsor, Lady Pickering."

Lord Lucien gave her a bemused look. "I know how desperately you want to come to the club, but I can't extend invitations to either one of you." He cast an apologetic glance toward Fiona.

"Have you even invited Aunt Christina?" Cassandra asked.

"No," he said slowly, stretching the tiny word out. "She would likely decline."

Cassandra took a step toward him, her expression pleading. "Will you please try? She likes you. She might surprise you."

"Father won't like it. Neither will Con."

"Since when do you care what they like?"

His lips spread in a devilish smile. "Never."

"I'm actually surprised you haven't invited her just to annoy Papa. And Con."

"You make an excellent point." He cocked his head. "Why haven't I?" He narrowed his eyes playfully at his sister. "You've always been far too smart."

Cassandra notched up her chin in faux haughtiness. "So you tell me."

Their warm and easy sibling banter teased an ache inside Fiona. She hadn't ever had siblings, of course, and she couldn't even say she'd had a close relationship with family. Seeing them, she realized she wanted that—a connection with others. A family.

Perhaps marriage wouldn't be such a bad thing, not that she'd ever thought it would be. But perhaps it wouldn't be detrimental to consider it sooner than later. Yes, she would keep an open mind, just as she'd told Overton she would.

"Fiona, you will come as our guest once Aunt Christina accepts the invitation," Cassandra said brightly.

"You're confident." Lord Lucien shook his head. "But then you always are. However, that doesn't mean you're always right. Do not be surprised if Aunt Christina does not want anything to do with the club."

"I find that difficult to imagine. Why would anyone—especially a woman—decline an invitation? I'd give anything to be a member."

"So you tell me at every opportunity," Lucien said wryly.

"Perhaps if you didn't tell me how delightful and wonderful it is, I wouldn't be so keen to get inside." Cassandra looked to Fiona. "You should have heard him while he was decorating the club before it opened, always discussing an expensive wallpaper or the marble he'd ordered for a fireplace or the massive painting of Pan hosting a bacchanalia that he commissioned to hang in the entry hall. He made sure I was positively seething with envy."

Lucien grinned. "It's a brother's duty to torment his younger sister. You forgot to mention the sister portrait featuring Circe and her nymphs as Odysseus's men bow to them in the ladies' foyer."

"I'd love to see that," Fiona said, more eager than ever to get into the Phoenix Club.

Lord Lucien's gaze strayed for a moment, and he lifted his hand to someone in greeting.

A blond gentleman strode toward them. He was tall and slender with a soft, hesitant smile. "Evening, Lord Lucien." His attention flitted toward Cassandra, Fiona, and Prudence.

"Good evening, Lord Gregory. Allow me to present my sister, Lady Cassandra, Miss Wingate, and her companion, Miss Lancaster."

Lord Gregory bowed to each of them in turn, starting with Cassandra as propriety dictated. However, his gaze settled on Fiona. "Would you care to dance the next set, Miss Wingate?"

Fiona was surprised that he asked her instead of Cassandra. She was prettier and possessed a much higher rank. Surely that mattered to a lord? She had no idea of his actual rank. Lady Pickering had encouraged her to spend time looking through Debrett's, but Fiona found reviewing people's titles and trying to recall their names far less entertaining than, say, poring over a map and recalling the names of countries and cities and rivers and so on.

She inclined her head toward Lord Gregory. "That would be lovely, thank you."

"In the meantime, shall we promenade?" Lord Gregory asked pleasantly.

Part of Fiona didn't want to leave her friend, but she was also feeling more confident about her dancing skill and wanted to see if she'd actually improved. Or perhaps she supposed nothing could be worse than what had happened the day before at the queen's drawing room. "Yes, let's." She curtsied to Lord Lucien and Cassandra and nodded at Prudence before taking Lord Gregory's arm.

"Pleasure to meet you, Miss Wingate," Lord Lucien said as they departed.

The Basildons' ballroom was much larger than the Edgemonts' had been, but then their house was bigger overall too. Hundreds of candles illuminated the space and mirrors probably made the size seem more impressive.

They started on a circuit of the perimeter. Fiona wondered if she would see her guardian.

"You're a friend of Lord Lucien's?" Fiona asked. "Lady Cassandra has become a dear friend to me since I came to London."

"I don't know him well, no. We've only recently become more directly acquainted. He attended Oxford with my older brother."

"I see."

"I *still* don't have an invitation!" a lady declared in an impossible-to-ignore shrill tone as they passed her. "I can't believe you do!"

Fiona glanced toward the woman who'd spoken. In her late thirties, her face was quite florid and her expression outraged.

"I'm sure yours will come soon," the other woman, who stood in profile to them, soothed in a calmer, quieter voice.

"I wonder if they're speaking of the Phoenix Club," Fiona said as they left the pair of ladies behind. "It seems to be quite the rage."

"It does indeed. I was recently invited, actually."

Fiona tipped her head to look up at him. "Were you? Well done."

He glanced down at her with a wry smile. "I didn't *do* anything."

"And did you accept?"

"I haven't decided yet. I only received the invitation yesterday. Lord Lucien did search me out at Brooks's last night to ensure I received it."

"I think you must accept, don't you? It seems a particular honor. You heard and saw that woman. Becoming a member of the Phoenix Club is important to one's standing."

"I'm not sure that's true. There are those who say it's beneath them, that to have a club that accepts both men and women, even if they are mostly separated, is beyond the pale."

Fiona nearly snorted. She could think of many things that were beyond the pale, and this was not one of them. "Well, I can't become a member because I am unwed. I would argue that is beyond something, if not the pale."

"My brother hasn't been invited, and he's the heir. Isn't that strange?"

"I'm not sure it is. It seems they invite very specific people —or not—and one must assume they have a good reason." She slowed. "Is it a they? Or does Lord Lucien make all the decisions?"

"From my understanding, there is a committee." He lowered his voice. "The Star Chamber."

Fiona briefly pressed her hand to her lips and met his gaze. "They don't really call themselves that."

He shook his head. "That's what others call them."

"Those who aren't invited, I'd wager." The Star Chamber was not exactly a favorable term. It also inferred secrecy. "Who is on this committee?"

"No one knows for sure, but Lord Lucien is obviously a member since he owns the club. Or one would assume anyway."

"I think that's a fair assumption. The rest are secret?"

"The ladies' side has four patronesses, and it is also presumed they are on the committee."

"Who are these patronesses?" Fiona wondered if they could be petitioned to somehow allow her and Cassandra entry to a ball. Perhaps one of them would be willing to act as a sponsor. She had no idea if any of that was even possible, but why not try?

"Mrs. Renshaw is one of them. She oversees the ladies' side in much the way Lord Lucien manages the gentlemen's. Lord Lucien explained that much to me last evening."

Mrs. Renshaw. Fiona would speak with Cassandra about her as soon as possible.

"I think you should feel flattered that you've been invited," Fiona said.

He didn't immediately respond. She looked at his profile, his long, dark blond lashes sweeping down as he blinked. "I hadn't thought of it that way, but I suppose I do. I am not, ah, typically at the top of anyone's list when it comes to social opportunities." A faint shade of pink briefly swathed his upper cheekbones. "I probably shouldn't have admitted that to you."

"Nonsense, I'm glad you did. I can wholeheartedly understand your position. I may be the ward of an earl, but I'm from a small village in Shropshire, and I've never been anywhere before. Then yesterday I was presented to the queen."

"That's quite an advancement." He grinned at her, and she

acknowledged he was rather handsome. "This is really my first Season too. I've spent the last several years teaching at Christ Church College at Oxford."

"How fascinating. What did you teach?"

"Religious studies. I'm intending to become a vicar, though my father hopes I'll be a bishop one day."

"Do you want that?"

The pink returned to his cheeks. "Honestly? Yes." He shook his head. "I can't believe I admitted that to you. It's rather immodest, isn't it?"

She laughed. "No, it is not. Ambition isn't bad, even for a man of God."

"God might disagree," he said drily.

"Except I'm sure your ambition is entwined with your desire to advance the word of God."

"The Phoenix Club is a distant second to you when it comes to flattery, Miss Wingate." He sent her a slightly sardonic look. "Perhaps I'm the type of religious man who only wants to find a living so that I may reap the benefits and will employ a curate who does all the work."

"Well, that sounds like the vicar in Bitterley." Fiona thought of poor young Tom Keeble, the curate. The vicar didn't do a thing beyond sermonizing, and he only did that once a month, leaving the rest to Tom. "I realize we just met, but I can't see you doing that. And if you did, you certainly wouldn't admit it. Nor would you think twice about accepting membership in London's most exclusive club."

He laughed. "You are a most logical young lady, Miss Wingate."

"Why thank you, my lord."

Fiona's gaze connected with a familiar pair of pewter eyes. Lord Overton stood to her left, his attention focused wholly on her. His expression was inscrutable, but something about his stance made her catch her breath.

Why?

Recovering her wits, she smiled at him and lifted her hand, not quite waving.

"See someone you know?" Lord Gregory asked.

"My guardian, Lord Overton. Are you acquainted with him?"

Lord Gregory shook his head. "I am not, but being relatively new to town, there are many people I haven't yet met."

"If you accept the invitation to the Phoenix Club, you will undoubtedly get to know him there. He's a member, and a close friend of Lord Lucien's." She looked over at him. "Are you going to accept?"

"I think I might, owing to your counsel."

"I don't think you'll regret it." Fiona noted the musicians were preparing to start the next set.

"I think it's time we made our way to the dance floor," Lord Gregory noted.

She hesitated, casting him an apologetic glance. "I should warn you that I'm not very good."

He didn't appear concerned in the least. "I'm sure you're more than accomplished."

"Aside from only recently learning most of these dances, I am apparently clumsy, a trait I hadn't noticed before coming to London."

He led her onto the dancefloor. "Surely you're mistaken. Or exaggerating."

She let go of his arm and faced him. Arching her brow, she looked him square in the eye. "I fell down yesterday while curtseying to the queen."

His eyes rounded with horror. "That was you?"

Of course, he'd heard the story. Fiona had noticed people staring at her tonight.

"It was indeed."

"And here you are tonight without a shred of embarrassment. You are a most astonishing young woman, Miss Wingate."

Smiling, she inclined her head. "I hope you still think so at the end of the set."

~

*I*t was the best she'd ever danced. She looked graceful and confident, and, most importantly, like she was having a grand time. So did her partner. Tobias diverted his attention from her and made his way to Lucien, who was standing with Miss Lancaster.

"Not dancing this set?" Lucien asked. "I expected you to have a full dance card."

"Allow me to just get it out and show you," Tobias said sarcastically. "Why aren't *you* dancing?"

Lucien let out a laugh. "I'll pretend you didn't ask that. Why are you in a mood?"

Was he? Tobias stroked his hand down his jawline. "I see you introduced Lord Gregory to Miss Wingate."

"That was the plan, wasn't it?" Lucien stared at him as if he'd gone daft.

Tobias glanced toward Miss Lancaster, who would likely repeat anything she overheard to Miss Wingate. Smiling, he begged her to excuse them before motioning to Lucien to walk with him.

"What's going on with you?" Lucien asked as they left Miss Lancaster.

"I don't want to discuss Miss Wingate in front of her companion. I assumed that would be obvious." Tobias waved his hand. "There's been a change in plan. I'm not pushing my ward into marriage. As you so helpfully suggested the other night, I'm giving her a break from this sudden turmoil in her life."

"Is this because she fell down in the queen's drawing room yesterday?"

Tobias heard the humor in his voice and sent him a glower. "That was very traumatic." Except she was laughing about it now, so perhaps it wasn't. "But no, it's not because of that. Not specifically." He brushed his fingertips across his forehead.

"You've come to like Miss Wingate very much," Lucien remarked softly. "That's very kind of you to give her a reprieve—just the opposite of what your father would do, in case you hadn't already noted that."

"I hadn't, but that does endorse the change in tactic, doesn't it?" Tobias came to a stop and pivoted to face the dance floor where dozens of dancers were moving in concert, including Miss Wingate. "For now, it's best that I focus on my own marriage goals instead of Miss Wingate's."

"Your time is dwindling, isn't it?"

Tobias shot him another dark stare. "Thank you for pointing that out." He scanned the ballroom and found Miss Goodfellow lingering in the corner with her mother. Good, he'd ask her to dance when he finished with Lucien. Looking to his friend, he asked, "What was the name of the widow you suggested to me?"

"Lady Alford, but she's already accepted a proposal. Lord Pettiford got there first, I'm afraid."

"That was bloody fast."

"Perhaps you should consult with Lord Pettiford for advice on how to move more quickly."

Annoyed, Tobias stared at Lucien. "Give me one good reason why I shouldn't haul you into the garden and plant you a facer."

"Because I'll give you one right back, and then you'll be horribly unattractive to your prospective brides." Lucien grinned, clearly enjoying needling Tobias about his wife hunt.

With a low grunt, Tobias started to turn. "Your company has been most helpful this evening. I'm off to *speed up* my endeavors."

Lucien snagged his sleeve. "Wait just a moment, if you don't mind."

Exhaling, Tobias gave him his full attention.

"Cassandra has asked me to invite our aunt to the Phoenix Club so that she may act as sponsor for Cassandra to attend a ball. And for Miss Wingate, since Lady Pickering has never responded to our invitation." He spoke in a near whisper, and Tobias moved closer so no one would overhear their conversation.

"Should we be discussing this in a ballroom?" Tobias asked softly. Who was and wasn't invited to the Phoenix Club was a topic of great debate and inquiry. Anyone over-hearing even a snippet of this conversation would most certainly crow about it.

Lucien lowered his voice even more. "No, but it's an urgent matter."

"You want to extend the invitation immediately?" Tobias smiled as he shook his head. "You are impossibly devoted to your sister." He often wished he had a sibling for whom he could care about in that way. Perhaps he should try to think of Miss Wingate in that manner. Yes, a younger sister he would oversee and protect.

"Someone has to be," Lucien said. "I'm merely trying to speak to as many of…us as possible. Will you stop by the club later?"

"I will. Are you prepared for your father and brother to be furious with you?"

Lucien smirked. "Always. Father will try to prohibit Cass

from going to the balls, but I'll win out in the end, particularly if Aunt Christina joins the cause."

"Do we really want her though?" She possessed an air of insincerity that pricked Tobias's ire.

"Think of another way for my sister and your ward to gain entry, and I'll support it. Now go dance with Miss Goodfellow."

"It's your bloody club," Tobias muttered. "If you can't find a way for your own sister to come, whose fault is that?" With a final look over his shoulder, Tobias took himself off to the corner.

"Good evening, Lord Overton," Mrs. Goodfellow greeted him. "How pleasing to see you this evening."

He bowed to both women. "The pleasure is mine. Might we promenade and then dance, Miss Goodfellow?"

"I would appreciate that, thank you."

Appreciate. What did that mean?

Christ, he *was* in a mood. And he still didn't know why. He exhaled the tension from his shoulders and gave Miss Goodfellow his arm and a bright smile.

~

*L*ater that night, when Tobias was settled in his coach with Miss Wingate and Miss Lancaster, he stretched his legs out, feeling much better than he had earlier. His promenade and dance with Miss Goodfellow had gone exceedingly well. He'd call on her Monday, and perhaps a week from now, they'd be ready to announce their betrothal.

"How was your evening?" Tobias asked. "I barely saw you."

"I danced a great deal. Did you happen to see?" Her eyes held a delightful sparkle. "I'm much better."

"I did, actually. Well done."

"Several people did ask me about the unfortunate situation at the queen's drawing room. Most commented that I looked well recovered."

Tobias wrinkled his nose. "Did that bother you?"

"Not at all," she said brightly. "Lord Gregory and I had quite a laugh about it, actually."

"Lord Gregory?" Tobias asked as if he didn't know who the man was or that he'd all but delivered him into her orbit.

"We danced. And promenaded, I suppose. I liked him very much." Her eyes sparkled in the lamplight. "He said he was recently invited to join the Phoenix Club but hadn't yet decided whether to accept. I convinced him he should."

"Did you now?"

"What possible reason could there be to decline it?" She stared at him intently. "It's a coveted invitation. I heard one woman carping about being ignored by the club, but she seemed unpleasant. And since everyone I know who is a member is *exceedingly* pleasant, it's easy to deduce that the membership must be of a high quality."

Enchanted by her reasoning, he curled his mouth into a faint smile. "Which members do you know exactly?"

"Er, you, of course. And I met Lord Lucien this evening." She looked up at the ceiling of the coach, as if she might find an answer in the brocade. "Very well, I don't know many, but *you* are exceedingly pleasant."

Feeling inordinately flattered, Tobias sat a bit straighter. "Thank you."

Miss Wingate tipped her head to the side. She brushed at a dark red curl grazing her temple. "What is the Star Chamber?"

Tobias stared at her. "The what?"

"That's what some call the club's membership committee."

"Is that true?" He glanced toward Miss Lancaster.

Her brows rose. "Why would I know?"

"No reason. I'm just...surprised." He laughed. "And amused. The *Star Chamber*, really?"

"Because it's so *secretive*," Miss Wingate said, lowering her voice and grinning as she said the last word.

"And because the committee has such power," Miss Lancaster put in.

"So you did know?" Tobias asked Miss Lancaster.

She shrugged, smiling faintly.

Miss Wingate nodded. "Yes, their power. I'd love to know who's on this committee. Besides Lord Lucien, of course. And the patronesses."

"Who said the patronesses are on the committee?" The question leapt from his mouth before he considered how it might sound. But it was silly to think they'd gather he was on the committee from just that.

"No one *said*," Miss Wingate answered breezily, not seeming to make any assumptions about his question. "Lord Gregory and I were only musing as to who the members might be. They seemed the most obvious candidates. I have not met Mrs. Renshaw. I understand she oversees the ladies' side."

Tobias knew what she was doing. "You're trying to maneuver your way into an assembly, aren't you?"

"Is that bad?" Her eyes narrowed slightly, and she pursed her lips. "You're certainly not helping."

"That's not true." He crossed his arms. "Why are you so bloody interested in going to a Phoenix Club ball anyway?"

She blew out a breath. "Didn't I just finish explaining how coveted an invitation to the Phoenix Club is? Truly, if you *want* me to have a successful Season, I must attend a Phoenix Club assembly. Only think of how attractive that will make me to potential suitors."

Laughter exploded from him then. "Attending a ball as a guest is not the same as being a member. I daresay there will be a number of young ladies who attend a ball who will not find themselves members in the future when they are eligible."

"So some of the attendees will be beneath the club's lofty standards, while I won't even be able to go." She clasped her hands in her lap and blinked at him.

Hell, he'd walked right into that. "I am working on how you might attend an assembly, all right?"

Unlacing her hands, she rested them on the seat on either side of her lap. "You are?"

"Don't be disappointed if it doesn't come to fruition."

"It's a stupid rule. *You're* a member and you're my *guardian*. I should be able to go with Prudence as my chaperone."

Once again, he couldn't argue with her reasoning. If she knew he was a member of the committee that could change such rules, she would never let the matter alone. "I'll speak with Lucien." Perhaps they should allow young ladies with male family members—or guardians—to attend the assemblies. And Lucien wouldn't have to invite his irritating aunt. Damn, why hadn't he thought of this earlier?

"Miss Wingate, if I haven't already marveled at your intelligence, allow me to do so again."

She inclined her head with a well-earned, smug smile. "Thank you, my lord."

Very smart. And amusing.

And far too beautiful by half.

"I must say, I did like Lord Gregory," she murmured, turning her gaze toward the window.

And she just might beat Tobias to the altar.

CHAPTER 9

*F*iona strode eagerly into the drawing room where the butler said Cassandra was waiting for her. Before Fiona could greet her, Cassandra waved for Fiona to join her on the settee.

"I have news," she said with a rather dire tone.

"Has your father betrothed you to someone?" Fiona asked with deep concern.

Cassandra's animated expression arrested. She stared at Fiona a moment, then blinked. "Whyever would you think that?"

"You just sounded so serious, and now you've lines etched into your forehead."

Laughing, Cassandra massaged her brow. "Better?" At Fiona's nod, she returned her hand to her lap. "Lucien told me our aunt is not getting an invitation to the Phoenix Club."

Disappointment blazed in Fiona's chest. "Why not?"

"Apparently the membership committee was not in favor." Cassandra exhaled. "It's no use being upset about it. I begged him to try again, but he said the committee's vote is final—and I'm not even supposed to know there was a vote. If I tell anyone, he said he'll send me to a nunnery."

"Then I suppose I'd best not tell anyone either."

"That would be most appreciated," Cassandra said drily.

Frowning, Fiona leaned back against the settee and stared straight ahead as if she could divine answers from the air. "I wonder why they voted against her."

"Because she can be haughty and insincere and just...irritating." Cassandra also leaned back. "Still, I'd hoped they would overlook her shortcomings since she's Lucien's aunt. What we have learned, however, is that Lucien doesn't have as much power as I'd thought, despite being the owner."

"That makes no sense," Fiona said. "Unless he isn't the only owner."

Cassandra sucked in a breath and turned to face Fiona. "I hadn't considered that. Perhaps we could find out if there's a secret, silent co-owner and use that information to extort invitations to the assemblies."

Fiona inhaled sharply, echoing Cassandra, her eyes widening as she pivoted on the settee. "You wouldn't do that to your own brother."

"Of course not. Unfortunately, my mind tends to come up with rather devious plans. I do try very hard not to launch any of them. Only when needs are critical." She paused and looked Fiona in the eye. "I would say our needs are now critical."

Feeling slightly puzzled, Fiona asked, "What needs are those exactly?"

"How we'll obtain a sponsor so we may go to the assemblies."

Right. "I did ask Overton why he couldn't just sponsor me, and why your brother couldn't sponsor you. They're members, and we're family. Well, you're family, and I'm sort of like family."

"Brilliant. What did he say to that?"

"He indicated he'd speak with Lord Lucien. Did your brother say nothing to you?"

"No, and he just called late this morning. Perhaps the membership committee wasn't in favor of that either."

"Are they in charge of all the rules in addition to membership?"

Cassandra wiped her hand across her forehead but didn't rub it this time. "I have no idea. I am beginning to lose hope that we'll attend an assembly. I would wonder if my father wasn't behind this, except Lucien typically ignores Papa's edicts. On the other hand, when it comes to me, Lucien doesn't push too hard. Damn, I really wanted to see that bacchanalia painting."

"And I want to see the Circe one," Fiona murmured.

"When we first met, you suggested that we steal inside," Cassandra said slowly, as if she were testing to see how it sounded out loud.

"I was jesting." Had she been? "Sort of."

"I think I may have a plan." Excitement sparked in her gaze.

Fiona was simultaneously thrilled and hesitant. "Didn't you just say your plans are devious?"

"I also said I only launch them when absolutely necessary."

"What's your plan?"

"We'll dress up as gentlemen and steal into the men's side of the club."

Fiona gaped at her. "*What?*"

"That's an awful idea." Prudence stood just inside the doorway with a tray of cakes and lemonade.

"Why are you bringing refreshments?" Fiona was still confused by the hierarchy of households. Prudence was not a servant and yet she did things that were similar to a servant.

"Because I was hungry and thought you might be too." She set the tray on a table near the windows that overlooked Brook Street. "Also, I didn't want to trouble anyone," she murmured.

Fiona understood that sentiment. If she wanted something late at night, she never rang for assistance. Indeed, she had trouble ringing for assistance at any time. The fact that she had a maid dedicated to helping her dress and taking care of her things seemed utterly excessive. However, Fiona completely understood—and appreciated—her maid's expert help with dressing for a ball, not that she needed that again anytime soon.

Fiona and Cassandra joined Prudence at the table where she was sipping lemonade but hadn't taken a seat.

"Aren't you staying?" Fiona asked, reaching for a biscuit.

Prudence eyed her and Cassandra guardedly. "That depends on whether you're actually planning to dress up like gentlemen and steal into the Phoenix Club."

"Do you have a better idea?" There was an eagerness to Cassandra's question and a glint in her eye that said she rather hoped Prudence did.

Setting her glass down on the table, Prudence perched on one of the four chairs. "Why are you trying to get inside?"

Cassandra sat across from Prudence. "Because it doesn't look as though we'll be able to attend the assemblies. And it will be incredibly diverting."

Prudence pursed her lips and gave them a disapproving look. "Those don't seem like very good reasons to take such a risk. I shouldn't listen to this conversation," she murmured, starting to rise.

"No, you shouldn't," Fiona said firmly. She truly didn't want to get Prudence into any trouble.

Prudence plucked a biscuit from the tray. "I'll leave you to your plans." She glanced toward the door, then lowered her voice. "If it were me, I'd dress up as one of the maids and steal into the women's side one morning—just act as if I'm going about my work. The maids wear a distinct costume of a gray gown with a dark green apron. And a white cap, of course." She took a bite of biscuit before turning and departing the drawing room.

Fiona wanted to ask how Prudence knew so much. Also, she still hadn't inquired as to how Prudence was acquainted with Lord Lucien.

Cassandra sat back in her chair, grinning. "You are so fortunate to have Prudence. What I wouldn't give for a companion like her. Or any companion," she added with a sigh.

Was she lonely? Fiona hated to think she might be. She knew how that felt, not that she'd realized that was what she'd been experiencing in Shropshire until she'd come here. Going from a small household, where it was just her and Mrs. Tucket, along with Mr. Woodson who came round regularly to help with things, to this grand house in Mayfair with its large complement of servants, plus Prudence, was just as much of a change as participating in Society.

No, she wouldn't go back to Bitterley—not now. And if that meant marrying, then she'd find someone tolerable.

In the meantime, Fiona was going to enjoy her freedom. "Where do you suppose we can find dark green aprons?"

Cassandra blinked in surprise. "Do you truly want to do it?"

"Your brother owns the club. If we were discovered, would there be any harm? Besides, if we go in the morning, no one will see us there, save the employees of the club. We'll just need to keep our heads down. Perhaps we need extra large caps to pull them down over our brow."

"Oh yes," Cassandra said with a warm laugh. "I think

perhaps it's time for our shopping trip to Cheapside. I'll arrange for Aunt Christina to take us tomorrow."

"Will she be available on such short notice?"

Cassandra narrowed her eyes. "She owes me a favor after all but abandoning me the other night at the ball. If I told my father, he'd cut off her allowance."

"Your father gives her an allowance?"

"He compensates her for acting as my chaperone."

Fiona kept the next question to herself—why would family need to be compensated for helping and supporting one another? She feared the answer as well as how it might make Cassandra feel. Fiona was beginning to realize things about her friend. She seemed so fortunate on the outside, with her family, wealth, and privilege. But if she was lonely and her family was as cold as Fiona was beginning to grasp, it was no wonder Cassandra had grasped on to Fiona and looked for entertainment. Again, Fiona wondered about Cassandra's mother, whom she now knew had died, but Cassandra never wanted to talk about her.

"Then I suppose she'll have to escort us to Cheapside," Fiona said with a smile. "I will not invite Prudence. That way she has absolutely nothing to do with this." Fiona froze, and she stared at Cassandra. "Are we actually going to do this?"

Eyes dancing, Cassandra faced Fiona. "I think so. You were right—no one will see us and even if they did, what harm would be done? We'll go on our merry way."

It sounded marvelous. Like an *adventure*. And hadn't the queen herself urged Fiona to enjoy her adventure? "I hope it's not our only visit. I do plan to ask Overton if he's spoken to your brother about my idea of changing the rules so that men can bring their unwed family members."

"I will speak to Lucien myself," Cassandra said. "Where is the earl today? I hope he's not lurking about eavesdropping." She laughed softly as she picked up a glass of lemonade.

"He's out paying calls."

Cassandra took a sip. "On prospective brides?"

"Probably." Fiona hadn't considered that, but it made sense.

"I wonder who he's considering? I hope she's pleasant and fun—you'll be living with her, after all."

Fiona hadn't thought of that. But if he wed soon, that's precisely what would happen. How would his countess feel about having to share her house with her new husband and his ward? The pressure for Fiona to wed would grow apace. "I'll settle for pleasant." And patient, for what if she didn't wed? What if his new countess hated having his ward here and insisted he send her back to Shropshire?

She would hope he didn't find a wife soon.

～

*D*iscordant notes from a pianoforte greeted Tobias as he entered his house and handed his hat and gloves to Carrin. "I hear it has arrived."

"Indeed, my lord. It has been placed in the sitting room as you directed. However, it will need to be arranged in a more pleasing fashion."

"Excellent." Smiling, Tobias veered left into the sitting room that faced the street. The small pianoforte stood in the corner, awkwardly situated between other pieces of furniture.

Miss Wingate stood in front of it, her fingers picking randomly across the keys.

"A lovely melody already," he said, drawing a gasp from his ward as she abruptly pivoted toward him. "My apologies, I didn't mean to startle you."

"I didn't hear you enter over the noise I was making. A

melody?" Her lips curved with amusement. "You're very kind, particularly after I cringed at your humming."

Tobias laughed. "True, I am quite magnanimous. Shall I hire a teacher for you then?"

"Surely I'm too old to learn." She glanced back at the instrument. "I didn't really think you were going to get one. And certainly not this fast."

He shrugged. "Lucien had an extra."

Her brows drew together. "Just a surplus pianoforte lying around?"

"Or something. Lucien is quite good at solving problems."

"Was not having a pianoforte a problem?"

"Of course not, but when I mentioned I wanted to get one for you, he said he could have one delivered today."

"You didn't tell me."

"It was a surprise. I'll inquire about a teacher tomorrow."

"Do you play?"

"Only superficially. My mother was quite skilled. We used to make up silly ditties when I was a boy." He hadn't thought of those in years.

Miss Wingate smiled broadly. "About what?"

The words of one came back to him. "Frogs are slimy, and they eat flies. Birds are downy, and they just fly."

She laughed, her eyes alight with mirth. "You were a true poet."

"Why lie about such a thing when you were unflinchingly brutal about my abysmal humming?"

"Did I say it was abysmal?"

"You said something was abysmal, and since you compared me to a cat in heat, I think that's probably accurate."

"I did not say a cat in heat." She held up her finger to make her point. "I said a cat in *mourning*."

"I can't decide which is more flattering."

"Definitely the bereaved cat." She turned back to the pianoforte and plucked out a few more notes. "Perhaps we can put on a musicale."

"For those who can't hear, I hope."

She grinned. "We'll make it for some indistinct future date. After we are wed." She clasped her hands and faced him once more. "Did you make good progress on that front?"

Her comment about them both being married jolted him, for his initial interpretation was them married to *each other*. As if his reputation wasn't bad enough. What would the ton say if he wed his ward?

It didn't bear consideration.

"Yes, I think so," he managed, directing his mind to the question she'd posed. "I called on Miss Goodfellow, and we had a nice visit."

Miss Wingate ran her slender fingers over the top of the pianoforte. "Does she play?"

"I don't know. That topic didn't come up. We mostly discussed the absurd war we just lost in America."

"Did you? What an odd thing for a young lady to discuss with a suitor. Or so I've been led to believe."

He snapped his gaze to hers. "Who told you that? It's terrible advice. Don't rely on the Fs for conversation." He shuddered.

"The Fs?"

"Fashion, food, and flowers. It's all most young ladies talk about. And the weather."

"You won't catch me discussing fashion. I can, however, wax rather effusively about Shropshire flowers. I tended a garden back home. What used to be home, anyway."

Used to be. "You don't think of it as home anymore?"

She exhaled and moved away from the pianoforte. "It's difficult to think of a place as home when you don't have family, and nothing really belongs to you. Home is solid and secure—permanent. I have felt rather transient in recent years. I suppose I still am."

Tobias realized Horethorne was the place he recognized as home. He lived here and at Deane Hall, but his mother's house, where he spent Yuletide and a few weeks in late summer, was where things felt most secure and...permanent. Which was why he'd never let it go.

He pivoted toward where she'd gone. "That's a beautiful sentiment, albeit sad. I want you to feel at home here."

She summoned a half smile. "I am as comfortable as I could possibly be. But this is temporary."

"You do have family—your cousin and his wife. And Mrs. Tucket is somewhat like family, isn't she?" The former maid had begun to assert herself as a kind of assistant house-keeper, much to Mrs. Smythe's chagrin. If she didn't stand down, Tobias was going to have to intervene. In fact, he should probably say something to Miss Wingate. Perhaps she could help.

"Yes, she is," Miss Wingate answered. "My cousin and his wife, however, are not. We have never been close. Actually, I've only met his wife three, maybe four times in the three years they've been married."

Tobias found that shocking. And horrible. Why didn't they regularly invite Fiona to dinner at their house? He couldn't send her back to Bitterley, knowing what she'd return to.

"It sounds as if things are going well with Miss Good-fellow then?" It seemed Miss Wingate didn't wish to continue speaking of her cousin, and Tobias would respect that.

"I believe so, yes."

"Did you call on anyone else?" Miss Wingate went to the settee where she gracefully sat at one end and arranged her skirt. She'd learned a great deal in the almost fortnight she'd been here. Perhaps she didn't need a break from Society after all.

"Not today." He deposited himself in the chair angled near her position, stretching his legs out.

"That's probably well and good," she said. "Best to take your time with finding the right countess." She smiled serenely. "When more people come to town, you'll have an even wider selection of potential brides."

He didn't disagree, but he didn't have the benefit of time. Nor did he like the idea of the Marriage Mart where he browsed young ladies like horses at Tattersall's. Furthermore, he'd done that two years ago, and the results had been disastrous.

"I'm not sure I care to participate in the full-fledged Marriage Mart. Better to settle on someone soon, I think."

"Settle? My lord, that doesn't sound romantic at all. Surely you wish to feel something for your wife? Another reason to take your time, to allow emotion to root and bloom and flourish."

He nearly laughed at her word choice, even as her perspective hit him square in the chest. He didn't love Miss Goodfellow. Not yet anyway. "You're using a flower analogy."

"Oh dear, does that count as an F?" she asked in mock horror.

"I'll allow it. And you'll have to tell me about your Shropshire flowers some time."

"Fritillaries, oh blast, another F, are my favorite. I love the checkered pattern on the blooms. They bloom in April and May. If you wait to get married until then, I could have some brought here for your bride's bouquet."

Was she trying to get him to put off his marriage? Why would she do that? Unless…

No, she couldn't know about his father's will. The only people who knew she stood to inherit Horethorne if Tobias didn't marry within three months of his father's death were his closest friends and his father's secretary. Who was now Tobias's secretary. Tobias had asked him if Miss Wingate would be notified of her potential inheritance, but Dyer had assured him she would not unless the three months elapsed before Tobias wed.

Tobias brought his legs up, bending them at the knee, and rested his elbow on the arm of the chair. "Why are you so interested in my marriage all of a sudden?"

"It's important to you, and it does affect me."

Tensing, he probed further. "In what way?"

"Your new countess will take command of this household, as she should. I am a member of this household. For the time being."

He stared at her as if by looking long and hard enough, he'd be able to divine what else she might be thinking. Alas, that was impossible.

"Cassandra visited earlier." Miss Wingate moved closer to the end of the settee. Closer to him. "Have you spoken to Lord Lucien about my idea to change the rules so you can bring me to the assemblies as your guest?"

"I haven't had a chance." He didn't really understand why this was so important to her. It was just another ball. That wasn't exactly true. It was a coveted invitation, like Almack's but so much better. If he were young and new to London, he'd probably want to go too. Hell, he was neither, and if he wasn't a member of the club, he'd be trying everything possible to garner an invitation.

She pressed against the arm of the settee, and her skirt brushed his boot. "Surely this is another problem Lord Lucien can solve. Particularly since this affects his sister, and *he owns the club.*"

"Put like that, it sounds rather achievable. Rest assured, I will speak with him on the matter."

"I must say, I don't understand why Lady Pickering hasn't been invited. She seems like precisely the sort of well-respected woman in Society that the club would want to include."

"How would you know that?"

"Because everyone always speaks of her with awe and admiration. Besides, didn't you say Lord Lucien helped you gain her support as my sponsor? That would infer they are at least friendly. Why wouldn't he invite her to his club?"

"Because it isn't just up to him."

"I think there are things you know about the club and its policies that you aren't telling me." She straightened, her eyes rounding. "Are you on the membership committee?"

"Why would you think that?" He'd responded too damn quickly and with too much vehemence. He forced a laugh. "If I was on the membership committee, I could ensure you were invited to the balls."

Setting her elbow on the arm of the settee, she rested her chin on her palm. "Could you? So the membership committee does more than invite members. They control every aspect of the club?"

"I can't say because I'm not a member of the committee."

"Not allowing women to become members until after they wed is a terrible policy, as is not letting them be invited to an assembly unless they are sponsored by a member."

Tobias ran his hand through his hair, then silently cursed himself for appearing agitated in any way. "It is not a terrible policy to disallow young, unmarried women membership. To do so would ruin the young woman."

She cocked her head, her hand still supporting her chin. "But it doesn't ruin older unmarried women?"

"They are already—" He snapped his mouth closed. He wasn't sure what he'd been about to say, but nothing would be good. He'd yet to determine exactly what made a woman a spinster and found that the idea genuinely intrigued him. "I don't disagree that the policy is unfair. However, it mirrors Society's rules, and we must abide by them." Except wasn't the point of the club to buck the ton's conventions and rigidity?

Yes, but they still couldn't lead young ladies to ruin.

She lowered her arm, keeping the elbow on the settee. "I apologize if I seem rather naïve about these matters. Society is unnecessarily complicated, in my humble opinion."

"I don't disagree with you," he murmured. "And I find your naïvete refreshing."

She leaned toward him. "Do you?" Her dark eyes met his with unabashed curiosity.

He found himself pitching forward as well so that their faces were only a few inches apart. "Utterly."

"My lord?"

Tobias and Miss Wingate jumped at precisely the same moment, their noses colliding with such force that they both fell back against their respective pieces of furniture with a collective "Ow!"

He held his face as numbness crawled up his nose. Miss Wingate did the same, her hand cradled over her nose and mouth.

"I beg your pardon," Carrin said. "Mr. Dyer is here for your scheduled meeting."

Hell, Tobias had forgotten all about that. And he'd even been thinking about Dyer a few minutes ago.

Tobias was unaccountably disappointed. Glancing toward Carrin, he slowly lowered his hand from his face. "I'll be there in a moment." Did he sound as if he had a cold?

Carrin inclined his head and departed.

Tobias instantly turned to Miss Wingate. "Are you all right?"

She nodded as she slowly removed her hand from her face. Wiggling her nose, she said, "I think so."

He couldn't stop staring at her reddened nose and the alluring way she was moving it. Because her lips also moved, and now he was fixed on them as well.

Hell.

Carefully, he rose from the chair, lest they suffer some sort of additional mishap. "I'm terribly sorry about that."

"It was an accident." She laughed softly. "I'm rather good at those since coming to town. I promise my agility wasn't this poor before."

"It's my influence. I'm making you clumsy."

"How can it be your fault?" She shook her head briskly. "I haven't noticed that you are clumsy at all."

"Given what just happened, I don't think you can rule it out. Perhaps you should rethink your plans to delay finding a husband so you may get away from me as soon as possible." He'd meant it as a joke, but the moment he saw the discomfort flit through her gaze, he regretted it. "That was a jest. All of this was a jest. Of course I haven't affected your agility."

"Of course," she murmured.

"I must meet with my secretary now. Keep hammering away on the pianoforte, if you like." He smiled at her on his way out.

As he made his way to his study, he wondered why, in addition to his still smarting nose, his lips were also tingling.

CHAPTER 10

"*H*ow do I look?" Cassandra sat straight in the hack as it rattled its way along Bond Street toward Piccadilly. She smoothed her hand over the front of her dark green apron and adjusted the white cap covering her dark curls.

"Like a Society miss dressed up as a maid." Fiona giggled.

Grinning, Cassandra flopped back against the seat. "Hopefully no one will look too closely."

Fiona settled her own cap over her hair, which she'd personally dressed into a tight, simple style. "I, on the other hand, probably appear quite normal."

"I've no idea what that's supposed to mean, but you also look like a Society miss in costume."

Did she? Fiona wasn't sure she believed that. She was barely a Society miss. And she didn't feel like one this week since she wasn't going to any events. Not that she could complain. Yesterday's shopping excursion to Cheapside with Cassandra's aunt had more than made up for anything Fiona was missing. Cheapside was a teeming, vibrant area with so many sights and sounds. She'd even tried caviar from a cart.

Cassandra's aunt had brought along a friend, and they'd all but ignored Fiona and Cassandra, so purchasing their costumes had been unremarked upon. They'd encountered some difficulty finding gray dresses that fit them properly. As a result, their garments were both a tad too large.

The hack turned onto Piccadilly, where they planned to disembark at Duke Street and walk to the club. Fiona's insides churned with excitement and anxiety.

After proclaiming themselves ill and stating their plans to remain abed all day, they'd both slipped from their houses and met where Brook Street met Grosvenor Square. Keeping their heads down, they'd hurried to Bond Street and caught a hack, which had been an exciting endeavor on its own. No one could say Fiona wasn't having an adventure.

The hack came to a stop at the designated location and disembarked. Cassandra paid the driver, then linked arms with Fiona as they started down Duke Street.

"I wish you were coming to the ball on Saturday," Cassandra said. "What will I do without you there?"

"Dance, make conversation, and generally shine like a diamond?"

Cassandra snorted. "The diamond part is highly debatable. My father is annoyed that no one has paid me a call yet."

"Why do you suppose that is?" Fiona hadn't received any either, but she wasn't surprised.

"The Season is in its infancy. If it were a person, it would still be drooling."

Fiona laughed. "Is your father annoyed just to be annoying?"

"Precisely." Cassandra looked at her askance. "I thought Lord Gregory might have called on you by now."

"Really, why?"

"It seemed you shared a connection. And that you liked him well enough."

"I did. I do." Fiona thought back to their promenade and dance. "What constitutes a connection?"

"Sharing things in common, finding things to laugh about, but most importantly a physical...magnetism where you're drawn together."

Fiona suddenly thought of the other day when she and Overton had crashed noses. Just before that had happened there'd been something...odd. What Cassandra described was somewhat how Fiona had felt, as if she were being pulled toward him. Additionally, they did laugh together. She found him rather engaging. It was hard not to when he went out of his way to do nice things, such as procure a pianoforte and hire a teacher who was coming to give her a lesson on Friday.

"You're thinking about Lord Gregory," Cassandra observed.

She wasn't at all, but Fiona wouldn't admit that. And she certainly wouldn't reveal who she *was* thinking about.

"Is that the servants' entrance up ahead?" Fiona asked. Near the corner of Duke Street and Ryder Street, there was a gate to a set of steep, narrow stairs that led down to the lower level of the women's side of the club.

"Yes." Cassandra quickened her pace, and Fiona hurried to keep up.

When they arrived at the gate, Cassandra took her arm from Fiona's and reached for the latch. Fiona tipped her head back to look up at the building. "So this is the Phoenix Club," she whispered.

"Try not to look at it in awe." Cassandra opened the gate and started down the stairs.

Fiona followed, pulling the gate closed behind her. At the bottom of the stairs, there was an area for coal storage as well as other items, but Fiona didn't pay close attention.

"Ready?" Cassandra asked, her hand on the door.

"Yes," Fiona breathed.

Then they were inside the rather dim interior of a corridor. Their plan was to find cleaning implements and make their way upstairs. Fiona had managed that part of the scheme. They'd polish furniture or clean floors. In truth, they'd do neither, but that's what they would pretend if they encountered anyone, which, of course, they would.

Immediately, as it happened.

As they made their way along the corridor, another maid —dressed in a gray gown and dark green apron, just as Prudence had said—walked past them without a word or eye contact.

"Excellent," Cassandra murmured.

Fiona glanced about, eager to find their props. She poked her head into one doorway, only to jerk it back out again after seeing two maids in conversation. "Not in there," she whispered.

Moving on, she tried another door, this one closed.

"Careful," Cassandra urged.

She *was* being careful. Fiona gently opened the door and peered inside. It was a pantry of some kind with…cleaning supplies! "Success!"

Removing a bucket and some rags, she turned and handed the former to Cassandra. "We should fill this before we go upstairs. Otherwise, we won't be convincing at all."

"Where do we do that?"

"There might be a pump in the kitchen?" Fiona wasn't familiar with houses like these.

Cassandra shrugged. "I'm not allowed on the lower level of the house. But at Woodbreak—that's my father's country estate—it's in the kitchen."

Creeping cautiously along the corridor, they found the kitchen and the pump. Fiona traded the rags for the bucket and filled it. Then, finally, they went in search of the stairs.

A few minutes later, they emerged on the ground floor, stepping out of the servants' stairway into a sitting room in the back corner with windows facing Duke Street and the back garden.

Decorated in delicate gold and ivory, the space felt warm and welcoming. It also, somehow, seemed to shimmer. Fiona strolled around the perimeter. "It's such a pretty room."

"Whoever designed this is brilliant," Cassandra said, running her fingertips along the back of a brocade settee. "I feel right at home here."

"How wonderful that women have such a splendid place to gather." They'd discussed whether they might run into any of the members today. If so, they'd just keep their heads down and hurry away from them. Fiona doubted anyone would recognize her, but they might Cassandra.

"What are you girls doing in here?" The high-pitched demand came from behind them.

Fiona let out a soft squeak as she whirled around. Tossing a glance toward Cassandra, Fiona was impressed to see that she didn't look as if she'd been caught somewhere she oughtn't be. But perhaps her heart was thudding as wildly as Fiona's.

The middle-aged woman, whose costume varied from the other maids in that her apron was white with an embroidered phoenix on the chest, narrowed her eyes at them. She stood in the wide doorway that led toward the front of the house. "I don't recognize either one of you."

Fiona froze. This was it. They'd been found out. The woman—the housekeeper?—would alert Lord Lucien, and perhaps even Lord Overton. Would he send Fiona back to Shropshire?

"We're new," Cassandra said evenly. If she was even half as terrified as Fiona, she didn't show it in the slightest.

She looked as if she might believe Cassandra. "Lord Lucien hired you?"

Cassandra nodded. "Yes."

The woman exhaled and shook her head. "Wouldn't be the first time he forgot to tell me." She glanced at the bucket Cassandra held. "You're supposed to be ensuring the ballroom is tidy." Her gaze flicked to the right. "Go at once, before the ladies arrive."

"We will," Cassandra said earnestly.

After the woman left, Fiona sagged, reaching for a nearby chair to steady herself. "I feared we were discovered." She stared at Cassandra. "However did you maintain your composure so well?"

"Years of avoiding my father's disdain when I did something he didn't care for."

"It was most impressive. And how did you come up with us being new?"

"My brother likes to help people in need and often assists them with finding employment."

"How lovely of him. And convenient for us. Do you think that was the housekeeper?"

"I do." Cassandra moved toward the closed door the housekeeper had glanced toward.

"Because of her fancy apron?"

"Mostly the authority in her tone," Cassandra said drily.

"Yes, that." A tremor rippled over Fiona's shoulders. "What ladies do you think she referred to?"

Cassandra shrugged. "Members? However, surely they wouldn't come this early in the day." It was not yet noon. "Who knows what she meant."

They stepped into the next chamber, closing the door behind them. A harp stood in one corner and a pianoforte in another.

"The music room, I suppose," Cassandra noted, her gaze

sweeping the chamber before narrowing at the open doorway on the opposite side.

"Aha!" Fiona said, moving past Cassandra. "The heart of the establishment—for the assemblies anyway." She strode into the ballroom and marveled at the high ceilings edged with elaborate cornicework. Two massive chandeliers hung from wide, ornate medallions. A wall divided the large room, but the sliding doors were thrown open between the two spaces.

"It's the *entire* ballroom," Cassandra said excitedly. "Meaning that part over there is the gentlemen's side. The forbidden realm." She added the last in a dark, playful tone as she set the bucket on the floor and twirled about. Her skirt brushed the bucket.

"Careful you don't knock it over, or we really will have to clean."

Cassandra laughed. "We wouldn't want that. I haven't the slightest notion."

Fiona did. She could scrub the floor and beat the carpets. She could even clean out the hearth, though that was her least favorite job.

"Come, we have to look." Cassandra was already striding toward the doors to the other side of the ballroom.

Dropping the cleaning rags near the bucket, Fiona hurried to join Cassandra.

The ballroom looked precisely the same on the men's side —tall windows that looked out to the garden, a gleaming oak floor, elegant chandeliers, and several mirrors on the wall opposite the windows which made the already large room seem even more grand.

Cassandra stood in the center of the floor with her hands on her hips, her gaze flitting about. "I'd like to know how wealthy my brother is. This was not an inexpensive endeavor. I realize we haven't seen everything, but so far every room is impeccably designed and beautifully decorated, just as he described. My father would never have given him money for this. He loathes the very idea of the club's existence." Cassandra turned toward her. "I am beginning to think it's *quite* possible my brother is not the sole owner."

"It would seem to support your aunt not being invited, though I suppose that could just be owing to the Star Chamber."

"Perhaps, but my brother is most persuasive. Whatever the cause, membership is evidently not entirely up to him."

Fiona was especially glad they'd executed their plan since it truly seemed they would not be able to attend the assemblies. "It's good that we came today. This will likely be our only entrée into the Phoenix Club."

"Until we are wed and duly invited." Cassandra's eyes darkened. "If my brother doesn't ensure I receive an invitation to join the club, I will sever ties completely. Won't that delight my father?" she added with a laugh that carried no humor.

Fiona thought of what Cassandra had just said a few minutes earlier about her father, as well as all the other times she'd mentioned his coldness. "Cassandra, if you ever—"

Cassandra lifted her finger to her lips. "Shh. Did you hear that?" she whispered, looking toward a closed pair of doors leading from the ballroom.

Without waiting for Fiona to answer, Cassandra grasped her by the hand and pulled her toward a wide archway cloaked with a thick curtain. She released Fiona and slowly parted the drape. "Stair hall." Inclining her head for Fiona to follow, she held the curtain until Fiona passed through.

Standing in the stair hall, they could see directly into the entry where a footman stood near the door. He didn't see them, but if he pivoted...

"Upstairs!" Cassandra whispered urgently, dashing for the

stairs. Fiona bolted after her. As they climbed, she muttered, "So close to seeing the bacchanalia portrait."

At the top of the stairs, they arrived at a landing. Across from them was a closed door.

Another voice, this one quite deep, prompted Fiona's heart to pound. Thinking they should have left after encountering the housekeeper or that they should not have come at all, she darted to the right.

In front of her was a door to the outside—presumably to a terrace since they were on the first floor. Before she could contemplate her next move, a door to her right opened and out stepped a gentleman.

Not just any gentleman. Her guardian.

Eyes wide, she stared at him, speechless.

His eyes reflected her keen shock. "Ah, I have a task for you," he said, grabbing her arm and steering her away from the door into a room that stretched along the back of the building.

Fiona turned her head to determine what had become of Cassandra but didn't see her. She did, however, observe a group of men—and a few women—departing the room Overton had just left.

"Turn around," he whispered with dark urgency. "And don't look back. If anyone recognizes you—"

She heard his teeth clack as he snapped his mouth closed. He dug his fingers into her arm, then dragged her out to the terrace and closed the door.

Bright sunlight washed over them as she tried to wrench her arm away from him.

"I'm not letting you go," he growled. "What in the bloody hell are you doing here?" He paused long enough to rake his gaze over her. "Is that one of the maids' costumes? How on earth did you get that?"

"I—"

"There's no phoenix on your apron, so it's not a costume, which means you are merely trying to *look* like a maid."

Fiona glanced down at her clothing and brushed her hand over the top of the apron. "There's supposed to be a phoenix?"

Overton dragged her across the terrace and pulled her down the stairs to the garden. As soon as they reached the bottom, he paused. He sent a guarded look toward the back of the building.

Turning back to face her, he released her arm and instead took her hand. "Stay close to me and hurry. We have one chance to get you out of here."

There was no time for her to respond, even if she'd been able to think of a thing to say. She did as he said and hastened to keep up with him as he pulled her across the garden, veering away from the building, but not too far.

Suddenly one of the doors opened. Glancing to her right, Fiona saw that it was the ballroom and there were people inside, unlike earlier when she and Cassandra had discovered it. *Many* people—at least a dozen. But surely no one would recognize her.

"Overton?" a feminine voice asked from the open doorway.

Fiona didn't know the woman.

"Is that—"

"Just a maid!" Overton said with a laugh.

"Whose hand you're holding." The woman squinted at them.

"Er, yes." He tugged Fiona toward the wall separating the two gardens, then cut to the left, practically running with her to the back corner. There, behind a rather tall shrubbery, he pushed open a door in the wall and pulled her through to the other side.

Reaching past her, he closed the door. She felt cold wood against her back.

"What in the devil are you doing here?" He clasped his forehead and stared down at her.

She expected his eyes to be frigid, as they'd been before when he was annoyed. However, he was perhaps not quite annoyed but something else instead. His eyes were liquid silver, hot and wild as he pinned her to the door.

"I'm—"

"Don't. It doesn't matter why you're here. You shouldn't be." His gaze dipped over her once more. "And you're dressed like this. And your hair is coming loose." He reached up and grasped a lock of her hair. "And they saw me with you."

"Did they recognize me?"

"I hope not. Thank God you're wearing this infernal costume." He was still clasping her hair, and his gaze was still boring into hers as it had the other day. No, not like that. This was something more. This was that *connection* Cassandra had talked about.

"I'm not at all sure how to get you out of here." He glanced toward the house, letting her curl slip from his fingers. "Shit. They're opening those ballroom doors too."

"I'll find my way," Fiona said, determined not to cause him any more trouble. "I'm so sorry. This was ill-advised."

His gaze met hers once more with the same fire and intensity of a moment ago. "You're damned right it was. We'll discuss it later. How the hell are you going to get home? You should wait for me, and I'll take you."

"Should I just find a place to hide in the garden then?"

He swore again, more violently than before. "Don't get caught."

"I won't." She stood on her toes. "I really am sorry." To punctuate her statement, she pressed her lips to his without thinking about the consequences of such an act.

The moment their mouths met, he pulled back, surprise flashing across his features. It was a brief pause, for in the next instant, he curled his arm around her waist and tugged her to his chest as he lowered his mouth to hers.

The sensation of his lips on hers was a wondrous delight. At first, the touch was fleeting, but then he cupped her face with his other hand. She felt as if she might melt against him.

A low groan vibrated from his throat as he angled his head and brushed his mouth against hers. His lips parted, prompting her to do the same. She clutched at his arm and waist, desperate for more of…everything.

"Well, this is *most* improper."

CHAPTER 11

*T*he woman's voice pierced the enraptured haze surrounding Fiona as she stood in Overton's embrace. Lifting his lips from hers in the most terrible interruption ever, Overton turned Fiona about so her back was to the woman who'd spoken.

"Ah, Lady Hargrove," he said a bit stiltedly. "I was just consoling this maid."

Despite the awfulness of the situation, Fiona nearly laughed. She quickly sobered, however, as she felt him stiffen behind her. His body was rock-hard with tension.

Panic began to build inside Fiona. Was she ruined?

"You sought to console her by kissing her?" Lady Hargrove demanded.

Fiona wanted to correct the woman—it was she who'd kissed *him*. And why on earth had she done that? He would certainly send her back to Shropshire now.

"She's a maid here, Lord Overton," Lady Hargrove said with considerable disdain. Though Fiona couldn't see her, she imagined a middle-aged woman with an austere, judgmental expression.

"Allow me," another woman said, her voice less outraged than Lady Hargrove's. Actually, she didn't sound angry at all, only concerned. "I'll just take her inside."

"Thank you, Mrs. Renshaw. I'm sure she could do with some tea. Or something." He guided Fiona toward a young woman, perhaps in her middle or late twenties, with glossy brown hair and a kind expression. There was an intangible grace about her, an air of confidence and capability that was instantly soothing.

Fiona had the sense Mrs. Renshaw took care of things and people, but then she did oversee the ladies' side of the club, so perhaps that was her nature. Careful to keep her head down, Fiona went eagerly to the woman's care. Mrs. Renshaw guided her toward the house, keeping them away from the small group of people who'd gathered outside. Fiona could only see them from the corner of her eye. She didn't dare turn her head.

When they reached the door to the house—that led into the ivory and gold sitting room in the corner—Fiona gave in to temptation. She turned her head and spied Overton walking back toward the ballroom. His body was still rigid, his head high, and his features inscrutable.

This was such a disaster.

As Mrs. Renshaw ushered her into the sitting room, Fiona thought of Cassandra. Where was she? Hopefully, she was hidden.

"I'm Mrs. Renshaw, and I oversee the Ladies' Phoenix Club. We'll take the backstairs up to my office."

Fiona hesitated, wondering if she should tell her about Cassandra. But Mrs. Renshaw was already moving into the narrow servants' cupboard that also contained the stairs down to the lower floor—the origination of this excursion that was not turning out to be the adventure Fiona had planned.

However, it was, whether expected or not, an *adventure*.

They went up instead of down, and Mrs. Renshaw led her into yet another gorgeously decorated room that was directly above the sitting room they'd just left. Bookshelves lined half of one wall, and tall windows looked out to the garden and Duke Street below. Between the two windows overlooking the garden stood a beautiful desk with turned legs and drawer pulls shaped like flowers. A small landscape painting that looked rather old hung above it. Fiona was drawn to the vivid greens and blues of the rolling country-side and cloud-free sky.

"That's a lovely painting," she remarked, perhaps hoping to avoid whatever must come next but, of course, realizing she could not.

"It was my mother's," Mrs. Renshaw said softly. She gestured to the gathering of furniture in the center of the room—a small settee and three chairs. "Would you care to sit? I would address you by name, but I don't know it. You are not a maid here." There was no hint of accusation, just a simple statement of fact.

Even so, Fiona tried to copy Cassandra's confidence from earlier. "Lord Lucien hired me recently?" Despite her attempt at assurance, the statement came out sounding more like a question.

Mrs. Renshaw smiled but didn't show her teeth. She was a very attractive woman. In addition to the comforting quality about her, there was a sophistication that made her seem older than she probably was. Fiona didn't think she could ever attain such an attribute.

"I would know if he had." Mrs. Renshaw still didn't seem even slightly bothered by what had happened or that Fiona was trying to lie. "You are not a maid here," she repeated, "so who are you then?" She sat on the settee, her back straight, and fixed Fiona with an expectant stare.

Fiona realized the time for prevarication had passed. She perched on the middle chair that was directly opposite Mrs. Renshaw. "I am Miss Fiona Wingate, ward to Lord Overton."

Mrs. Renshaw's dark brows arched briefly before settling back into their gentle curves. "I see." To her credit, she didn't say a thing about them kissing.

Oh God, they'd been *kissing*.

"And why are you here dressed like a maid?" Mrs. Renshaw prompted.

"I, ah, wanted to see the inside of the club. It was a terribly foolish endeavor. I'm rather new to town."

"Yes, I've heard you mentioned. You hail from Shropshire?"

"A very small village there. I have no experience with..." Fiona looked about before continuing. "Any of this."

"So you thought dressing like a Phoenix Club maid and stealing inside to have a look around would somehow help with your experience?"

"Er, I suppose." Fiona again wondered about Cassandra. They'd clearly gone separate ways when they'd heard the voices on the men's side. While Fiona had walked straight into her guardian, Cassandra had gone...where? "I wanted to see the inside of the club. It was a lark. And a foolish one at that. What is going to happen now?" Fiona plucked at the edge of her apron.

"Now that I know who you are, I'll make sure you're delivered to Lord Overton's house."

"Should I wait for him?" She didn't really want to face him at the moment, but she would have to eventually. Unless he directed her return to Shropshire without even seeing or speaking to her. Fiona could imagine him doing that and indeed wondered if that's what she deserved. After impersonating a maid and, even worse, kissing him.

"No, you needn't wait. I imagine you'll discuss this…
matter at home." She exhaled, and her brow creased.

"Am I ruined?" Fiona hated that she was so naïve about
these things. The earl had talked about ruination, but what
did that mean exactly?

"I don't think so. It doesn't appear anyone got a good look
at you or knows who you are, and your secret is completely
safe with me. I would never want to contribute to another
woman's downfall." She smiled kindly at Fiona. "The scandal
of what happened in the garden will rest solely on Lord
Overton."

Horror spread through Fiona. She clutched the arms of
the chair in a knuckle-whitening grip. "It was a scandal?"

"He was seen kissing a maid. Yes, that's a scandal. My
goodness, you *are* new to town, aren't you? Gentlemen
shouldn't be kissing maids out in the open." Her eyes
narrowed. "They shouldn't be kissing them at all, really, but
that's a topic for another day. Overton's reputation will
suffer for it, which is too bad since he's been working so hard
to repair it."

"What's wrong with his reputation?"

Mrs. Renshaw blinked. "Perhaps I should leave that
between you."

Fiona sat forward in the chair, which meant she almost
slid to the floor. She grasped the arms even more tightly. "He
won't tell me." She wasn't entirely certain of that, but she
wasn't sure she wanted to ask. She did, however, need to
know what the woman meant. "He's an earl. What could be
wrong with his reputation?"

"Overton is a rake. Rather, *was* a rake. He's been trying to
rehabilitate himself, and he'd been doing so well." She
frowned briefly. "He gave up his mistress, and he's spent
several evenings at White's in the company of Lucien's
brother." Mrs. Renshaw squared her shoulders and gave her

head a shake. "He's been attempting to demonstrate his worthiness, that he's left his roguish behavior in the past now that he's the earl."

And she'd ruined it. Fiona pressed her hand to her mouth. She'd utterly devastated his hard work. A chill raced over her as she lowered her hand to her lap. "How will this affect him?"

"I would say it would not since so few people witnessed what happened, however Lady Hargrove can't resist a piece of gossip if she thinks it's helpful to others. And in this case, she will undoubtedly think so because Overton is hunting for a wife. She'll see it as her duty to ensure his prospective brides know that he is still carrying on with other women."

Fiona wanted to cup her face in her hands, but she made herself sit straight and still. "I feel terrible. What can I do?"

"Nothing, nor would he want you to. If you were recognized, you would be ruined. And while the earl can survive this—socially—you would not. It would also reflect rather poorly on him since he is your guardian. Many would think he took advantage." Mrs. Renshaw's nostrils flared. "Did he?"

"Not at all," Fiona said quickly. "I kissed him." Then he'd kissed her. And she'd kissed him back.

"I see. Well, if there is something between you, I encourage you to determine what that is with the utmost haste." Mrs. Renshaw scooted forward and reached across the space to graze her fingers against the back of Fiona's hand. "Don't fret. I can see you blame yourself for what happened, but Lord Overton is a grown man. While you did err in coming here, what happened was just an unfortunate turn of events."

Mrs. Renshaw stood. "Now, let's get you home. I'll hail a hack to deliver you."

Fiona couldn't leave Cassandra behind. She tipped her

head back and summoned the courage to speak. "I, ah, wasn't alone."

Mrs. Renshaw's jaw dipped in surprise. "Indeed? Who is this other person?"

"My friend." Fiona didn't want to reveal her identity, but when they found her, there would be no helping it. She'd leave that for when she was found. *If* she was found. Perhaps Cassandra had been able to escape. Would Fiona have done that? No, she couldn't have left her friend behind, just as she wouldn't now. "We were separated over on the gentlemen's side. On the first floor."

"I'll take care of it. You relax here for now." With a parting smile, she left, closing the door behind her.

Fiona practically leapt from the chair to the window. The garden below was empty. Where was Overton now? And what could he possibly be thinking of her behavior?

Wringing her hands, she paced across the room and back again. Why *had* she kissed him? She'd never kissed anyone besides her mother. This was a wholly different kind of kiss, of course. It was the kind of kiss she'd seen depicted in a certain book hidden in the bottom corner of her father's library. Before her cousin had taken it along with the rest of the books.

Perhaps her lingering curiosity about the things she'd seen in that book had prompted her to kiss him. Or the fact that the magnetism Cassandra had talked about had swept through Fiona, driving her to the earl. He'd been angry, and she'd felt awful. So she'd apologized. Then she'd wanted to do something to make amends.

Such as kiss him?

Coming to a halt, Fiona squeezed her eyes closed and put her hand over them. She forced herself to breathe, to calm the racing of her pulse. Everything was going to be fine. The worst that could happen was that she'd end up right where she started in Bitterley.

Her insides churned. That would be truly terrible. She didn't want to go back. The only person she would have missed, Mrs. Tucket, was here with her. And here she had Prudence, Cassandra, Lady Pickering...and Lord Overton.

Dropping her hand to her side, she went back to the window and looked down at the garden once more. More specifically, she focused on the back corner where the door was partially disguised by a vine. She felt the cool wood of the door on her back and the warmth of the earl pressed to her front. Heat spread through her as she recalled the way he'd clutched her waist and pulled her against him, the feel of his bare hand cupping her face, the brush of his lips against hers.

The entire encounter had been over far too soon, and she'd no expectation it would happen again. Nor should it. He was her guardian. He was also, apparently, a rake who'd recently given up his mistress and was trying to improve his reputation.

An overwhelming sense of frustration and failure washed over her. She hadn't meant to cause him so much trouble. She hadn't thought of him at all, and for that she was horribly sorry.

A few minutes later, the door opened. Fiona turned from the window as Cassandra rushed inside. They met in the center of the room and hugged.

"I was so worried about what happened to you." Cassandra gave her a fierce squeeze before they parted.

"As I was about you." Fiona darted a glanced at Mrs. Renshaw, who stood near the open doorway. "Were you found?"

"Not until Mrs. Renshaw came." She sent her a grateful

smile. "I was huddled in the servants' cupboard trying to decide what to do."

"And now you must both be on your way, quickly, before those who are downstairs take their leave."

Cassandra started toward the door, and Fiona followed. Mrs. Renshaw led them down two flights of stairs to the lower level, and they retraced their steps to the door they'd entered earlier. Then Mrs. Renshaw accompanied them up the stairs to Duke Street, where a hack was already waiting.

She turned to Fiona and Cassandra. "I've instructed the driver to deposit you each near, not in front of, your perspective homes. He has already been paid, so you needn't worry about that."

"How can we ever thank you?" Fiona asked, still over-whelmed with regret as well as disappointment in herself.

"By not doing anything like this again." She smiled at them. "I understand what it's like to do something foolish. You feel bad about it now—and you should—but you'll learn from this and emerge wiser. To do anything else would be the true failure."

Fiona took her words to heart, silently vowing to learn from this mistake. "From now on, I will consider my actions from everyone's perspective."

Mrs. Renshaw fixed her gaze on Cassandra. "I will not be telling Lord Lucien you were here."

"I could hug you," Cassandra said, blinking. "Thank you."

"Go now." She waved them toward the hack and stood on the pavement until they'd climbed inside and the vehicle rolled away.

Sitting beside Cassandra, Fiona leaned her head back against the seat. "That was such a bad idea."

"It was not my finest," Cassandra said wryly. "I'm so sorry. What happened to you?"

"Nothing happened to *me*, but I think I ruined Lord Overton."

Angling herself toward Fiona, Cassandra gaped at her. "What?"

"When we heard those voices, I panicked. I ran to the right—where the voices were coming from."

"I did wonder why you went that way. I dashed over to the door across from the stairs. It was a servants' cupboard."

"You were smart." Fiona exhaled lest she rush the retelling of what had happened. "I was not. I ran directly into Overton. He recognized me immediately and pulled me away before anyone could see me."

Cassandra's eyes lit with delight. "Brilliant! Then he brought you to Mrs. Renshaw's office?"

"Not directly," Fiona said slowly as the events ran through her mind for the dozenth time. "He took me out to the terrace, then down to the garden. I'm not sure he was thinking of where we would go, just that we shouldn't be where everyone else was." How she hated that she'd put him in that position.

Her face falling, Cassandra pressed her lips together. "Right. You said you ruined him." She winced. "How could you possibly do that?"

"Er, it's complicated. When we were in the garden, there were people in the ballroom. They opened the doors, and someone recognized him. We ran to the other side of the garden—to the ladies' side—and I thought we were safe."

"But you weren't?" Cassandra tensed, her shoulders bunching.

"I felt terrible about the entire situation. He was angry, I apologized, and the next thing I knew, I was kissing him." She covered her eyes, afraid to see Cassandra's reaction. That didn't stop her from hearing it, however.

Cassandra's gasp filled the hack. "He kissed you?"

Fiona wiped her hand down her face and rested it in her lap. "No, I kissed him. Then he kissed me. It all happened so fast."

"Did you enjoy it?"

That was not a question Fiona expected. She jolted, her mind going right back to that moment and the pleasure of his embrace. "Yes." The word was a bare whisper, an almost silent affirmation of what she dared not admit and yet couldn't seem to withhold.

Fiona rushed to say something else, to distract from what she'd revealed. "He's going to send me back to Shropshire immediately."

"Is that what he said?"

"No, but why wouldn't he? I deserve nothing less."

"How did you ruin him? If you were seen kissing, you'd be the one ruined, not him."

"Because no one recognized me. They assumed, based on my costume, that I was a maid and that Lord Overton was having his way with me."

Cassandra grimaced, her brow creasing as her jaw tensed. "Now I understand. And he's been working so hard to improve his reputation."

Fiona stiffened. "You knew about that?"

"Vaguely." Cassandra waved her hand. "He has a reputation as a rake, as do a good number of gentlemen, including my brother. I mean Lu, of course. Con is the most staid gentleman you'll ever meet. Poor Sabrina."

"Sabrina?"

"His wife. She's lovely. Hopefully she'll come to town so you can meet her." Cassandra frowned and then touched Fiona's arm. "This is all my fault. I never should have suggested this endeavor. You must lay the blame entirely upon me."

"I can't do that. We were in this together."

"I don't want Overton to send you back to Shropshire. Please say whatever you must."

Fiona smiled and took her friend's hand. "I would never make you the scapegoat, just as you didn't abandon me at the club."

"I couldn't! I honestly didn't know what I was going to do, but I wasn't going to just leave you there." She squeezed Fiona's fingers. "Though we only recently met, I have never had a friend as dear as you."

"I haven't either, which is why I won't mention you at all. Overton won't even know you were there. And Mrs. Renshaw is going to keep your secret too."

Cassandra blew out a breath. "I don't deserve any of that. I maintain this is my fault."

They stared at each other a moment before collapsing into a hug against the seat until they were both laughing.

They separated, and Fiona flopped back against the squab. "I don't know how I can find amusement in this. I'm quite anxious to see Lord Overton."

"If he tries to send you back to Shropshire, you must allow me, or better yet, Lu, to intervene. I won't let you go. How can I possibly survive this Season without you?"

Fiona appreciated her friend's support, but it was more than that. She didn't want to return to Bitterley either, and she would do whatever necessary to prevent it—whatever her guardian insisted.

What if that included kissing? It would never, of course, but she might dream that it did.

CHAPTER 12

*T*obias stood stoic as he watched Evie Renshaw lead his ward away through the Ladies' Phoenix Club garden. Inside, however, he was raging. Not in anger—well, not entirely in anger—but with a wholly unexpected, unwanted, and unsuitable desire.

"Overton, I must insist you cease that sort of interaction with our maids at once." Lady Hargrove stood with one hand on her hip as she glowered at him from perhaps five feet away.

"It was just one maid," he muttered. Who wasn't even a maid. But he couldn't make that clarification without answering questions as to who she really was. Better for everyone to just think she was a maid.

And he was a lecher.

"One maid, five maids—it should be no maids!" Lady Hargrove turned to Lucien, who was staring at Tobias with a mix of pity and disbelief. "Lord Lucien, if you can't keep a rein on your friend, we may need to consider expulsion."

Tobias's eyes widened briefly. In over a year of the club's existence, they'd never expelled anyone. There was no process. Yet. Hell, Tobias refused to be the first. Could they even toss someone who was on the bloody membership committee? As if he could hear Tobias's question, Lucien gave him the tiniest shake of his head. It did little to improve Tobias's mood.

"Let us continue with our discussions for the upcoming assemblies, beginning with next week." Smiling blandly, Lucien gestured for those who'd come into the garden to return to the ballroom.

As Tobias walked past his friend, he said nothing. Lucien, however, murmured, "We'll discuss this after."

Tobias could hardly wait.

Inside the ballroom, Mrs. Holland-Ward, one of the ladies' club patronesses, announced the plan to have a series of themed balls, beginning with the first of the Season on the second of March. Though it wasn't yet spring, it would be a celebration of the new season and of beginnings. Those gathered, which included the other patronesses, the membership committee—which the patronesses did not realize was the membership committee—as well as a few other chosen members from each side of the club. The latter group had been invited so as to not only include the membership committee in order to keep their identity secret.

Tobias thought about how Fiona wanted to come to the balls. Could he allow that now? Would someone here recognize her from today? He'd tried to keep her hidden from everyone, and no one realized she was his ward. However, Evie would know. What was Evie doing with her now?

And what was Tobias going to do with her?

Anger—solely directed at himself—rose inside him, and he worked to keep the scowl from his face. In one moment, he'd completely ruined all the good he'd done the past fortnight. For a kiss. But what a kiss... He could still feel the sweet softness of her lips, the eager clasp of her hands on his shoulders, the delicious press of her body against his.

She was his goddamned *ward*.

She was also a massive pain in his arse. What the hell had she been thinking coming here dressed as a *maid*? Clearly, this had been a well thought out, premeditated scheme. No, it hadn't been well thought out. It had been utter madness. She'd come horribly close to being seen by everyone. If he hadn't been the first person out of the room upstairs and seen her before anyone else... It didn't bear thinking about.

He ought to send her back to Shropshire tomorrow. Or ensure she was wed with the utmost haste—before she could ruin herself. She'd come damned close today. He realized she didn't want to marry right away, but she'd quite forfeited her wishes with her impudent behavior.

"Did you hear any of that?" Lucien asked quietly from his right.

Blinking, Tobias realized people had broken off into groups and some were leaving. The men—Wexford, MacNair, and a few other fellows—walked into the men's side of the ballroom, presumably to go upstairs.

"You can tell me what I missed," Tobias said, eager to be on his way and...what? Find Fiona? Was she even still here? Evie hadn't yet returned.

Lucien moved to stand directly in front of Tobias and narrowed his eyes. "You missed the bloody issue you raised earlier—whether to allow unmarried relatives of members into the assemblies."

"Hell, I missed that? I'm rather, ah, distracted."

"I should think so." Lucien shook his head. "Yes, you missed it. Three of the four patronesses were in support, so it passed. Young ladies with relatives who are members may attend, but they must have a chaperone."

"Let me guess, Lady Hargrove was not in favor." Tobias slid

a glance toward the woman. In her late forties, she was his least favorite of the patronesses, so, of course, it was her who'd seen him kissing Fiona. Lady Hargrove was an esteemed member of the ton, however, and her husband was a jovial and generous gentleman, the best sort really, which was the primary reason she'd been selected as a patroness. In searching for appropriate women for the role, they'd looked to the wives of gentlemen who'd accepted some of the first invitations of membership. Lord Hargrove was one of those men.

"You are correct," Lucien said. "So now my sister and your ward can attend the assembly next week. Except I need to find Cass a chaperone."

"She can use Miss Lancaster. Fi—" Tobias realized he'd started first-naming her in his head. Which seemed logical since they'd been kissing a short while ago. However, he couldn't display such familiarity. Hell, he shouldn't even be *thinking* it. "Miss Wingate won't be coming." Tobias thought it a very bad idea to bring her back to the scene of the scandal. Not that it was a scandal for her. Hell, if no one knew it was her, she could probably come to the damned ball. Except she had that bloody dark red hair that stood out. It was possible no one would make the connection since she'd been wearing a cap today, but it hadn't covered her hair entirely.

"Why not? I thought this entire proposition today was so your ward could attend."

"It's… Never mind." Tobias wiped his hand over his face.

"You're still distracted," Lucien said. "By the maid. A maid? What the hell were you thinking?" He gave Tobias an icy glower. "Also, don't fuck with my maids."

Before Tobias could say something stupid, such as she wasn't one of his maids, Evie strode into the ballroom. Leaving Lucien behind, Tobias went to meet her.

"Where is she?" he asked.

"On her way home." Evie gave him a look that told him everything he needed to know—she knew *exactly* who the "maid" was, and she wasn't going to tell anyone.

Tobias briefly clasped her hand. *"Thank you."*

He left the club without a backward glance.

By the time he reached his house, he'd considered several ways he might approach Fiona. *Miss Wingate.* As he walked inside, he asked Carrin to summon her to his study. There, he waited anxiously for her arrival.

He did not have long to wait.

Now dressed in a floral-patterned gown with her vibrant hair in a severe style without a curl falling loose as it had in the garden, she tentatively stepped inside.

"Close the door." He shouldn't have her do that for propriety's sake, but this was a private conversation.

She did as he said and moved to the middle of the room. She looked lovely, despite the obvious tension in her frame. Her jaw was tight as she regarded him with well-earned wariness.

He stood near his desk, his arms folded, willing himself not to look at her mouth lest he recall kissing her. "Why were you at the club dressed as a maid?"

"I wanted to see the inside. I thought it would be safe to go at that time of day."

"You thought it would be safe?" He ran a hand through his hair before dropping it to his side. "There is nothing safe about disguising yourself and stealing into a private club, even one where women are allowed."

"I understand that now," she said softly.

"I should bloody hope so. The irony is that you chose a truly awful day for your excursion. There was a meeting to discuss this Season's assemblies as well as whether family members—and wards of members—could attend."

"And can they?" she asked in a voice that grew smaller and higher with each word.

He stepped toward her, glowering. "It doesn't matter to you because you won't be going."

Her eyes rounded briefly. "Because you're sending me back to Bitterley."

"I bloody well should. What were you thinking dressing as a maid and—" He stopped short, frowning. "How did you even know how to dress as a maid?"

"I'm clever."

Yes, she was. "Who helped you?"

"No one."

"I don't believe you. Why aren't you telling me the truth?"

She lifted her chin and stared him in the eye unflinchingly. "If you're going to send me away, just do it, please."

He closed the space between them so that she had to tip her head back. "You are fortunate you weren't recognized because you would have been ruined."

"Did I ruin you?" She lowered her gaze as her brow furrowed. "It seems I may have."

Could a man be ruined? Probably, but it took a great deal of effort, especially for an earl. "I established my reputation long before you came along."

She looked up at him once more. "But you've been trying to rehabilitate it, and I ruined your efforts."

"Did Evie tell you that?" He saw the confusion in her eyes and added, "Mrs. Renshaw, I mean."

"It's important that I understand the consequences of my thoughtless actions, which I now do. I'm so sorry."

He could see her remorse, could feel it coming off her in waves—so much so that he was tempted to take her in his arms and console her. Which would be the worst idea in the history of ideas. "What should I do with you?" He asked that question of her as much as of himself.

"I promise I will be a model young lady going forward."

"You think I should allow you to continue with your Season? I was of a mind to insist you wed immediately."

She nodded. "I understand, and I will work to that end so that I am no longer a burden to you."

He flinched. "You aren't a burden."

"I was today."

He couldn't argue with that. While he may not be ruined, she'd made his objective of finding a wife much more difficult.

"I would do anything to go back and not do what I did."

The kiss exploded in his mind. But she likely didn't mean that. "Go to the club?"

"Well, that too." Faint swathes of pink swept up her cheeks. "I was referring to kissing you. I don't know why I did that. I just felt bad, and it seemed the right thing to do."

The right thing... How could that be possible? She was his ward, and he was responsible for her well-being, for her future.

He looked at her mouth then, at the plump curve of her lips, and recalled how she'd felt in his arms. An over-whelming urge to take her against him once more came over him. The right thing indeed. "It can't happen again." His voice sounded rough.

Taking a step back from her, he exhaled some of the frus-tration from his body. Sexual frustration, if he were honest with himself. Deciding honesty was overrated, he attributed the tension to the impact of today's events on his marriage plans. He was running out of time.

"Go upstairs now," he said. "And stay there until tomor-row." He sounded autocratic and obnoxious, like his bloody father, but he needed to. However their relationship had changed today, he had to get them back to where they needed to be—he was her guardian, and she was his ward.

"I get to stay?"

"Apparently. Don't make me regret my decision."

"I won't. Thank you." She turned to go but hesitated at the door. Looking back over her shoulder, she said, "I really am sorry. If there's anything I can do to help you, I hope you'll let me."

You could marry me. That would solve my problems.

The idea came from nowhere and shocked him to his core. He said nothing as Fiona left, his heart pounding at the notion that had just crept into his mind.

He was in trouble where she was concerned. Especially if he couldn't even stop thinking of her as Fiona instead of Miss Wingate. She was his ward, not a woman he desired.

Unfortunately, she was both.

CHAPTER 13

*M*rs. Tucket yawned loudly as she rushed to put her hand in front of her mouth. "I must to bed, girls." She started to rise from her chair in the sitting room Fiona shared with Prudence but wobbled.

Fiona jumped up from her chair and went to help Mrs. Tucket to her feet. The older woman smiled and patted her hand. "Thank you, dear."

"You should have brought your cane." Fiona had taken her to get one over a week ago, but Mrs. Tucket was not using it consistently.

"Bah, I haven't got very far to go, and I'm not going up and down stairs."

"At least let me help you to your room," Fiona said, still holding the older woman's arm.

"That won't be necessary. If I can't walk that far on my own, I'm a lost cause. You stay with Miss Lancaster." Mrs. Tucket sent a smile toward Prudence.

Fiona reluctantly released her. "You promise you're going to your room? That you aren't going down multiple flights of stairs to bother Mrs. Smythe?"

"No, I'm not doing that." Mrs. Tucket sighed. "I was only trying to help with directing the maids. This is such a large household, and I thought Mrs. Smythe could do with the support."

"You're retired now, Mrs. Tucket," Fiona said kindly. She'd had to speak with her the day before about intruding on the housekeeper's domain. "You don't have to do any of that. Just relax and let others do the work."

"It's very hard to stop managing things when you've been doing it your whole life. Since I was eleven, mind you, when my mother died and, as the oldest, I had to take charge of everyone, including my poor father." She shook her head as she meandered to the door. "Good night."

"Good night," both Fiona and Prudence called after her.

"She's such a sweet woman." Fiona retook her chair near Prudence's, picking up the book she'd set on the seat when she'd leapt up to help Mrs. Tucket. "I do wonder if she'd be happier in a cottage back in Shropshire. I should speak to Lord Overton about it. Although, she really isn't his concern. I should probably wait and let my husband decide what to do. He'll be the one to support her." She turned her head to Prudence. "Will he support her? I suppose Mrs. Tucket won't be his concern either, but she's as good as family to me."

"Then you'll only choose a husband who understands and values that."

Fiona wasn't sure it would be that easy, but she would take the advice to heart. "You're so wise."

"I'm not sure that's accurate," Prudence said with a frown. "I should have put a stop to your plans to go to the Phoenix Club, not stand idly by while you secured costumes and executed a reckless scheme."

Fiona had told her what happened as soon as she'd arrived home. Not everything, of course. She'd left out the kissing part. "You are not to blame for what happened. I did want to ask how you knew about the maid costumes." She hadn't had a chance earlier because she'd been summoned to the earl's study.

Prudence was focused on her embroidery, her hand moving the needle perhaps a bit more slowly than a moment before. "I don't remember where I heard about them. Probably overheard something." She didn't look up.

Fiona wasn't sure she believed that but wouldn't press her. "I've also been meaning to ask how you knew Lord Lucien. The night I met him, you two were already acquainted."

Now Prudence sent her a furtive glance. Her hand stopped, but only for a moment before poking the needle into the fabric again. "Lord Lucien helps people. I used to work at a school, but I didn't like it." She spoke slowly and deliberately, which only made Fiona more curious. "I heard about him from a friend and asked for his help to find new employment."

There was clearly more to her story, but it seemed equally evident that Prudence didn't wish to share it all. She wasn't making eye contact, and her body was tense. "I didn't mean to make you uncomfortable, Prudence," Fiona said softly. She thought of what Cassandra had told her about Lord Lucien helping people and was glad he'd done so for Prudence. "I hope you're happier here."

Prudence looked up then, her gaze meeting Fiona's. "I most definitely am. Perhaps I shouldn't admit this aloud, but I just wanted a chance to be in Society, even though I'm not actually *in* Society, if that makes sense. I prefer it that way, actually. I don't like to be in the center of anything." Her shoulder twitched.

"It does make sense because I feel somewhat the same. Although, I suppose I don't mind being the focus of attention, except that I have a tendency to be a disaster."

"The queen's drawing room was just one occasion." Prudence gave her a small smile.

"True, but the Season is young yet," Fiona said drily. And it seemed she was here for the duration, which still surprised her. She rather expected Overton to change his mind and return her to Shropshire anyway. In fact, if she inquired about Mrs. Tucket, he may just decide it was convenient to send them both.

"Good evening, ladies." Overton's voice drew Fiona's attention to the doorway. He stood just inside the room, his gaze moving from Fiona, as if she'd caught him looking at her, to Prudence.

"Good evening, my lord," Prudence said, setting her embroidery down in her lap.

Overton stepped further inside. "I came to inform Miss Wingate that her break from Society is over." He looked at Fiona then, his gaze cool. "You'll attend the Dungannon ball on Saturday. You must be on your best behavior, for Lady Dungannon is a Phoenix Club patroness."

Meaning she had a great deal of power. Did that really matter to Fiona since she would not be attending the club's assemblies? She couldn't bring herself to ask. "Will you be coming to the ball?"

"Yes."

She stared at him, wanting to ask again if there was anything she could do to repair the damage she'd caused to him. But she knew there was not. "I shall be an exemplary model of a young lady. My dancing form will be perfect."

The corner of his mouth inched up, but he pressed his lips together and straightened. "Good. Have a pleasant rest of your evening." Then he was gone.

Fiona stared at the empty doorway for several moments. Exhaling, she flipped open the book in her lap, looking for the page she'd left off on earlier. After trying to read the same paragraph three times, she snapped the book closed. "He's still angry with me."

"I daresay he won't stay that way," Prudence said. "He doesn't strike me as someone who holds grudges."

Except perhaps when it came to his father, but was it truly a grudge when the relationship was fraught? "He has every right to be angry with me." For far more than Prudence knew, of course.

Prudence didn't look up from her embroidery. "No harm came of it—your reputation is intact. He'll come around."

Guilt weighing on her, Fiona blurted, "But his is not."

"His reputation?" Prudence's brow furrowed.

"I didn't quite tell you everything that happened. I didn't want to, but I need help. I don't know how to fix this."

"What did you leave out?"

"The part where Lord Overton was seen by one of the patronesses to be kissing a maid." Fiona felt the heat in her face but didn't look away from Prudence.

"He kissed you?" Prudence stared at her, her eyes narrowing in outrage.

"Not at first. I kissed him."

"Are you very certain he did not take advantage? Men are inclined to do that." Prudence pursed her lips.

"He did not take advantage. We were in the garden at the club. It was a...tense moment. I don't really know why I kissed him." Other than she'd simply wanted to. "I do know that it adversely affected his reputation, which he was trying to improve."

"It should," Prudence said firmly. "He shouldn't have kissed a maid. Er, you."

"As I said, *I* kissed him. And now he will continue to be seen as a rake."

"Did he step away when you kissed him?"

"No."

"Then he was an equal participant and deserves whatever judgment comes his way."

"That hardly seems fair. I won't suffer at all, apparently."

Prudence stared at her a long moment. "I will never think this is an unfortunate situation. On the contrary, I revel in your emerging from this without any impact to your standing. It's absolutely brilliant. We women must take whatever victories we can."

"It doesn't feel like a victory."

"Trust me, Fiona. Lord Overton will recover. You, on the other hand, would not. At least not in the eyes of Society." That was almost precisely what Mrs. Renshaw had said. They were both rather adamant in their statements, which made Fiona wonder about their past experiences. Neither could have been ruined for they wouldn't be in the positions they were. Would they?

"But the earl is trying to find a wife, and this will have a negative effect."

"Still his fault, not yours. Nor is it your responsibility to rescue him from his behavior—even if you could, which you can't."

So much for Prudence providing any assistance to help Overton.

Fiona stood. "I'm going to retire."

"You've a caring heart, Fiona. I understand that you feel responsible for what happened at the club, but it wasn't entirely your fault. Don't carry a burden you don't have to."

"Thank you, Prudence." Fiona retreated to her chamber, closing the door behind her. Setting the book on the table beside her bed, she considered Prudence's counsel. While she understood what Prudence was saying, Fiona didn't agree that it wasn't entirely her fault. If she hadn't been foolish enough to go to the club in the first place, none of it would have happened.

She would find a way to make things right with the earl. In the meantime, she'd ponder why she hadn't simply ignored the impulse to kiss him. She'd found other men attractive—Lord Lucien, Lord Gregory. Even so, nothing about them appealed to her in the same way as her guardian.

~

*I*n hindsight, Tobias should have insisted they skip the Dungannon ball. Between the rumors swirling about his debauchery with an "innocent maid" and the fact that Miss Lancaster was ill, and Mrs. Tucket was acting as chaperone, he should have realized it would be uncomfortable, to say the least. He only hoped it didn't turn into a full disaster.

Really, could anything be more disastrous than what had happened at the club the other day? As soon as he'd entered the ballroom with Miss Wingate and Mrs. Tucket, he'd been aware of the stares and the whispers. He'd gone directly to the gaming room for a drink.

As he reentered the ballroom, he considered whether he should leave entirely. He shouldn't abandon Miss Wingate, but she had Mrs. Tucket and Lady Pickering.

The latter woman saw him come in, her gaze meeting his and then narrowing. She left the group she was in and came striding toward him, her focus fixed entirely on him.

Tobias was reminded of how he'd felt when his mother had caught him pilfering cake from the kitchen. "Good evening, Lady Pickering," he said brightly, hoping he might stave off a lecture.

It was, however, a foolish notion.

She steered him toward the wall. "You have quite bungled things." She frowned at him, her green-blue eyes flickering with disapproval.

"Mmm."

She cocked her head. "That's all you have to say?"

He arched his shoulders. "What should I say?"

She exhaled and pivoted, her gaze surveying the ballroom. "It's a pity, for I'd planned to introduce you to two women who are eager to wed. They are not, however, interested in marrying a rake. They'd like to find a gentleman they will love or at least hold in high esteem."

Damn. "They sound like precisely the sort of countess I am looking for."

"More's the pity then." She swept her head back to toss another glower in his direction. "A maid? What on earth were you thinking?"

"I wasn't really." Fiona had kissed him, and he'd temporarily lost his wits. Which was no excuse. He never should have kissed her back. He'd taken a bad situation and made it a thousand times worse.

He edged toward her, whispering, "Is it really that bad? It really was just a fleeting kiss. There was nothing more."

"Well, I suppose that's something. Except it isn't to the masses. They would much rather recount your bad behavior over and over again, which ensures they all believe you were carrying on a torrid affair with a maid at the Phoenix Club." Her brows elevated as she regarded him. "I might expect the mysterious membership committee to expel you."

He wanted to assure her they would not, but that would only raise questions or suspicion. Besides, he was only one member. Could they vote to expel him?

"What if I told you she wasn't even employed by the club?"

Lady Pickering's brows went so high they almost disappeared into her hairline. "Is that true?"

He blew out a breath and directed his gaze to the dance

floor where Miss Wingate was dancing. With Lord bloody Gregory. "It doesn't matter."

Tobias tried to find Miss Goodfellow, but it seemed she wasn't in attendance this evening. He was disappointed, but at least she couldn't overhear all that was being said about him tonight.

"Do you think my chances with Miss Goodfellow are ruined too?" he asked.

"It's difficult to say. Her mother might cool toward your suit, but that's because her father was a rector and she's rather committed to her religious beliefs. On the other hand, you are an earl and neither of her other daughters married so well."

"That tells me how Mrs. Goodfellow might think of me, but I am not marrying her. What of *Miss* Goodfellow?"

"Well, this is her fourth or fifth—sixth?—Season, and she is generally considered to be on the shelf. I am not sure she'll have another Season after this. She would be a fool to decline your suit. Unless she doesn't want to wed, which is sometimes the case with women who end up as spinsters."

Tobias saw a chance to have his question answered. "How does a woman become a spinster? Is there some number of Seasons or some age that defines this designation? Why does it even happen? There is nothing about Miss Goodfellow that ought to suggest she isn't marriageable."

Lady Pickering stared at him as if he'd spoken a language she didn't understand. "What a strange question. I suppose after a woman fails to marry, Society just thinks of her differently."

"It's ridiculous. At least with Society's regard of me, *I've* done something to alter their perception or opinion."

"Some would argue a young lady on her fifth Season with nary a proposal has done something. Perhaps it can't be identified, but there is a reason she is not wed."

"I still maintain it's ridiculous. What if the young woman is shy or just hasn't met the right gentleman?"

"Are you trying to decide if you should wed Miss Goodfellow? I don't think it should matter to you that she's on her however many-th Season."

He gave her a wry look. "It absolutely does not. However, it may be too late. I called on her yesterday, and she wasn't receiving. Perhaps her mother's stringent opinions extend to her."

Lady Pickering inclined her head in sympathy. "I am sorry to hear it. You'll have to find another young lady who is in danger of finding herself a spinster. I shall search for a suitable candidate if you like."

"I am good enough for women whom Society has deemed probably not good enough." He shook his head in dismay.

"You could also take your time, do a better job of rehabilitating your reputation, and see what new crop arrives over the next few weeks."

"I think I'd prefer a near-spinster." And not just because he wasn't keen to wed a young lady on her first Season.

None of that mattered since he was nearly out of time. His father had died December twelfth. Which gave him just fifteen days to *be* wed. Not *identify* a prospective countess but marry her. In a fortnight, he would be sharing his name, his home, his bed.

His entire body chilled. Not just because it was a daunting task, but because he couldn't see it happening. Miss Goodfellow was pleasant, and he liked her, but to take her as his wife...

Once upon a time, he'd wanted to fall in love. As he'd told Fi—Miss Wingate, he had an ideal woman in his mind. However, his father's demands had made any hopes or dreams Tobias possessed nearly moot. He began to feel morose about the entire situation.

"I'm not at all certain you should have brought Mrs. Tucket as Miss Wingate's chaperone this evening." Lady Pickering frowned toward the corner.

Tobias followed her gaze. Seated in a chair, head bent with her chin resting on her chest, was Mrs. Tucket, her eyes closed and her mouth hanging open.

He should have stayed home tonight. They all should have stayed home.

"Is she asleep?" Lady Pickering asked.

"It appears that way." He scrubbed his hand down his cheek. "I'll go and wake her."

As he made his way to Mrs. Tucket, he realized Lady Pickering was following. They passed a few ladies who, based on the direction of their attention and their whispered murmurings punctuated with "Overton's ward," were clearly discussing the snoozing chaperone.

As Tobias neared the woman, she jerked. "Goddamn bloody hell!"

Everyone in a ten-foot radius turned toward her immediately, their eyes wide. A hush fell over the corner as each person stared at her in expectant silence.

Mrs. Tucket had fallen back into her restful state, her chin on her chest, her lips parted. At this distance, Tobias could hear her snores.

Refusing to make eye contact with anyone, he gently touched the chaperone's shoulder and whispered, "Mrs. Tuck—"

She jumped so violently that she nearly fell from the chair. Tobias had to clasp her elbow and throw his arm across her middle to keep her seated. Slumped, but seated.

In her confusion—at least he hoped it was confusion—she brought her other hand around and socked him in the jaw. He stumbled back, letting go of her elbow, which allowed her to use that hand to shove him over onto his arse.

The silence around them was deafening, and somehow the music for the dancing seemed quite far away. Then there was chattering and...laughter. Small at first, the amusement grew until Tobias could no longer hear the music at all.

Scrambling to his feet and tidying his clothing, Tobias went back to Mrs. Tucket who, blinking and yawning, straightened in her chair. She looked up at Tobias as if she hadn't just knocked him over.

"Did you have a nice nap?" he asked quietly, forcing himself to smile. He needed to send her home, which left him as Miss Wingate's chaperone. How could he act in that capacity when it was taking all of his energy just to think of her as Miss Wingate and not Fiona, the woman who had quite invaded his dreams the past three nights? *Goddamn bloody hell* indeed.

"I fell asleep?" She waved her hand. "Just for a moment. Where is Fiona?" She squinted toward the dance floor.

"Dancing with Lord Gregory." Tobias glanced over his shoulder and noticed that Lady Pickering was only a few feet away, her expression a mix of humor and pity. He looked at her pleadingly and mouthed the word, *"Help."*

Thankfully, she came toward him with alacrity. "I'll be delighted to take over as Miss Wingate's chaperone." She gave Mrs. Tucket a warm smile. "You go on home and get your rest."

"I don't need to go home," she said stubbornly.

Tobias feared this was going to turn into even more of a scene than it already had. As if his current notoriety wasn't bad enough. Pivoting so that he faced the wall and had his back to most everyone around them, he fixed Mrs. Tucket with his most serious stare. "If you don't go now, it's going to reflect poorly on Miss Wingate," he said quietly. "I'm sure you don't want that to happen."

Concern darkened her features. "How can that be?"

"You did that…thing you do when you sleep. The cursing. Then you hit me and knocked me over."

Her face turned a rather ghastly shade of gray. "I understand. And I offer my gravest apologies."

"I'll escort you downstairs, and my coach will take you home. Lady Pickering will take care of Miss Wingate. All will be well." He offered his arm, assisting her to leverage herself up. Thankfully, she'd brought her cane this evening. It had fallen to the floor, probably when she'd demonstrated her remarkable pugilistic skill.

Tobias bent and swept it up, handing it to her so she could make her way to the doorway. He worked very hard not to look at anyone as they left.

Once he'd turned her over to a footman who promised to see her settled in the coach when it was brought round, which the man had promised would be quickly, Tobias returned to the ballroom. His steps grew slower as he passed through the doorway, and he asked himself why he wasn't leaving too. Not returning home with Mrs. Tucket, but there were so many other places he could go.

White's. Where there were probably even more wagers about him, as well as Trowley and others like him waiting to pounce. So perhaps not there.

The Phoenix Club, of course. He'd kept to the library the past few nights to avoid talking with anyone about the incident with a maid who wasn't even a bloody maid.

Barbara's. His former mistress would welcome him back eagerly. She'd continued to send him notes every few days, encouraging him to change his mind. Yesterday's had been angry, however, as she'd heard about his affair with a Phoenix Club maid. She'd accused him of being a lying ass. Not Barbara's then.

As if he would have gone there. She was no longer an option. When he thought of a woman who he wanted to spend time with, he increasingly imagined Fi—dammit, Miss Wingate. He thought of their charming discussions about maps and geography, teaching her to dance, listening to her learn the pianoforte. He thought of her hunger for life and thirst for information, and he wanted a first-row seat as she experienced everything she wanted, everything she felt her life had been missing.

When she'd kissed him, something had unlocked inside him. Now, he wanted his ward and having her was impossible.

Before he could retreat and leave as he should have, she was coming toward him smiling, her hand on Lord Gregory's arm. Tobias deeply regretted not leaving.

"Thank you, Lord Gregory," she said, taking her hand from his sleeve. Her cheeks were prettily flushed from their dancing. Her eyes were also alight, probably due to his charm or good looks.

"The pleasure was mine, Miss Wingate. I'll see you soon." He winked at her, then bowed his head to Tobias. "Lord Overton."

"Lord Gregory," he muttered as the man turned and walked away.

Fiona glanced toward the corner, then looked to Tobias in alarm. "Do you know where Mrs. Tucket is?"

"I sent her home."

She stared at him in surprise. "Why?"

"Because she fell asleep and gave everyone in her vicinity an earful."

Lifting her hand to her mouth, she looked at him in abject horror. "Oh dear. I am so sorry, my lord."

He didn't want her to call him that. He wanted to hear her say Tobias.

That was never going to happen.

Lady Pickering was coming toward them. Good. Now he could leave.

"Lady Pickering is going to act as your chaperone for the remainder of the evening," he said.

"How was your dance?" Lady Pickering asked Fiona as she came up beside them.

"Lovely, thank you. I have finally mastered the steps. I didn't trod on his feet once." She looked quite proud, and while Tobias was happy for her, he was also disappointed that Lord Gregory's toes hadn't suffered.

"Splendid," Lady Pickering said.

"I'm going to leave," Tobias announced.

"Probably for the best." Lady Pickering leaned toward him, her gaze dipping to his jaw. "Looks like you might have a bruise come morning."

Fiona stepped closer to him and lifted her hand, as if she meant to touch his face. His eyes widened at the implication of it, here in the middle of a bloody ballroom where everyone had already been staring at him all night.

She seemed to realize the error too, thank goodness, for she quickly brushed a nonexistent curl behind her ear. "What happened?"

"Mrs. Tucket hit him when he interrupted her slumber."

"*Oh no.*" Fiona winced. "I'm so sorry," she whispered.

"I'll be fine." He touched his jaw and easily found the tender spot. Yes, he may well have a bruise. A brilliant culmination to a brilliant few days.

If he could assume his bad luck was over. He probably should not.

Turning to Lady Pickering, he asked, "You'll see Miss Wingate home?"

"Of course. Have a good evening, Overton. And *behave*," she added in a reproving whisper.

Boring as that sounded, Tobias could do nothing else.

CHAPTER 14

The maid arranged the flowers Lord Gregory had brought and set them atop a side table in the sitting room. Fiona thanked her before she left, then returned her attention to her guest, who occupied a chair opposite the settee where Fiona sat. Prudence was present but removed from them in a chair near the window that looked out onto Brook Street.

Fiona surveyed the bouquet of daffodils and snowdrops. "Thank you again for the flowers, Lord Gregory. They're just beautiful. I find daffodils so cheerful."

"I'm glad you like them." He sat straight in the chair, his frame stiff as if he might be a tad uncomfortable. One leg was slightly extended while the other was bent at the knee. He almost looked as if he were posing for a portrait. And what a handsome portrait it would be with his blond hair waving jauntily over his brow and his mouth drawn into a slight smile.

"It's lovely of you to call today." Fiona glanced toward Prudence, whom she could just see from the corner of her eye. She could not, however, offer any help. Not that she knew Fiona needed any. "You are my first caller," Fiona said, deciding to be honest about her inexperience.

Lord Gregory's smile widened. "You are my first call."

Fiona laughed softly. "We are well matched then."

"I thought so too," he murmured.

Realizing the potential implication of what she'd just said, Fiona worried she'd made a mistake. She didn't want him to think they were courting. Were they courting? What constituted a courtship exactly?

"I'm pleased to inform you that I've accepted the invitation to join the Phoenix Club. I am looking forward to the first assembly on Friday evening. You will be there, I presume?"

"Oh, well done," she said, pleased that he'd taken her advice. "Alas, I will not be there."

His smile completely fell away. "I expected you would be since your guardian is a member."

"I believe we had already accepted an invitation for another event." It was an outright lie, but she didn't know what else to say.

"I see. Well, that is disappointing." He glanced away, then looked back to her with a light of hope in his gaze. "Which event? I shall see if I can also accept an invitation."

Fiona darted another look toward Prudence. Their eyes connected, and Prudence gave her a slight shrug.

"I don't recall at the moment." Since the earl had reinstated Fiona's social privileges, she hadn't asked him what invitations they'd accepted. But then she'd been rather avoiding him. More accurately, he seemed to be avoiding her. She'd only seen him in passing since the ball on Saturday. "I can send word later or tomorrow."

"I would like that very much." His shoulders relaxed the barest amount. "If the weather improves, perhaps we can promenade in the park."

Fiona had been waiting for that in particular, of course. There was just something about walking amongst the ton in a place she'd been looking at on a map for years. "I would enjoy that immensely."

Lord Gregory sat forward in his chair, his gaze fixing intently on hers. "It seems we are in accord. I am so delighted. I look forward to our next meeting—soon." He stood and bowed before departing.

Exhaling, Fiona let her body relax completely as she slumped back against the settee. She hadn't realized just how nervous she'd been.

Prudence came to sit in the chair closer to the settee—the one Overton had occupied when they'd bumped noses. "There can be little doubt about Lord Gregory's intentions. Are you pleased?"

"Forgive me for being obtuse, but exactly what intentions are those?"

"Courtship, marriage. One follows the other. He was clear with his intent to see you again soon." Prudence gave her a satisfied smile, which said something because she rarely smiled. "As you told him, you are well matched."

Fiona groaned and dropped her forehead into her hand for a moment. She had said that, but she hadn't meant it like that. She'd only meant that they shared the fact that it was their first social call in common. Should she have clarified the matter so he didn't have the wrong idea? *Was* there a wrong idea? Didn't she *want* to be courted by him?

Wiping her fingers across her eyes and down her cheek, she looked over at Prudence, who was no longer smiling. "I was speaking about our newness at social calling."

"I don't think he realized that," Prudence said softly. "Nor did I. If you aren't interested in courtship, you should tell him as soon as possible."

"I don't know what I'm interested in."

That question plagued her through the day and past dinner, which they had once again eaten without the earl. The question was still uppermost in her mind as she tried to distract herself with maps in the library later that evening.

She'd just immersed herself in the topography of southern Europe when Lord Overton came in. At once, the air changed, filling with a thick tension. Her heart rate picked up speed.

"Good evening, Miss Wingate."

She straightened in her chair at the table upon which the map was spread. "Good evening, Lord Overton."

He strolled to the other side of the table. "I apologize for missing dinner again. I was caught up at Westminster."

"No need to apologize. Speaking of apologies, however, Mrs. Tucket is keen to offer another one to you about the ball the other night."

He smiled and ran his fingers over the faint bruise on his jaw. "She could have a future as a pugilist if not for her dependence upon the cane."

"She would argue about the need for the cane, so please don't tell her that."

His brow arched. "You think she'd actually want to take up fighting?"

Fiona recalled the way she herded chickens and goats. It wasn't fighting, but she possessed a temperament that was good at commanding others. Fiona imagined that would be a welcome quality in a fighting match. "I would not be surprised. More importantly, I think she would be frightfully good at it."

He looked down at the map. "Topography of southern Europe?"

"I am trying to imagine how the French army invaded Portugal. Their path seems difficult."

"It was." He moved around the table and stood at the

corner, rather near her. His fingertips traced over the Tagus Valley. "Napoleon wanted a shorter route, but it's more remote and rugged."

"I close my eyes and try to imagine how it looks."

"There are drawings, I'm sure. Perhaps those are the books we should look for next."

He spoke as if they would be together like this for some time. They would not, of course, since they would each likely be wed in the short term.

She tipped her head back to look up at him, only to find his gaze on her instead of the map. He took a few steps to his right—away from her.

"I came to tell you that I've changed my mind about the Phoenix Club assembly. We'll go on Friday."

She bolted from the chair in surprise. "Why?"

"I heard Lord Gregory accepted his invitation. I thought you might want to attend the ball since he'll be there." He focused his attention on the map.

Confusion swept through her. "You keep changing your mind about me. I mean, about things I'm allowed to do." She added the last in a rush, thinking the first thing she'd said could be interpreted in multiple ways. Perhaps she should take more time to consider her words since she seemed to be doing that often. At least today.

"It seems Lord Gregory is courting you." He flicked a glance toward her. "You like him, don't you?"

"I do," she responded. Had Prudence said something to him? How else would he know about Lord Gregory accepting the invitation?

"Then you must go. Once a gentleman calls on you in London, it's a signal that the courtship is progressing. If he calls on you again, and you continue to dance together and otherwise spend time in each other's company, a betrothal will be expected."

Fiona swallowed. "And if it doesn't happen?"

"It depends on the situation, but in many cases, the woman will be seen as somehow wanting."

"The woman, not the man?"

His lips stretched into a brief, humorless smile. "It's not particularly fair."

"It's a wonder anyone is able to make a match. How can you determine if you will suit without spending a great deal of time together? And it seems if you do that, you're committed. Whether you suit or not."

"That can happen, I suppose. My mother thought she and my father were suited, but after they married, she realized that was not the case."

Fiona thought of her own parents and exhaled. "This doesn't just happen in London, of course. Things might be more relaxed in the country, but there are still expectations. I believe my parents did not suit." She offered a small, commiserative smile. "Perhaps our parents' failures have made us more cautious. How are things progressing between you and Miss Goodfellow?"

He looked away from her again. "A bit stalled at the moment." He pivoted so that his hip was against the edge of the table. "It occurs to me that there will be a waltz at the assembly on Friday—it is always the third dance. You should dance it with Lord Gregory. Do you think you can?"

She wanted to ask why things had stalled with Miss Goodfellow but suspected it was her fault because of what had happened at the club in the garden. Because of what *she'd* done to affect his reputation.

Instead, she answered his question about dancing. "My only waltzing experience has been with you."

His brows rose slightly. "Then you need another lesson, I think." He offered her his hand. "I promise I won't hum."

She put her fingers against his palm. His hand closed

around hers, sending a rush of heat up her arm. As she stood, her entire body tingled with awareness, and she found herself looking at his mouth, recalling their kiss.

Best not to think about that.

Leading her away from the table, he kept hold of her hand. "Do you remember how to position yourself?"

She nodded, facing him and putting her hand on his shoulder. Their clasped hands shifted, and he put his hand on her waist. There were several inches between their chests, but Fiona was intensely aware of their proximity and that enduring magnetism that continued to draw her to him.

"Ready?" he murmured, his pewter gaze locked with hers.

"Yes."

He began to move, gently steering her about the room, gliding with masculine grace as he avoided the furniture. And he did so without looking, for his attention was focused wholly on her. She could not have taken her eyes from him, even if she wanted to. Did he feel the same?

Without music, the room seemed somehow smaller, more intimate, and the space between them charged with a specific energy that only they could generate. Without music, it was not really a dance, but a joining in which they used the waltz as an excuse to move as one.

After a few circuits, he said, "I think you've mastered this."

"I'm only following your lead. I suspect I may only be as good as my partner."

He smiled. "Not true. You've become quite good at the other dances you learned. I saw how well you danced at the ball the other night."

He'd watched her? "Did you?"

"It is my responsibility to supervise you." The words should have disappointed her, for she wanted to be more than a responsibility. However, the way he continued to look at her made her feel a bit giddy.

"Do you like me at all, my lord?" She'd meant to tease him, but she found she wanted to know the truth. She was his father's ward, and she'd caused him a great deal of trouble and expense since coming into his life.

He slowed until they came to a stop. "Fiona."

Her heart beat fast and hard. He'd said her name, not Miss Wingate.

His thumb stroked her hand, and his fingers moved like a whisper along her spine. "I like you very much," he breathed.

Fiona slid her hand along his shoulder until she met the stiff, vertical collar of his shirt. She leaned slightly toward him, erasing half the distance that separated them. Focusing on his lips once more, she could almost taste his kiss...

He abruptly released her and took a step back. A cold disappointment washed over her. She wrapped her arms about her middle. He didn't want to kiss her again—he'd said they couldn't. He was her *guardian*. But what of this magnetism or whatever it was she was feeling toward him? She'd have to find a way to put a stop to it.

"I'd say you are more than ready to waltz with Lord Gregory," he said, his features stoic. "He is an excellent match."

She was growing tired of hearing people say that. "I know. However, marriage between us is not a foregone conclusion. I am still not quite ready to make that leap." Except she'd told the earl that she would. She owed it to him to stop being a nuisance. Particularly when he clearly saw her that way.

"You'll have to decide soon. Lord Gregory is not stupid, and you are an excellent catch."

"Why? I'm a nobody from the country."

"You're intelligent, beautiful, and you have a rather large

dowry," he added wryly. "Thanks to my father. As a second son, that will undoubtedly be enticing to Lord Gregory."

"I'm a good investment," she muttered.

"It's an added benefit. Lord Gregory may have pursued you even without it."

Fiona froze. Cocking her head, she stared at him a moment. "He knows about my dowry?"

"I would assume so."

"Why? Is there some publication where eligible young ladies are listed with their pedigree and monetary worth?" Anger bubbled inside her.

"Of course not. But when a young woman enters the Marriage Mart, certain things are shared."

"So you shared—with who, the entire ton—that I have an oversized dowry?"

"I made it known, yes." His brows dug down as his eyes narrowed. "That is how things are done, particularly when a young lady is not, as you put it, pedigreed."

"I see." She would never know if any man was ever interested in her for her or for the money she could bring him. Money that wasn't hers, but with which she could change her life and be independent. Of course, women were never afforded that option. Just imagine if a father—or a bloody guardian—said, *"This is your dowry, but if you choose not to wed, you may take it for yourself."* She nearly laughed out loud.

"You seem angry," he said slowly.

"I feel trapped. I am utterly reliant on you and my future husband. I don't even know what to do about poor Mrs. Tucket. She'd probably be happier back in Shropshire, but I can't make that happen. I have to ask you or my husband to provide a retirement for her. Apparently, I have a dowry that I *could* use, except that I can't because it isn't really mine."

Lines burrowed across his forehead. "You aren't trapped. I am doing my best to give you the best opportunities."

"As dictated by Society. I must learn to dance and how to behave so that I may find a husband."

He frowned more deeply. "I also obtained books and maps for you, as well as a pianoforte. I've tried to give you things you've never had and that you clearly enjoy."

Some of her ire dissipated, but the sense of being in a cage did not. She thought of returning to Shropshire with Mrs. Tucket, but she'd be without choices there too, since her cousin would marry her off just as Overton was doing. "I am grateful, my lord, for everything. And I shall repay you by marrying Lord Gregory, provided he proposes. It seems that is the preferred, and best, course. I bid you good evening."

She turned and left the library without tidying the maps. Because to stay another moment in his presence might have completely broken her spirit.

~

*A*fter a particularly long day at Westminster, Tobias went directly to the gaming room at the Phoenix Club where, over the course of an hour, he lost a considerable sum of money. Most of it went to Mrs. Jennings, a sharp, witty widow around forty years of age.

As he took his leave of the table, she did the same. "You seemed distracted as we played, Overton," she said as they walked between the tables.

Between his troublesome ward and his lack of marriage prospects, Tobias was more than distracted. One might even describe him as morose. "My mind is cluttered," he admitted. "It was a busy day at Westminster."

"I don't miss that about Mr. Jennings," she said. "He spent far too much time there, which was probably the cause of the fit that killed him."

Tobias recalled that he'd died—in his seat in the

Commons—two years previously. "Mr. Jennings was a strong voice."

"He was indeed. Is that what you were doing today?" she asked, peering at him askance with her bright blue-green eyes. "Pontificating?"

"Heavens no." Tobias made a slight face for comedic effect. "I try never to do that. I did deliver a small speech about voting reform, but there aren't many who support that."

She smiled approvingly. "Mr. Jennings would have been proud of you."

Tobias's father would have been horrified, which Tobias counted as an added bonus. "Are you going upstairs to the members' den?" he asked, intending to offer his escort.

"I am." At her confirmation, he presented his arm and an invitation. "Thank you. Can I attribute anything to your behavior beyond polite kindness?"

He guided her toward the staircase hall. "What do you mean?"

"I understand you are searching for a wife. I am probably too old for you. However, my younger sister is not. She is, however, on the shelf and not currently in London."

Tobias liked Mrs. Jennings, but this was an odd conversation. Did he appear desperate?

"I heard about your...situation last week here in the garden." She gave him a sympathetic look as they started up the stairs. "I wondered if you might seek to find a bride who would not be troubled by your...activities." Lowering her voice, she added, "My sister would not mind. In fact, she'd be happy to engage in an arrangement in which she provides you an heir and beyond that you lead separate lives."

Tobias caught his foot on the next stair and had to clasp the railing. Mrs. Jennings gripped him more tightly and let out a soft chuckle. "I didn't mean to startle you."

"I was not, ah, expecting you to say any of that." His mind scrambled to think of an appropriate response. *Was* there an appropriate response?

"Such things aren't typically discussed so brazenly, but I don't see a need to mince words. You seem in want of a wife and find yourself in a difficult circumstance. I only wanted to offer a solution."

"Brilliant, thank you." He summoned a smile. "I shall take your thoughtful offer under advisement."

They'd reached the top of the stairs. "I'm for the library," he said, deciding at the last moment that he'd rather not risk the chance of having to sit with her in the members' den. He didn't think he could withstand any further attempts at "assistance."

She took her hand from his arm. "I thank you for your distraction earlier. My modiste will be quite happy to receive my next order." Smiling widely, she took her leave and sauntered toward the members' den, which would be quite full of ladies this evening since it was Tuesday.

Tobias hesitated. He should go. What if his bride was there and he had only to go in and find her?

Scowling, he turned on his heel and went to the library. There, he strode directly to the liquor cabinet and promptly swore when he couldn't find any Scotch whisky.

"Waiting on a shipment, I think," Wexford said from a table behind him. "There's Irish though!" Grinning, he raised his glass.

"Irish," Tobias muttered as he poured some. He joined Wexford at his table and sipped the whisky. "Not bad."

Wexford narrowed his eyes jauntily. "After you finish that glass, you won't go back. I'll put ten pounds on it."

Tobias shook his head. "No more wagering. I lost enough downstairs already."

"I heard." Lucien, a glass of port in his hand, took another chair at the table. "I just came from the members' den where Mrs. Jennings is crowing about her winnings."

"I hope that's all she's talking about." Tobias winced inwardly to think of her sharing the proposition she'd offered him with anyone else. Surely she wouldn't. He didn't know her to be the kind of person who delighted in salacious information.

Both Lucien and Wexford stared at him, their eyes wide.

"Are you shagging her too?" Wexford asked, incredulous. "I mean, she's bloody attractive, but aren't you trying to take the tarnish *off*?"

Tobias growled low in his throat. "I'm not shagging her. Or anyone else." He took a long pull on the whisky. Wexford might be right about becoming a convert by the bottom of the glass. But was that because it was good, or because Tobias would have downed the cheapest gin if it was in front of him?

"Never mind," Tobias grumbled, setting the glass down and leaning back in his chair. "She was trying to be helpful. I've twelve days to marry and zero prospects."

"She offered herself?" Lucien asked.

"Not exactly." Though she'd hinted at that too. "Can we forget about Mrs. Jennings and focus on the matter at hand?"

Lucien arched his brows. "Which is?"

"Finding a damned wife. If I'm going to race to Scotland, I need to leave in a few days."

"Since you have no prospects at present, I take it you're referring to a kidnapping then?" Wexford sent a smirk toward Lucien, who tried not to smile and failed.

"I can't believe Mrs. Jennings was actually trying to be more helpful than you lot." Tobias swept up his glass and finished the whisky. He started to rise, but Lucien waved him back down.

"We apologize," Lucien said soberly as he cast a quelling

glance toward Wexford. "You need help finding an appropriate bride, one whom you can whisk away to Scotland or marry by special license."

"Yes." Tobias settled himself in the chair and folded his arms over his chest.

"What happened with Miss Goodfellow?" Lucien asked.

"Her feelings toward me—if she even had any—may have cooled." Tobias couldn't even say for certain because he hadn't seen her.

Cupping his glass atop the table, Lucien tapped his finger against the rim of the tumbler. "That's a shame. Things seemed to be going well. You danced, you called on her, and she is in a position to eagerly accept a courtship. One wonders why you didn't propose days ago." There was a hidden question there, but Tobias wasn't entirely certain what it was, nor did he like it. He also didn't like that Lucien was getting to the heart of something—namely, Tobias's heart and the fact that he was having trouble committing to marriage without engaging said organ.

Wexford furrowed his brow as he studied Tobias for a moment. "This shouldn't be so difficult. You're a wealthy, reasonably attractive earl. Plenty of women would say yes to you, even if you are shagging a maid." He held up his hand in self-defense. "Not that you are. Anymore."

"Wexford makes a valid point," Lucien said slowly. "About your options. It all depends upon how desperate you are, and it seems you may be nearing the point where you might, ah, broaden your prospects or lower your expectations? And that isn't to say you should propose to just anyone, only that the thing you would normally require might be ignored."

Such as falling in love. Tobias had genuinely hoped that might happen. However, he'd run out of time.

"Hell, you could start for Scotland tomorrow and find a woman on the way!" Wexford suggested completely unhelpfully. "Or you can find one in Scotland. Does MacNair have an unwed sister or a cousin?"

Lucien shook his head. "He has two sisters, but I think they may both be wed. Even if they weren't, I'm certain he would no sooner want his sister to marry a rake like either of you than I do."

"I wasn't suggesting myself," Wexford said with a bit of heat. "Furthermore, you know I am not interested in marriage for at least three more years."

Tobias uncrossed his arms and set one palm atop the table. "And I am no longer a rake."

"Last week's maid was just a fleeting relapse?" Wexford asked.

"She wasn't a relapse. She wasn't even a maid." Tobias picked up his glass before realizing it was empty. Fortunately for him, a footman in the corner noted his lack of whisky and came to rectify the deficit. Tobias looked up at him in gratitude as he retrieved the empty glass. "Thank you."

Lucien's eyes glittered as he regarded Tobias across the table. "Yes, about that. I have since learned that the woman you dallied with was not, in fact, an employee. The ladies' housekeeper said she and another young woman she didn't recognize were in the sitting room that morning. They said they were new and that I had hired them. I did not."

Fiona had been with another young woman? She hadn't mentioned it. Was it Prudence? Perhaps Fiona had been protecting her, which was smart. If Tobias learned it was her, he would toss her out immediately.

The footman set down Tobias's whisky. He murmured another thanks before busying himself with a long sip.

"I can see your mind working." Lucien seemed to realize Tobias was trying not to participate in the discussion of these women's identities. "Do you know this woman?"

Tobias didn't want to reveal his ward. But if he didn't,

they'd think he was kissing someone he'd just met in the garden while they were supposed to be meeting about the club. Did it even matter? They'd already cast him in the role of incurable lothario.

Lucien squinted at him briefly. "Perhaps you are trying to recall. Her hair seemed red."

"Doesn't your ward have red hair?" Wexford mused.

Tobias tensed. He didn't particularly want to look at Lucien. Or Wexford.

Lucien muttered something before taking a drink of his port. "Why was she here dressed as a maid, and who was she with?"

Leveling an icy stare at Lucien, Tobias, said, "I didn't confirm it was her."

"You don't have to," Lucien said quietly. "It all makes sense now."

Wexford leaned toward Tobias. "Do you have a tendre for her?"

"No." Tobias didn't know what he had for her. One thing was certain, he thought about her too damned much.

Lucien stared at him intently, repeating, "Who was she with, and why were they here?"

"I didn't know she wasn't alone." That was the absolute truth. "She wanted to see the inside of the club. It was foolish, and she knows it. That's all I'm going to say on the matter."

Wexford continued to look at him intently, as if he were trying to puzzle something out. "Why can't you just marry *her*?"

"She's young and not yet ready to marry. She already has a perfect suitor in Lord Gregory, and she is completely unenthused."

Sitting back in his chair, Wexford let out a hollow laugh. "Clear proof that she's immature and simple-minded."

"Or that she's perhaps interested in someone else." Lucien sipped his port.

Tobias gritted his teeth. "Stop playing matchmaker, both of you. How would it look if I were to court my ward? As if my reputation isn't bad enough."

"That seems an excellent argument to marry her," Wexford said with a shrug. "If people already expect the outrageous from you, give it to them."

Hadn't Tobias done exactly that after his failed courtship two years ago? He'd considered eloping to Gretna Green with his prospective bride—after she'd already become betrothed to another man. Thankfully, he'd seen the error in his rash thinking. More importantly, he'd realized the young woman hadn't ever loved him. She'd loved the idea of marriage to whomever she was with, and the idea of running away to Scotland had titillated her. That was the moment Tobias had come to his senses and changed his mind, telling her to go forward with her betrothed. Afterward, she'd told everyone he'd tried to kidnap her. While many did not believe that of him, the ton's consensus was that he'd behaved poorly by trying to elope with her. They cast him as a rogue and a scoundrel, and he'd decided to become just that.

Perhaps he *was* actually a rogue and a scoundrel, and a rake and a reprobate. He *had* proposed elopement to someone who was already betrothed, and he *had* kissed a maid—*his ward*—without concern.

"He's grown awfully quiet," Lucien observed. "I think he's considering it."

"I am not." Tobias took a drink of whisky. "Can we please talk about something else?"

Otherwise, Tobias was absolutely going to envision Fiona Wingate as his wife.

CHAPTER 15

"*T*hank you for serving as my chaperone today as well as Fiona's," Cassandra said to Prudence as they sat down at Gunter's to await their ices.

Fiona situated her skirts around her chair. "She may as well, since she'll be chaperoning both of us at the Phoenix Club assembly on Friday."

"I am still a bit surprised we are able to go. My father was not pleased, and he said I can only attend this *one*." Cassandra made a face. "It would serve him right if I met my future husband there."

"Speaking of future husbands," Fiona murmured. "Apparently, I have a dowry, and my guardian has been dangling it as bait to attract suitors. What a disgusting practice."

"It's commonplace, I'm afraid," Cassandra said with sympathy. "I didn't realize you didn't know that."

Fiona blinked at her. "Did you know I had a large dowry?"

"Not specifically, but Con mentioned you were potential competition for me—and please don't take that personally because Con is a bit of an ass—so I presumed you had a dowry."

A shard of hurt sliced through Fiona. "Why, because I couldn't possibly compete without it?"

Cassandra blinked in surprise. "Not at all. Con, like my father, believes the most important things a woman can bring to a marriage are position, land, and money. Since you don't have the former two, it seemed you must have the latter."

"Because of what your brother said." Fiona ducked her head sheepishly. "My apologies. I should have realized, and I should not have been so naïve about this. And everything else."

Cassandra, seated to her left, reached over and briefly clasped Fiona's hand. "No need to apologize. I just hope you aren't angry with me."

"Not at all. You've been nothing but a good friend."

"Except for dragging you to the Phoenix Club." She frowned with regret. "I can't believe *you* aren't angry with *me*. Especially since I was safely hidden in a closet."

Fiona laughed. "Only because you were smarter than me."

Cassandra grinned as the ices were delivered to their table. It was their second visit to the tea shop, and this time Fiona was keen to try the chocolate flavor while both Cassandra and Prudence had ordered the orange flower.

Picking up her spoon, Fiona returned to the matter of her dowry. "I just wish I could receive the dowry instead of my husband. Then I could ensure Mrs. Tucket could retire. She confided in me last night that she wants to return to the country."

Prudence gave her a sad look. "I'm sorry to hear that."

"She's horribly embarrassed about what happened at the Dungannon ball the other night. She's afraid she'll ruin things for me." Fiona dipped her spoon into the ice cream. "If

I had money, I could make sure she had a small cottage and could live in comfort and peace."

"Your cousin in Shropshire won't see to that?"

"I don't see why he would. Mrs. Tucket has been my family's maid-of-all-work since before I was born. He would feel no obligation toward her." Fiona tried the chocolate and immediately appreciated the dark, rich flavor.

"Have you spoken to Lord Overton about this?" Prudence asked, surprising Fiona because she simply didn't say much.

"Not directly, but he is aware of my…frustration in not being able to use my dowry," Fiona said. "I plan to discuss it with my future husband, which at the moment seems to be Lord Gregory. However, I don't want to be presumptuous, so I must wait until he proposes."

Cassandra regarded her with a bit of shock. "Are you really considering marrying him?"

"I *must* consider it."

"Is that what you really want though?"

For some reason, Fiona thought of Overton. Probably because he'd made her position untenable. If he'd never brought her to London, she and Mrs. Tucket would be living the life they'd long enjoyed.

Enjoyed? Fiona had been bored in Shropshire, horribly so in hindsight.

"What I really want is independence," she said softly before digging her spoon into the ice cream and taking a large, decadent mouthful.

Cassandra swallowed a bite of her ice cream and gave Fiona a wistful look. "Wouldn't that be wonderful? Perhaps Lord Gregory will be the sort of husband who will allow you the freedoms you desire. And he may very well support Mrs. Tucket, especially if he loves you and sees how important she is to you. I think a marriage with love or at least mutual respect and care is the greatest freedom we can hope for."

Love? Fiona hadn't contemplated that at all. She was fairly certain her parents hadn't loved each other. She wasn't sure what that even looked like. She did know that she hadn't loved anyone, not beyond her parents, and that was different.

"Why do you think that?" Fiona asked.

"Because marriage is the societal ideal. Without it, we will always be lacking in the ton's eyes, whether we have the financial ability to live independently or not. I hope I can find a caring husband. It's just easier than the alternatives," Cassandra said, plunging her spoon into her dish. "My father insists I become betrothed by the end of May or he's going to arrange a suitable marriage. I suspect that will diminish my chances for an amiable union."

Prudence lifted a shoulder. "Occasionally, an arranged marriage works out well. King George and Queen Charlotte were quite happy before, well, before."

Fiona knew what she meant—before the king had become ill and his son had been made Regent.

Cassandra waved her spoon. "While that may be true, his eldest son and his arranged wife quite despise each other."

"There is only one solution," Fiona declared. "We must pool our pin money and run away. Where shall we go?"

Cassandra giggled.

Prudence raised her hand. "If I also contribute funds, may I come along?"

"Of course!" Fiona and Cassandra answered in unison before they all dissolved into laughter.

"Sounds like you're having quite a gay time."

Fiona recovered herself and looked up at the woman who'd approached their table. Petite with pale skin and blonde hair, the woman fixed her blue eyes on Cassandra first. "Good afternoon, Lady Cassandra."

"Lady Bentley."

Fiona noted the tightness in Cassandra's voice and surmised she didn't care for the new arrival.

Cassandra offered Lady Bentley a weak smile. "Allow me to present my friend, Miss Fiona Wingate and her companion, Miss Lancaster."

Fiona rose and curtsied, as did Prudence. "It's a pleasure to meet you." She tried to remember who Lady Bentley was. The name was familiar, probably from Debrett's, but Fiona couldn't place the title.

Lady Bentley turned her bright blue gaze on Fiona. "Miss Wingate, are you Lord Overton's ward? It seems you are. I heard about your presentation to the queen."

Of course she had.

"How charming of you to bring that up," Cassandra said, her voice and features carrying a sharp edge.

"Yes, well, it was quite the story." Lady Bentley laughed, a soft but wholly grating sound. At least to Fiona. "I did feel sorry for Overton. He's had such a bad time of things since I chose Bentley over him."

Fiona couldn't think of what to say to that surprising revelation. Why on earth would this woman have chosen anyone besides Overton? He was witty, thoughtful, handsome, caring. "Has he? He seems in rather good spirits to me." Fiona looked to her tablemates. "Wouldn't you agree?"

"Most definitely." Cassandra blinked in what appeared to be mock ignorance at Lady Bentley. "Did you actually choose Bentley, or was the choice made for you? I can't imagine why you'd choose him over the earl." Her eyes rounded briefly before she leaned toward Fiona and whispered, though not quietly enough that Lady Bentley couldn't hear, "Bentley's opinion of himself wasn't quite so inflated then. Also, his father *is* a duke." She pursed her lips.

Lady Bentley's eyes narrowed. "He didn't attempt to kidnap me to Gretna Green, as Overton did. Overton would have made a terrible husband. Autocratic and cold, as his father was known to be."

Fiona didn't believe for a moment that her guardian would kidnap anyone. Nor did she believe the other things Lady Bentley said about him. "I've never known Lord Overton to be anything but warm and kind. Perhaps you misunderstood his intentions."

"Oh yes, that must be it," Cassandra said eagerly. "I'd wager the truth is that he offered to kidnap Bentley so he could avoid the parson's trap."

"You are not at all amusing," Lady Bentley said with considerable affront.

Cassandra adopted a sober expression and lowered her voice to a remorseful tone. "My apologies. I thought you were jesting, and we were simply playing along."

"Well, good day." Lady Bentley turned on her heel and stalked toward the door, her maid following quickly behind.

"What an unpleasant woman," Prudence murmured.

"Indeed," Fiona agreed. "Did Overton really want to marry her?"

Cassandra shrugged. "I recall that he'd had his heart broken, but I don't pay attention to gossip. And, of course, I wasn't out then."

He'd had his heart broken. Fiona felt a surge of sympathy for him. "I realize I don't know him extensively, but he's never seemed cold or autocratic to me. Yes, he's been demanding and rather managing when it comes to my future, but even then, he seems to change his mind in favor of allowing me to do things as I choose. Friday's assembly is a prime example. He wasn't going to let me go and then changed his mind."

Cassandra cocked her head as she studied Fiona. "I wonder why. Has he developed a particular affection for you?"

"It may be that he is striving to not be like his father," Prudence suggested. "I have heard talk from the servants about Lord Overton. His relationship with his father was fraught, especially after he didn't marry as expected two seasons ago. If the prior earl was autocratic, it makes sense that the current earl may reverse decisions that could be seen in the same light."

That did make sense. Fiona wanted to ask him about it. Would he open up to her about his father and about whatever had happened with Lady Bentley? Was it even any of her business? Not really, but she thought they had some sort of connection—if not as family, at least friendship?

"I did hear something this morning that made me curious," Prudence said, setting her spoon down since she'd finished her ice cream. "The housekeeper and the butler were discussing the earl's need to wed."

"Why would that make you curious?" Cassandra asked. "He's an earl and needs an heir."

"They said something about his father putting him in a terrible situation." Prudence looked to Fiona. "I suppose that could refer to some disagreement they had before he died."

And Fiona hadn't improved his situation with her behavior last week. She'd reminded everyone that he was a rogue and perhaps not the best marriage material, earl or not. "Cassandra, is there anything I can do to help him? His current predicament regarding his reputation is entirely my fault."

"Unfortunately, there is nothing you can do. But you do give me an idea." She tapped her finger against her chin briefly. "My brother Constantine is completely above reproach. He can probably assist Overton in ways we can't. I'll speak with him."

Fiona was so glad to hear this, even if she didn't understand how he could help. "What can he do? While we've been sitting here, I believe you referred to him as an ass."

Cassandra laughed. "That much is true, but in this case his pomposity is an advantage. He can speak on Overton's behalf, spend time with him so that people will see the earl with a new perspective. The only thing Overton must be careful of is spending *too* much time with him, for then he may be found dull." She flashed a smile. "I am joking. Con is not always as boring as Lu says he is."

"That would be wonderful," Fiona said, grateful for her friend's support. "I feel so terrible about what happened."

Cassandra gave her an encouraging smile. "We'll do what we can. Now, let us discuss what we are wearing on Friday!"

Fiona turned her mind to the assembly and seeing Lord Gregory. Was she really going to accept his proposal should he offer it? She didn't see as she had any other choice. At least he was kind, and she enjoyed his company. She could do far worse, such as the vicar that her cousin apparently had in mind.

Furthermore, she expected Lord Gregory would be amenable to caring for Mrs. Tucket, but she'd have to ensure that was the case before she agreed to anything. In fact, she'd speak with him about it on Friday at the ball.

In the meantime, she meant to offer whatever support she could to her guardian, *if* he would take it.

~

"May I come in?"

Tobias looked up from the papers he was reading at his desk after dinner to see his ward framed in the threshold of his study door. Her simple green gown was a rich contrast for her vibrant red hair. Captivated by her beauty, he stood, as if he were pulled by an invisible rope. He moved around the desk but forced himself to stop.

"Please." He went to the small settee near the hearth and hoped she would sit beside him, even if it did invite temptation.

She came forward, the hem of her pear-colored skirts skimming the carpet as she joined him.

"I hope I'm not intruding on your work," she said, glancing toward his desk.

He angled himself toward her and rested his arm along the back of the settee, bending it at the elbow so his fingers didn't reach her shoulder. "Not at all. I'm grateful for the respite, actually. Is there something you wish to discuss?"

Her gaze dropped to her lap where she fidgeted with her gown. Straightening her hands so her fingers flexed, she placed her palms on her lap and gave him a tremulous smile.

"You seem nervous," he said. "Is aught amiss?"

"No, nothing's wrong. I went to Gunter's today with Cassandra. And Prudence, of course." She hesitated before adding, "We encountered Lady Bentley."

Tobias gritted his teeth to prevent himself from swearing out loud. "I see," he said slowly. "How was this…encounter?"

"She came to our table, and Cassandra introduced us. She, ah, mentioned something about you trying to kidnap her…" She looked away again, and Tobias couldn't quite tell what she was asking.

"Did you believe her?"

Fiona's gaze snapped to his, her pupils dilating in what he thought was outrage. "Certainly not! It was the most preposterous thing I've ever heard. In fact, I'm not even sure I believe you wanted to marry her. She was rather odious."

Tobias couldn't keep himself from laughing. "She is that, but in my defense, I didn't realize it at the time. I was in want of a wife, and she was enchanting. I thought we suited perfectly."

Her lips pressed into a straight line that screamed her disagreement. "After meeting her, I can't imagine that was remotely possible."

Another laugh escaped him, and because he tried not to let it, the sound was somewhere between a snort and a cough. He had to clear his throat after. "You determined that from a single encounter with her?"

"Easily. I'm surprised you found her tolerable, let alone courted her."

He winced as he rubbed his hand down the side of his face. "I was eager to wed. My father had decreed it was time, and I didn't have an objection to doing so. Lady Priscilla, as she was known then, made me feel as if I was the most important person in the world. I was certain we would wed. I was on my way to tell her of my intention to ask her father for her hand when I learned she'd already accepted Bentley's proposal. It was, I'm now loath to admit, upsetting."

"Why did she say you kidnapped her?"

"Because I offered to elope with her to Gretna Green. I was certain her father had pressured her to accept Bentley's proposal. As the son of a duke, he outranked me. I had to know if the decision to choose him was hers, so I arranged to get her alone at a ball."

"Isn't that rather scandalous?"

He arched a brow at her and tried not to smile. "This from the woman who disguised herself as a maid and stole into a private club?"

She blushed. "And was the decision hers or her father's?"

"Her father's, but she seemed willing to do whatever he wished, like a good, biddable young lady who understands that a marital alliance is perhaps the most important thing she can do."

Fiona made a face, her nose wrinkling as her mouth twisted. "How perfectly horrid. But isn't that what you expected me to do?" She spoke softly, but the volley of words managed to pierce straight into his chest.

Wincing, he dipped his head. "Yes. I deeply regret it. I hope you'll accept my apology. It is, unfortunately, the way of Society—for women and for men. Who I married was of the utmost importance to my father."

"Was he angry when she chose to marry someone else?"

The old, familiar tension gripped Tobias, but only for a moment. With his father gone, he knew he didn't have to suffer the man's dissatisfaction anymore. "He was disappointed. Our relationship never recovered from that."

"How come?"

Tobias gripped the top of the settee's back as he recalled that night at whatever ball they'd attended. "When I suggested to Lady Priscilla that we elope, she was extremely titillated by the idea—not because it was a chance to marry the man she loved, but because it would spark notoriety and popularity. I saw my mistake in thinking she would be a good wife, and I encouraged her to wed Bentley."

"You changed your mind?"

"Yes. She then told everyone that I attempted to kidnap her." He made a sound of disgust low in his throat. "Most didn't believe her, thankfully, but it was dodgy there for a while. I was given the cut direct on several occasions, and my father was furious with me. I was labeled a rogue, a scoundrel, and a rake—the worst sort of reprobate. I grew frustrated with everyone's judgment, especially since I'd ultimately done the right thing. I decided to become what they accused me of."

She was quiet a long moment. "I can't imagine your father approved."

"Not at all. He was livid. We didn't speak for some time."

He looked toward the portrait of his father that hung on the wall to the left of the desk. In it, the former earl stood with his pony when he was about seven or eight years old. The portrait was his father's favorite because of his love for the animal. Tobias had always hoped his father would speak to him with the same tender fondness with which he recalled his horse, but he never had. Now, Tobias wondered why he hadn't removed the painting. Perhaps Tobias was still hoping, even now, to find some glimpse of affection from the man.

"When I learned he was ill, that he was dying, I thought we would repair things, but he wasn't interested in such sentiment." Instead, he'd focused on what Tobias needed to do when he was gone—take care of his ward and marry as soon as possible or suffer the consequences.

"I'm so sorry," Fiona said softly.

"He found my behavior abhorrent, and I must admit I did my damnedest to ensure he felt that way. His disapproval was the best approval I could earn." He shook his head. "Looking back, that was not a terribly wise choice considering that I would need to marry at some point."

"I did not help matters with my behavior." She grazed her fingertips against his leg, sending a flash of heat through him. From the moment he'd glimpsed her in the doorway, his body had thrummed with a steady, insistent longing. Her touch amplified the sensation so that need pulsed through him, sending blood rushing to his cock.

He shifted in an attempt to get his coat to mask his desire, but it was fairly hopeless. Perhaps she wouldn't notice.

"Please don't continue to fret about what happened," he said thickly. "My reputation was well known before you dressed up as a maid."

"Still, you were on the way to improving things, and I ruined that."

He stared at the pale column of her throat where her pulse beat strong and sure, and perhaps a bit quickly. "Did you?"

Her lips parted, and he wondered if she felt the same arousal as him, if that was even possible. For he was powerfully drawn to her and wanted nothing more than to lay her out on the settee, lift her skirts, and bury himself between her legs.

"What are you asking?" she whispered.

"I'm not really asking anything." In his mind, he peeled her stocking away and kissed the backs of her knees before skimming his tongue along her thigh. Clearing the lust from his throat, he continued, "I'm merely pondering whether you had anything to do with it. Perhaps I am truly what my father and everyone else believes—a reprobate, a rogue, a *scoundrel.*"

"Of course you aren't."

"No? Then why is it that when I look at you, all I can think about is kissing you? And not just your mouth. In my mind, I strip away your clothing so I may kiss you everywhere. That is surely improper, for you are my ward. No, it's beyond improper, it's scandalous." He straightened his arm and allowed his fingers to graze her shoulder—first the part that was covered with the sleeve of her gown, then her bare flesh as he moved toward her neck. "It's positively shameless."

"Would it be so bad if it was just one kiss?" the question was higher than her usual tone. Her eyes were wide, her pupils dilated with unmistakable desire.

"But what if it wasn't?" He trailed his fingertips up the side of her neck to a spot behind her ear. He gently pressed his thumb to her jaw.

She leaned forward and put her mouth on his, shocking him, as she'd done that day in the garden. No, it wasn't shocking like that. He'd never imagined they would share a kiss before that. But in every moment since, he'd hoped for the chance. Now, it was here.

Cupping the side of her head, he brought his other hand to her side where he splayed his fingers along her back and tucked his thumb beneath her breast. He slanted his lips over hers, rising slightly from the settee.

She curled one hand around his neck, clasping his nape. He brought his thumb forward and pressed against her chin. Pulling back for the barest moment, he whispered, "Open your mouth just a bit so I can show you—"

Her lips parted, and once again she shocked him as her tongue met his. She gasped at the contact, and he lost himself in the wonder of her response. He forced himself to go slowly, to show her every divine progression of this ritual, of the sweet and dazzling moments when one first learns a lover's terrain. Perhaps she would find it was like studying a new map. He hoped she found it that entrancing.

The kiss deepened, each of them exploring the other. Her fingers dug into his head and neck, and he thrust his hand into her hair, desperate to pull the pins away so he could bury himself in her softness.

He did not, however, because to do so would be to completely lose himself. That, he could not do. She was his ward, and while they were in a private place, the door to his study was not closed.

Despite that, he did not pull away. He didn't want to interrupt this magnificent moment. Pressing her back into the corner of the settee, he brought his hand to her front where he cupped her breast. She gasped again but didn't withdraw. In fact, she clutched him more tightly and arched up against him.

A deep growl rose in his throat as he tore his mouth from hers. Not to leave her, but to further survey the map before him.

He kissed her chin, her jaw, then her mouth once more, eagerly devouring her. She tipped her head back and pulled on his hair as he trailed his lips down her throat. He clasped her breast more firmly and dragged his thumb across the bare skin above the neckline of her gown. How he longed to rip the garment, and those beneath it, away, to expose the landscape of her body.

"Oh yes." She let out a delightfully dark and gritty moan followed by a whimper that made Tobias even harder. He licked along the edge of her bodice and suckled her flesh.

She cried out and he put his hand over her mouth. Looking up at her, he saw the stark desire etched into her features and nearly lost all control. He put his finger against her lips. "Shhh."

"My lord," she breathed before sucking the tip into her mouth.

"Tobias," he hissed. "My name is Tobias."

Her only response was a nod and the press of her hand against his neck. Tipping his head back down, he tried to make sense of her gown. It was the sort that gathered at the front, so he could loosen the tie tucked into the front of her bodice and the garment would open.

Testing his theory, he pulled the tie. The gown gaped, exposing the corset beneath. And beneath that was her infernal chemise. "I hate women's clothing," he muttered.

Undeterred, he reached down for the hem of her gown, lifting her skirt until he found it. Raising it farther, he exposed her leg until his fingertips found her bare thigh. She parted her legs, but instead of taking that as encouragement, he froze.

What on earth was he doing? She was still his bloody ward, and this *was* shameless.

Tobias released her and sat back, his chest still rising and falling rapidly, even though his pulse had finally begun to slow. Because it had to. This wasn't just shameless, it was madness.

She stared at him, her gaze confused. "Did I do something wrong?"

"No, I did. I never should have allowed any of that to happen."

"You say that like you're in charge. Why don't you manage your body and your choices, and I'll manage mine." Giving him a look that was somehow both prim and enticing, she tied the lace of her dress, cinching the bodice back so it covered her undergarments. "I welcomed everything that just happened, and I enjoyed it."

"Fiona, I am your guardian."

"Thanks to your father." She rose and smoothed her hands down her rumpled dress. "Now I think I may harbor a particular dislike for him too."

What was she saying? "This can't happen again." The words came out low and harsh because he had difficulty summoning them.

"You said that before, and yet here we are."

Satisfied that he could stand without displaying the crux of his desire now that his erection had somewhat waned, he stood. "Please forgive my lapse in judgment. I shall resist temptation in the future. I told you what I am."

Her gaze moved over him, stirring his cock once more. "A rogue. A rake. A scoundrel. A reprobate." She spoke with soft deliberation, and it was sweet poetry. "Yes, I can see what you are, and contrary to what you may think, it isn't bad." With a flick of her skirts, she turned and left the study.

"Christ," Tobias murmured as he sank back down onto the settee, his body deflating with unquenched lust.

Not only did he want his ward, but he was also now beginning to consider if he could actually marry her. The question was whether she would consider it too.

CHAPTER 16

*A*fter a night of sleep in which torrid dreams awakened her several times, Fiona spent the morning feeling agitated and uncertain. She'd managed to keep herself together while in Tobias's presence, but as soon as she'd reached her room, she'd collapsed against the door in a quivering mass of unsatisfied desire.

As she lay in bed, she'd closed her eyes and recalled the book she'd found in her father's library. Complete with detailed drawings, the treatise outlined ways in which men and women gave and received pleasure. She'd been horrified when she'd first found it, and then over the years, she'd returned to it as her curiosity had grown. If not for that book, she wouldn't have had a clue about what might happen with Tobias. As it was, she *knew* what could have happened, and she was wholly disappointed when it hadn't.

It also meant she knew how to provide herself with at least a modicum of relief.

He'd opened her eyes to what she was missing, to what marriage could bring. She'd been foolish not to consider this physical aspect and the fact that it was directly tied to the magnetic pull she felt toward him. It was desire, pure and simple, and she'd never felt it for anyone else, including Lord Gregory.

Frowning, she finally emerged from her room and immediately found Prudence in their sitting room. Seated at the small round table near the windows, she looked up from the newspaper she held. "Are you feeling all right today?"

"I didn't sleep well." Fiona didn't want to tell her what had happened. She wasn't sure she agreed with Tobias that it was shameless, but it was most certainly improper.

"Were you able to speak with Lord Overton about our encounter with Lady Bentley?" Prudence knew Fiona had gone downstairs for that purpose. Thankfully she'd been abed when Fiona returned.

"Briefly," she said. "Apparently, he did court her, and she did choose Bentley over him. He did not, however, attempt to kidnap her." Fiona rolled her eyes.

"Of course," Prudence murmured. "I noticed you were downstairs for quite some time."

There was no question, but Fiona heard her curiosity quite loudly. "I went to the library to spend some time with the maps."

The butler stepped into the sitting room just then. "Pardon my intrusion, ladies. Miss Wingate, if you are free, your presence is requested in his lordship's study."

A wave of heat spiked through Fiona, followed closely by a crisp burst of anxiety. What could the earl want? Would it be awkward to be with him in the place where they'd embraced so intimately the night before?

"I'll be right there, Carrin," Fiona said, brushing her hand over the back of her upswept hair.

After the butler departed, Prudence said, "You look fine. Actually, you look very pretty."

Darting a glance toward Prudence, Fiona dropped her hand to her side. "Thank you." And blast because Fiona didn't want anyone, including Prudence, knowing that she cared what she looked like in Tobias's presence.

Tobias. She really oughtn't call him that, even in her head.

Fiona walked downstairs, her pace altering between fast with anticipation and sedate with trepidation. By the time she reached the study, she felt as if she'd taken a few laps around the house.

As she stepped over the threshold, she nearly tripped. Tobias wasn't there.

His secretary, a round-faced gentleman with dark, receding hair and a warm smile, stood from where he sat in a chair beside Tobias's desk. "Good afternoon, Miss Wingate. Thank you for coming to meet with me. Will you sit for a moment?"

She glanced toward the settee but didn't want to sit there. Instead, she took another chair on the other side of Tobias's desk. "I didn't realize I was coming to see you, Mr. Dyer. Carrin only told me that my presence was required in the study."

"I see, well, my apologies. It wasn't my intent to surprise you. With the deadline for his lordship's marriage in ten days and his lack of a bride, I thought we should discuss the specifics of your inheritance."

Her what? Fiona stared at him as words utterly failed her.

"Now, the twelfth is a Sunday, so the property will officially transfer to you on the thirteenth. The property does have a steward who was hired by Lady Overton, and you will likely wish to retain him, at least for a while—"

Fiona held up a hand and finally managed to push forth speech. "What inheritance are you speaking of? I am not aware of a property or anything else, for that matter."

Mr. Dyer's complexion paled by at least a shade. He

shifted in his chair and glanced down at the papers in front of him on the corner of the desk. "Oh. I thought his lordship had informed you of the terms of his father's will."

Outrage warred with disappointment inside her. "He has not. I pray you will enlighten me since it seems to involve... me." She somehow summoned a smile but feared it wasn't at all pleasant. She clasped her hands so tightly in her lap that her fingers started to go numb.

Dyer hesitated. No doubt he was perplexed as to why his employer hadn't told her a thing about any of this. He certainly seemed confused.

The secretary coughed. "Well, this is irregular, as I thought his lordship had told you of the situation. His father's will states that his lordship must wed within three months of the prior earl's death, and that date is the twelfth of March."

Now Tobias's search for a countess and his seeming inability to find one made sense. He wasn't looking for a wife because he wanted one but because he had to marry. The servants' chatter that Prudence had overheard also made sense.

"What happens if he doesn't wed by that date?" Fiona asked.

"If he remains unwed, one of his properties will be transferred to you."

"How can that be? Aren't an earl's properties entailed with the title?"

"It varies, but in this case, the estate in question belonged to Lord Overton's mother's family—that is, the current Lord Overton. Upon her marriage to the prior earl, Horethorne became his property."

Fiona's mind spun. She was to own an entire estate? That would change everything. She wouldn't have to worry about

Mrs. Tucket or herself, never mind when or whether she should marry. Her heartbeat thundered in her ears. It was rare for women to own property. She wondered if her cousin was aware of this and whether he could prevent her from claiming it.

"The estate will be mine? It won't belong to a gentleman who will hold it for me?"

The secretary shook his head. "The instructions are clear —you will be the owner."

She stared at him in utter disbelief. This was beyond unexpected. It was a bloody miracle. "Does the estate have income?"

"Enough to support the house and provide a modest living for the inhabitants."

This was unbelievable. "You said it's called Horethorne?" The name was familiar.

Dyer smiled. "Yes, it's a lovely estate in south Somerset." As soon as he said Somerset, Fiona remembered where she'd heard the name of the estate. And with that, she recalled precisely what it was before the secretary even finished. "His lordship spent most of his childhood there."

Her stomach sank. "Lord Overton told me about his mother's house," she said softly, her heart aching at his father's cruelty. "Why would the previous earl write such a thing into his will?"

Dyer averted his gaze. "I'm sure I don't know."

"How can that be? You were his secretary, were you not?"

"I was. His lordship was an exacting employer, and he did not suffer inquiries, particularly regarding his intent. Such curiosity was insubordination in his eyes." The secretary's chin seemed to quiver a moment before his jaw tensed. "I cannot disagree that this act was singularly ruthless."

Yet while it was terrible for Tobias, it was wonderful for

her. Again, she wondered why Tobias's father had involved her in any of this. It was one thing to be her guardian, but to see she had an extravagant Season, a large dowry, and now an estate?

"If Lord Overton weds by the twelfth, I will not inherit Horethorne, is that correct?"

Dyer nodded. "The likelihood of him doing so is quite low, however. He would need to marry by special license or perhaps run away to Gretna Green." He said the last with a smile, then quickly sobered. His neck flushed. "Please forget I said that."

Fiona wasn't sure if the man was aware of the rumors about Tobias and Gretna Green but thought he must be. Why else would he react that way? Her mind returned to earlier in the interview. "You were surprised I didn't know about this. Did his lordship tell you I knew?"

Again, the man hesitated, and his neck remained a faint pink above the crisp white collar of his shirt. "He did."

When had he planned to tell her? Or had he decided to leave it to his secretary?

She released her hands and gently flexed her fingers to restore feeling. "Is there anything else I need to know?"

"Not at present. Do you have any questions for me?"

"No." She rose, and he jumped up from his chair. "Thank you, Mr. Dyer. I hope you don't feel as if this put you in an awkward position. You are only doing your job. Lord Overton—*this* Lord Overton—will not be upset with you." If he was, Fiona would kick him. Repeatedly.

"I hope not."

"He is not like his father." At least, he tried not to be. She started toward the door, then stopped abruptly. Turning back to face him, she said, "I do have one question. What happens to my dowry if I don't wed?"

"If you aren't wed by the age of twenty-five, the funds will go to you."

"Remind me, please, how much is it?"

"Six thousand pounds."

Such an enormous sum! And just three years until it could be hers. Her birthday was in less than a week, and she would be twenty-two. Three years, and she could be a financially independent woman with an *estate*.

"I beg your pardon, but I suppose that was two questions and now I have a third. It is the last, I assure you."

"Ask as many as you like."

"Is there any way his lordship can retain Horethorne if he doesn't wed?"

Dyer's eye twitched. "I'm afraid not."

The property was all but gone to him then. Unless he decided to actually kidnap someone to Gretna Green.

"Thank you, Mr. Dyer." She inclined her head and left the study, her mind swimming with ideas and plans she hadn't possessed a mere half hour ago. Her life was going to completely change, and she had Tobias's tragedy to thank for it.

What a terrible, horrible mess.

∽

*T*obias stepped into the sitting room outside his bedchamber and froze. A figure lay upon the chaise angled near the fireplace. Quietly moving closer, his gaze moved from the pale green blanket covering the person's lower half up to the thick dark red braid that seemed to glow in the light of the low fire.

Fiona's back was to him, but there was no mistaking the hair. Or the gentle slope of her shoulder and the dip of her waist. He let his eyes feast on the curve of her backside. It was impudent of him, but she'd come into his domain. She had to expect he would at least look.

What the devil was she even doing here? Had she come to rekindle last night's madness? He could *not* let that happen. His best course of action would be to ignore her and go straight to his bedchamber. Except if someone found her asleep in here...

Hell. It was fortunate no one had discovered her yet.

He had to wake her. Stepping closer, he inhaled the unmistakable scent of lavender. Of Fiona. Of temptation and promise.

"Fiona," he whispered. When she didn't stir, he repeated her name but louder. Still no movement.

He reached for her shoulder, his fingertips grazing along her upper arm. "Fiona," he said more firmly.

She rolled toward him, her eyes closed. A soft sigh escaped her parted lips, and Tobias was nearly overwhelmed with longing. She blinked, her lashes fluttering, before her dark gaze settled on him, narrowed at first and then widening slightly.

"My lord," she said, pushing up to a sitting position. "I must have dozed off."

"In my private sitting room. What are you doing in here?"

"I needed to speak with you, and it grew quite late." She brushed a lock of hair from her forehead. "I couldn't think of another way to ensure I saw you tonight."

"Surely whatever you need to discuss can wait until tomorrow." He tried not to look at her dressing gown, which exposed a V of flesh from her elegant throat to the alluring valley of her breasts. "And surely it didn't require you come here to wait for me."

"It absolutely did." She rose in a graceful movement that caused the blanket to cascade down her leg and drape over the side of the chaise. "I met with Mr. Dyer today, and he gave me some rather startling information."

The pleasure of watching her clashed with her words, jarring him into a state of dissonance. "Dyer?" *Shit.* There was only one reason Dyer would speak with her, and yes, it would have surprised the hell out of her.

"He told you about my father's will."

One of her auburn brows arched, and the edge of her lip curled. "He thought *you* had. Imagine his mortification when he realized I was ignorant of the entire matter. That wasn't very kind of you."

"I didn't see a need to tell you unless it came to pass. I never expected that would happen—that I wouldn't wed in time. Rather, I didn't allow myself to think of that." Losing Horethorne was unimaginable.

There was a bare hiss as she exhaled quickly. "Apparently, you didn't allow yourself to think of me either. But then I am no one of import, just your ward for whom you are responsible and for whom you have been charged with settling into an advantageous marriage."

"Which you have indicated you aren't interested in at the moment."

"You also failed to mention the sum of my dowry. Six thousand pounds! Or the fact that it would be mine should I fail to wed by my twenty-fifth birthday."

He shifted his weight, uncomfortable beneath the weight of her stare. She was right—he hadn't thought of her. He'd seen it as his duty to manage the situation because she was his ward, and it had never occurred to him to inform or consult her. Why would he when he hadn't expected any of these things to come to pass? "Just as I failed to consider that I wouldn't marry as outlined by my father, I also didn't imagine you wouldn't wed by then. I thought your reluctance was in the short term, as you acclimated to London, and that in three years' time, you would undoubtedly be married. Unless you plan to reject every proposal you receive."

"I might. Particularly now that I know I'll have six thousand of my own pounds if I do." She stuck out her chin. "But again, you discounted my right to know, let alone make choices. How am I to make decisions about my life, about my future, when I am not fully informed?"

She stepped toward him, her eyes wide, her features serene. But she wasn't entirely composed. A tension radiated from her, so thick he thought he could slice it like bread.

He flexed his hands. "I'd planned to tell you after the assembly tomorrow night, when I will know for certain if I will marry or not."

"That is still a possibility?" She sounded surprised.

"It is." Miss Goodfellow would be there tomorrow night, and he was going to ask if she would entertain marriage to him. He would be clear about why he was asking and his expectations that they would hopefully form a romantic attachment. At the very least, he expected them to be friends and behave as a married couple should. It was not the union he'd dreamed of, but it was all he could expect given the deadline his father had imposed.

In that moment, he realized he'd planned to afford Miss Goodfellow a courtesy he had not given Fiona—the truth.

Suddenly overheated, he shrugged off his coat and draped it over the back of a chair near the hearth. "Fiona, I'm sorry. I should have told you everything from the start. I didn't know you then. I expected a young chit from the country who would be eagerly wed and removed from my responsibility."

"I don't know what's worse, that you didn't tell me after you came to know me, or that you assumed I would be a simple-minded automaton who would bend to your will. You try to not be like your father, but you are not entirely successful."

Her words cut into him, inflicting a sharp, deep pain. Because there was a veracity to them. He had handled this —*her*—as his father would have. "Please don't compare me to him," he whispered.

"As a woman, I have been and will always be subject to a man's whims—my father's, my cousin's, your father's, yours." Now she looked angry, her eyes blazing. "I am entirely dependent on whatever scraps you have for me. Until now. If you do not marry and I do not marry before I'm twenty-five, I have the chance to be independent, to own my choices, to decide my future. It's the closest thing to a miracle I will ever see, and you wanted to keep all of it from me. I thought you'd grown to care for me. You can be so kind, so considerate, and you seem to realize when you display despotic tendencies—"

"Despotic?" He flinched.

"And you rein them back. But then I learn that you've kept me ignorant of things that would change my life and my perspective, and I feel as though I don't know you at all."

He closed the distance between them and took her hands. "My father set all of this in motion to cause the maximum pain. I wonder if he somehow knew I would grow to care for you, that I would fail to marry because of the distraction of you." He shook his head. "Distraction sounds terrible, but it's true. You're my *ward*. I am not supposed to be attracted to you in the way that I am." He let go of one hand and clasped the lower half of her braid between his fingers. Dragging his thumb down the silken coil, he couldn't help but smile softly. "I am so sorry for not telling you. Please understand. Horethorne is my dearest possession. To lose it would be to lose my mother all over again."

Her eyes glazed as she stared at him, and she stroked his hand with her thumb. "I know. This is an awful situation. As angry as I was to learn you'd kept this from me, I don't know that I wouldn't have done the same in your position." She brought his hand up and kissed his knuckles. "I'm sorry, Tobias."

He sucked in a breath. "You said my name. Again. Please."

"Tobias." She kissed his hand again, keeping his flesh pressed to her lips as she said it a third time. "*Tobias*."

"I just realized our names share three letters in common —all vowels. Surely that means something."

She tipped her head to the side.

"What?"

"I have no idea." He gripped her braid and moved his other hand to her back, drawing her against him as his mouth covered hers.

She put her hand on his lapel and slid it up to the side of his neck, her thumb moving from the front of his throat up to the underside of his chin. With a soft groan, he opened his mouth and licked inside hers. She met his thrust with a parry and slid her hand to his nape, her fingers tugging at his hair.

Tobias climbed his fingers up her braid and cupped the back of her head, holding her as he plundered her mouth. She responded in kind, clutching him fiercely and kissing him with a wildness he'd never known.

A tiny voice at the back of his mind told him to stop, but a stronger chorus urged him to take what she offered. What if they were caught? There was slim chance of that, for he'd closed the door behind him, and no one would disturb him at this hour unless he asked for assistance.

He slid his hand forward, under her arm, and found the swell of her breast. There was no gown or corset to deter him tonight, just her dressing gown and presumably a night rail beneath. Stroking her through the layers, he felt her nipple harden. He tugged at the tie on the front and slipped his hand inside the garment. Now there was just a thin piece of lawn separating him from her. He cupped her breast and kissed down her throat, encouraged by her soft whimpers and the insistent pressure of her fingers against his scalp.

Pushing the dressing gown off over her shoulders, he let it fall to the floor. His entire focus was on her breast as he tugged at the neckline of her night rail. It was wide enough to allow him to pull it down, exposing her flesh so he could take her bare nipple into his mouth.

She gasped, her fingers digging into his flesh. *"Tobias."*

He wanted more. He needed *more*.

Rotating her, he gently guided her down to the chaise. On the descent, she loosened his cravat and pulled it from his neck, tossing it away. Her hands worked at the buttons of his waistcoat, and when she'd released them all, he shrugged out of the garment and threw it to the side.

She was so beautiful in the glow of the fire, her hair radiant and lush, her skin gleaming like a pearl. He kissed her again, and she ran her hands and fingers through his hair, over his neck, and inside the collar of his shirt, her warm flesh teasing his.

Trailing his mouth down her body, he found her breast once more, eagerly devouring her nipple as she arched up into him. *"Tobias."*

Every time she said his name, a thrill shot through him. There was a stark intimacy in the way she said it or perhaps in the way she touched him and looked at him. He couldn't precisely remember when she began to command his thoughts, but it had happened wholly, and he didn't want to return to before.

He'd planted his knee between hers as he leaned over her and kept his other foot on the floor. She clasped his waist and pulled while he felt her rise from the chaise, her body seeking his. Finding the hem of her night rail, he lifted the garment to her hips. He gently caressed her thighs, then her mons, delighting in the shivers that twitched across her flesh.

She moaned as he stroked across her sex, his fingertips sliding over her soft crease.

Moving beneath him, she gripped his waist and his neck. "Tobias, please."

She seemed to know what she wanted or at least that she wanted something. He did not want to disappoint her.

He lifted his head and kissed the side of her throat beneath her ear. Slipping his finger inside her, he whispered, "Is this what you want?"

"Yes." She pulled on his hair and guided his mouth to hers. Sealing her lips against his, she kissed him over and over, teasing him with her tongue. "*More.*"

His body shook with need as he stroked into her, pressing his finger deep until she jerked up, gasping into his mouth. Her muscles clenched around him, urging him to move faster. He alternated between massaging her clitoris and pumping into her, meeting her thrusts with his own.

Her cries grew as her body arched more frantically beneath him. He could feel how close she was, and he wanted to send her blissfully over the edge into oblivion. Tearing his lips from hers, he moved down, pushing her night rail up to her belly. He put his mouth on her sex, his tongue flicking over her clitoris as he plunged his finger into her sheath.

She let out a string of unintelligible words as her body began to shudder. Her thighs quivered around him as he licked over and into her sex, parting her flesh with his fingers. Her muscles clenched, bearing down around him as she let out a high, keening cry. He reached up and touched his finger to her mouth. She sucked him between her lips, and his cock responded, twitching against his clothing, desperate for release.

Gradually, she began to quiet, her movements slowing. She released his finger, and he glanced up to see her casting her head back against the chaise. He kissed her thigh, her hip, the slope between her belly and her sex.

She reached for him, grabbing his shirt over each shoulder. "You can't be finished."

He pulled his shirt from his waistband and looked down into the dark, glossy chocolate of her eyes. "Not by half. But if we are to continue, I need an affirmative answer to a critical question." He stroked his fingertips along her cheek. "Will you marry me?"

CHAPTER 17

*M*arry him?

For the second time that day, Fiona was at a complete loss for words. He didn't want to marry her. He wanted to shag her.

She pushed at his chest, sending him off balance so that he landed on his arse at the end of the chaise. "You don't really want to marry me."

He stared at her, a slight frown tugging at his lips. "Why not?"

"Look where we are, what we were doing. I may be from the country, but I am not a fool."

"I'm very confused. Were you not enjoying that? I thought you were."

"Of course, I enjoyed it." She'd finally experienced a real release—orgasm, as the book had called it. The book had contained drawings of what he'd just done, but she'd never imagined the devastating wonder of it. She pulled up the neckline of her night rail, covering herself completely.

"Then marry me, and we can do it over and over again."

That was exceedingly tempting. She looked at him once

more, her gaze dipping to the V of his shirt, which exposed a tantalizing expanse of his chest, some of it dusted with dark hair. Her hands practically itched to explore him the way she devoured a new map, her fingers tracing over every fascinating revelation.

"This is not a good reason to get married." She reached down for her dressing gown and stood from the chaise.

"It's sure as hell not a bad one. People have married for far less."

She had only to think of her mother and father to know that was true. They hadn't shared some grand passion. No matter how hard she tried, Fiona couldn't recall even one moment of intimacy between them—no stolen glances, no touching, and certainly no kissing. Still, having that...*connection* wasn't enough. Especially not when independence was in sight, something a woman like her could never have expected. An amazing life—and *adventure*—was within her grasp. Even the queen had advocated she seek that. And if she did marry, she didn't have to settle for anything less than the man of her dreams, a notion *Tobias* had put into her head.

Drawing her gown on over her night rail, she fastened the front. "You should marry the woman of your dreams," she said softly. "Especially after what happened with Lady Bentley. Furthermore, I deserve to find the man of my dreams—if he exists."

He stood, and with the fire behind him, his face was inscrutable.

"We both deserve to be loved." She thought of how he'd lost his mother and the ensuing years of a difficult relationship with his father. Yes, love. And for herself, she also wanted freedom. "None of this changes where we are." Except if she married him before the twelfth, she'd lose Horethorne. "Did you ask me to marry you because of your mother's house?"

"No." He blew out a breath. "But I'd be lying if I didn't say that was an added benefit. I could obtain a special license, and we could be wed next week."

"Or I could repeat my answer—it's still no—and I'll inherit the house in a matter of days."

"Is that what you want?"

She heard the anguish in his voice, and her heart twisted. "I want...freedom." She thought of her mother's warning, that she be sure before making a lifetime commitment. There had been regret in her counsel, and when Fiona recalled her mother's occasional melancholy, she knew she didn't want to feel that way. As though she were trapped with no choices, no freedom. "This is awful."

"Just the way my father liked things."

"You believe he envisioned this would happen?"

"I believe he set me up to fail." Tobias raked his hand through his hair, and his shoulders drooped. "Or he knew me better than I know myself. Whether he expected me to surrender to temptation with you or someone else, he seemed to have been betting on the fact that I wouldn't be able to wed in three months." He let out a soft, humorless laugh. "I came close though."

Until she'd ruined his chances.

"Fiona, I understand the lure of everything my father has dangled before you, but please reconsider. I don't know what I'll do if I lose Horethorne."

"You wouldn't lose it. I'd allow you to visit whenever you like." Allow him. He would need her permission, and that wasn't the same as calling it your home. Fiona understood that distinction and couldn't ignore the guilt cutting through her. Could she really consider this a dream come true when it came at the expense of Tobias's dreams?

"But that isn't quite the same, is it?" He bent and retrieved his waistcoat and cravat. Pivoting toward the chair, he swept up his coat and laid it over his arm with the other garments. "Good night, Fiona."

She said nothing as he disappeared into his chamber, the door clicking shut behind him.

Coming here tonight had been a terrible idea. What had she hoped to accomplish?

Conflict battled inside her. Tobias had admitted he'd never wanted to be her guardian, and he'd repeatedly done things that indicated his lack of genuine concern for her. But then he'd also done the opposite—listened to her and changed his mind, given her things and experiences that brought her joy and showed how much he cared.

He hadn't asked to have her in his life or to steal the thing that meant the most to him in the world. The real miracle was that he didn't despise her. Still, her presence was likely a painful thorn.

Well, then she would remove it. As soon as she inherited Horethorne, she would go there immediately. Then she wouldn't be his concern any longer.

Or you could marry him.

She shook her head, as if the question had been spoken aloud and the speaker could see her reaction. His proposal had been made in haste, in a completely heated moment. Even if it hadn't, could she ever truly know if he wanted her and not just his mother's house? Did she want him to want her?

Stalking from his sitting room, she stopped short as she took in her surroundings, looking for anyone who might be about. It was quite late. Even the servants would be abed, wouldn't they?

Fiona went to her room and, removing her dressing gown, slid between the covers, shivering for a few minutes until the bed began to grow warm from her heat. Or was it his lingering heat?

What a blissful interlude that had been. Totally unexpected.

Totally?

After their kiss last night, a small part of her hoped it would happen again, but she hadn't expected the combustion that had flared between them. She'd dreamed it perhaps...

Now, she must accept that it would never happen again. Not after she took his house. They would go their separate ways, and she would hold on to tonight as a cherished memory.

Except they wouldn't go their separate ways. How could she when she owned his beloved Horethorne? They would be linked together, through the estate, forever.

She forced herself to think of the assembly the following evening, or more accurately, tonight, given the lateness of the hour. Since working so hard to be able to attend, she should be filled with anticipation. Instead, her emotions were bittersweet. It was likely to be her first and last Phoenix Club ball.

She would just have to ensure it was memorable.

~

*W*hat a wretched night of sleep.

Tobias yearned to lay his head down on his desk, but he needed to go to Westminster before coming home to dress for the assembly. Before he could stand, Carrin came into his study. The butler looked...harassed.

"My lord, the dowager countess has arrived. Did I, ah, somehow miss the fact that she was coming to town?"

Jumping to his feet, Tobias smoothed his hair back with his hands. "If you did, I did as well. I suspect this is an intentional surprise." His grandmother had done this to his father at least twice that Tobias knew of.

Carrin sagged with relief. "Very good, sir. She's waiting for you in the drawing room."

"I'd best not keep her waiting." Tobias hurried past the butler, then stopped and swung back around. "Where are we to put her? The best rooms are all occupied by our guests."

"It's probably easiest to move Mrs. Tucket to a smaller chamber upstairs," Carrin suggested.

"Yes, do that at once. With my apologies to Mrs. Tucket. Hopefully, she will understand." Tobias felt bad she would have to climb an additional flight of stairs with her mobility issues. Perhaps there was another option. He'd think on it.

Carrin nodded in response, and Tobias turned on his heel to dash up to the drawing room. His grandmother was a diminutive woman with an immense personality. Or at least she was intensely intimidating. Perhaps those were not the same thing.

Affixing a smile on his face, he swept into the drawing room to find her seated near the hearth. "Welcome, Grandmother. I wish I'd known you were coming. I would have ensured we had a room prepared."

"They're taking care of it now, although I was told my usual chamber is currently occupied by your ward." Her slender upper lip gently curled.

Though she was seventy-five, she looked more than a decade younger—she still had some dark hair mixed in with the gray, and the lines that etched her face were few and gentle, most of them occurring around her mouth, likely owing to the way she pursed her lips. Which she was doing presently.

"Shall I have her removed to another chamber?" In his mind, he was already shuffling her to Miss Lancaster's room and transferring Miss Lancaster to Mrs. Tucket's room.

The dowager waved her hand. "Don't bother. I don't think I'll be here more than a week." That was a relatively short stay since the journey took two days each way, and that assumed decent traveling weather.

Tobias sat near her. "I'm quite surprised to see you here."

"As you were supposed to be. I kept waiting for an invitation to your wedding, but when one did not arrive, I decided to come see what the devil is going on."

A horrible sinking feeling settled in Tobias's gut. "Why did you think I was getting married?"

"Because your father's last letter to me said you would be doing so at the start of the Season."

"Is that all he said?" Tobias wondered if she knew about his father's marriage requirement.

Her still-dark brows arched. "Yes, why?"

"No reason. I'm pleased to see you, Grandmother." And shocked. She rarely came to town, and he was flattered she'd want to come check on him. Even if it was strange.

She hadn't even come to London when her son had become gravely ill. But it had been December, the absolute worst time to travel. Instead of visiting, she'd sent a letter every day, and in return, his father had his secretary draft a response every three days. Because he was a jackass like that.

"How are things with your ward? Is she amenable? Attractive? Betrothed yet?"

"Not really, yes, and no." His honesty about Fiona surprised him. "Marriage is not high on her list of priorities."

"What balderdash. Isn't she nearly on the shelf?"

"She'll be twenty-two next week."

"Then yes, she's almost past the point of marriageability."

"Why? How is it that I am twenty-eight, and no one says I'm ineligible for marriage?"

His grandmother stared at him, her blue-gray eyes the color of frost. "You can't really be that obtuse. You're an *earl*. And a wealthy one at that."

"What I mean is, why is she—or any other young lady—

suddenly unmarriageable? It's not as if they've done something to lower their worth." He hated the way that sounded, once again equating them with a product.

"Haven't they? If they haven't found a husband in the first year or perhaps two of being out, there must be a deficit. I suppose your ward can be excused." Her lip curled again. "Because she hasn't had a Season yet."

"She's attracted at least one suitor," Tobias noted. That did not include him, because he wasn't a suitor. He was merely the man who'd taken advantage of her.

"Then there is absolutely *no* reason for her to be unwed," the dowager said firmly. "Give her an ultimatum."

Tobias bit his lip to keep from laughing. "I, er, somewhat tried that. Miss Wingate has suffered some...challenges in adjusting from country life."

"Your father should have seen that coming. I told him not to give her a Season, but he was adamant." Her shoulders twitched, and her features displayed such a sharp expression of distaste that Tobias's curiosity was pricked.

"What do you know of Miss Wingate? I don't understand why Father made such a commitment to her. He could have settled a modest dowry on her and left it up to her cousin to see that she was wed."

The dowager sat straighter, her interest clearly piqued. "She has a cousin?"

"She resided in a cottage on his estate."

She emitted a thoroughly unladylike sound of derision. "That makes absolutely no sense. Your father was a fool not to let him handle the matter. Instead, he's made her your problem. I am sorry for the way he's treated you, Deane." She pursed her lips again. "Overton, rather. This will take some getting used to."

"It won't bother me at all if you continue to call me Deane." He smiled. "I prefer that, in fact."

"That is unsurprising given the estrangement between you and your father. But you mustn't take any of it to heart. You couldn't be more different from him, what with his scandalous tendencies." Her gaze softened but only slightly. "You would have no idea of those, however, since you are not aware of the reasons for his...*commitment* to Miss Wingate."

His father had "scandalous tendencies" and that made him different from Tobias who also possessed...scandalous tendencies? Oh no—had his father carried on a liaison with Fiona's mother? Was she his half-sister? Perhaps the "friendship" with Fiona's father had been a ruse. Tobias's blood went cold. "Was he having an affair?" He barely forced the words out.

"Since Oxford." Again, her lips pursed. "At least he was skilled at keeping it hidden. I don't think anyone ever knew about his vile sins against nature."

Since Oxford. Had Fiona's mother been a maid there? Wait. *Vile sins against nature...*

Tobias froze. "Who was he having an affair with?"

"That Wingate miscreant! They met at school. The only reason I know about it is because I saw them once." A shudder passed over her once more, and she pressed her hands to her cheeks.

"They carried on an affair all those years?" So many things made sense all of a sudden, including the cold relationship between his father and Tobias's mother. To her credit, she'd never denigrated him to Tobias. She'd only said that he wasn't capable of loving her, and she accepted that, especially since she had Tobias to love and love her in return. It was after learning this that Tobias had vowed to love his wife. Which would be impossible if he adhered to his father's requirements. Perhaps *that* had been the man's goal—to ensure that Tobias wouldn't have time to fall in love.

"Yes," his grandmother responded. "Your father traveled

to Shropshire a few times a year. On occasion, Wingate came to Deane Hall, but I put a stop to that when you grew old enough to converse with visitors."

Tobias thought back and tried to recall male visitors but couldn't. Much of the ire he felt toward his father lessened as he tried to imagine the life he'd been forced to lead. He was still angry, however, for the hurt he'd caused Tobias's mother.

Swallowing, Tobias looked to his grandmother. While she seemed disgusted by her son's behavior, Tobias only wanted to understand it. "Did he love Wingate?"

His grandmother froze for a moment, her lips parted as her eyes seemed to stare at nothing. At length, she said, "I hadn't considered that." She blinked and focused on Tobias. "Could that have been true?"

"I hope so," Tobias said softly, feeling as though he was finally glimpsing his true father. "Where you see vile, sinful behavior, I see a man who was trying to find happiness in a world that wouldn't accept that which would make him so."

"I hadn't considered that he might have loved Wingate." She frowned, but it seemed to be directed inwardly. "Still, that doesn't excuse his treatment of your mother. She deserved better and so did you."

A sudden burst of love expanded in his chest. "I appreciate you saying that. I was sad that my parents didn't seem to love each other."

"You have a romantic nature, just like your grandfather. He and I were fortunate to be a love match."

Tobias barely remembered his grandfather. The man had died when Tobias was six. "You think I'm a romantic?"

She looked at him as if he had a third eye in the middle of his forehead. "Aren't you?"

Tobias laughed with great warmth. This had to be the

most remarkable conversation he'd ever had with his grandmother.

"I do believe you're correct that your father must have loved that man," she said.

Tobias agreed. "It now makes sense why Miss Wingate was so important to him. She was the daughter of his love, and as such, was like a daughter to my father." The association made him quickly add, "But she has no relation to me."

"Of course not."

He exhaled with relief. If Fiona had been his sister… God, it didn't bear thinking about any more than he already had. He'd spend a great deal of time erasing that thought from his mind.

"I'm surprised he had so little interaction with her," Tobias said. "Like me, she had no clue as to why my father took such a vested interest in her future. We assumed our fathers had a close friendship and nothing more."

"Do you plan to share this information with her?" The dowager wrinkled her nose. "Warn her that she must keep it secret."

"I must tell her. She will want to know." He could never keep this from Fiona, and not just because he'd already stupidly kept other things from her. Although on that score, he'd learned his lesson. Too late, however.

Tobias studied his grandmother for a moment. "Did you really come to inquire about my marriage, or was it to tell me about my father and Wingate?"

She waved her hand again. "I suppose I also wanted to meet your ward and offer assistance." That didn't answer his question, but he didn't think she was going to. "I should not have declined to help you before. I was angry at your father for making you deal with her."

"I haven't really minded." He had at first, of course, and had even told Fiona that. Inwardly wincing, he made a mental note to apologize for that again. He'd been an enormous ass.

"Haven't you? It sounds as if she's a disaster—refusing to marry and struggling to fit in."

"She fits in fine, actually. She's become quite close with Lady Cassandra Westbrook."

"Your ward counts the Duke of Evesham's daughter as a friend? Is this the same chit who fell down in front of the queen?" the dowager asked incredulously.

Tobias eyed her with curiosity. "You've been paying attention."

She huffed. "I receive the newspapers from town. Which is how I also know you have been misbehaving. Are you still up to your antics and evading the parson's trap?"

"Actually, I was hoping to marry. I've just been...distracted." Wholly. Irreparably. Wonderfully.

"By that troublesome ward. It's good that I'm here. I'll take over managing the chit, and I'll toss her back to the countryside if I must. I can't imagine—"

Tobias pinched the bridge of his nose. "Please stop. She's not troublesome, and you're not tossing her anywhere. She's quite lovely, actually. She's smart, charming, never fails to make me laugh, and she possesses a unique perspective that none of the other ladies in town has demonstrated."

The dowager gaped at him. "Good heavens, Deane, you sound as though you're in love with her."

A queasy, giddy feeling swept over him. *Yes,* he *was* in love with her. That's why he wanted to marry her. Not because he was desperate to shag her—though he was that too. And not because he wanted to keep Horethorne—though that was, as he'd said, an added benefit. The primary reason he wanted her for his wife—the only reason that mattered—was that he loved her. He couldn't imagine her leaving. Just the notion of his grandmother "tossing her back to the countryside" made him want to vault out of his chair, rush to Fiona's chamber, and beg her to stay.

Except he'd already proposed—*badly*, he now realized. Had she refused him because of the inadequacy of his proposal, or did she not feel the same? Was he heading straight for another Priscilla situation where he would be thrust aside, his heart broken?

He couldn't compare Fiona to Priscilla. He'd thought he was in love two years ago, but that was nothing compared to what he felt now. Just the thought of seeing Fiona made his chest compress and then grow light with anticipation.

"I can tell from your silence that you have realized you do." The dowager exhaled with what sounded like resignation. "What do you plan to do about it then?"

"I'm not certain yet, but we're attending an assembly tonight. I'd invite you to come along, but you're probably too tired."

"I am, but I want to meet this chi—this young lady—before you go. I shall require a respite for a couple of hours. Then she will present herself to me here."

Tobias wished he had time to prepare Fiona, but he was already late for Westminster. "I'll inform Carrin, but now I must go." He stood and went to take her hand, giving her a light squeeze. "Thank you for coming. I am glad to know the truth. I think perhaps I understand my father a little better."

"I don't see how that's possible, but I'm pleased for you." She smiled up at him. "You're a good boy."

With a soft chuckle, Tobias released her hand and left. On his way out, he told Carrin about the scheduled meeting between Fiona and his grandmother. "You may wish to ensure Miss Lancaster and Mrs. Tucket are present. Miss Wingate could use the support." He winked at the butler before striding outside to his waiting coach.

As he leaned back against the squab and the vehicle began

moving, he considered his grandmother's question: what was he going to do about being in love with Fiona?

First and foremost, he needed to stop behaving like a self-involved ass. To do that, he had to stop thinking of himself and his predicament.

He also needed to convince her that he didn't want to marry her because of his father's will. And to do that, he could think of only one thing that would matter. Something that had always been a tangible reminder of the only love he'd never known.

But he realized now that love was more than a house. His mother—and her love—were a part of him, as was his father. Tobias felt the incessant pull to please him, and it wasn't entirely due to the trap he'd diabolically laid. The anger he'd long felt toward his father evaporated. Tobias didn't want it anymore. Nor would he cling to Horethorne.

He would choose love.

CHAPTER 18

Seated in the drawing room with Prudence and Mrs. Tucket, Fiona awaited the arrival of Tobias's grandmother, the Dowager Countess of Overton. Fiona had been surprised to be summoned to meet her, but now she was just nervous. Prudence had learned from the servants that the dowager countess had been unexpected. Prudence also shared Fiona's curiosity as to why the dowager sought an interview.

Without her grandson present.

Fiona had asked Carrin if his lordship would also be there, and the butler had explained that the earl was at Westminster. He would hopefully arrive home in time to accompany her and Prudence to the ball, but if not, he would meet them there.

At ten minutes past the appointed time, the dowager countess arrived. Petite with surprisingly dark hair for a woman of her age, Lady Overton marched in with the agility of someone much younger. Or perhaps Fiona was comparing her to Mrs. Tucket, who, though a few years younger, suffered much more difficulty. It was no wonder when one compared the life of a dowager countess to the life of a maid-of-all-work. Thinking of it made Fiona even more committed to ensuring Mrs. Tucket's comfort. She would be free to relax and find comfort at Horethorne.

The conflict flared inside her as it had since the day before. Fiona was at once excited by the prospect of inheriting an estate and deeply troubled by Tobias's loss of what would have been his most cherished possession.

Prudence made a sound, startling Fiona. She looked over and saw that Prudence had stood from the settee. Fiona scrambled to do the same as a flush of embarrassment washed up her neck.

Mrs. Tucket did not get up. "Pardon me for not standing, my lady," she said. "My hip is bothering me more than usual today."

"You must be Miss Wingate's maid from Shropshire," the countess said, her gaze assessing as it moved over Mrs. Tucket, then Prudence, and finally Fiona. "And you must be Miss Wingate."

Fiona dipped into a curtsey. "Good afternoon, my lady."

"I hope you aren't going to fall down as you did at the queen's drawing room."

"I shall try not to." Fiona rose and waited for the dowager to settle into a chair before retaking her place on the settee next to Prudence. "Allow me to introduce my companion, Miss Lancaster."

The dowager looked toward Prudence, her lips pursing. "You're too pretty to be a companion."

Prudence's cheeks turned a faint pink, something Fiona had never seen before. "Thank you, my lady," Prudence murmured.

"How fortunate you all are to be here," the dowager announced. "I imagine it must feel quite extraordinary to be part of an earl's household."

"Indeed," Mrs. Tucket said quickly. "It's overwhelming, if I'm being honest. I'm looking forward to getting back to Shropshire."

The dowager smiled faintly. "And when will that be?"

Mrs. Tucket shrugged. "Not until Fiona decides she doesn't need me."

"I shall always need you," Fiona said warmly.

"What about you, Miss Wingate?" the dowager asked. "How are you finding London? Is the Season everything you hoped it would be?"

"Not really," Fiona said honestly. "I was looking forward to exploring London, but I've been more restricted in my activities than I anticipated."

"Of course you are, dear. It's London, not some backwater village in Shropshire."

Fiona tried not to take offense. The way she was raised was likely as foreign to the dowager as London had been to Fiona when she'd first arrived. "Once the weather is warmer, there will be more to do and see."

"You'd be less restricted if you were wed. What are your plans on that front?"

"She has attracted the attention of the son of a marquess!" Mrs. Tucket beamed proudly.

The dowager cocked her head as she surveyed Fiona. "The heir?"

Fiona clarified, "No, his second son, Lord Gregory Blakemore."

"Witney's spare." The dowager pursed her lips again. "He's an academic with an eye toward obtaining a living in the church, isn't that right?"

"It is," Fiona said. "You are well informed."

"Just because I'm not in town doesn't mean I don't keep up on everything." Evidently, since she'd mentioned Fiona's mishap in front of the queen. "Who else has caught your eye?"

The only man that came to Fiona's mind was Tobias, but she couldn't very well admit that the dowager's grandson had caught more than her eye. He'd captured nearly every thought in her head. "No one in particular."

"How can that be? I realize the Season is young, but you should have multiple suitors. You're a beauty, despite that red hair, and my grandson tells me you are not empty-headed."

Fiona stifled a laugh. She was willing to bet Tobias had not used that description. What had he said? That he would flatter her to his grandmother made her feel surprisingly wonderful. "Perhaps I've not been attending enough events." She didn't draw attention to the fact that Tobias had kept her from going out for a time.

"Well, I'm not convinced Lord Gregory is a suitable choice. While your pedigree is unremarkable, you have enough pleasing attributes, including a very generous dowry, to obtain a better match."

What would be better than the second son of a marquess who was kind and charming? The same name as before came to mind, and Fiona shoved it away. A frustrated voice in the back of her head asked why, when that very gentleman had actually proposed.

Except he didn't really want to marry her. Not for the right reasons anyway.

And it was his fault that she wasn't enthused to wed Lord Gregory. Tobias was the one who'd put it in her mind that she shouldn't settle for anyone other than the man of her dreams.

"Is there something wrong with Lord Gregory?" Mrs. Tucket asked with a touch of alarm in her voice.

"Wrong is not the right word," the dowager said haughtily. "I am confident Miss Wingate can—and should—do better." She directed her icy gray-blue gaze on Fiona. "You've still plenty of time left in the Season to make a match. I understand Lady Pickering is your sponsor. I will speak with her and, if necessary, take over myself. Matchmaking is an important task and should not be overlooked."

Fiona thought of the match her cousin wanted to make and disagreed vigorously. Matchmaking should be completely abandoned. She did not voice that opinion, however. How on earth was she supposed to respond? She settled for, "Lady Pickering has been lovely."

Mrs. Tucket's brow creased, forming deep dimples just above the edge of her brows. "Would it be bad if she accepted Lord Gregory?"

Another lip purse from Lady Overton. "I am advising her not to accept Lord Gregory." She turned her attention to Fiona once more. "My advice should not be ignored."

This was all so odd. The dowager coming to London without advance notice. This audience in which she apparently wanted to stress the importance of matchmaking. Her stark lack of support for Lord Gregory, who seemed not only suitable but admirable.

What was going on?

The dowager abruptly stood. "Thank you for the enlightening conversation. If I was not fatigued from my journey, I would attend the assembly with you tonight. I will, however, accompany you to see Madame Moreau tomorrow evening."

An opera singer was performing at someone's house. Fiona did not recall the specifics. She rose, as did Prudence, and remained that way until after the dowager departed.

"Well, she was an odd bird," Mrs. Tucket said with a cluck of her tongue in the way she described a pudding that didn't turn out properly.

"She's a dowager countess." Prudence made the statement as if it explained everything.

Fiona thought about not just the woman's title but her family. "She's also Tobias's father's mother." And given everything she knew about the former earl, it seemed logical that his mother would be an intimidating, exacting force of nature.

Mrs. Tucket pushed herself to her feet. "Time to climb more stairs so I may have my nap."

Fiona hated that she was another floor higher. She needed to be in a cottage with one level of living. "Why don't you nap in my room?" she suggested.

"Nonsense, you need to start preparing for the ball." Mrs. Tucket waved her hand toward Prudence before she could offer her chamber. "As do you. I'll get a footman to help me up. I like that Baines fellow. He's a strapping lad." She sent them a wink and chuckled on her way out of the drawing room.

Fiona turned to Prudence. "It seems the dowager has come to manage me. Why?"

"I can't imagine." She looked at Fiona intently. "But the more pressing question in my mind is why you referred to his lordship as Tobias."

Had she said that? Fiona hoped she appeared nonchalant. "I misspoke. How bizarre."

"Quite," Prudence murmured. "Shall we prepare for the assembly?"

"Yes, let's." Fiona was looking forward to donning her favorite and as yet unworn purple gown. No, she was looking forward to focusing her attention on something that did not involve her guardian, the ways he'd withheld information from her, or the manner in which just the thought of him made her quiver.

She needed to look forward to the life she would lead without him.

~

he line of carriages outside the Phoenix Club was quite long. Both entrances were open and thronged with people. Had it been like this all evening? Tobias was an hour late due to his business at Westminster. He'd rushed home but had missed escorting the ladies. Now he was quite anxious to get inside.

To see Fiona.

Since realizing he was in love with her, the anticipation of seeing her was almost painful. He kept smiling at odd times, provoking questions and puzzled stares.

At last, he was here. He only hoped he could find her easily with so many people about.

Avoiding the crowds at the entrance, Tobias slipped down to the lower floor, where the employees of the club bustled here and there. He had to sidestep someone more than once and apologized profusely. He'd thought this would be an easier entry and was clearly wrong.

When he finally reached the stairs, he hurried up to the ground floor only to find that he couldn't really get into the house. So he went up one more and emerged on the first floor of the gentleman's side.

Low voices and the sound of glass hitting glass emerged from the Star Chamber—what he and the others on the membership committee now called the room after hearing the nickname—where the membership committee met to discuss invitations and other issues. Tobias veered from his course of finding Fiona and poked his head into the room. Just Lucien and Wexford sat inside drinking.

"Why are you hiding up here?" Tobias asked with a smile.

"We aren't hiding. We're fortifying." Wexford set down his glass and leapt up from the chair. "What can I pour you?"

Tobias stepped inside. "Nothing. I'm eager to get downstairs."

Lucien arched a brow. "Eager? Miss Goodfellow will be there this evening. Dare I assume she's the source of your anticipation?"

"She must be the reason," Wexford said after downing a gulp of his Irish whisky. "Deane is nearly out of time. Less than ten days, is it?"

Tobias dropped his chin in a single nod. "Yes, but it's not going to happen—the marriage, I mean. Not before then anyway."

Both men stared at Tobias.

Wexford's brows drove down as he narrowed his eyes. "You're giving up?"

"Not at all. I still plan to wed." He inhaled and corrected himself. "I *hope* to wed." He could not assume Fiona would accept him. She'd already said no once.

"What about Horethorne?" Lucien asked the question softly, almost reverently. He knew how much the place meant to Tobias.

"It will be well taken care of by its new owner." He felt such joy when he thought of her having a place she could permanently call home for the first time.

Lucien didn't look convinced. "How do you know?"

"Because in the event that I fail to wed by the dictated date, which I will, my father has given it to Fiona, rather, Miss Wingate."

Nostrils flaring slightly, Lucien pinned him with a knowing stare. "Who is it you hope to marry? I do not think it is Miss Goodfellow."

Lucien had always been too bloody astute, not that Tobias felt a need to keep his plan secret, at least not from them. "It is not. I hope that Miss Wingate will become my countess."

Wexford let out a chortle. "Oh, well played!"

Tobias turned his attention to the laughing Wexford, as did Lucien. "This is not a game."

"Deane's not hoping to marry her to gain his mother's house. He's in love with his ward," Lucien clarified.

Wexford's laughter died immediately. He gaped at Tobias a moment and then leaned forward, his elbow on the table. "So you *did* have a tendre for her?" He grinned. "Spectacular."

Setting his empty glass down, Lucien stood. "Come, let us go find your countess-to-be."

"You assume she'll say yes," Tobias said, suddenly more nervous than he'd been all day. No, more nervous than he'd been in two years. The memory of learning that Priscilla had chosen someone other than him rose sharp in his mind.

"There's a chance she won't?" Wexford also stood, finishing his whisky as he rose and depositing the empty tumbler on the table.

"She may have already refused me."

Wexford winced, and Lucien moved to clap Tobias on the shoulder. "I'm sorry to hear that," Lucien said. "Why did she say no?"

"Probably because she'd just learned that she's to inherit Horethorne if I don't marry."

Lucien nodded, his eyes alight with understanding. "Like Wexford, she assumed you wanted to wed her to obtain the estate."

"Can you blame her?" Wexford asked.

"Not at all. In fact, if I'm honest with myself, that was part of the reason I asked. That, and we were half-naked at the time."

Wexford shook his head. "Christ, Deane, you're supposed to have rehabilitated your behavior. Have you no shame?"

Lucien took his hand from Tobias's shoulder and turned his head toward Wexford. "Leave him be." He returned his attention to Tobias. "What is your plan?"

"I don't really have one. She just rejected me last night. I can't imagine she'll change her mind today."

"Have you mentioned the love part?" Wexford asked. "I suspect that might help your cause."

"No, but what if it doesn't?" Tobias hoped they shared something beyond the physical attraction that had bloomed between them. They were friends, perhaps even confidantes. But more than that? He didn't know. And given that he'd completely misread his relationship with Priscilla, he didn't entirely trust himself to get this right.

"There is only one way to find out." Lucien regarded him with determination. "Just vow to us you won't devolve into an even bigger degenerate if she refuses you again."

Tobias couldn't promise that at all.

~

At the midpoint of the main staircase, there was a landing with a doorway that led to another staircase, which in turn led to a gallery that ran along one side of the men's ballroom. Emerging onto the gallery with Lucien and Wexford, Tobias had a bird's eye view of the ballroom below.

"What is she wearing?" Wexford asked, peering down into the throng.

"Purple, I think? At least that was her plan a couple of days ago." Tobias looked until he had to blink to regain some moisture in his eyes.

"Let's move to the ladies' side," Wexford suggested before moving along the gallery and opening a door to an identical gallery that overlooked the other side of the ballroom.

"Over there?" Lucien pointed to the opposite side of the ballroom near the doors that led out to the garden.

Yes, that was her. Even from this distance, she was unmistakable, and not because of the purple of her gown. It was the vivid red of her hair, the graceful slope of her neck and shoulders, the poise with which she held herself—a solitary, gleaming pearl amidst a stretch of unremarkable sand.

"Is that Lord Gregory with her?" Wexford scowled.

Tobias tensed. "Yes." They stood rather close to one another, and she was smiling up at him.

"You need to get down there." Lucien started toward the other door that would take them to the ladies' staircase, and Wexford followed.

Only Tobias couldn't move. His feet were rooted to the floor and his gaze was fixed on Fiona. And Lord Gregory.

A moment later, he felt a tug on his sleeve. "Come on."

Tobias didn't look at Wexford. He couldn't tear his eyes from Fiona as she laughed at something Lord Gregory said. Tobias's body went completely rigid as Fiona touched Lord Gregory's arm.

He finally turned away. "I can't do it. Yes, I'm a pathetic coward. I had my heart broken once before, and since Fiona has already rejected me, I should expect failure again."

Lucien scoffed. "Priscilla didn't break your heart. You said so yourself at the time."

"Well, it bloody well felt like it. I was humiliated." Not because she'd chosen someone else over him and everyone knew it, but because he should have known better. He should have realized there was nothing really between them, that Priscilla had only taken their courtship as seriously as her father told her to. And once someone with a higher rank came forward, that was not at all.

What if Tobias had this wrong too? What if the things he imagined Fiona felt for him were only in his mind? "This is different," he whispered, staring at the painting hanging on the wall opposite but not seeing any of its detail. "I don't think I can survive a rejection from Fiona."

"Christ, you're being melodramatic." Lucien gave him a gentle shove. "You'd rather let Lord Gregory do his worst and not even try?"

"Come on, Deane, if you love her, she's worth the risk. And the pain, if it comes to that." Wexford thumped him on the back. "I wager it'll hurt even worse if you don't fight for her."

They were right. They were more than right. This was nothing like Priscilla because Fiona was, well, Fiona. He knew precisely who she was, and more importantly, she did too. She wasn't some social-climbing miss looking for the best marriage. In fact, she'd declared her intent *not* to do that. She was utterly unique, and he loved her unequivocally.

"So much for my attempts to stop being an ass," he muttered. He started toward the door that led to the stairs. "Do either of you have any idea what set they're on?"

Lucien consulted his watch fob. "If they are on schedule, they are likely in the second."

Tobias practically ran down the stairs, which were thankfully not crowded. The hall below was, however, and getting into the ballroom took longer than he'd hoped. By the time he stepped inside, he feared the set would be drawing to a close.

Hurrying between people and ignoring those who tried to speak with him, he arrived at Fiona's side, breathless, just as the music stopped. "Miss Wingate, it's time for our dance."

Fiona stared at him, clearly confused. And why wouldn't she be? They'd made no plans for dancing or anything else.

"She's already agreed to partner me," Lord Gregory said affably.

Angling his head, Tobias smiled at Fiona. "Did you forget?" He narrowed his eyes slightly and tried to silently plead with her to agree.

"You can dance with Lord Gregory later," Miss Lancaster

put in from just behind Fiona, proving that her eavesdropping skills were quite advanced. "There's another waltz."

Fiona turned to Lord Gregory with an apologetic smile. "I hope you don't mind delaying our dance. I seem to have forgotten that I promised this one to my guardian."

Tobias flinched inwardly, wishing she hadn't called him that. He didn't need any further reminders that he should not be doing what he was about to do.

"Of course, I don't mind. Now I have something splendid to look forward to." Lord Gregory stepped to the side.

Fiona took Tobias's arm. As they walked toward the dance floor, she looked at him askance, her expression dubious. "Did your grandmother put you up to this?"

iona's question made Tobias stop, but only for the barest second because the music was starting. He swept her into his arms just as the waltz began.

It was heavenly. The sparkling candlelight reflected by the glass chandeliers and the mirrors. The blur of color as they swirled around the dancefloor. The lush notes of the music rising in the air and propelling the dancers.

"We've never had music before," she said, her eyes locked with his. He looked splendid this evening in a black coat and silver-threaded waistcoat. When she'd imagined her guardian on her journey from Shropshire, she'd never envisioned a handsome man who made her pulse race.

"Not true. I hummed the first time." The corner of his mouth ticked up. "On second thought, I believe we determined that didn't qualify as music."

She very much appreciated his ability to laugh at himself. "Perhaps with practice, you will gain the skill as I did with curtseying. *After* the queen's drawing room debacle."

"I doubt that," he said wryly. "But I'm willing to try, and you can tell me if I'm successful. Now, why did you mention my grandmother? And tell me about your interview with her."

"It was…enlightening," Fiona borrowed the dowager's word. "I see where your father might have inherited his autocratic tendencies."

"Oh dear, what did she say?"

"She went on quite a bit about matchmaking and the importance of it. She's considering becoming my sponsor in place of Lady Pickering."

Tobias wrinkled his nose. "That will not go well. The only woman who is perhaps more formidable than my grandmother, at least in my experience, is Lady Pickering."

"I have a hard time imagining that. Lady Pickering is so pleasant." Fiona liked her very much. "Not to say your grandmother is not," she hastily added.

Tobias laughed softly, a dark, throaty sound that never failed to make her want to smile in return. "I don't mind admitting she can be rather intimidating on occasion. I was shocked when she arrived earlier today. I was not expecting her."

"That's the impression I had from Carrin."

Tobias pressed his palm more firmly against her back, and it was hard not to recall his touch upon her the night before. She tried not to shiver and failed. His pupils darkened, and she knew he'd felt it. "Tell me why you think my grandmother provoked me to dance with you."

"It wasn't about you. She was not in favor of Lord Gregory's courtship. I wondered if she asked you to prevent me from spending time with him. It seemed a logical conclusion since you've never asked me to dance before." He had though. "At least not in public." She ought to look away from him because the intensity of his gaze was making it hard for her to focus on the waltz.

She did not.

"What is her quarrel with Lord Gregory?" Tobias seemed to hold his breath a moment.

"She never actually said, only that I could do better. She did, however, say quite plainly that she was not in favor of the match. I still don't understand." Fiona frowned. "Lord Gregory comes from an excellent family, and he's a very kind and interesting person."

"To you, he's a good match." Tobias broke eye contact, and she suddenly felt off-kilter. She clasped his hand and shoulder more tightly. "If you think you'd be happy with him, you should marry him." Tobias sounded strained, as if he struggled to force the words out. Was he upset?

Why shouldn't he be? He'd proposed marriage to her last night, and she'd refused him. Just as Lady Bentley had done two years before. Even worse, now he was also facing the loss of something he deeply cherished.

Her chest squeezed as she thought of how he must be feeling. Yet here he was at this assembly, and in what seemed to be a good mood. She wondered if there was a reason for it. "I saw Miss Goodfellow a short while ago. I'm surprised you didn't waltz with her."

His gaze found hers once more, and there was a warmth to the pewter depths that made her heart beat a little faster. "I have no intention of dancing with Miss Goodfellow or anyone else this evening. I came tonight to see you enjoy this ball that you've been so looking forward to, and to tell you I'm not getting married before the twelfth. Horethorne will be yours."

She missed her step, but he held her fast, keeping them from faltering as he continued to steer them behind the couple in front of them. Had she heard him right? She can't have. "You're giving up?"

"Not at all. I'm choosing not to allow my father's control to guide me. I was approaching marriage the way *he* wanted me to—as a business arrangement—instead of the way *I* wanted to."

Her breath tangled in her throat. "And what way is that?"

"With love and hope for a happy union. With the woman of my dreams."

The ache in her chest grew more pronounced. "Oh, Tobias. That's lovely."

His nostrils flared and his lips parted. "You shouldn't call me that in the middle of the ballroom, particularly after you declined my marriage proposal." Though his body tensed, he said the words with a light humor that she suddenly realized was as much a part of what drew her to him as anything else —his generosity, his care, and so much more.

"Furthermore, I don't deserve such familiarity from you when I seem to keep behaving like an ass. On that note, I've had a temporary bedchamber set up on the first floor in the antechamber off the drawing room for Mrs. Tucket. Now she will only need to bother with one set of stairs."

"That's incredibly thoughtful of you. Thank you."

"I should have thought of it immediately." He pressed his lips together and appeared disappointed—in himself. "I'm sorry I didn't."

Fiona moved her hand toward his neck, wishing she could wipe the lines in his features away. "It only matters that you did." And he was also giving her his mother's house. She knew that wasn't precisely the case, but his actions, or inaction, made it seem like a gift.

They danced without speaking then, and Fiona was only aware of the way they moved together and the touch of his hands upon her. He smelled of sandalwood and...maps. Probably because she associated them with him now. He'd increased the quantity of them in his library so that she had yet to peruse them all.

"Are you going to take my grandmother's advice?" he

asked, startling her slightly but not breaking the spell between them.

"To be honest, I'm still trying to decide what to do. I have made one decision though."

The music drew to a close, and the dance ended.

"What's that?" he asked.

"I need to settle Mrs. Tucket somewhere—either in Shropshire or at Horethorne. I plan to discuss it with her tomorrow." She realized they were still standing on the dancefloor, their hands clasped, as if they would continue dancing if only the music would begin again.

Tobias seemed to recognize this too, for he released her, only to tuck her hand around his arm and lead her from the floor. "Has she expressed a desire to leave London?"

"Yes. The incident at the ball last Saturday was rather embarrassing for her."

"I am sorry for that. Please let me know what I can do to help. Although, I am not sure your cousin would allow her to live on his estate. He was quite relieved that your invitation to London included your maid."

Fiona had thought of that. It was another reason she was glad to have Horethorne. "Yes, that is a concern. Is there someplace she could retire on the estate? Just a small cottage would be acceptable."

"I'm not certain, but Mr. Davies is the steward, and he can help you. He's incredibly kind and knowledgeable."

"You know him well?"

"My whole life."

She couldn't discount the sensation that this wasn't right, that Horethorne should be his. They were heading toward the garden, she realized. The doors were open, and the air in the ballroom was quite warm. "Are we going outside?"

He slowed. "Do you want to?"

Her eyes met his, and instead of answering, she continued

through the open doorway out onto the terrace. Lanterns lit the walkways, and an oval pool in the center reflected the light. She'd somehow missed that aspect of the garden when she'd rushed inside with Mrs. Renshaw the week before.

"If there's nowhere suitable for Mrs. Tucket at Horethorne, I will find a place for her at Deane Hall."

Fiona paused near the pool. "You would do that?"

"Of course."

"Your father's support of me is such a mystery, and now you are continuing it. I will be forever grateful. And indebted."

He shook his head and guided her along the pool, then veered away from it toward the wall that divided this half of the garden from that of the men's. It was less illuminated here and more secluded.

"It is no longer a mystery." He stopped and turned to face her. "My grandmother explained why our fathers were so close."

Fiona withdrew her hand from his arm. She could just make out his features in the shadows. "Why?"

"They were lovers. Since Oxford."

Sucking in a breath, Fiona felt as though she'd found a long-missing piece of a puzzle. "That explains why my parents' relationship always seemed so aloof." It also explained why certain pages of that book Fiona had found in her father's library seemed more worn than others—specifically the ones with drawings of only men engaged in sexual acts. "Did they love each other?"

"They must have. Look at the lengths to which my father went to provide for your future." He smiled. "I admit I was glad to learn my father had known love. I was also jealous, since he wasn't ever able to bestow any upon me."

Fiona reached up and cupped his jaw. "I'm sure things were very difficult for him."

"Certainly, yes. I can't imagine the life they were forced to lead. I am sad they had to live falsely, which perhaps resulted in our mothers' unhappiness. However, without that, you and I would not be here. I must also admit that when my grandmother first began to reveal this to me, I thought she was going to tell me that we were somehow related."

Gasping, Fiona took her hand from his jaw and covered her mouth. "Oh, that would have been awful."

"I thought so too, but then I wondered if it mattered since it seems we do not have a future together."

She lowered her hand between them. "Tobias—"

He put his gloved finger on her lips. "Just let me say one more thing. When I spoke earlier about the woman of my dreams, I meant you, Fiona. I love you, and not because you're inheriting my mother's house or because I desire you above all other women. Which, I do, by the way. I love you for your sweet nature, your inquisitive sensibilities, and your hunger for life. You make me laugh, provoke me to think about things I don't usually, and you inspire me to be a better man."

Her throat constricted, and it was a moment before she could speak. "So your grandmother was playing matchmaker when she deterred me from Lord Gregory. She was trying to drive me to you."

"If that's true, she did an exceptionally poor job of it," he said with a laugh. "Did she say anything to encourage you to reconsider my suit?"

"I suppose not, but she didn't really need to. And she was wrong anyway—Lord Gregory is more than suitable, and he'll make someone a fine husband. Just not me. He is not the man of my dreams, and someone I respect and admire once told me I shouldn't settle for less than that."

"You've decided what the man of your dreams should be?"

"He's the man who's made all my dreams come true.

Dreams I didn't even know I had. I thought I wanted freedom—and I did. I didn't want to feel trapped and alone like my mother did. Cassandra once said to me that a marriage with love was the best freedom a woman could hope for. I think she might be right."

He drew her into his arms, pulling her deeper into the shadows. "If you aren't talking about me, say so now." His lips hovered over hers.

She wrapped her arms around his neck. "Of course, it's you. It's only ever been you."

Their lips met, tongues and teeth clashing as they kissed with a new and desperate abandon. Nothing stood between them now, just clothing and a rather inconvenient location.

She pulled her mouth from his. "This is where I kissed you the first time."

He glanced around briefly and grinned. "So it is. I may have a plaque placed on this very spot."

Giggling as he kissed her jaw and neck, she asked, "What would it say?"

"Don't get caught."

He devoured her laugh with another kiss, turning her body until he pushed her up against the door in the wall. Yes, exactly the spot. She thrust her hands into his hair as he kissed down her neck and licked along the rise of her breast above her neckline.

"Should we go back inside?" she asked between rasping breaths.

"Where inside?" His voice was low, dusky, and made her want to beg him to kneel down between her legs and repeat what he'd done to her last night.

"To the ball." She gasped as he cupped her breast, pushing it up as he suckled her flesh.

"I suppose we should, but there is a bedroom—a few, actually—on the second floor of the men's side. Or we could wait until we get home..." He kissed up to the hollow of her throat, making her body quiver until she wanted to whimper.

"Except your grandmother is there," she managed.

"Bollocks."

She reached inside his coat and pulled him against her as she licked the edge of his ear and whispered, "Upstairs it is."

His hand moved behind her, and the door gave way. He didn't let her fall, holding her close against him as he propelled them into the other garden. Closing the door swiftly, he set the latch before taking her into his arms again and kissing her thoroughly.

Weak-kneed, she clutched his hand as he led her to the back of the building, seeming to trace the same path they'd taken the week before. He was cautious, looking from side to side and up at the thankfully empty terrace before taking her into a side door that led into a back stairway.

Fiona held onto him as they walked along a narrow corridor lit with sconces. "This is convenient."

"We sometimes have parties in the garden. This provides direct access for the employees to come and go from the kitchens downstairs with food and drink." He inclined his head to the stairs that led down, moving quickly to turn the corner where he took her upstairs.

She hesitated, pulling on his hand. "You know far too much about this club to be an ordinary member. You must be on the membership committee. Don't bother denying it."

He turned, the light from the sconce illuminating the resignation in his features. "I'm supposed to deny it. The committee is very secret." A smile teased his lips. "How did you know?"

"You've said things that made me wonder, but I really should have known the day that I was here as a maid. You said there was a meeting to decide if a member's family could attend assemblies. How would you know that if you weren't part of the *Star Chamber*?" She dipped her voice as she uttered the last two words and shook her head. "I can't believe I didn't realize it then. Was everyone else who was here also on the committee?"

"That I won't say." He pressed his lips together, then led her up to the second landing. As they ascended, he continued, "And you must promise to keep the secret. If not, Lucien may toss me out."

"My lips are sealed."

When they reached the landing, he pulled her into his arms and gave her a wicked smile. "For this, I would ask you to unseal your lips." He kissed her again, his tongue licking into her mouth with delicious strokes. She moaned softly, eager to get wherever they were going. They needed to be fast. They would be missed if they were gone too long.

Except their absence was likely already noted. Could they explain it away as a lengthy promenade in the garden? Naïve as she was about most of what went on in London, Fiona had no idea. Nor did she particularly care in this moment. It was hard to be concerned about rules that had never applied to you before.

Tobias swept her into his arms, and she let out a soft squeal. Laughing, she encircled her arms around his neck as he dashed up the rest of the stairs. At the top, he set her down gently and put his finger to his lips before opening the door carefully.

Glancing about, he took her hand once more and quickly guided her to another closed door. "Please let there be no one inside," he murmured.

Before Fiona could protest, he ushered them both inside. Throwing the latch, he turned, only for her to shove him lightly in the chest. "You were concerned someone might be in here?"

He lifted a shoulder. "The chance of that happening at this early hour is incredibly unlikely. Especially with the assembly going on. Besides, a smart person locks the door." He pivoted to set the lock, then faced her once more as he drew his gloves off and tossed them toward a table. "Now, where were we?"

Waggling his brows at her, he took her hand and removed the glove. Then he moved to her other hand and did the same. Tugging her against him, he kissed her again, this time taking his time exploring her mouth and stripping away the last of her defenses.

Well, if she'd had defenses, he would have stripped them away.

Ending the kiss abruptly, he took a step back. "I don't want to muss your gown. Please tell me this isn't a nightmare to remove."

"It's not exactly a nightmare, but I will require your assistance with the buttons on the back." She turned her back to him, which forced her attention to the primary piece of furniture in the room—a large four-poster bed. Covered in a lush, dark purple coverlet, the bed looked fit for royalty.

There were only five buttons, and Fiona felt each one as Tobias plucked them open. Then he loosened the tie that cinched the dress around her middle until the fabric parted in the back. He lowered the gown, and she carefully stepped out of it.

Turning her head, she saw him gently lay the garment over a high-backed chair. "The best I can do, I'm afraid." His gaze swept over her. "You are so beautiful."

Fiona pulled the tie at the back of her petticoat and slid the narrow straps from her shoulders. She was not quite as cautious as she let the garment fall to the floor before stepping aside and plucking it up.

"Allow me." Tobias took it to the same chair and laid it

atop the gown. "I suppose we should leave your corset in place." He sounded disappointed.

She pulled at the laces until the garment was loose and she could push it down over her hips. "Too late." Keeping her gaze locked with his, she kicked her shoes from her feet. "I'm about to be nearly nude, while you are completely clothed."

He scrambled to remove his coat, letting it fall to the floor unheeded before moving on to his dancing slippers and stockings, which required him to perch on a chair.

"I'll just wait over here," she called, climbing onto the bed where she sat back against the headboard.

A low growl crept across the room from his lips to her ears. His body followed as he prowled toward her, discarding his cravat and waistcoat along the way. When he reached the side of the bed, she met him there, first on her knees, then putting her legs over the side of mattress on either side of him.

She reached for his shirt, pulling it from his waistband, and he hastened to help, casting the garment away before she could blink. Then she couldn't because her gaze was transfixed on his bare chest. She splayed her hands over his flesh, her fingertips pressing into him. "A new map," she murmured.

He cupped her head and kissed her, claiming her mouth and her utter surrender. He had that and more—everything she could offer.

She fell back, pulling her chemise up until he took over and tore the garment over her head, flinging it away. Before he could kiss her again, she touched his cheek. "I love you too, Tobias."

"Oh, thank God." His mouth met hers once more as he caressed her body, trailing his hands across her shoulders, down and around her breasts, pulling at her nipples until she whimpered into his mouth. Then his hand was between her legs, stroking across her sex, gently at first before becoming more insistent, his thumb and fingers finding those sweet spots that made pleasure unfurl inside her.

Desire pulsed within her, centered in her sex where he worked her flesh, driving her toward that unfathomable ecstasy. "More," she urged him, clutching at his shoulder and his waist. She ran her hands over his bare back, glorying in the muscular terrain and anticipating more time when she could explore every peak and valley.

He settled himself between her legs, forcing them wider. His cock, hard beneath his clothing, pressed against her sex. A jolt of pleasure shot through her, the promise of what was to come.

Fiona slipped her hand between them, trying to find his buttons. He rose up and unfastened his fall. "Take them off," she ordered. "Completely."

"You're still wearing your stockings."

"Then take those off too. I'll wait. But not long. If you dally, I'll pleasure myself."

"Bloody hell, Fiona. You know how to do that?"

"I'm not as accomplished as you." She put her hand on her sex. "But I think I've learned a thing or two." She rotated her fingertips over her clitoris.

"God, stop, please. I'm going to embarrass myself." He worked to remove his breeches and smallclothes as quickly as possible. When he settled back between her legs, he put his hand over hers and pressed her finger inside her, making her gasp. "To hell with your stockings."

He thrust her finger into her twice, three times before lifting her hand and lowering his head simultaneously so he could suck her digit into his mouth. She felt the vibration of his groan along with another pulse of need.

"Please, Tobias." She reached between them and found his cock, closing her hand around the warm flesh.

He closed his eyes briefly. "Move your hand. Just for a moment. Please."

She slid her palm up and down, reveling in the hard yet silken feel of him. "Like this?"

"Yes. Just like that. Faster. No, don't. I won't last." His hand covered hers as he opened his eyes. "Ready?" He put the tip of his shaft to her sex.

She looked up at him, losing herself in the piercing pewter of his eyes. "Now."

He pushed inside her, his flesh stretching hers. It was so much more than his fingers, and it took her a moment to grow accustomed to him. He kissed her temple and her cheek before whispering, "Just breathe. We'll go slow for a bit."

He waited, quietly filling her and holding still until she began to relax.

"Ready," she said.

"Wrap your legs around me, love." He withdrew, but not completely, then slowly drove forward again. Again and again, he removed and returned until she began to move with him.

"Yes, that's right," he urged. "Now we'll go a bit faster." He picked up speed and the friction was delicious.

She gasped, arching as he filled her. "I like faster. I think I want harder or deeper. I don't know. I want *more*."

"Hold onto me." He leaned down and kissed her, his mouth tantalizing hers as he built a new momentum. She gripped him with hands and legs and tried to move with him, her body becoming frenzied as she careened toward her release. Digging her fingers into his back, she cried out as she came apart, her muscles tightening as a torrent of pleasure washed over her.

Tobias moved even faster, his body snapping into hers

with a blissful precision. She closed her eyes and cast her head back, surrendering herself to the soul-deep rapture.

Just as she began to float back to earth, he cried out, a low, guttural sound that she felt in her bones. He thrust deep, and a smaller second burst of pleasure sparked. She held him tightly between her legs as she stroked his back and kissed his neck, his shoulder, his chest.

When he was spent, he fell to the side, his chest heaving. Fiona rolled to face him. Skimming her hand along his abdomen, she felt the ripple of his muscles from his chest to his belly. "What an unusual terrain. What would this be, I wonder?" she murmured to herself somewhat nonsensically. "Perhaps this is the Overton Steppe."

"Are you referring to the hair on my chest? There isn't *that* much. Isn't a steppe grassy?"

"Not necessarily." She giggled. "If not a steppe, then a plain, I suppose, but it's not flat." Inspiration struck. "It moves like water, particularly if you laugh." That made him laugh, proving her point. "The Sea of Overton."

"You astonish me, Fiona."

She rose up over him and a lock of her hair fell free, grazing his chest. "Oh dear, I worry my hair is a mess."

"I think it's best if we don't return to the ball. I'll say you became ill and I saw you home."

"Won't that still spark disapproval?"

"But I'm your guardian!" His eyes widened in mock horror.

"I was rather hoping you would be my husband instead."

He bolted up, forcing her to sit too. "I was trying so hard not to be an ass anymore, and I completely forgot to propose to you again." He wiped his hand over his face and gave her a sheepish look. "Miss Wingate, will you do me the honor of becoming my wife?"

"I think I must at this juncture." She giggled again, then

forced herself to be serious. "Yes, I'll marry you, and not because I must. Actually, it *is* because I must, for to not marry you is no longer conceivable."

Grinning, he leaned forward and kissed her, drawing a deep sigh from her chest at how right everything felt, from that beautiful waltz to this enchanting moment.

She ripped her mouth from his and gasped. "The waltz! I'm supposed to be waltzing with Lord Gregory!"

"Shit!" Tobias leapt from the bed and dashed nude to the mantel where a lantern burned. There was also a small clock, which he surveyed. "I have no bloody idea when that waltz is, but we can't have been gone that long." He faced her, his hands on his hips. "Still, we should go home. Better yet, I should send you home. Because you're ill."

"I can't leave without speaking to Lord Gregory." Fiona climbed from the bed and found her chemise, quickly drawing it over her head. "I must explain to him that I cannot proceed with a courtship."

Tobias, who'd started putting on his clothing, stopped. His breeches were on, but the fall hung open. His chest was still bare, the lantern light casting alluring shadows over the hard planes. Fiona averted her gaze lest she become irreversibly distracted.

"I feel bad about Lord Gregory. I know people noticed your…interest in each other."

"It makes you think of your experience with Lady Bentley." Fiona went to him and caressed his cheek. "This is different. I am not Lady Bentley."

He smiled, then turned his head to kiss her palm. "Thank goodness for that. You'll be kind and considerate."

"And I love you. Lord Gregory will understand."

Clasping her waist, he looked into her eyes. "How did I get so fortunate to find you?"

"I believe you have our fathers to thank. I wonder what

they would say if they could see that their offspring would unite their families."

"I think they would be very glad. And while it pains me to please my father in any way, I am glad too." He bent his head to kiss her as the door crashed open.

"What in the devil is going on here?"

CHAPTER 20

*T*obias recognized that feminine voice. He reached for his shirt and quickly drew it over his head. Then he realized Barbara was not alone.

"This room is occupied, obviously," Tobias said. "How did you even get in here? And who are you with?" He stalked to the doorway where the gentleman stood in profile.

Constantine Westbrook, the Earl of Aldington, darted a glance toward Tobias, then promptly turned and stalked away.

Tobias ran past Barbara, who held the door as she stood inside the room. "Aldington, wait! Why are you here?" It wasn't really the question he wanted answered, but he was flustered.

"This was a mistake," Aldington said without stopping. "Please don't follow me out." He disappeared through the doorway Tobias and Fiona had used earlier as they'd come up the backstairs.

Looking about, Tobias was relieved to not see anyone else. Pivoting, he hurried back to the bedchamber, tucking in his shirt and buttoning his fall as he went. He arrived to find the door still open, Barbara standing inside, and Fiona lacing her corset.

Tobias closed the door firmly and faced Barbara. "How in the bloody hell did you get in here? You aren't a member, and neither is Aldington."

"His brother is the owner, however," Barbara said rather unhelpfully.

"You're saying Lucien let him in?"

Barbara shrugged, her pearl earrings bobbing. "Aldington knew a door by which to get in, and he had a key to this room. We did not realize it would be occupied." Her eyes narrowed as she surveyed Fiona at length. "I should have expected you'd find someone younger to warm your bed. All that nonsense about improving your reputation and getting married. What a load of rubbish."

"As it happens, he *is* getting married," Fiona said as she finished with her corset. "To me." Smiling pleasantly, she fetched her petticoat and drew it over her head.

Barbara turned her head toward Tobias, who was feeling rather proud of his betrothed. She didn't seem the slightest bit ruffled by Barbara's presence. But then she didn't realize who Barbara was.

"Pity you're getting dressed." Barbara sauntered toward Fiona who'd donned the petticoat and was now reaching behind to her back to pull the drawstring to cinch it around her middle. "May I?"

"Thank you." Fiona presented her back.

"I would've asked to join you," Barbara purred. "I am quite expert at what Toby likes."

Tobias had drawn on his waistcoat and stalked to Barbara. "Please take your hands from my betrothed."

Fiona took a step and swung around toward Barbara. "You were his mistress?"

"Until very recently, yes." Barbara folded her arms over

her chest and pouted. "Until that chit—his ward—came to live with him."

"Barba—"

"Oh, you mean me?" Fiona laughed, and Tobias had no idea if it was genuine or an act to beat Barbara at whatever game she was trying to play. She sent Tobias a warm smile. "How lovely that he stopped seeing you when I arrived." Their eyes locked, and he marveled at her confidence and composure.

Fiona picked up her gown from the chair. "Now, you must excuse me, for I need to return to the ball."

Barbara frowned at her, and Tobias prepared himself to jump to Fiona's defense. "You can't go like that," Barbara said. "Your hair's a fright. Let me help you."

"Oh, would you?" Fiona asked brightly. "That would be wonderful."

"Here, let's get you dressed first." Barbara took the gown and helped her into the garment. Then she situated it over Fiona's undergarments and fastened the back.

Tobias stared at them, completely flabbergasted. "What is even happening right now?"

"Your former mistress is helping your betrothed." Barbara shook her head. "I should think that would be obvious."

"I fear I will never understand women," he muttered as he buttoned his waistcoat, then went to sit and don his stockings and dancing slippers.

"There, I think that will do," Barbara announced as she stepped back and surveyed Fiona's repaired hair.

Fiona moved to the small mirror that hung over a dresser between the pair of windows that looked down to Ryder Street below. "Brilliant. I can't thank you enough." She patted the back of her head and turned from the glass, looking to Tobias in the chair. "I'll see you downstairs later?"

Tobias stood and took her hand. "Good luck." He kissed

her knuckles, his body stirring as he wished to do much more. "I love you," he whispered.

She smiled softly. "I love you too." Leaning forward, she kissed him, her lips lingering on his for the barest moment before she drew back, her eyes sparkling. "See you later."

Barbara handed Fiona her gloves. "Don't forget these." She smiled at her. "I apologize if I was rude at all. I was—am—quite fond of Toby. I'm glad to see he's found someone who will make him happy."

"I will work very hard to do so." Fiona sent him a look of promise that sparked a heat inside Tobias that he knew would never diminish.

When she was gone, Tobias found his cravat and went to the glass, pulling the fabric around the collar of his shirt.

Barbara joined him. "Let me help you too."

"I'd rather not."

"Do you want to look as though you haphazardly repaired your costume, which will only contribute to your notoriety?"

He hated that she made sense. Dropping his hands to his sides, he surrendered to her ministrations. "Why were you here with Aldington?"

She arched a dark brow as her fingers worked beneath his chin. "I should think that would be obvious."

"But how? He doesn't consort with courtesans. He's as staid as the bloody Archbishop of Canterbury."

"Do you promise not to say anything?" She looked him in the eye, and he knew she wouldn't reveal a thing if he didn't.

"Yes. Explain."

"Since you abandoned me"—she sniffed for some sort of dramatic effect—"I've attended a few Cyprian balls to find a new protector. As one in my position must do."

Tobias felt bad about that, but Barbara had always said how much she enjoyed her work, especially when she could find a kind and generous benefactor such as him. "I believed

I gave you enough of a settlement that you wouldn't have to look for someone new right away. Or even this Season."

"You did, but I am easily bored. And I believe you know that, unless you weren't paying attention. Which I know can't be true because *you* never bored me in the slightest." She patted his lapels and stood back, surveying her work. "You'll do."

"Did you meet Aldington at a Cyprian ball?" Tobias was shocked to hear this. He couldn't imagine Lucien's brother would want to be recognized at such an event, and he surely would have been.

"A masquerade a few nights ago." That made a bit of sense at least. "He very awkwardly approached me for a liaison—nothing permanent, at least not yet. He was extremely nervous. I had the impression he'd never negotiated with a courtesan before."

"That would not surprise me." Tobias plucked up his coat and pulled it on. Lastly, he returned to the mirror and smoothed his hair. Satisfied he no longer looked like he'd just shagged his soon-to-be-wife, even if he certainly felt like it, he went to fetch his gloves.

He paused at the door. "Barbara, do me a favor, please?"

"Anything." She sauntered toward him, her hips swaying. "You know you may have any favor you like."

"Not that kind. If I wasn't clear before, I have no intention on bedding anyone other than my wife. Ever." *Wife.* How he loved the sound of that. He pulled on his gloves. "If Aldington returns to you, ensure that he truly wants to engage in a liaison. I would hate for him to do anything he would regret." He met her gaze. "And that is not a reflection on you. I just know him well enough to believe this behavior is so outside who he is that he may be filled with remorse. In fact, I would strongly advise you move on to another candidate."

Her lush red lips curved into a soft smile. "You're a good friend, Toby."

"I try to be—and I will be to you. Always. Good night, Barbara."

Tobias wondered how Fiona had found her way downstairs and hoped she hadn't encountered anyone here on the men's side. Even though there was an assembly going on next door, many gentlemen were simply at their club, spending their evening in the gaming room or the members' den. He ought to have discussed that with her before she left.

Hurrying down to the first floor, he didn't pause to see who might be in the members' den. He did, however, nearly run into Lucien, who came toward the staircase from that very room.

Lucien glanced up the stairs. "You're coming down? What were you about on the second floor?"

It was a valid question since the only rooms up there were Lucien's office, the bedchambers Tobias had mentioned to Fiona, and a storage room. "I was, ah, dallying with my bride-to-be."

Lucien grinned. "Congratulations. All of your worrying was for naught then."

Tobias rolled his eyes. "I encountered a most peculiar person up there."

"Not your betrothed?"

"Your brother. In the company of my former mistress. He had a key to the room we were in. He can have only obtained it in one way."

"By stealing it from me?"

Tobias narrowed one eye at him. "Is that really what happened?"

"No. I gave it to him." Lucien exhaled. "It's my bloody club, Deane. If I want to give my brother access to a bedchamber so he can shag someone, I will."

"You're helping him commit adultery?"

"He's viciously unhappy."

"Hasn't he always been? According to you anyway." Tobias remembered a time or two when Aldington had laughed.

"I will help him do anything if it will remove the stick from his arse, even a small amount. But I am sorry they troubled you."

"I just think allowing non-members access to the club is problematic."

Lucien's eyes grew cold, which didn't happen often, but when it did, you knew he was angry. "I didn't invite all of bloody London. He's my brother."

"I do wonder if your brother's disposition might improve if he could find some happiness with his wife. Perhaps you should help him with *that*. Since you are so fond of—and skilled at—providing assistance."

"I've actually suggested that. It's not as if Sabrina is awful or a bad wife. I truly don't understand why they are estranged. But then it's none of my business according to Con, and he's right."

MacNair came up the stairs then and greeted them both with a smile. "Have you had more than enough ball for one night as I have?"

"Not at all," Tobias said with a smile. "In fact, I am on my way downstairs."

"Lucien, you should come up to the members' den with me," MacNair said, pivoting.

"I should check on the assembly, converse with Mrs. Renshaw, and make sure all is well."

"You can do that later." He reached for Lucien's arm. "Come and have a glass of port with me."

Lucien's eyes narrowed. "Is there some reason you don't want me to go downstairs?"

Tobias was itching to get to the ballroom and see how Fiona was faring. He hoped her absence hadn't caused a stir. "I'm going then."

"I'm coming with you." Lucien started to descend with him.

MacNair let out a groan. "Lucien, your sister is dancing with Wexford."

Lucien swore and increased his pace down the stairs. Tobias looked up at MacNair. "Why would you tell him that? You know how he is about Lady Cassandra and...any of us."

"Better he knows what he's about to see than be surprised." MacNair inclined his head toward the lower floor. "You'd better ensure he doesn't do something stupid, such as call Wexford out."

"He wouldn't do that," Tobias said with a snort. Still, he followed after Lucien with alacrity. "Wait, Lucien. It's just a dance." Tobias caught up to him in the staircase hall, but Lucien didn't slow.

"That's all it better be."

Tobias caught his friend by the arm, pulling him to a stop. "Why are you upset? Wexford is our friend, and he's only dancing with her."

"Dancing with someone means something, as you bloody well know, and I wasn't jesting when I told you all to leave her alone. Don't forget how well I know you all, and while I might have been able to tolerate her forming an attachment with you or MacNair, Wexford is completely unacceptable."

"But he's our friend."

Lucien's features darkened. "That doesn't mean he should be dancing with my sister." He tugged his arm from Tobias's grasp and stalked into the ballroom.

∿

*F*iona retraced the path she and Tobias had taken from the ballroom. However, instead of going back into the ballroom from the garden, she went to the other door she'd used with Mrs. Renshaw the week before. The beautiful gold and ivory sitting room was being used as a ladies' retiring room. Once inside, she ducked behind a screen and was grateful to find the space empty. After a short while, she emerged and conversed briefly with a pair of ladies who were resting.

Apprehension threaded through her as she left the room. What would she encounter when she reentered the ballroom? Were people already gossiping about her and how she'd disappeared from the ball for an hour? She honestly had no idea how long she'd been gone.

Taking a deep breath to fortify her anxiety, she walked into the ballroom and immediately looked for Lord Gregory. Before she could find him, Prudence bore down on her wearing an expression of what could only be described as extreme distress.

"Where have you been?" she whispered urgently, drawing Fiona away from anyone who might want to listen in on their conversation.

Fiona smiled. "Could you try to look less concerned and upset? I was, er, ill. I just came from the retiring room." That much, at least, was true.

"You were gone a very long time after you disappeared from the ballroom following your dance with Lord Overton. Were you with him?"

"Yes." There was no reason to lie, not to Prudence. "We are betrothed."

Prudence grabbed her hand. "Truly?" At Fiona's nod, she smiled broadly. Indeed, it was the happiest Fiona had ever seen her. "Then I am sorry for my behavior. Still, it was ill-advised to disappear. Your absence has been noted. You missed a dance with Mr. Arbuckle."

"Blast. I will find him and apologize. But you must say you knew I was ill."

"That won't be difficult since that's what I told him." She arched a shoulder. "I had to say *something*."

Fiona squeezed Prudence's hand before letting it go. "Thank you. I don't know how I would have survived these past weeks without your support. Now, I must find Lord Gregory and tell him I am in love with someone else."

Prudence winced. "I don't envy you. I think he's on the other side."

"Brilliant, thank you."

"I'll come with you." Prudence linked her arm through Fiona's. "Not when you actually speak with him, of course."

They threaded their way to the other side of the ballroom, passing through one of the wide doorways into the men's side. This was where the food was located along with some seating. Fiona saw him standing near the doors to the garden with another gentleman. She took her arm from Prudence's. "Wish me luck."

"Good luck."

Fiona considered what she might say. None of it sounded right. But was there any *right* way to tell someone you didn't return their feelings? Actually, she didn't even know his feelings. Perhaps he would be relieved. Yes, she'd hope for that to be the case.

Lord Gregory saw her when she was still several feet away. He excused himself from the other gentleman and met her. "Miss Wingate, I trust you're having a pleasant evening."

"I am, actually. Might we take a stroll in the garden?" It wasn't particularly warm out, but she wanted at least a modicum of privacy and the ballroom was quite stuffy, which only added to her discomfort.

"That would be delightful." He offered her his arm and escorted her outside.

The garden on this side was similar to the other half, except the reflecting pool was rectangular and had a large statue of Aphrodite in the center. She rose from the water as in the myth, a shell behind her feet.

"Our waltz should be soon," Lord Gregory said as they began a circuit of the reflecting pool. The lantern light danced across the water.

Fiona saw no reason to prolong the inevitable. "You may not want to dance with me after I tell you something."

"Well, that sounds ominous." He stopped, turning toward her. They stood on the other side of the pool from the club.

She looked up into his warm brown eyes and felt a pang of guilt. But why should she feel guilty? She genuinely liked him, and if Tobias hadn't fallen in love with her or she with him, Lord Gregory would be a wonderfully acceptable husband.

Acceptable did not inspire emotion. So yes, she would feel guilty.

"You are a lovely gentleman, and I've enjoyed our time together very much. However, I find that my heart is engaged elsewhere."

He blinked. "I rather thought we suited." It wasn't a declaration of love, and she now realized she wouldn't have been able to settle for anything less than that.

"We would have, most likely. However, I am in love with someone who makes me feel as though the world is at my feet. I want for you to make someone feel that way too."

"But it isn't you." A sad smile flitted across his lips. "I admit I'm disappointed, but I must also confess that I am not in love with you either. Though I expect it was only a matter of time until that happened," he added softly.

Fiona felt terrible. "You're incredibly kind."

"This other gentleman loves you in return?"

"Yes. You deserve the same."

They continued walking around the pool. As they neared the house, a footman rushed to greet them. "My lord, a message was delivered for you requesting that you return to your father's house at once."

Fiona felt Lord Gregory tense and withdrew her hand from his arm. "Is everything all right?" The question was for the footman, but she looked at Lord Gregory.

"Did the missive say anything else?" Lord Gregory's brow creased. He was clearly surprised and concerned by the summons.

"I'm afraid not." The footman bowed, then retreated to the house.

Lord Gregory turned to her. "Forgive me, I must go. Not that we were still going to waltz." His mouth curled into a half smile.

She touched his sleeve. "I would have been honored to waltz with you. I will pray that everything is well at your father's house."

"Thank you. Good night, Miss Wingate." He turned and went into the ballroom.

Fiona started forward as Mrs. Renshaw came out to intercept her. "Good evening, Miss Wingate. I see the footman found Lord Gregory. I received the message for him. I do hope there is nothing too troublesome."

"He seemed unaware of whatever prompted the request. I shall be thinking of him and his family." She dearly hoped it wasn't bad news, particularly after she'd just disappointed him.

"You look rather concerned," Mrs. Renshaw observed. "Dare I assume the two of you share an attachment?"

Fiona blinked and shook her head. "Ah, no. As it happens,

I had just told him that my affections are toward another gentleman."

"Oh!" Mrs. Renshaw put her hand to her mouth briefly. "You mustn't feel guilty. You had no idea he would receive that note."

"While that is true, I still regret the sequence of events." If she'd just taken a few minutes longer to find him… But then she may not have had the chance to tell him face to face that she was no longer interested in pursuing a courtship, and he'd deserved that consideration. "It had to be done, however, for I am in love with someone else and we're to be married." She bit her lip. "Perhaps I should not have said that. We have not discussed when we will make this announcement."

"Is it who I hope it is?"

Fiona blushed. "If you're referring to the man I kissed in the garden last week, then yes."

Mrs. Renshaw's eyes sparkled with glee. "Splendid!"

"Perhaps you can offer some advice. I'm worried Society won't be kind since he is my guardian."

"Society is seldom kind." Mrs. Renshaw sent a sharp glance toward the ballroom. "You are right to be concerned. However, happiness trumps everything else. You're fortunate to be marrying an earl. People will overlook a great many transgressions for such a lofty rank."

"That hardly seems fair."

Mrs. Renshaw gave her a wry look. "When is anything fair?"

Fiona started back toward the ballroom. "I do hope you'll keep my news a secret for now. We have not discussed anything. I only just accepted his proposal this evening."

Mrs. Renshaw fell into step beside her. "Of course. I am not like most of Society. I know how to keep confidences, and I value friendship."

"Thank you." Fiona smiled at her askance, glad to have another friend.

They stepped into the ballroom, and Prudence immediately came toward them. Fiona introduced the two women, and Mrs. Renshaw took her leave.

"I saw Lord Gregory come back to the ballroom and then he left immediately. He appeared quite distressed. Was he devastated by your news?" Prudence's eyes were lined with worry.

"He was disappointed, but that's not why he left. He received a summons to return home at once without any explanation."

"I do hope it's nothing serious."

"As do I." Fiona saw Cassandra striding toward them from the ladies' side of the ballroom.

"There you are at last!" Cassandra said as she arrived at Fiona's side. "Where did you go after dancing with Overton?"

"We strolled in the garden, and I accepted his proposal of marriage."

Cassandra's eyes rounded, and her jaw dropped. She let out a sound of joy that provoked a few people near them to turn their heads in curiosity.

Fiona turned toward the corner and motioned for Cassandra and Prudence to follow. She looked to Cassandra. "We haven't announced anything yet."

"Certainly. I didn't mean to react so...exuberantly. I'm just so shocked! What happened?"

"I realized, rather belatedly, that I have fallen in love with him, and thankfully he has with me as well."

"How wonderfully convenient and orderly." Cassandra grinned. Then her eyes narrowed. "You were gone an awfully long time. I danced two sets."

"Prudence was quick enough to tell anyone who inquired that I wasn't feeling well. And I made sure I was seen in the retiring room. Have I completely ruined my reputation?"

"That depends on if you were seen in the garden with Overton and whether anyone put that together with your subsequent absence for an hour or however long you were gone. If you announce your betrothal quickly, perhaps tomorrow, all should be well."

Fiona relaxed, her body loosening from a tension she hadn't realized she'd been carrying since returning to the ball. Probably because she'd also been too giddy to notice. "That is exceptionally good to hear."

Seeing Cassandra reminded Fiona that her brother had been upstairs. With a courtesan. She pondered whether she ought to tell Cassandra. On the one hand, he was her brother, and on the other, his...private affairs were just that —private. Even if he was married and shouldn't have been dallying with a courtesan. Fiona decided it wasn't her place to involve herself.

Glancing toward the wide doorway from the staircase hall, she wondered when Tobias would come downstairs and how they would need to act toward each other. It would be very difficult when all she wanted to do was to proclaim to the world that he was hers and she was his.

As if conjured from her thoughts, Tobias came toward them. He wore an absurdly bright smile that reflected Fiona's joy.

He was not alone. Lord Lucien was at his side, and if Tobias looked utterly delighted, Lord Lucien was the personification of irritated. His brow was deeply furrowed and his jaw clenched.

"Where is he?" Lord Lucien demanded of his sister without preamble.

"Who?" Cassandra appeared perplexed.

"Don't be clever. Wexford. Why were you dancing with him?"

Lord Lucien was angry because his sister was dancing with someone? Who was Wexford? Fiona looked to Tobias, who barely shook his head, his eyes silently communicating that he'd explain later.

"As if it's any of your concern, I was avoiding an overzealous gentleman." Cassandra's eyes glittered with an ire that seemed to match her brother's. "Actually, perhaps it is your concern, since this is your club. Mr. Upton had clearly over-imbibed and was not accepting my refusal to promenade in the garden."

"Sounds as though Wexford performed a great service," Tobias said genially.

"Wexford should have taken Upton into the garden for a beating." Lord Lucien's mouth twisted. "I'll speak with him later. And with Upton." He exhaled. "I'm relieved to discover the dance was nothing more than that."

"And if it had been, it still wouldn't have been your business. I don't know why you and Con and Father seem to think you can manage every part of my life. I won't tolerate it." Cassandra glanced toward Fiona. "I'm for the retiring room." She left in the direction of the ladies' side of the ballroom.

"Perhaps you should go with her," Fiona suggested to Prudence.

Prudence flicked a glance toward Tobias before saying, "It seems you're the one I should stay with."

Fiona laughed softly. "I promise I will stay right here."

Prudence hesitated but ultimately departed after Cassandra. Lord Lucien, who continued to frown, turned to Tobias and Fiona. "Allow me to offer my most heartfelt congratulations. However, I hope you'll excuse me."

"Thank you and yes." Tobias gave him a meaningful look. "You heard what your sister said."

"That I'm like my brother and father? Yes." A slight tremor passed over him. "I'm going to find Upton." He stalked off.

"Uh-oh, alone again," Tobias murmured, moving to stand as close to her as propriety would allow. His fingers grazed hers.

"You can hardly call this alone." She swept her gaze over the crowded ballroom and smiled.

"I suppose not. I'm just glad to be with you again, hopeless as that sounds."

She couldn't keep herself from staring into his eyes. "I feel the same."

"Were you able to speak with Lord Gregory?"

"I was. He was disappointed, but he was also glad for me."

"What did you tell him?"

"That my heart was engaged elsewhere. He wanted to ensure my feelings were reciprocated. I assured him they were."

"If there is any question, my love," he whispered, "let me confirm that I adore you most fervently. Did you tell him I was the gentleman who stole you away?"

Fiona briefly clasped his fingers and hated to let them go. "You didn't steal me—I willingly chose you. I did not tell him it was you. We did not discuss anything about getting married, and I didn't want to inadvertently spread gossip about myself."

He chuckled. "An excellent consideration. We can send the announcement to the newspapers tomorrow and have the banns read on Sunday."

"But then we'll have to wait three weeks, and that will be after the twelfth."

"I already told you I don't need to wed by then. Anyway,

something tells me the new owner of Horethorne will invite me to visit often." His eyes gleamed with mirth.

"I want you to be the owner." She almost touched his mouth when he parted his lips to argue. "I feel very strongly about this—it was your mother's house, and it should be yours."

"That is incredibly wonderful of you. However, all that matters to me is that our son or daughter inherits it someday."

"We are agreed on that." It was a struggle not to put her arms around him, to kiss him, to hold him. "I have an alternate idea to reading the banns on Sunday. What if we eloped to Gretna Green? I understand that's something you've longed to do."

He laughed a bit loudly, and again some people around them turned their heads. "I must admit that holds an appeal. I know how much you'd love to travel."

"Especially with you. If we leave tomorrow, we can surely arrive and marry before the twelfth. Then you will have met your father's deadline."

He stared into her eyes. "You mean this in earnest." At her effusive nod, he took her hand and brought it to his lips. "Yes. I'll elope with you to Gretna Green tomorrow." He kissed her knuckles and reluctantly released her.

Heat sparked along her hand and arm and spread, making her body hum with desire. "Well, in that case, I think we should go home and get some rest in anticipation of our journey."

"Another excellent idea. We should probably also pack."

"Let me stop into the retiring room to tell Prudence and Cassandra we are leaving." She hesitated. "What about Prudence? What will happen to her now that I am getting married?"

"She will become companion to another young lady. I'll ensure she's taken care of until then."

"Perhaps Cassandra's father would hire her." Fiona suspected she would have a bit less time to spend with her friend after marrying Tobias, and she worried that Cassandra would be lonely. Actually, she already worried that Cassandra was lonely. "Would you speak to Lord Lucien about it?"

"Anything for you, my love," he murmured. "It's an excellent idea—for both Miss Lancaster and Lady Cassandra. You are a wonderful friend. But then I would expect nothing less."

His words warmed her. "Shall I meet you in the entry?"

"No, let's leave in a way that will garner less attention," he said. "Can you meet me downstairs?"

"Now who has the brilliant idea? I'm so pleased to be marrying such a clever gentleman. What a fortunate young woman I am."

His eyes gleamed with love and pride. "The fortune is all mine."

EPILOGUE

Eight days later...

"**D**o you think your father is scowling or laughing because you wed on the eleventh of March?" Fiona snuggled more closely against Tobias in their bed at the Bell and Broomstick in Gretna Green.

After a fortunately pleasant journey north, they were now being blanketed with snow. Which Tobias found rather lovely, for there was nowhere he would rather be than bundled up with his wife in a cozy four-poster bed at an inn.

"I would say scowling probably, but I'm going to imagine him laughing. It's past time I let my negative feelings about him fade away. Anyway, there is really no room for them with all the love I have for you." He turned to kiss her, and her stomach made a loud rumble.

She giggled. "Oh dear."

A knock on the door made Tobias leap, nude, from the bed. He grabbed his banyan and cloaked himself. "Our tea has arrived just in time." He waggled his brows at her as she burrowed beneath the coverlet.

Tobias opened the door to see Mrs. Insley, the innkeeper's wife, holding a tray. She grinned. "I hope you're hungry. There will be less travelers today owing to the weather, so the cook gave you extra portions."

"Come in." Tobias opened the door wider so Mrs. Insley, an efficient and warm-hearted woman in her late thirties, could place the tray on the table.

"There's tea, ale, cheese, bread, biscuits, and some special cake we give to all the newlyweds." She winked at Tobias. "And the latest newspaper from London."

"This looks wonderful. Thank you, Mrs. Insley."

"Will you be coming down for dinner?" she asked.

"If it's not too much trouble, we'll take it up here, I think." He was loath to leave the cocoon of their room.

"Not at all. That is not an unusual request for those who visited the blacksmith shop earlier in the day." Winking, she took her leave.

Fiona pushed back the coverlet and quickly donned her dressing gown. "I'm famished." Her dark red hair caressed her face and shoulders in a riot of unkempt waves. She looked as if she'd been thoroughly shagged—which she had.

A joy and satisfaction Tobias had never known settled over him. He *did* possess a romantic nature, just as his grandmother had said. He'd always wanted to find a woman like Fiona, and to experience a love like they now shared. That he'd discovered both was still a shock.

They settled at the small round table in front of the window that overlooked the yard below. The Bell and Broomstick was a smaller coaching inn and not as busy today because, as Mrs. Insley had indicated, of the weather.

"Do you think we can still leave day after tomorrow?" Fiona asked before taking a bite of cheese.

"I suppose we'll have to see what the weather decides. If it keeps snowing like this, however, I would say no."

She smiled, her mouth full, and her eyes danced with glee. "That would be a pity." She put her hand in front of her mouth and tried not to laugh.

They ate ravenously for a few minutes, then Fiona poured tea. Tobias plucked up the newspaper and scanned the headlines. Opening it, he found the column with news from the ton and read aloud.

> It has come to this author's attention that the Dowager Countess of Overton was the sole instrument in matching her grandson with his ward, Miss Fiona Wingate. Their shocking elopement to Gretna Green caught everyone by surprise. Well, everyone but the dowager countess. She insists she was part of the planning, and that the couple has her full endorsement. When she arrived in London, she immediately realized they were perfectly suited, and the match was made. Indeed, they were so perfectly matched that they wished to wed and honeymoon at the same time. The old rumors of the earl trying to dash off to Gretna Green with another young lady have finally been put to rest, and this author wishes the earl and his new countess a very happy life together.

Fiona goggled at him. "That's what it says? You didn't just make that up?"

He laughed and handed her the paper. "See for yourself." That was what his grandmother had said she planned to tell everyone and anyone that asked and to those who didn't. That she'd successfully made their perhaps scandalous elopement into a romantic tale was more than Tobias could have hoped for. "Now, this would make my father scowl." He chuckled as he lifted his cup of tea.

Fiona set the paper down, a look of warm happiness on her face. "That was really lovely. I do like your grandmother."

"And she likes you. I can hardly believe she's staying in London until we return so that she can spend time with you." He shook his head. "You, my love, are a miracle in so many ways."

She stood briefly and then slid onto his lap, curling her arms around his neck. "I am just a simple, ordinary girl from the country, my lord."

"Not true. You are a countess and there is nothing simple or ordinary about you." He nuzzled her neck.

"To think, I could have been a spinster. I did consider it."

Tobias pulled his head back and looked up at her. "I asked Lady Pickering and my grandmother about how a woman achieves spinsterhood. They could only say that a woman eventually arrived there after failing to wed. There are no rules, apparently."

"I realize I am still somewhat naïve when it comes to Society, but I think there are more than enough rules."

He laughed at her sarcasm. "True. The Phoenix Club has invited a few spinsters to join. I think we need to invite more. I've decided to make it a specific goal."

Her brow pleated and her mouth flirted with a smile. "Why?"

"Because I think they're an underappreciated segment of the population. If the Phoenix Club's aim is to include those who are excluded, I can think of no more deserving group. Can you?"

"I can't," she said softly, lowering her head to touch her nose against his. "Tobias, you are the very embodiment of a true hero."

He slid his fingers into her hair above her nape. "I don't know if I can agree with that. I've done some rather unheroic things, especially with you. It pains me to think of them." He looked into her eyes. "I'm so sorry."

"I'm not. Every moment with you, even the ones you

might regret, is such an adventure. When Her Majesty told me to have one, I never imagined this." She rotated on his lap and straddled him, parting her dressing gown so that only his banyan came between their sexes. Grinding her hips down, she kissed him. "I think perhaps I'm hungry in another way now."

"You are never satisfied," he said throatily, desire burning through him. "But let me try." He kissed her thoroughly, his hand tangling in her hair.

"Not true," she murmured breathlessly against his mouth. "You are quite adept at satisfying me. Over and over and over again. Perhaps you need to remind yourself." She reached down and pushed the sides of his banyan apart, then curled her hand around his shaft.

"Hmm, I'm not sure I remember. Keep going, if you don't mind."

She guided him to her sheath, taking him into her body as he thrust up. "Is this helping?" Kissing him again, she moved over him, her hips rising sharply and pressing down as he held her tightly.

"Oh yes, I remember now. This is also deeply satisfying for me. How convenient that it is mutually beneficial." He slid his fingers between them and teased her clitoris. She moved faster, crying out as her muscles clenched around him when she came.

Tobias tugged her hair, glorying in the sounds of her pleasure as he poured himself into her. Breathing heavily, it was several minutes before he could form a coherent thought.

He clasped her against him and rose from the chair, carrying her to the bed where he laid her down gently. She gazed up at him, her dark eyes glossy with satisfaction—and love.

Removing his banyan, he climbed into bed beside her.

She'd also tossed her dressing gown away and they snuggled together, nude, their bodies warm from their activity.

"I'm sorry we don't have time to visit Horethorne before returning to London," he said before kissing her temple.

"I understand. You have duties to attend. I am anxious to get back to Mrs. Tucket—and to see Prudence and Cassandra. I'm so glad they are together." Tobias had sent a note to Lucien the night of the assembly and the matter of Prudence's employment as Cassandra's companion had been settled before he and Fiona had left for Scotland.

"I wish we'd been able to settle Mrs. Tucket." Tobias had suggested sending her to Deane Hall or Horethorne, but the maid had insisted on waiting in London for Fiona to return. She was so proud of "her girl" and couldn't wait to see her as a countess.

"For now, she's quite content in her new first floor accommodations on Brook Street."

"And we needn't worry she'll harass Mrs. Smythe. My grandmother will not allow it."

Fiona chuckled. "No, I can't imagine she would. She is a most proper dowager countess."

"She's also a fierce matchmaker. Without her arrival, I may not have realized the depth of my affection for you in time. You might have attended the assembly that night and found yourself married to another man entirely."

She shuddered against him. "Never. I realized I couldn't marry without love. Perhaps that was why I resisted your efforts to see me wed. I simply couldn't countenance it. Until I could." She looked into his eyes with love and joy. "Until you."

Tobias gathered her close and kissed her.

"Rogue." She kissed his chin. "Rake." Her lips trailed along his jaw. "Scoundrel." She snagged his earlobe with her teeth.

"*Reprobate*." Pushing him to his back, she rose over him. "Husband."

"I am all of those things." He cupped her face, love searing through his chest. "I am yours."

～

Don't miss the next book in THE PHOENIX CLUB, IMPASSIONED!

Find out what happens when a countess demands her estranged husband give her a child and they discover their secret desires that have lain dormant ...

Would you like to know when my next book is available and to hear about sales and deals? Sign up for my VIP newsletter, follow me on social media:

Facebook: https://facebook.com/DarcyBurkeFans
Twitter at @darcyburke
Instagram at darcyburkeauthor
Pinterest at darcyburkewrite

And follow me on Bookbub to receive updates on pre-orders, new releases, and deals!

Need more Regency romance? Check out my other historical series:

The Untouchables
Swoon over twelve of Society's most eligible and elusive bachelor peers and the bluestockings, wallflowers, and outcasts who bring them to their knees!

The Untouchables: The Spitfire Society
Meet the smart, independent women who've decided they
don't need Society's rules, their families' expectations, or,
most importantly, a husband. But just because they don't
need a man doesn't mean they might not *want* one...

The Untouchables: The Pretenders
Set in the captivating world of The Untouchables, follow the
saga of a trio of siblings who excel at being something they're
not. Can a dauntless Bow Street Runner, a devastated
viscount, and a disillusioned Society miss unravel their
secrets?

Wicked Dukes Club
Six books written by me and my BFF, NYT Bestselling
Author Erica Ridley. Meet the unforgettable men of
London's most notorious tavern, The Wicked Duke.
Seductively handsome, with charm and wit to spare, one
night with these rakes and rogues will never be enough...

Love is All Around
Heartwarming Regency-set retellings of classic Christmas
stories (written after the Regency!) featuring a cozy village,
three siblings, and the best gift of all: love.

Secrets and Scandals
Six epic stories set in London's glittering ballrooms and
England's lush countryside.

Legendary Rogues
Five intrepid heroines and adventurous heroes embark on
exciting quests across the Georgian Highlands and Regency
England and Wales!

If you like contemporary romance, I hope you'll check out my **Ribbon Ridge** series available from Avon Impulse, and the continuation of Ribbon Ridge in **So Hot**.

I hope you'll consider leaving a review at your favorite online vendor or networking site!

I appreciate my readers so much. Thank you, thank you, *thank you.*

ALSO BY DARCY BURKE

Historical Romance

The Phoenix Club

Invitation

Improper

Impassioned

Intolerable

The Untouchables

The Bachelor Earl

The Forbidden Duke

The Duke of Daring

The Duke of Deception

The Duke of Desire

The Duke of Defiance

The Duke of Danger

The Duke of Ice

The Duke of Ruin

The Duke of Lies

The Duke of Seduction

The Duke of Kisses

The Duke of Distraction

The Untouchables: The Spitfire Society

Never Have I Ever with a Duke

A Duke is Never Enough

A Duke Will Never Do

The Untouchables: The Pretenders

A Secret Surrender

A Scandalous Bargain

A Rogue to Ruin

Love is All Around
(A Regency Holiday Trilogy)

The Red Hot Earl

The Gift of the Marquess

Joy to the Duke

Wicked Dukes Club

One Night for Seduction by Erica Ridley

One Night of Surrender by Darcy Burke

One Night of Passion by Erica Ridley

One Night of Scandal by Darcy Burke

One Night to Remember by Erica Ridley

One Night of Temptation by Darcy Burke

Secrets and Scandals

Her Wicked Ways

His Wicked Heart

To Seduce a Scoundrel

To Love a Thief (a novella)

Never Love a Scoundrel

Scoundrel Ever After

Legendary Rogues

The Legend of a Rogue

Lady of Desire

Romancing the Earl

Lord of Fortune

Captivating the Scoundrel

Contemporary Romance

Ribbon Ridge

Where the Heart Is (a prequel novella)

Only in My Dreams

Yours to Hold

When Love Happens

The Idea of You

When We Kiss

You're Still the One

Ribbon Ridge: So Hot

So Good

So Right

So Wrong

ABOUT THE AUTHOR

Darcy Burke is the USA Today Bestselling Author of sexy, emotional historical and contemporary romance. Darcy wrote her first book at age 11, a happily ever after about a swan addicted to magic and the female swan who loved him, with exceedingly poor illustrations. Join her Reader Club newsletter for the latest updates from Darcy.

A native Oregonian, Darcy lives on the edge of wine country with her guitar-strumming husband, incredibly talented artist daughter, and imaginative son who will almost certainly out-write her one day (that may be tomorrow). They're a crazy cat family with two Bengal cats, a small, fame-seeking cat named after a fruit, an older rescue Maine Coon with attitude to spare, and a collection of neighbor cats who hang out on the deck and occasionally venture inside. You can find Darcy at a winery, in her comfy writing chair balancing her laptop and a cat or three, folding laundry (which she loves), or binge-watching TV with the family. Her happy places are Disneyland, Labor Day weekend at the Gorge, Denmark, and anywhere in the UK—so long as her family is there too. Visit Darcy online at www. darcyburke.com and follow her on social media.

facebook.com/DarcyBurkeFans

twitter.com/darcyburke

instagram.com/darcyburkeauthor

pinterest.com/darcyburkewrites

goodreads.com/darcyburke

bookbub.com/authors/darcy-burke

amazon.com/author/darcyburke

CPSIA information can be obtained
at www.ICGtesting.com
Printed in the USA
BVHW031705170521
607560BV00001B/36

9 781637 260159